IStanbul

D5656561781878

Ottery Books

IStanbul

Published in Great Britain by Ottery Books
Ottery St Mary

First published 2017

ISBN 978 0 9955035 3 3

Typeset in Palatino

Cover picture by author, cover design by Short Run Press

This novel is a work of fiction. The names, characters, incidents and
locations are the product of the author's imagination and any resemblance
to actual persons, places or events is entirely coincidental

website: jehallauthor.com

A full CIP record for this book is available from the British Library

Printed and bound by Short Run Press, Exeter

To

Rosie with all my love, recalling our adventurous spring days in the beautiful city of Istanbul where this sequel to Flashbacks finally took shape. A city whose rich history, diversity of peoples and religious traditions lies in the borderlands of east and west. Facing huge challenges from within and without, the people we met and the vibrant colours of tulips we saw, stood as colourful reminders of Istanbul as a place of hope, life and a future.

Sadly, since writing, recent IS and Kurd bombings, and a summer coup have shown Turkey to be a place very much in the front line in the struggle against extremism.

I also dedicate this novel to the people of Turkey and Istanbul.

ALSO BY J E HALL

Flashbacks

Acknowledgements

I would like to thank my family who have encouraged and contributed in so many ways. Their interest and support enabled me to press on.

Thanks also to the people of Istanbul who made Rosie and I so welcome and charmed us with their amazing city and pointed us to places, like the atmospheric Basilica Cistern, we might otherwise have missed. Following recent terrorist incidents it saddened us to see so few foreign tourists in the central area. It deserves better. How fickle the travel business is!

This novel, IStanbul, is in no small measure the result of the feedback I received on the publication of Flashbacks. Many people wrote or asked me directly when the sequel would be available. Libraries, book club discussions and messages from many individuals also played their part. Well, here it is and thank you for demanding it from me!

Many dear friends contributed to improvements to the text. Christopher Lamb spotted gaps in my understanding of Islam. Eleanor Piper saw the shortcomings in my grasp of the use of English and the Ottery Writers spotted where my story-telling took a wrong turn. Sheila Walker and Ruth Ward attended closely to my draft. It is always an invidious task to try and name people, but to these people especially and the many more who helped along the way, thank you.

I am once again indebted to the team at Short Run Press, Exeter for their professionalism in getting the story to the printed page and to local independent bookshops for their support. These include Adrian Lea at the Curious Otter Bookshop and Carl East at Winstones.

"Islam was never the religion of peace.
Islam is the religion of fighting."

Abu Bakr al-Baghdadi
IS Leader, 2015

"Humanity is but a single Brotherhood:
So make peace with your brethren."

The Qur'an 49.10

"The parrot looking in the mirror sees
Itself, but not its teacher hid behind,
And learns the speech of Man, the while it thinks
A bird of its own sort is talking to it"

Jalal ad-Din Rumi
Sufi 1207-1273

1

It was very dark. Rising vapours shaped the air. Above, barreling domes supported by colossal stone pillars divided the space. Below, pooling black water swirled and hid ancient mysteries in its depths. The giant columns stood in rows of serried ranks; silent, guarding witnesses.

Water dripped down as time stood still in the ancient Basilica Cistern. Splashes and ripples as strange fish with barbels twisted and turned on the surface before mysteriously disappearing as suddenly as they had come. There was another world higher above. Little did the cold city know what was throbbing beneath its citizens' feet in its rebellious heart.

It was with untold human suffering the roman emperor Justinian called this palatial space into being. Today, Istanbul's cavernous underground vault awaited its latest visitors. Meant to deliver life giving fresh water, those days were long passed. Presently, with the day's excited tourists gone, it was once again a place of the night.

Footsteps echoed. Three ghostly figures were silhouetted in the gloom. They moved slowly as they paced the walkways to approach three simple chairs left for them. They had assembled to hold a conference of war on this strange subterranean island. Drawn together on the low wooden floor surrounded by unfathomable water in every direction, their shimmering shadows seemed to float. Their features hidden in the gloom, the men sat down in turn without exchanging a word, clutching their winter garb close. Even down here there was a chill in the air.

They knew this dark concealed world afforded them anonymity. They needed security from listening ears, escape from an outside world full of electronic surveillance and ever-watchful eyes. Nearby the sculpted goddess Medusa with her hair of snakes looked sideways on; her former place of magical power when once she turned men to stone, usurped by these modern successors in turn intent on transforming men to lifelessness. Her unfeeling, inscrutable gaze was fixed on the unfolding proceedings.

Certain they would not be interrupted, introductions were made. The one wearing a black robe spoke first. As he cleared his throat, the noise was magnified and reverberated sonorously. Nothing down here was as one expected it to be.

'Salaam alekum. I am Salim Ismat. I represent the true Caliphate, the Islamic State of Iraq and the Levant. I have the mandate of our illustrious leader, Abu Bakr al-Baghdadi, to speak for IS. I am so very pleased you have both decided to join me. Though we haven't met before, I know we share a common goal, the destabilisation of Turkey and the opening of a new future for both our peoples. Please...' He bowed and invited the bearded man to his left to speak.

A pause followed as the second man reached into an inside pocket. This action drew anxious looks, but it was only to pull out a piece of paper which glowed eerily in the half-light. The three shuffled in their chairs, all uneasy, men well-used to anticipating treachery.

'I have instructions from the Kurdish PKK High Command Group. My name doesn't matter. Call me Tahir if you like. Before I say anything further I need to hear from you this meeting never happened. Either it's secret and always stays so, or I leave now. Understood?' he said, looking from face to face for an answer.

The other two men looked at each other, then nodded in agreement. 'Of course,' added Salim. 'We all appreciate that not everyone will be ready to accept what we want to do. Even our own. Discretion is always the better part of valour. We're happy to keep quiet.' Salim thought the man foolish to make such an unrealistic demand; such a request made him feel more in control. This Kurd must be stupid, after all, who does he think is going to enforce this "secret" agreement not to tell? Salim looked across to the third man in the group, his opposite number, the local IS commander in Istanbul. Salim

2

wished he knew him better. It was his turn to introduce himself.

'I'm Zaid Jamal. I live in Istanbul; look after IS interests here. Salim, with all due respect, you are just a visitor. I know this city and what happens here. The safety of my men is my call, anything we agree, well it's on my watch. Already, Turkish Police Special Operations make life hell for us here. I have to mind my own back all the time, that's why I'm still alive.'

'Yes, yes, my brother, but what's your take on this request for secrecy?' asked Salim.

'I want out. I can't make any binding or lasting promise of secrecy. Those locally who serve our cause wouldn't hear of it. As I see it, Kurdish nationalism and ways of doing things are not IS's concern. We must not allow ourselves to be distracted Salim. We have to be open. All I will say is that nothing of this meeting will be shared unless absolutely necessary. For the moment I will keep quiet, but you listen here, Tahir, I will not be silenced by the likes of you. That said, I'm prepared to listen to what you have to say.'

Salim thought he really should have spoken to Zaid earlier. Zaid had shown he had no awareness what it had taken to arrange this meeting with the Kurdish leadership. His edgy provocation was about to undo everything; it was time to step in. There was no need for this needling, not at this juncture, not when IS needed the Kurds.

'Hold it there! Patience my friend. I agree. Let's see what our Kurdish friends have to offer before we reach too hasty a conclusion as to what we say or don't say to our men,' Salim gently chided, before turning his attention back to Tahir. The Kurdish man was still holding his precious sheet of paper, as if waiting for permission to read it. 'Let's hear what your commander wants and see if we can oblige him.' As the man looked up, Salim could see he was still on board, and for the moment Salim still had a glimmer of hope he might bring IS's plan to life. Tahir looked down again at his paper, his eyes squinting in the gloom as he tried to capture its message from the small text.

3

'The PKK commander in chief was interested to receive your proposal suggesting mutual cooperation in our military campaign. There is, he says, strategic merit in IS and Kurdish forces working in synchrony at this point in time to destabilise further the present, misled, Turkish government.'

'Good, very good. Please continue,' said Salim encouragingly.

'But, he is not wanting our collaboration to be made public, nor is he willing to go so far as mounting joint operations; there is no question of agreeing to a single head of command. The PKK will not surrender any sovereignty to IS now or ever. For the crimes you have committed against our people in recent years, driving many from their homes, these are deeply felt. For now, remember it is only a small number of our Kurdish people who are prepared to work with you.' Tahir waited, knowing that he'd made a significant offer of alliance, but that there were limits as to how far his Kurds would go to accommodate IS demands. So Tahir, not having confidence in the two facing him, his requested condition of secrecy leaving him feeling exposed, now wanted to take measure of IS's response to the three conditions attached to his offer of strategic cooperation before going further. He carefully re-folded his paper and pushed it back inside the folds of his coat, and waited.

'That is excellent news. There is such good sense in setting aside past difficulties and in looking forward to a new future. Of course IS is willing to cooperate with you and we will be pleased to see a legitimate Kurdistan arise from Turkey's ashes in the coming days. Be assured, IS sees a future where Kurds and Islamic State live side by side in peace, as true Muslims, working together and growing ever closer in union. Don't you think this a most welcome development Zaid? An unprecedented opportunity just waiting to be taken?' said a beaming Salim, looking to his local commander to press the green button. Unfortunately, an echoing shuffle from Zaid's sandals on the wooden floor suggested Salim was going to hear more words of reticence from his reluctant colleague.

4

'I don't like it,' said Zair. 'The only way it would work would be if we have completely separate areas of operation. I command my forces in Istanbul, you mind yours, Tahir. Of course I'm happier if we keep away from each other as much as possible. I propose you Kurds take on Ankara, whilst we do what we know best, tip the balance of power here in Istanbul. No disrespect, but I've never met you before and not for one Turkish Lire would I trust any Kurds I know in this city to work with us. There's too much history between us. In fact there are traitors everywhere, spies and informers on every street. Success will only come if I can count on my men one hundred percent, and that means I use only my own men and we both stick to our own neighbourhoods.'

At this Tahir began clenching and unclenching his hands, stifling his rising anger, before permitting himself to respond.

'That suits me just fine. The lack of trust you describe is entirely mutual. We wouldn't work with IS here. You've too many unreliable operatives. Take a good look at your front line troops – the mentally ill, the foreign mercenaries; all people who don't belong and who are watched by everyone. Your guys are the unreliable ones. Yes, you attack Istanbul, we take Ankara. There's no other option. Agreed?'

There was another pause. Salim had anticipated this might be the outcome. It wouldn't be ideal but it would do. This arrangement would put great pressure on IS's ability to deliver the necessary result but, they would cope. In agreeing to such a separation of operations and forces, he knew he still needed the Kurds' logistical support in getting the necessary arrangements and personnel in place in Istanbul. Without this the project would go nowhere. But how was he going to get this across to Tahir without actually admitting IS's weakness?

'I think we can agree to this. It would be in all our interests to keep tight control of operations, a separate focus on the two cities. It's agreed. There are some other, contingent steps, lesser but still important matters, we need to discuss and agree to if this enterprise is to go ahead – the date, the logistics, some basic coordination in getting forces in place, that kind of thing,' Salim added, bringing up the subject of Kurdish facilitation as gently as he could. Indeed, IS success in this venture would depend upon their cooperation.

'Of course. On the question of timing. Turkey is fragile, its government desperately trying to hang on to control, taking ever more repressive measures. We Kurds are gaining new international friends all the time. As we build our base with American help in Iraq and elsewhere, we know our time has come. The time for action is now, to tip the balance our way. Now, now, now,' Tahir said, clearly sold on a plan for action, punching the palm of his left hand with his right fist.

'I share your analysis and impatience, but let's not lose sight of the need for careful preparation, the selection of suitable targets and the training of the right personnel. No disrespect to local ability, Zaid, but we will want to bring in our best commander from Mosul to take charge. Our assessment is that the Turkish government will remain unstable, not just for weeks, but many months, meaning we have time to ensure we get this absolutely right. A precise date is not required right at this moment, but an aspirational, notional timeline would help us both, don't you think? My thinking is that a date in six months, late summer, would be ideal. How does that sound, Tahir? Might we agree on this too?' offered Salim.

'We've been fighting for our freedom for generations, and more blood's been shed in recent days than gets reported. You newcomers on the scene might need more time. We're part of an ongoing daily struggle. My people are used to betrayal. IS attack us, Turkey watches. Turkey attacks us, IS watches. That's what we're used to. A few months more, the summer you say, why not? If this cooperative effort is to succeed we need to create a tipping point moment when our combined attacks on one day instil such fear and terror, the balance is finally turned in our favour. You know, I think we can do this. Very well, we can tie down a date in the summer later. Better we do that last minute. Security considerations,' Tahir said with a sneer looking disparagingly at Zaid.

'And we will need assistance with transport and ordinance. To bring things in from Mosul. It will be so much more convenient with your help. We could do it alone, but just to guarantee things, to ensure everything moves smoothly into place, to show good faith.....' advised Salim stroking his beard thoughtfully.

'Hmm. I follow you. It's possible. You'll be able to see how we can do a proper job. Your outfit would need to pay up front, any problem with that?' asked Tahir.

'None whatsoever. Funds are never a problem. Don't forget we have the oil,' said Salim smiling and holding wide his arms in a gesture of beneficence. 'Our benefactors are so very generous.'

'We'd need to bring the necessary additional resources from Mosul into Istanbul. More high explosives will be needed than we have presently,' said Zaid. 'That's if, as you say, we want this to be really big, to make the difference.'

'Very big, the biggest there's been. So big the people of this city will wake in terror,' said Salim.

There was a noise to their right. All three turned as one to see what it was.

'Oh, it's you Matuk, our helpful Basilica Cistern Security Guard. We're so grateful you opened up this, err, conference facility for us. I think we've just about concluded our business meeting,' said Salim rising and stepping towards him smiling.

'That's fine. No problem. Once you've gone, I'll just lock the place up and be on my way,' said Ahmed eyeing the three curiously.

Tahir reached up and with a sudden movement tipped the man's head quickly back, stroking across and slicing deeply into his neck, a dark blade flashing. Holding him from behind so the splashing blood did not fall on his own clothes, he let the young security man, choking and gurgling, slide and fall slowly into the black water, an expanding pool of deep red water just visible in the encircling gloom.

'Like yourselves, we Kurds take no chances. I like to guarantee our conversation stays secret. You'll have to lock up for yourselves now,' said Tahir, turning on his heels. 'You'll be hearing from me, with a date for the summer,' his echoing voice called out as he walked quickly towards the exit.

Salim and Zaid looked at each other and then at the man floating face down in the water. Zaid was still staring into the water as Salim took him by the shoulder.

'I suppose we don't have to pay him now. Come on. Let's get out of here and find somewhere to eat. We have something to celebrate. It looks like, come the summer, IS can turn the corner in Turkey. Just think where that might lead. Consider today as the beginning of victory.'

As Salim cast one last look around at the dark waters and pillars beyond, he saw Medusa's stone face watching. For one unsettling moment he was sure he had seen her smile.

2

It was bitingly cold, an icy blast from the frozen heart of Russia created a deep chill outside. Ali Muhammed wrapped his robes more tightly around him. He didn't get back to Mosul until the New Year, long after they'd buried his younger sister, Fatima. She was his only sister, her kind and sweet nature so undeserving of such a thing. Nineteen was no age to die. She was his innocent good side and now he saw only darkness ahead of him. As a youngster she'd enjoyed music and singing but it had been years since she had dared make any sound like that. He missed her. Try as he could he couldn't remember when she last smiled. His heart was a cold and lifeless thing. He knew Fatima was dead because of him.

Ali had no doubt that it was his sensational Islamic State attack in London on 11 November that led directly to his home being targeted and for that surely he was entirely to blame. In the same bombing, his brother Mo's five-year-old son, Ahmed, had been injured and was still in the hospital with a broken leg, Mo staying there with him. The doctor had said there were complications. Broken bones heal, a dead sister leaves a permanent wound, thought Ali, feeling his distress welling up inside him again. Ali didn't want to have to face Mo just yet.

Life was bitter and had dealt him the cruelest of hands. His family suffered for IS whether he complied or not. Right now he wasn't in a place to offer Mo any comfort.

All this bad news was given him as he bumped along the trail in the dark. The van carrying him back to Mosul had crossed secretly from Turkey into IS controlled northern Iraq. He'd been told the devastating drone strike on his home had happened three days ago. His driver had said, as if to reassure him, how everyone had then rallied round to find and pull out those still alive; that it was only because of the rescuers' efforts more lives were not lost.

The family house, surrounding courtyard buildings, and all they possessed were no more than heaps of orange-red brick and rubble around a central crater. After two months as a hunted fugitive, Ali had returned to discover there was no home for him to come back to.

Sleeping at roadsides, behind bus shelters, sitting up against tree trunks, he'd first made his way of escape by bicycle from London to the Essex coast. There he'd spent six days waiting, hungry, watching, despairing, hoping Dave would visit his yacht moored at the Maldon quayside. When, he eventually appeared, the Channel crossing had proved easy, and once across, his contact in Calais addressed the logistics involved in getting him back east. Delays meant hiding up in safe houses in Brussels, Strasburg and three weeks in Berlin. This van ride was the final leg. Ali watched his driver picking at the white edges of the red eczema on his hands as he grasped the wheel. It disgusted him.

According to the driver, Fatima's funeral had been the best attended for many years, and because she was Ali's sister, the local leaders had honoured her. They'd even organised and paid for everything. His uncle, as head of the house in Ali's absence, had led the mourners and her body now lay buried with all the proper prayers and tributes having been said.

Ali pictured the nearby cemetery with its stones and markers, thinking all that it needed after so many recent additions was a 'full' sign. The customary mourning processes and handling of the deceased was in her case, he was told by his driver, all done in the best possible manner; the head Imam beautifully recited the Qur'an and prayers.

Ali's mother had apparently taken it very badly, crying without ceasing, people said.

'She will rejoice to have you home,' he added, rather too optimistically to be convincing. Ali understood that this new family loss had brought back all the grief from his father's untimely death. The driver thought it best Ali ought to be forewarned of his mother's delicate emotional state, he didn't want Ali to be unprepared.

Ali's memory all too often reminded him of his father, something he didn't want to be reminded of; images of his father's shooting by an Iraqi soldier five years ago started replaying in his mind, time and time again, like bulletins on the news channel, an endless repeat of the moment of death, flailing arms, a dancing body as the bullets hit flesh, then blood in the dusty road.

None of this cheered Ali whose heavy heart was already torn by what he had done in London, not least to Kaylah. Her image replaced that of his father in his mind. He pictured the stunned look of sheer horror as she saw him that last time, a face that screamed at him, 'what have you done?' How could he forgive himself for the way he had groomed and used her in his determination to fulfil his attack on the political and military leadership gathered unknowingly to await his bullets of judgement outside parliament that day.

Now he just couldn't cast Kaylah's face from his mind. Everywhere the world he touched seemed a cruel and hostile place and he felt fate had dealt hands of death wherever and however it chose. Feeling incredibly tired after all the recent travelling with its constant fear of discovery, he wondered whether the weight of the despondency and despair he now felt was the greater burden and the real source of all his deep weariness. He pulled the black robes the driver had given him round himself tighter in a futile but natural act of self-comfort.

By now it was early evening, the wind had dropped, a cool and pale winter sun had set long ago. Word had got out that he was back and people were coming into the streets of Mosul to catch sight of Ali, the great hero of the Caliphate, the warrior who had struck a deadly blow to the heart of the infidel. But to Ali's mind the people looked worn and battle-weary, their faces wore haggard looks and eyes stared much more so than when he'd left last summer. They had the frightened look of people whose enemy was at their very door.

Astonishingly, and with a careless disregard for security that surprised Ali, street and other lights were being switched on as if it were festival time. Indeed, since Ali's van had been spotted on the outskirts of his home city people looked in his direction, smiled and cheered; he found himself acknowledging their waves and smiling in spite of himself and waving back to them in return.

Ali wondered whether Adam Taylor would have got such a reception after his escape from Mosul and return to London. Would he have been feted by the people and the media like this? He couldn't imagine it. London just didn't have that sense of community. It was a godforsaken place. Maybe if Adam had a media-led celebrity status then that's how it would happen. Perhaps on Facebook and Twitter he'd get his million hits. Well, good on Adam for escaping from Mosul and getting back to London. How had he done it? He'd find out one day, he thought. Maybe Adam had a stroke of good fortune, like himself. Fate and good luck settles more than we know, he told himself. Could the two of us be brothers in another life? Probably not, he quickly concluded, there's no room for non-believers in the Ummah.

His driver stopped with a jolt and Ali realised he was back in the heart of his own district. They'd pulled up on the dirt road next to his CO's residential apartment block. The building had escaped unscathed, securely placed, nestling between hospital and gym. He wondered whether he would have to make a speech to the gathering crowd. The moment of panic that came with the thought soon passed as he had other things to think about.

There was his CO, Salim Ismat, smiling confidently, standing in the doorway to his residence, waiting to receive him. Ali tried to exit the van with as much dignity as he could muster, wondering what kind of disheveled and broken image he presented at what was supposed to be a significant public moment of homecoming. A hero to everyone else, he decided he must try at the very least to look the part as he stepped forward to be greeted.

'Salaam alekum! Welcome!' his CO beamed, embracing him as a returning long lost friend. Taking Ali's shoulders, he spun Ali round on the step to face the gathering crowd. Ali felt like a character in a puppet play, having a principal part to affirm and strengthen yet bigger parts than his. As he looked around him, he saw the occasion being filmed by the CO's media guy, who moved discreetly through the crowd to get his best propaganda shots. Then at a signal from the CO there was a rattle of shots into the air, a deafening celebratory fusillade, before Ali was swept into the CO's home with assurances that a feast fit for a Caliph awaited him!

First, he was permitted to refresh himself and some fresh clothes were put out allowing him to change. Then he joined a small group of men in the lounge where he was invited to sit in a pre-prepared seat of honour. At the CO's beckoning each man rose to introduce himself and to deliver a statement of appreciation for what Ali had achieved. Some were military leaders from neighbouring districts, others local administrative or religious figures. There were smiles all round. Some brought small gifts and placed them on the table in front of him. An expensive watch was given, a decorated ancient Qur'an and a piece of calligraphy for his wall. Then they all sat, a prayer in Arabic was intoned and, from the adjacent room, trays of food were brought in and left before them; the feasting began.

As ever, Salim Ismat personally took close care of Ali, never leaving his side. For five years, since he had watched as Ali saw his father shot in the street, he had taken him under his wing. He had prepared this intelligent young man, carefully making him the most exceptional jihadist he had trained. Every now and then he would slip Ali a question, testing out how he was. Ali in reply tried to be confident and assured. From under his robe the CO produced an envelope which he placed in Ali's hand, saying there had been a gift offering with contributions made by them all. He was to treat the money as an expression of love and gratitude from his brothers and sisters in the Caliphate. Ali slipped it into an inner pocket out of sight, embarrassed but still able to reply with polite words of appreciation.

Ali realised how, having been away so long he was slipping quickly back into old patterns, living again as

13

directed by his CO. He was serving him automatically as his right-hand man and he found himself wondering when the next order would come. The thought terrified him. It suddenly dawned on him that he hadn't returned to freedom; he would be called upon again. The waiting to know began to gnaw at him and he stopped eating, placing the lamb bone he'd been chewing the meat from back on his plate.

'What am I going to do next?' he asked Salim.

'What would you like to do?' came the reply, momentarily throwing him off-guard.

'My family needs me. They've suffered much. I need to grieve my sister Fatima. I hear Mo's son Ahmed is still in hospital and our home has been almost totally destroyed. My uncle, my mother, Mo and his wife and son need somewhere to live. I need to help them.'

'You are such a good man, for the success of dunya we must not overlook our blood kin. Allah, suhanahu wa ta'ala, would be pleased for you to care for them. I will provide you with three of my best men to show you your new home tomorrow; I have found somewhere very suitable for your family. Take a month, no take six, to get your family and yourself restored, back on their feet again. There will be a few little tasks for you to do round here, but you need to look after yourself, care for your family. I have a new Hilux truck for you waiting outside. It's yours, my brother, a personal gift from me. Here's the keys, but don't leave them in the vehicle next time!'

A momentary steely look crossed Salim's face, and Ali understood how Adam had got away. Adam had used Ali's Hilux, taking advantage of the fact the keys were always in the ignition, to make his escape. The remark and look that went with it were a reminder that his CO would never entirely overlook his failings. Ali just knew that at any moment, should he step out of line, the fact that Adam, a prized hostage, had been given the opportunity to escape, could be brought up to condemn him. Inside, he shuddered, hoping it didn't show, as his CO moved the conversation on.

14

He spoke up, everyone turning to listen, drawing Ali closer to him under his arm.

'My brother, you are a great man. You have led the most celebrated act of courage in our campaign and because of you the Prime Minister of Great Britain is dead. A commander of such ability will surely be telling me what we do next. Now tell me, Ali, where do you think you should lead us to strike next?'

His raised voice now had everyone's attention. All eyes in the room were suddenly turned to him and all other conversation quietened as they waited to hear Ali's response. He paused, then looked up.

'If an engineer wants to build a bridge, he first surveys very carefully the ground on which it is to be built. He looks around, he plans carefully, he counts his resources and the materials he will need. He judges when the best time will be to build, when the weather and river level will be most in his favour. It is the same for us in IS. The death of a prime minister here or a president there will not win us the war. It helps, yes, but what we really need to do is to take steps that carry guaranteed strategic benefits that we can count on. I've come back home knowing we are under pressure from outside, the infidel tries to hurt us. He tries to drive us from our strongholds, but I know that the resilience of our people, as they have shown tonight, is great.' There were nods and grunts of approval at this.

'What we need to do now is strike in a place where the destabilisation caused will inevitably lead to chaos, people being forced to choose whether they are true Muslims or heretics. Look around us, our so-called Muslim neighbouring nations pretend they are secure and faithful, but they are not; everywhere, just under the surface, there is instability and revolution in the air. We saw it with the so-called Arab Spring, but now we need to use these underlying destabilising forces at work to our advantage in what we do next.'

Ali paused for a moment, long enough to see everyone's eyes were fixed on him, listening intently to his every word.

15

He'd had time to think as he'd travelled back. His CO gestured to him to carry on speaking.

'Ali, my friend, this is good. Please share your ideas. Come, you are among your friends.'

'You will know that I have travelled through Turkey twice in recent months. This is a country ready to fall into our hands. Why? Well, we have many of our people now living there and they will rise up with the right encouragement. Individuals have already martyred themselves in Ankara, in Istanbul and elsewhere, and their sacrifice is honourable to the almighty. What we need now is to do something that will tip the balance, to undertake a strategic act that will be decisive, making a turning point in our struggle. Give the Turks a little fear and terror and they will come over to us.' Salim stood up to interrupt him.

'When Ali has rested and recovered, he will indeed be leading us in a decisive campaign in Turkey. But enough for now. Walls have ears and tonight is a night for feasting, for celebration, not for planning the next battle. There will be time for that in the months ahead. Today we praise Allah for Ali has triumphed. He succeeded. He overcame many obstacles and has come home to his friends, and you are all my welcome guests. Bring in the dates, figs and pomegranates.'

Ali felt Salim's heavy arm over his shoulder pressing him down, and smelled his greasy, lamb breath in his face. He was being made to sit down again. His CO leant across to speak privately in his ear.

'Ali, you are quite the strategic commander now aren't you? You will have some months off, take some time at home with your family. Then I will call you. As you rightly guessed, Turkey is indeed where we strike next and you will be leading the fight. Istanbul and Ankara is where the action will happen. As they bring the war to us, we will take the war to our enemy. This is the new battlefront and their efforts to destroy us in the desert will, as they are already coming to believe, crumble into the sand and dust. As they think they

16

are closing in, we will just spread our wings. I have such faith in you Ali. I truly know there is nothing you cannot do.'

With that he leaned back releasing his grip on Ali, smiling round at all his guests. Ali had had his fill, the sweet dates he had just eaten sticking to the sides of his mouth and on his teeth. The bitter taste of more pain and struggle to come welled up like vomit waiting to come from deep inside him. He was over-full, but out of duty added a gracious last word.

'Thank you my commander for this and for your care of my family. The Caliphate will flourish, enshallah, Allah willing, with your help. I am so glad to be home once again with my people.'

The party rolled on. Ali circulated amongst the guests, being forced to relive memories of what he had done in London which he would much rather forget. For them, it was a glorious story of heroism in an exotic foreign land. But for him, this was a party he felt increasingly uncomfortable with. There were moments when he could see all too clearly the ingratiation, the outward politeness, the dead-hand of control exercised by these leaders enslaved to an outdated and traditional way of life; he felt the cold reign of fear and terror they exercised which was suffocating him. For all the man of contradictions he knew that he was, his very survival would depend on keeping all his rising doubts buried well out of sight.

In the early hours he was shown to the guest room in his CO's house. Tonight he would stay here. Tomorrow, it had become clear, he had family to see to, and then, well, he was back where he was once before, being prepared for service, on this occasion for a secret, clandestine operation in Turkey.

As he lay down his head, he wasn't sure whether he hadn't talked himself into the military idea he had spoken of to those gathered, or whether in reality his CO had really been lining him up for it all the way along? Either way he'd said the right thing. They would have been pleased with the evening and his part in it. Ali realised he was back, albeit all too briefly.

Someone else also knew he was back. Authority was given for a drone bombing raid. The target was so important any collateral damage had been permitted. Buttons were pressed, a missile was launched, Ali Muhammed was the target.

3

Adam Taylor changed the bike's saddle. It wasn't a logical move, but he'd learned that not everything he did in life he did logically, instincts played a part too. That Ali Muhammed's arse had been against his saddle made the bike a taboo he couldn't overcome. He never rode it again until the puzzled Fred Striker at his Wood Green High Road Cycle Shop had provided and fitted a replacement. The fact it was secondhand and to all appearances exactly the same, a Brookes leather saddle but with none of the unpleasant resonances, greatly bemused Fred – who was happy enough to take back the original in a straight exchange and had the respect not to ask Adam why he was changing like for like.

Customers asked for strange things in Fred's experience and, as he had learned in a lifetime of selling bikes, the customer was always right. Adam had wanted to change the handlebars too, but settled on allowing Fred to re-tape the hand grips. For these latter changes Adam insisted on paying. He also bought himself a new set of front and rear lights together with a chain and lock, before preparing to leave the warm, oily smell of Fred's Aladdin's cave of cycle parts.

Fred knew all about him for there was no escaping the media exposure Adam had been subject to in the weeks since it had all happened last November. Adam knew that Fred knew what he'd been involved with and nothing was said; it was an understanding they had between them, reached without words. The celebrity thing came out into the open when Fred insisted on taking a mobile picture of Adam standing by his bike before he would let him go. Adam didn't mind.

He'd known Fred for years and he knew Fred to be a collector of customer stories as much as of bicycle parts. It was this, not the money, that kept him in the business and why everyone liked him and kept coming back to him. It kind of warmed Adam to think he had his own story on Fred's board, alongside the stories of past and present racing cyclists, of veteran tandem competitors and pictures of those who had broken their collar bones more than twice. This shop was a place for the dedicated cycling community to touch base with. It was personal shopping, shopping as part of a shared cycling obsession.

Fred's shop was a lonely icon to a disappearing shopping experience. All this was betrayed in its ironic name, 'The Chain Store.' Over the years, as one after the other of the one-man cycle shops had closed down in North London, Fred had picked up all their spares, filling wooden and metal shelves from floor to ceiling with cables and gears, frames and wheels. Whether imperial or metric, if Fred didn't have the part, no-one did.

As he was leaving, and before pushing open the shop door with its tinkling bell, Adam watched Fred. Fred had already printed off his mobile picture on the printer beneath the counter and cut it out with ancient scissors, chained prisoner-like to the countertop. Carefully, Fred found a place on the crowded pin-board above his workstation and added Adam to the colourful mosaic collage of all the cyclists, past and present, who had crossed his path.

Adam took one last look at the latest bikes for sale in Fred's window – only to see what there was, for he had no intention of buying. It was about keeping in touch with the cycling world. This was a special place to visit and Adam liked to browse and chat with Fred. As he wheeled his bike outside, he mentally savoured this long overdue visit. Call it nostalgia, whatever, it gave him a feel-good factor every time he came. Maybe, he thought, 'The Chain Store' wouldn't still be there when he next returned. After a last look over his shoulder as if to commit the place to memory, he began getting ready to leave.

With the new parts in place and after the previous day's deep wash he'd given the frame and panniers, only now did Adam feel his bike was clean and truly his again. Helmet on, he climbed in the saddle, cleats clicking in place as they locked on the pedals. He pulled away, enjoying the experience, the wind increasing against his cheeks as he built speed. It felt so good to be free.

Though pleased his bike had been returned to him, it wasn't the same as before. It was as if the bike had matured, no longer a child, it had grown up. Its marks and scratches were testament to its formative journey; and truth be told, Adam quite liked the secret life-story his bike had now written for itself.

He recalled how the previous summer, at the end of his gap year, he'd cycled his Marin bike across Europe as far as Eastern Turkey. There he'd been taken hostage and held in Mosul, Iraq. His IS captor, Ali had then brought it back to London pretending to be him, dropping it on the front lawn of his home in Muswell Hill and making out that he, Adam himself, was back. How spookily strange was that?

Adam still couldn't reconcile himself to what had happened – Ali's attack on the Armistice Day parade – the Prime Minister and others who had died. It was so nearly him too. He couldn't bear the memory of it. He grabbed his bike handlebars to focus, and told himself to get a grip. It took ages to get it back, for his bike had become police 'evidence' and it took forever to remove all trace of the forensic officer's white powder residues from the dark frame.

Soon he was passing Alexander Park Station, a passenger train whooshing under the road bridge as he cycled over. He swung sharp left, pointing his trusty steed up in the direction of Muswell Hill and home. This bike, he thought, as he coaxed it over the heights of Alexander Palace, was an extension of himself. He knew it held and told his story too.

He needed his bike, for cycling allowed his body and mind to flow more widely, to possess life fully and to let him feel more truly alive; it gave him freedom and satisfied his need to explore places. Its simple mechanics, now rhythmically working once again in power-giving, responsive, harmonious propulsive raw energy, gave him a buzz. Today, more than ever before, it was the bike that made him feel free rather than imprisoned or enclosed, and where he wanted to go the bike was sure to follow. For Adam, life without his bike would be impoverished and inconceivable. This morning, as he approached home, he found himself smiling again; things had suddenly got a whole lot better.

A fortnight later, in the chill of early January, the bike came with him on the slow train from Waterloo to Exeter. The front and rear panniers, together with a new rucksack filled with all he would need to survive the coming term at university, came too. He'd already visited the University of Exeter once in December, just as everyone there was winding down for the Christmas and New Year break.

Reflecting on it, he had to admit that they'd been really helpful, finding him a room in halls and filling him in on what he'd missed in what was to have been his first term. He couldn't entirely escape the feeling they were pleased to have a celebrity student join them, but they didn't overplay it. To his mind, they'd found an acceptable balance between supporting him enrolling late on the Islamic Studies course without referring too often to the events of the previous summer and autumn.

They'd also chosen to handle what they called, 'any potential psychological baggage' Adam might have brought with him by offering him free 'counselling services' through the university pastoral support scheme. They had insisted on that first visit he actually met his psychotherapist, Inger Walker, at her campus office.

The urban sprawl of London, stretching out well beyond Clapham Junction's vast rail and signalling matrix, eventually gave way to fields and downland before the much richer greens and smaller fields of Dorset and Devon countryside came into view. For someone born and bred in the city, he felt a deep rapport with the increasingly open, rural vista.

After three hours in the short, diesel multiple-unit slow train, much of it single track, they finally laboured the remaining few metres to roll into Exeter St David's station. An elderly couple were complaining that the driver had failed to stop at Feniton station just outside Exeter and would now have to find another train back. It was late afternoon.

Once he and his bike were off the platform, out on the street, it was then only a short cycle ride, in the welcome fresh air, to the university halls. On arrival, he dumped his panniers and rucksack in his new room and returned to his bike to take himself off on an exploratory ride around the hilly campus, a journey which didn't take long.

He then pedalled off downhill, taking care for the road surface was wet and greasy. It was a short uphill push to the mainly modern, shopping-experience-designed, city centre itself. A few minutes more and he'd seen four nearby cycle shops and a surfeit of pubs to try, which lifted his view of the place.

Pulling off the High Street, he wheeled his bike down an alleyway to find himself facing a statue of a seated Bishop Richard Hooker, a tudor-looking cleric with a severe and bearded face, who together with the visiting crowds on the surrounding green were almost barring his route and vista of Exeter Cathedral behind them. Must have been an important guy in his day, thought Adam, but I haven't a clue why. Muswell Hill doesn't do statues, he mused.

Maybe if I hadn't come back from Mosul, they could have put up a white ghost bike statue of me – that would be a first! The flashback moment was unexpected, initially no more than a bright idea before dragging him down into something unpleasant. He thought of the days locked up behind grey concrete walls sitting on dirt floors, being blindfolded, being hit. Clutching his handlebars tightly he moved on, mentally and literally, and thankfully, the moment of painful memory quickly passed.

As the pale, chilly, winter afternoon sunlight disappeared and dark shadows lengthened, the cathedral floodlights came on and Adam decided it was time to get back, to meet other students and discover the new undergraduate world lying before him. Anyway, he was long overdue a drink, his ride showing him enough fine-looking pubs to try. After a couple of wrong turns he was nonetheless back at his student halls within fifteen minutes, bike locked away and busy introducing himself to his new room-mates.

23

'Hi, I'm Adam, just arrived from London,' he said to a tall girl with purple hair. She was busily boiling pasta.

'Hi Adam, it's Gemma. Do you want some pasta, seem to have put too much on for me. There's some pesto in the bottle, grated cheese on the table. Grab a plate. Forks are in the middle drawer.'

The casual informality of it all struck him. This was an open-feel living space and self-expression was king in a laid-back, pseudo-relaxed way.

By seven-o-clock he was with the six others from his halls' group. Now all back for the start of the new term, they wanted to show Adam where the best student places were for a drink and a night out in Exeter. The pace of social engagement had wonderfully lifted and Adam found himself swept along, happy to be included, delighted to be allowed to be simply himself. Charlie, Alex, Gemma and the others milled around him, laughing and joking as they headed for town.

The first pub was bright and garish, a two-storey place specialising in shots and cocktails. He joined in. When it came to competitive drinking, he told himself, he didn't want to be the one holding back.

Later, three or was it four pubs later, they were in the High Street going through the door of an Australian named pub in a crocodile line. This Aussie watering hole had banks of TV screens behind the bar and a sports match being played on each. Local beers were bought and Adam realised he'd not had quite so much to drink for a very long time. But this was only the start; on they went, bar after bar, pub after pub, rolling, leaning, becoming ever more noisy until he knew he was in a such a state of inebriation, he was totally dependent on his new friends to guide and return him back.

As each drink had gone down, so he got to know another name, another person and their world; he felt he'd been initiated into their circle, as just another student, which is exactly how he wanted it to be. For that, he was more than pleased. In fact, for the first time in what felt like years, he felt deliriously happy, finding himself disappearing in a fog of clouded laughter.

The drink made him feel less inhibited and released him and he began telling them his story. They liked to listen to his story and tonight he liked to talk. Of course they knew who he was, but he was one of them, Adam the student. By one, or was it two or three in the morning, they were all linked arm in arm across the width of Queen Street, boy, girl, boy, girl, Adam in the middle, heading back, ever so slowly, voices loud, rocking and rolling, returning to the halls, where he knew he would collapse into what he hoped would be an unbroken sleep.

On their return, on the notice board by his room, Adam saw an unmissable white envelope had been pinned up, his boldly-typed name and address clearly marking it for his attention. It eluded his grasp the first time, then with Gemma's help, it was captured in his fist at his second. He tore it open to see the name, 'Inger Walker, Psycho-therapist'.

'What's it, what's it?' he muttered, staggering forward.

Gemma took it from the envelope and read it to him.

'You've an appointment to see Inger the shrink, at 08.30 next morning, or should I say in four hours' time,' and she burst out laughing.

'Fuck,' was the last thing he said, as, still clutching the letter, he collapsed fully clothed on his bed. Gemma shut his door behind her as she let herself out.

Next thing he knew, a phone was ringing somewhere. It hurt his head. Please would someone bloody well answer or switch it off, he thought. It stopped and then started again. Hell, it could be mine, he reasoned, his arm sliding towards his jeans pocket to retrieve it.

'Hi, Adam. Are you there? Adam?' Some distant female voice seemed to be calling him.

He grunted.

'Inger,' a female voice cheerily replied.

'What time is it?' asked Adam, trying to raise himself.

'8.40. Wondered whether you had got my note?'

Adam was trying to think hard, but his brain wouldn't work. She kept talking and was explaining to him where her room was and how he could get to it and how many minutes it took and that she was free now until 10am if he could still make it. When he saw the screwed up appointment letter on his bed, only then did things begin to fall into place.

Adam didn't know what to make of Inger and her 'counselling support'. He knew that it was something offered to people who had been through some crisis or loss, or maybe had difficulties at home or mental health problems. However, he didn't place himself in a 'needy' category, nor did he want therapy, but by the time he put his mobile down he found he'd agreed to meet up simply because not to have done so would have been more difficult than turning up. He'd just not been able to get his brain sufficiently into gear to find a reason not to go.

'Yeh! Yeh! Sorry, sorry, I'll be with you in ten, make it fifteen minutes,' he told her.

Slowly he moved into a vertical position, dragged himself to the bathroom and was horrified by his appearance in the mirror. Hair dishevelled, needing a shave, eyes bloodshot, he splashed cold water on himself. He drank water, more water, trying to wash the sour, stale taste from his dry mouth and throat. Trying to rouse and shake himself into life, he knew it was not going well. Thankfully he saw he was still fully dressed, saving him precious minutes.

He stepped outside. The cold January air hit him like a shock wave, bringing some further awakening as he hurried on, briskly walking the short distance across the campus. Wondering what he smelled like as he arrived, he timidly knocked on Inger's door with its smart, anodised, aluminium nameplate.

'Come in Adam, so nice to see you again, would you like something to drink?'

'Drink?' His thoughts still on the previous night, Adam's mind stayed with the word drink, making him mouth by way of reply, 'Yes, drink,' as he lifted a weary arm and pointed in the direction of a tin of Diet Coke. She showed him to an easy chair, so clinically clean looking he was unsure whether to sit in it. Perching herself opposite at a respectful distance, she was a creature part parent, part medical, part bureaucrat, thought Adam. She wore a light-blue jumper, dark skirt and a multi-coloured scarf, an altogether well presented lady. She began to speak in a very deliberative kind of voice, choosing her words carefully.

'It's so good to welcome you to Exeter. How are you finding things?'

He did his best to answer her questions, wondering as the polite conversation continued, why she never told him anything about herself or what she thought about anything. Is she simply a mirror, a non-person of some kind? Adam then wondered how much of what was happening was really about covering backs, ticking boxes.

He felt she needed to know from him that the University had indeed provided him with good accommodation, good room-mates and all the support someone who had been through what he had might need. He was a listed, 'at risk' student, who fell under their 'safeguarding and duty of care' umbrella. Counselling was really to serve their interest, he thought, a cynical rather than genuine service provided for his benefit. Negative thoughts aside, he found he was tiring of all this talk and his head was throbbing. Finally he got the opportunity to ask what he really wanted to know.

'Excuse me, but what's the point of me coming here?'

This caught her somewhat off-guard and he could almost hear the cogs inside her head turning in such a way as to produce in due time a well-constructed thought out answer. He imagined he could see what was going on behind those grey eyes. Why does she wear such boring middle-class clothes? Normal people don't have conversations like this, thought Adam. She interrupted his thoughts.

'Well, you've been through a lot since last summer and these things affect different people in different ways. It's good to talk, reflect on things, put them in their place, assess what effect it's all had and what you might want to do to move on, make the most of your future.'

'You mean, I was captured by ISIS, held in solitary in Mosul, suffered like I never knew whether the next moment I would live or die a horrible death. That I was hurt, got pulled into a horror movie back in London not of my own making, in which people died and I very nearly did too – that kind of thing.' He looked her straight in the eye. She nodded.

'What the hell would you know about any of that? If I want to talk about it anywhere, I'd talk to my mates down the pub, like I did last night.' He realised he'd rather betrayed himself, emotionally overreacted perhaps, but it was the truth, wasn't it?

'Yes,' she said calmly, 'it's all those things, and how they stay with you.'

Trying to correct for his outburst, wanting to show himself to be a reasonable kind of guy, he said more quietly, 'If you must know, I don't always sleep that well, but I'm not stupid, I know about post-traumatic stress disorder. I wake up sweating sometimes, I never used to. Another thing, I don't like small rooms now, I don't know why but I can guess, I've not got over that yet. It'll take time. Oh, and I don't trust people I don't know. I'm much more wary, guarded, bought a new lock for my bike, that kind of thing. Lots of things are different now.' He paused, she was still listening.

'I've changed, but that's life, well it is for me. My parents are well meaning, but insufferable, though I could never say that to them. They're so over-protective, it's like being cocooned, drowning in cotton wool. They signed up to the health and safety charter before those words were invented, always asking if I'm alright and telling me to be careful. I put it down to both of them being teachers, a profession scared stiff of accidents and litigation. Don't get me wrong, I love my parents, but it's my bloody life, not theirs! So, to tell you the truth, I'm glad to be here in Exeter and to have left all that behind. I'm moving on, up for it, no looking back, I'm the one in control, right.'

28

The more he talked the less sure of himself he became. He wondered why he spoke so angrily at times these days; meanwhile a little voice was saying, 'liar, who are you kidding?' in the back of his head.

And with that, Inger said their hour together was over. Adam couldn't believe it, an hour had passed already! Inger said she'd be in touch and 'next time,' the cheeky assumption of it, thought Adam, 'it might be quite helpful to hear your thoughts on how you came to choose 'Islamic Studies' for your time here at Exeter.'

As Adam escaped the sterile air of the therapy room with its pale-green walls and red rug on the floor, he knew that she, with the magic-grey eyes, had peered inside his head and turned over a few nasty dark things resting in the corners. The demons didn't like it much and he thought they'd take it out on him later. It might not be today, this term even, but he knew Ali and his demons were waiting, biding their time, his name still on their hit-list. They'd got to him once and they'd do it again.

Grabbing the sides of the chair tightly, he stood up. It was time to go and see if any of his new found friends were up and ready for a trip into town, hair of the dog and all that. He chucked the empty Diet Coke can with a well-aimed throw into a bin on his way outside. The loud clatter reminded him he was still feeling fragile.

4

The spring term was a whirlwind of making up for lost time, lectures, seminars and assignments; it passed in a flash. As the summer term was coming to a more leisurely end, everything changed and the student atmosphere became more relaxed and laid back. Adam's end of year one dissertation on 'Multiculturalism in the UK, with particular reference to the place of Islam in contemporary society,' had gone in late, but they'd still accepted it, marked it, and given him a good enough grade, along with passes for the other tests and assignments which had regularly punctuated his progress through the academic year. It was all very surprising to Adam that he'd done so well, since he'd missed a whole term's study at the outset.

Looking at the academic blackboard on his laptop and seeing all his marks smiling back at him, he reckoned that, in sum, they were more than good enough results to please his parents. These marks also implicitly stated he'd done well enough to come back for year two in October. The sense of achievement, summer warmth and stretching empty days ahead did him good.

First however, there was the not insignificant task of finding the right way and the appropriate place to spend the coming two weeks in a summer placement he was supposed to have already arranged. This was to be time spent in an Islamic context. The university had given the students all manner of options from which to choose, but it was the student's personal responsibility to arrange it. Consequently, some had opted for placements in their local mosque, though mosques were few and far between in south-west England; others had chosen to travel abroad to destinations like Egypt, Malaysia and even Indonesia. The exercise was easier for the overseas students from places like the Gulf. They could simply go home for the summer and write something up, but what was he, Adam, going to do? He wasn't sure if part of the problem was that he was unwilling to venture out into what might be an unsafe place for him, but then again, it might be that he genuinely had no idea where to go for the best.

This lack of clarity filled him with a growing apprehension as the deadline for agreeing his summer placement approached. The Islamic context would take him outside the closed and protected ivory tower world of the university institution, where he'd found himself a new identity, cocooned as a student. Drinking, partying, socialising and having fun, mainly with those in his student hall group, had filled his time. Some of the overseas students on his course had opened his eyes to the very different worlds there were within Islam and also helped him as he'd struggled to familiarise himself with learning basic Arabic.

Being on the course had been a kind of bi-polar experience. One minute he'd be learning Arabic and then some familiar words from his time in captivity would come back, like the word for 'eat', 'akl', but sometimes he would hear a word of control or uncertainty, or words from when he was the subject of an IS propaganda video. These were flashbacks to a time when he never knew whether that word would be the last one he would ever hear. Such words would bring back with them uninvited and unexpected moments of terror and panic. Sometimes he had to quickly exit the teaching room, to take in fresh gulps of air once outside.

With just a couple of days to go in which to make his summer arrangements before term finally came to a close, Adam was at the sink putting crocks away in the kitchen cupboard. One of his room-mates, Raqiyah from Oman, came across for some water and told Adam she didn't particularly want to go home for the whole summer.

'I'd much rather go somewhere I haven't been before...' she said, leaving her sentence hanging in mid-air.

Adam wondered whether there were other reasons she wasn't revealing why she didn't choose to go home, but she wasn't giving anything away.

Then, half an hour and two mobile calls later, there were four of them together, the only four not to have fixed anything up, talking over salad and fruit juices for lunch in the cafeteria of the university's Institute of Arab and Islamic Studies. It was a fine looking modern building, airy, solid, almost out of place, given its oriental appearance. It had been generously provided by one of the Gulf States a generation or more ago.

'Why don't the four of us go to Turkey?' asked Raqiyah, her eyes suddenly lighting up enthusiastically. 'Have any of you visited, been on holiday there?'

Adam hesitated, he could picture Turkey now and one of the demons his therapist had stirred in an earlier session was rattling its cage inside his head.

'Yep, been there,' he said, 'last year. Done that. Got the T-shirt.' But to Adam's alarm the direction of the conversation wasn't for turning.

'Tell us. What's Istanbul like?' asked Bilal.

'Well, it's big, a city much like any other city with its fast-food outlets and shopping. Much bigger than Exeter, historic, and amazingly, I think more than anywhere it's where East meets West.' Adam hesitated before adding a rider.

'But to be frank, I'm not especially keen to go back. I got spied on by IS and set up whilst I was there. So, when I got out into rural Eastern Turkey last summer, and believe me that is somewhere else, I got kidnapped. It was all a bit of a nightmare for me, so I'm not keen on Turkey really. Can we choose somewhere else?'

'But the city of Istanbul itself would be safe, and if we all went together we'd watch out for each other. I've got an uncle who lectures at Istanbul University. It's the oldest university in the city and it's not overrun by terrorists or spies or anything. He's been there forever, it's on the European side and they'd find us somewhere to stay on the campus, I know it,' said Raqiyah before taking a breath and adding, 'knowing my uncle, he'd fix somewhere up for us to stay for free! The air fares are cheaper now as fewer tourists

32

have been going, so we'd be able to afford it I'm sure.' There were two sets of approving nods and noises facing Adam. He could feel the tide turning against him.

Sophie, always quiet, usually the last to speak, added her support for going to Istanbul, giving as ever a considered view.

'I like the idea. Istanbul is where secular and Islam have an interesting history. It raises questions like, what does it mean for a mainstream Islamic nation to join secular Europe? It's also got some great tourist attractions and coffee houses and traditional shops. Come on Adam, if you've got any other ideas you'd better spill the beans now.'

Another ten minutes, and Adam knew he'd lost the argument and he could hear his demons cheering 'loser!' as he told the others that on second thoughts, what a great idea it was, and that he'd be glad to show them round some of the places he'd seen like the Hagia Sofia and the Sultan Ahmed Mosque.

It was settled there and then; they promptly wrote on Adam's laptop to submit the group's online proposal by email to the lecturer in the 'Islamic Studies' department who had been chasing them for days. It was all done before leaving the cafeteria. By the time Adam, Raqiyah, Bilal and Sophie had returned to halls, they had the green light, a brief, stark message stating, 'visit approved'.

Adam then had to call his parents to explain his summer.

'Yes,' he had told them, 'I will have to do some university work for two weeks from late August until the beginning of September,' but in his earlier conversation about it, he'd said he thought he might be staying at home to do it in London.

Unsurprisingly the call went badly. His mother was making him feel he'd made a bad decision. Within ten seconds he could tell she was losing it, politely shrieking down the phone, the way the middle-classes do, to say with restrained emotion and clipped words what a stupid decision he'd made to want to go back to Turkey. She felt sure the university wouldn't mind if he told them that, on reflection, he wanted to reconsider and in any case she and Adam's dad had arranged their summer on the basis that he would be at home with them. Finally, she added she was certain there were plenty of Muslim placement options in North London.

Adam listened on. He felt bad, knowing he was going to cause pain to his parents again, but knew the die was cast. Life had moved on and the pull of his new friends was winning. He was going to Turkey come what may, and he braved the remainder of the conversation, batting back the answers to his mother's questions the best he could. He hated it. As an only child, he felt he bore all their expectations and hopes. He felt the full, not the shared weight of their expectations resting on his shoulders alone. They had, as they frequently reminded him, not spared him any opportunity in life. Only when it crossed his mind to tell his mother how well he'd done this year and he was through to his 2nd year did he manage to leave the conversation on a better note.

The trouble was he felt glad and guilty at the same time. Glad he wouldn't be at home but with friends whose company he preferred, yet guilty for how he'd left his parents and how he'd now upset his mother. Something for my grey-eyed shrink to sort out for me, he told himself. Now there's a thought, he told himself, if I could tell them she'd agreed with my decision, that would help, surely. He made his goodbyes, promising to be home late the next evening, a fleeting time-window at home before he left.

As soon as he was free, he immediately sent an email message to Inger who almost instantaneously replied, agreeing to see him the next morning at 9.30.

Meanwhile, his three friends and would-be travelling companions were already searching online to book the cheapest flights and asking Adam to find his passport number. They'd settled on going towards the end of August, allowing everyone to have a bit of a break beforehand. Raqiyah had already called her uncle Abdul and he'd said, 'Of course. Come, bring your friends, it can be arranged.'

34

The flight looked like a trip to a London airport for the cheapest route and Adam knew he would have to make another difficult, salt in the wound call to ask his dad to put them up for the night and take them all to the airport. He thought he'd play for some extra time on that one for now. One bad call home a day was enough.

Next morning, he arrived at Inger's therapy room and sat himself in the now familiar easy chair. He'd got used to the routine, opening polite exchanges and at your ease chit-chat, the offer of a drink, which he always accepted, varying between Diet Coke and sparkling water. Then it was to the business in hand. They had, he had to admit, covered quite some ground in their sessions together.

As time had gone on he'd gained a growing respect for her ability to allow him to set and express himself on agendas he might usefully address. She never pushed him, was always patient, gentle and unruffled and, with her open questions and provision of a safe space for him to talk, he wondered, but didn't know for sure, whether she'd actually helped his life feel a little easier. In a subtle, unnoticed kind of way their times together had fallen into an organised journey through his life-story both chronological and emotional.

Unexamined instincts made hard working task masters in life, he'd learned. After six months of fortnightly visits he believed he knew himself better and was more equipped to keep his demons, those so far identified at bay. His bouts of unpredictable anger, his descent into dark moments, his fear of small spaces, his inability to trust, his nightmare moments and occasional terror flashbacks and his ambivalent attitude towards Islam all featured heavily in their conversations. Having initiated today's visit he knew she would ask him why he wanted to see her, so her question was no surprise when it came.

'You asked to see me this time, what prompted you to call me?'

'I have to do some uni work over the summer and I've decided I'm going back to Istanbul with three other students.'

'How do you feel about that?'

'I won't be on my own, there's four of us, and we're just going to Istanbul, staying at the university. Initially, I didn't want to go. You know what happened there. I know it won't happen again, but it makes me feel, well very insecure, not in control, not confident, maybe a little scared. And it's more complicated. We've talked about my parents and it's hard for them and this makes me feel I'm hurting them, messing up their summer plans and I care about that. But it also makes me feel I need to show them I run my own life, that my student friends are important too, that I feel stronger in myself. But, I wouldn't much welcome another conversation with my parents like the one I've just had and, I feel, well, guilty. I really want to be with my friends rather than them. So how's that for how I feel? All a bit shit really. Sorry about that. Is it the right call? It all seems very rushed, pressured. Did I make the right decision?'

'What do you think Adam?'

'Yeah, still thinking on it, I don't believe in demons, but .if I did, I'd hear them thinking they might reach me again. But yeah, I'm OK about it, but I want to know you agree with my decision. Do you? Have I made the right call?'

'The right decision, you would say, is the decision you take. It's your decision not mine.'

'So it is the right one and you won't disagree or try to persuade me to see it any other way.'

'What other ways are there to see it?'

'My parents' way for one. But I can't please both them and me, so that's it, settled.'

'Are you absolutely sure your decision has considered all the important matters here?'

He hesitated and silence fell between them.

'There's one more thing. I don't want going to Istanbul to trip me up. I don't want to freak out in the first mosque I go into or feel paranoid walking down the street whilst I am there, feeling that people in the street are stalking me to do me harm. I don't want to re-awaken things I think I'm moving on from. But all that's manageable I think. If things feel bad,

I'll come straight back, I won't be a prisoner there now, will I?'

And with an interrupting persistent knock on her door from another student pressing for help, Inger quickly wound things up and Adam was on his way back to his halls, thinking of the call to ask his dad to put them up and take the four of them to the airport.

'Hell,' he said to himself, 'I'm Adam and it's my sodding life. Its time to live it. Bring it on.' For good or ill his mind was made up.

Days later he was in his now familiar study-bedroom, his stuff half-packed up in his panniers and rucksack. He pulled some pinned up papers off the wall: letters from the estate agent lettings office, and folded them into his pannier. All the rooms had to be cleared for the summer vacation. Term-time students and most undergraduate students had already left the campus. He struggled downstairs with his things, collected his locked bike from the cycle store and loaded up.

This time last year, he told himself, as he stuffed the remaining things into panniers, things were very different – me, a prisoner of IS with no prospects. How things change! Next term he'd be out in digs, somewhere near St David's Hill, sharing a flat with Raqiyah, Bilal and Sophie. He reminded himself he had a few mobile calls to make; top of the list a call to alert his parents to the arrival of his three friends. Well the calls could wait for now, and besides, they would help fill the time on that interminably long slow train back to London later in the afternoon.

A year at uni all done and dusted. Pretty cool. Now for two weeks with mates in Istanbul, and time alone with Raqiyah. Hmm, he thought, I quite fancy her, can't be bad, can it?

In the dark interior of the cycle store he saw a reflection in the door's window pane, and just for a moment, he thought he saw a smiling Ali looking back at him, beckoning him to bring it on. He caught his breath. 'Bloody demons,' he said out-loud, 'Fuck off!'

It was time to move off. Grabbing all his stuff he shuffled awkwardly and as quickly as he could out of the store, away from his hall, and minutes later he and his loaded bike were heading downhill fast, just a few minutes more until he caught the hourly train soon to leave Exeter St Davids station for several weeks in London and then, yes, Istanbul.

5

A deep deep drag, that would help. Concentrating hard, she filled her lungs and instantly her head felt light and fluffy. She was floating, drifting off to white noise of exploding pin-prick stars, a legal high. Somewhere nearby her friend Melissa was speaking, but her voice was distant, shrill and strained. Sooner or later Kaylah knew it would wear off, reality would come back and her body explode.

'Thought you'd just put on weight, I did,' said Melissa. 'But looking at you now, big belly, big tits, it's obvious, fucking obvious. Now bloody well push like they keep telling you to.'

Melissa glanced up at the clock, less than two minutes since the last contraction, and then at her college friend on the bed, face in a mask, drawing deep on the gas and air.

'Why is it so long drawn-out? Why are we made this way? A bird drops an egg into a nest like so,' she let her arm fall down to the bed. 'Us humans, well it's such hard work. When you asked me to be your birth partner, I didn't think you'd take all day, so push, push now, now.' She watched her struggle and pant and then fall back on the white pillows. She rather regretted she had agreed to be with here for this.

Kaylah wriggled slightly and groaned some more, another wave of pain was screwing up her insides and doing her head in. Once again, she sucked deeply on the gas and air, her hands screwed tight clutching anything in reach – the white sheets.

'Ow! Get off me!' Melissa yelled, 'your nails are digging right in. You're the one supposed to be having the pain, not me.'

Kaylah released her, and then laughed, and laughed again.

'You're mad,' said Melissa, and began laughing herself.

A plumpish, comforting sort of midwife heard the noise and looked in. She stepped up to the end of the bed, picked up the clipboard, then prodded and poked, and looked up at the bleeping array of figures, lines and diode lights on the silver-grey monitor.

'I'd better hang around. Your baby's well on its way,' she declared.

Melissa was relieved, not only knowing professional help was on hand for her friend, but because all this was stuff about which she hadn't got a clue. More pressing, she could now attend to her phone whose excited chirping demands she had been forced for all too long to ignore.

'Phones are like babies,' she offered, pleased to be saying something she thought might be useful; 'they never let up.'

She wasn't sure Kaylah heard her. Kaylah was screwing her eyes shut now. Not since the May exams two months ago when college invigilators had been ruthless in their mission to silence mobiles, had Melissa and her pink phone with starry case been so estranged. As the midwife chatted to Kaylah, Melissa flipped open the lid with familiar dextrous ease, a quick glance, then some fluid screen tapping. She thought, this coloured screen served as her own life monitor, its ebb and flow, its flashing and colours showing just how much she too was alive. When nothing's coming in, she told herself, I feel as good as dead.

'Cool. Baby will be born on Friday 21 July. Easy one to remember that! Listen Kaylah, pay attention, says here, it's the birthday of my favourite actor of all time, Robin Williams. I loved watching "Mrs Doubtfire" when I was a youngster. The lengths that man went to to see his own kids. You remember it don't you Kaylah? He wore a wig and make up and took that job as a housekeeper to fool his ex-wife, just so he could be with his kids. He was brilliant! Such a good dad he was, really cared, made an effort...'

Kaylah was listening but not responding. She found it kind of comforting to have Melissa there wittering away about anything, anything to take away this surging, all

40

enveloping pain, even if she was going on about dads in films, dads who weren't there. No way was this baby's dad going to be near his kid, that bloody terrorist, life-wrecker, manipulative bastard.

'Bastard!' she yelled.

There was movement down below, it felt different, she could feel her baby pushing out, the warm wetness of it sliding into the world. The midwife was bending down and reaching between her legs.

'One last push,' she said gently, her hands carefully taking the weight of the emerging baby.

'And Robin Williams, he was so good as a woman. He fooled his former wife completely. She had absolutely no idea and I think he fooled himself too. Hey, you never told me who the kid's father is. You never told nobody. He should be here not me, that's what's normal. But then nothing has been normal innit? You bloody well didn't know you was having a child until you'd done your exams, did you? Just thought you'd been eating and eating and getting fat. Surprised us all with your end of year results, you did! A 100% in baby making! Not much less in your Business Studies, what was it, 85%? Two achievements with distinction. Bloody brilliant! How's that baby doing nurse? Is it, is it, is it...'

Melissa's voice drifted into silence as her eyes began to fall on blood and mess. Monitors beeped and took over as the midwife rose, clutching a bloodied but quite definite baby boy. A gurgling sound and then yelling cries pierced the air just as the midwife turned to catch the fainting Melissa, or rather leaned into her to break her fall. Who made the loudest noise, Melissa or the baby, would be argued about later.

Kaylah couldn't concentrate on Melissa. She was totally engaged in delivering her baby, her life governed by earthy pain and bodily demands. As the midwife struggled, Kaylah's arms reached forward and tenderly embraced her child as Melissa declared she was feeling unwell.

A couple of hours later, Kaylah and her now checked-over, healthy baby boy with a dark, not black complexion and curly but not tight frizzy hair, were wheeled across to a

41

recovery ward. It was an ungainly royal procession. Kaylah was propped up by several pillows like the Queen of Sheba on some mobile throne, the baby like some precious sceptre of gold across her regal chest. Melissa, her fainting now behind her and fully recovered, was scurrying alongside almost hopping, trying to take ever more mobile photos, whilst at the same time there was the clicker-clatter as she wheeled along Kaylah's pink suitcase full of her things and what she had hastily got together for the baby.

'Can I send the pictures out on Facebook?' Melissa cried. 'You look amazing!'

Kaylah was too exhausted to answer, but smiled meekly, which Melissa took to be consent. Minutes later Melissa reckoned everything was 'done now' and she excused herself, leaving Kaylah trying to tease her crashed hormone-spinning brain into life. There was a hug and a kiss from Melissa on both of Kaylah's wet cheeks and then she'd gone.

It was now just her and her baby boy. She gazed at the new life now sleeping in her arms. It was the tiny fingers clutching hers that mesmerised her.

'Perfection,' she said. Tired and not daring to give in to sleep for fear of dropping her baby, she knew that any sleep she might have would be short-lived. The crisis past, life began to slow down and she began to contemplate her new situation and status. She looked around her post-natal ward at the Enfield Hospital; she noticed other mums and their babies and wondered at the new world she was in.

Motherhood had arrived unexpectedly and quickly, stealing her past life and terrifying her with the new. She'd had so little time to prepare and she had been scared, really scared. The months had simply flown since last autumn's whirlwind affair with Ali, and when it had all ended so disastrously, she'd been left feeling so embarrassed, such a fool, so angry, and very alone. She gazed again at her new baby, she was momentarily alarmed, she saw glimpses of Ali in his face and for a second feared he'd be coming back.

Her mobile buzzed, it was her mum. She took the call.

'A boy,' was all she could say. 'Please come and see me mum,' and then she cried. The tears wouldn't stop and she swallowed and burbled like a child, quite unable to speak. What an idiot I must sound, she thought.

The phone went quiet. She could still hear the tension back at home. Her mum wanting to come, her dad hovering over her saying, 'She's made her bed and had better lie on it.'

'I'm coming, on my way,' her mum finally said, before the call went dead.

Her mum's words, when they came, were all Kaylah wanted to hear, and she threw her phone down on the bedclothes. There were more tears, this time of relief, she told herself, but she had really no idea why she felt so emotional. Dad had taken it all badly, a 'family honour' and 'shame' thing, he'd said. For months he'd avoided talking to her, even encountering her, taking to hiding in the back room or going out when he knew she was in. Mum had hovered between the two of them and, but for Mum, she knew she'd have been out on the street. Her brother Clive would want to know about the baby, she thought, and at that moment a call from him came in, the phone glowing with life on the bedclothes.

'Nice pictures,' he said cheerily. 'Some a bit gory for my taste. When am I going to meet my nephew then?'

The realisation came that Melissa had actually posted the pictures.

'Hell! What must I look like?' she blurted out, before telling Clive she appreciated his call and hoped he'd come in to see them both. That was strange, saying 'see us both' she thought. It brought it home to her that it wasn't just her anymore. And, as if to remind her, her baby wriggled and shook its little lower jaw before letting out a cry out of all proportion to his little size. Looking round desperately she called out.

'Nurse, nurse,' and when the blue-uniformed figure appeared, asked, 'Please, tell me, what do I do now?'

She was allowed to stay in hospital just 24 hours as it had been a very normal, routine birth, though Kaylah thought it had been pretty grim. Her mum, driving the old family

Volvo estate came to pick her up from the hospital. Mum had been brilliant, proudly embracing her daughter and introducing her into the world of sisterhood through motherhood. Kaylah's experience was an awakening in her mum of the trials and suffering of her people, and where else did one stand when the chips were down, but alongside the needy and the heart-felt cries of one's own. In a new enthusiasm, some deep flame had been re-ignited in her life.

'Jamaica,' she told Kaylah, 'was built by its women folk. Don't you forget it. Your ancestors did not let the birth of children defeat them, nor will you; don't you mind what that father of yours says, leave him to me. You, my child, are coming home with Mama, with your beautiful baby boy.'

She was as good as her word. Their Edmonton, North London, 'Huxley Estate' brick-terraced home in Cheddington Road, was transformed with a single purpose. All became centred on the baby's needs. It proved infectious. Clive proved happy to help out as never before and, rather more quickly than Kaylah might have ever imagined, her father took her little baby in his arms and declared him, 'a fine looking fellow,' gently pinching and puckering her baby's cheeks.

For days, everyone kept asking Kaylah, 'What's his name?' Kaylah was irritated and each time fobbed them off. As his latest feed was coming to a contented end and her baby's eyes could no longer sustain the battle between open for more milk and closed for sleep, she was watching daytime TV. It was just the two of them together, warm, relaxed and content, when she said out-loud, 'Jacob! You are my Jacob!'

And that was it, he was Jacob Kone, taking his Mother's surname. The name went down well with the family, and her Mum even said it was a name deep in the roots of their family history, though she could no longer be sure which branch. As the family gathered round in the front room in mutual admiration of Jacob and shared their happiness, Kaylah knew in her heart it couldn't last.

There was also no way she could have known that, even then, Melissa's pictures had travelled far and wide and, in

Mosul, Ali Muhammed, now back from London, was being shown some new Facebook baby pictures by his beaming IS commanding officer.

'What a handsome son you have, Ali,' Salim said before flicking the laptop shut and turning his attention once more to pressing military matters.

In that brief moment when he saw his son and Kaylah on the screen, he knew that when the opportunity came he would be resuming his calls to Kaylah and making his claim upon his son Jacob, but that was not something he could tell anyone.

6

Kaylah grew more contented and fulfilled with each passing day, and she knew a fondness for another human being she'd never believed possible. Love flowed from her every touch and caress. People said she was a natural mother, and what at first had been guesswork and instinct became practised and familiar as the days passed and Jacob's feeding, changing and sleeping became an easy routine.

Yet her new life was not perfect for her. Past torments assailed her, especially during the night, when her mind turned to thoughts of Ali and his betrayal. There were flashbacks of the day she almost died and others actually did. But for Adam's instinctive catch and throwing of the grenade meant for them, she would be dead. It was after the night feeds, when she had put Jacob down again, Ali would appear phantom-like in long black robes drifting into vision, wanting to gaze upon her child, a spectral image that hovered between life and death. She wondered, would his ghost haunt her forever?

The real Ali had made a desperate, pleading, mobile call to her at the beginning of the year, just as she was leaving college for the weekend. It was a real shock; she'd taken him for dead. He sounded so near, although where he actually was she wasn't sure, but there was no doubt from the very first words he spoke, it was him. Ali didn't say he had made it back to Mosul, but that was what she assumed. He spoke to her in a pained kind of way, his final sentence short, just a faltering, 'I'm sorry.'

His 'sorry' was never received, all the pent up anger and rage she never knew she was capable of spewed out as she'd told him to 'Go to hell!' That call should have ended things right there and then. She would have had the final word, won the argument, and maybe felt better and moved on. But life doesn't let you move on, she thought, the past messes up your insides and its stickiness never disappears from the touch.

Lena Bloom at the Israeli Embassy was partly to blame for the bind she was in. It was charming Lena, in the smart clothes, with the coolly professional manner, who had asked her if she ever heard from Ali again, 'Would she mind keeping a channel of communication open?'

Kaylah recalled how she'd willingly assented to Lena's request, only afterward when it was too late regretting it. Back then, in agreeing to help Lena, she had been thinking it might be a way of getting back at him. For Kaylah, everything since last November's unbelievably terrifying events had been reduced to the personal, and she more than anything else wanted to hurt Ali badly, and if Lena could help her do that, then that was fine by her.

The fact of Ali being an A-list wanted terrorist, a dangerous extremist who might strike again, was what concerned others: but, for Kaylah, the pain he had caused most was what he had done to her. He'd taken and used her for his own ends, dragging her into his evil world, tainting her life with darkness, leaving her a legacy of nightmares and now a baby – now all she wanted was to hit him back hard.

When two weeks later Ali had called again, this time pleading with her for forgiveness, begging to be understood, trying to say he'd had no choice; saying she just had to try and understand, she was ready for him. She'd prepared herself for his second call as thoroughly as if it were a college assignment, and everyone knew that she was a high mark chasing, focused, hard-working student when it came down to it.

So when Ali called that evening she was fully in control, framing the conversation as if it were a piece of macabre fishing. She was the bait and she was going to hook him. She knew the Israelis only saw Ali as a terrorist, using his betrayal of her as a lever to lure him into their net. She wanted all of that, but most of all, she wanted the satisfaction of her own revenge.

47

This time Ali told her he was back in Mosul, but wouldn't be drawn as to how he'd achieved that. He'd told her some of his family had died and the family home had been destroyed because of what he'd done and he was trapped in a nightmare. She did not feel an iota of sympathy and needed to control her desire to express pleasure at this news of his suffering.

After Ali's call she'd called Lena the following morning. From the moment they began talking Kaylah intuitively knew that Lena had heard every word of the previous night's conversation and she instinctively recoiled at the subterfuge, eyes-everywhere culture, that Lena represented. Nonetheless, she was polite and accommodating, Lena giving a few further ideas for the next conversation. This was cold deliberate fishing, and she was part of a trap being set.

It became a pattern. Ali called at the end of every month, and with each call she sensed her own anger had begun to dissipate. Though knowing they were being listened to, she never let that detail slip to Ali. She got the impression he was making his calls to her secretly. When he spoke, he never pushed her and never seemed to find her anger at him too much. She thought he had told himself that was what he was to expect given the way he had treated her.

The last time he'd called at the end of June was when she'd finally realised she was pregnant, but never for a moment did she think of telling him. On this last call, Ali had once again seemed so lost, this time asking her how her brother Clive was, and whether she would apologise to him on his behalf as he'd deceived him too. Things were tough in Mosul, he said. He'd be on the move again shortly, he said, because it wasn't safe to stay in one place for long for fear of a drone attack. She didn't believe him and guessed there might well be another explanation for Ali being 'on the move again'.

This last time had been the most difficult conversation to date. So in control in earlier conversations, this time Kaylah found she simply didn't know what to say to him. She knew he could sense that, and when he'd asked her, ever so gently, how she was, rather than answer him, she'd put the phone down. She was feeling pulled in one direction by an exploding anger, and in the other by the man who seemed to control her like some string puppet. He didn't ring back. Indeed, she wondered whether he would ring again.

Now with a new baby boy, Ali's baby as well as her baby her thinking became more conflicted. One moment she wanted him dead, another moment, she wondered how she would ever explain things one day to her boy Jacob. Over time, something she now knew for certain was that she wasn't going to play Lena's fishing game any longer. If Ali died, for Jacob's sake she personally didn't want his blood on her hands. But how was she to tell Lena of her decision?

When she made her call to Lena next day, all she could say was, 'My life's changed and moved on. I don't want to be reminded of all this any more. You've no idea what it's been like with the media, the inquests, the interviews and articles. I'm done with it.'

Strangely enough, Lena just accepted what she said.

'I totally understand,' she said, 'I just want you to know you've been an absolute marvel, so really helpful these past months. With news that Ali is on the move again, we know to keep an eye on him.'

When the line went dead Kaylah knew she had just made a big mistake in thinking that that was the end of it. She also recalled she hadn't actually told Lena that Ali had said, 'I'm on the move again'.

The messes in my life are getting bigger, Kaylah mused, but looking down at Jacob's innocent face she was soon distracted. As she gazed into his dark eyes, she wondered how Ali must have looked as a baby, and what had happened to him to rob him of his innocence, to make him into someone upon whom she still desperately wanted to inflict revenge and lasting pain. That fleeting moment passed as a bubbling cloud on a summer's day and, as she looked again into Jacob's eyes, she found such joy, and all else was instantly dismissed.

Meanwhile Lena, now back at the Israeli Embassy in Kensington Palace Gardens, had just been told by her boss Dan Abrahams, the Political Secretary, that she'd made a mistake. Bearing over her and leaning on her desk, resting his weight on both fists, he made her feel both uncomfortable and vulnerable. Looking her straight in the eye, he then addressed her in a tone of seriousness which made it absolutely clear what was expected and where her real duty lay in the coming days.

'Kaylah Kone is to be kept on board at all costs; by whatever means, we get Ali, right!' he thundered.

7

Salim, his CO, was as good as his word, giving Ali a full six months to recover and attend to his family. Things changed for them. The CO had made available a large apartment above his own and provided help on demand with their move into their new home. Ali guessed he had been waiting for the right person to move in, and Ali had seemed to him to be exactly that right person.

With the move here, to the local centre of operations in Mosul, he felt the constriction as he was ever more closely held in the tight grasp of the IS leadership. Part of him felt fine about it, being treated as a trusted insider, an elite at the heart of operations, but deep inside another part of him felt that the door to any personal freedom had been permanently and irrevocably slammed shut and locked. His life was, more than ever, no longer his to lead and he felt doubly cornered because what was left of his family were with him.

There were always two or three of Salim Ismat's entourage offering to help with the move and associated practicalities, so much so he felt their new home was intimately connected to Salim's men. In fact it went further than that. Over the coming months they sourced all manner of furniture and fittings, pots and pans, blinds for the windows and white goods for the kitchen, rugs and a telephone – much of it quite unsolicited. Ali imagined that most had been purloined from empty houses where families had fled. He was being set up, fitted up in every sense, bound to his CO. He didn't like it, but outwardly couldn't show it, meekly thanking his providers every time they turned up with yet more goods.

For his part Ali liked the security from outside attack which the place offered, nestling between hospital and school, but he wasn't happy at the thought of being on such intimate terms with his CO. His every move and that of his family were known and under scrutiny as never before. Furthermore, he knew his family would find the adjustment from their traditional family compound to living city-style in the confine of an apartment a mixed blessing. In the past the family had often idly talked about moving into a flat, like most of their neighbours, but had valued their independence and in the end never wanted to make the transition.

But why was he thinking in terms of 'family' whilst in reality only his ageing uncle and mother were actually living there? Mo, his wife Sara and Ahmed seemed to be spending most of their time at the hospital waiting until Ahmed was well enough to complete his rehabilitation at home. It had been many weeks of waiting for the complicated injury to his leg to heal. As he reflected to himself, Ali realised his home meant little to him anymore. It was a shadow of what it had been.

Maybe it was all for the best to make such a change now, Ali mused. Mo would need to take his son to the hospital regularly for some months to come, and as it was next door that would make life easier for them. As the surviving family was small in size now and the old compound hard work to keep going and keep clean, the easy to use apartment was a good arrangement. The older ones, his mother and uncle, well, they could manage their lives better in a flat, and if they kept in with the CO then they would share in some of the benefits, the largesse, the spoils of war he would sometimes distribute to those near him.

Once the months of resting were over, he was summoned downstairs. It was July, the summer heat unbearable outside and not much better inside with only occasional electricity to run the air-conditioning. People sat quietly in the shadows, never far from an open window in the hope of catching the slightest breeze. Ali no longer had a walk and time to think before speaking to his CO, now the family phone served as a direct intercom by which Ali could be immediately reached. Today, once his sandals were on, he was downstairs with Salim in less than five minutes.

52

The usual formalities of greeting and the offering of refreshment were observed before the two of them sat down in silence facing one another. It was here in this very room last summer, Ali knew, that Adam had been forced into reading a statement and a film had been produced. He wondered what had happened to it. Adam's escape was so great an embarrassment, he for one was certainly not going to mention it. He knew his own family would be viewed as entirely responsible for that and, if they or he ever made another slip, the matter would very quickly be brought up and used against them. He had no doubt about it. It was the way things worked. His CO shuffled in his chair. It was time for Ali to listen carefully.

'You spoke well on your arrival home back in the winter, my brother. You had everyone's respect, as you still do.'

'Thank you. It is good to be home, and to have had time with my family.'

'And as you rightly said back then, we need to be thinking about where we next take the battle against the infidel. You have a highly developed strategic sense. In fact you would never have succeeded in London, and made it home again, had you not got such amazing abilities.'

'Thank you, but it was the will of Allah. Enshallah.'

'Hmm. You are a competent and experienced warrior, quite able to command others in our cause. I have spoken with the elders and we are entrusting you with a responsibility that has every chance to turn things. It involves once more taking the fight to the very doors of the enemy. I thought a lot about what you said when you came back and the leadership have come to their decision. We are sending you into Turkey.'

'I have been there before.'

'We are sending you to Istanbul. This will be a very complex and ambitious mission that will so destabilise that country it will create a new opportunity for us.'

'I realise it has huge strategic significance for our cause.'

Salim said, asserting his authority, 'I doubt you realise the half of it. A great deal of work has been going on behind the scenes to prepare for this, so listen carefully'.

'For some considerable time we have been intending to shift warriors across the border into Turkey where we have many more sympathisers than people realise, both trained fighters and supporters. The millions of refugees and the hitherto open door there has enabled us to prepare the ground very well. Yes, there has been a steady drip drip of occasional IS attacks to remind them we exist, but they have no idea what will hit them next. How do you think this will happen?'

Ali could do nothing but shrug his shoulders. It was the right reply, for he knew his CO wanted to tell him all. His CO stood up and paced the room, ready to give a leader's speech.

'The Kurds have been getting ever more ready to fight for their own independence.'

'But we are not on speaking terms with them,' said Ali.

'That my friend is not the current position. Over recent weeks, we have been talking to the PKK leadership in terms of shared interests, common ground, cooperation and mutual benefit. I have been there myself and talked with them. They want to establish a sovereign state – their beloved Kurdistan. They want a slice of Iraq, a piece of Iran, a corner of Syria, but most of all a large slice of south-east Turkey. Now most of the world thinks that means IS and the Kurds are in fierce competition for much the same land. Truth to tell, I find that when you talk reasonably to people who have long chased their dream and you offer them the hope of achieving it they listen very carefully to what you have to say to them. For nearly half a century the Kurds have nurtured a dream of a homeland. I told them they could achieve it!'

'How?' asked Ali, intrigued to hear how this could be.

'If we work together, if we coordinate our planned attacks, double our efforts and effectiveness then the Ottoman Empire, their stumbling block and ours, can be destabilised and the fighting front moved west. Think about it – the airbase for those American infidel planes would have to go. Turkey has many Muslims who will be brought to a point of decision – the time to make their mind up to serve the Caliphate, the true Caliphate – and given the opportunity I'm sure enough of them will.'

'But surely the Kurds will fear that we will turn on them next?'

'We will, but they don't know it; and we will not and cannot do so for now. As a strategist you will appreciate the advantage of giving up a little in the short term for the sake of winning the long game. The Kurds are desperate for the win that has stayed forever just beyond their grasp; the promise of success we offer working with them has proved just too much for them to resist. We have agreed with them a joint initiative, a simultaneous massive attack on eight targets. We will each take separate responsibility for our attacks and without threat to either their or our command structures. They can live with that.'

'What can we offer them that is so decisive?'

'That is where you come in. I'm having you prepared to go into Turkey, to a cell in Istanbul where you will be the new IS commander for the fight for Turkey. An international cadre of fighters is being gathered together, including Omar al Britani from England. We already have a large multinational force of loyal IS warriors here and in Turkey who will, under your direction, coordinate their efforts to achieve a mighty victory. You will be travelling with three of our best fighters under your personal command at the end of July.'

'What targets do you have in mind? How do the Kurds come into it?'

'We have to attack several key targets simultaneously. These targets have been chosen very carefully. At the same time as these military attacks, we have in mind working with our allies to launch a cyber attack from here which will confuse and disable their key response bodies. Our method, to create sufficient fear and terror to mould the will of the people our way, should do the rest. There will be no going back for Turkey.'

'What targets?' Ali repeated, wide-eyed at the audacity of the programme being suggested.

55

'Listen! Attacks led by the Kurds will take place in Ankara. The IS unit, led by you, will cut off the head of the snake in Istanbul. Targets include: first, the heart of government, the parliament building; second, the heart of learning, a university; third, the busiest tourist site of the Blue Mosque. Elsewhere we hit the international football match between Turkey and England at the Galatasary stadium. I'll see you get proper orders with your targets fully specified. The Kurds have agreed to attack key military and police targets simultaneously with your attacks. It will be enough. There will be panic, fear and chaos. The country will disintegrate and fall into our hands. No western tourist will visit again. No true Muslim will dare question us.'

Ali then realised this was either the dream of a madman or something quite brilliant, but he had no means of knowing which, and in the present company it had to be the latter.

'Ali, on leaving here this afternoon, I want you to directly report to the training unit where you were prepared for London. I'm sure you remember it well.' He grinned. Ali noticed, not for the first time, that his CO failed to clean his teeth properly.

'It still operates from the gymnasium opposite. You will meet our visiting Kurdish commander and you will work together over the next week to finalise plans. This military mission is bigger than any bridge you thought of designing at Mosul University when you were an engineering student, bigger than anything you've done to date. This will be the most glorious thing Ali, and you are the one chosen to deliver it. Anything you need, anything you are uncertain about, then I want to be the first to hear of it. My door is always open, and since you are my neighbour, I would like to see you calling to see me very regularly to keep me updated. You will understand I have to report on this to our leaders myself. Much is expected of us both.'

Ali nodded to indicate he both understood and assented. It was time to take his leave. As he was about to stand, his commander's hands told him to stay sitting. He turned and opened the wall-unit cupboard behind him.

'I have something for you. A gift.'

He passed Ali a wooden box wrapped in a small blue and red traditional prayer mat. Ali opened it, grasped the gift and lifted it above his head. An AK47, his favourite weapon, and a timely replacement for the one left behind in London. He smiled at his CO in genuine appreciation.

'With this in my hand, with Allah's blessing, nothing will stop us. Thank you my master.'

Ali replaced the machine gun in its box, wrapped the prayer mat around it, and left clutching it under his arm. As he climbed the stairs back to his family's apartment he felt on the one hand excitement and pride and equally, on the other, apprehension and terror. He knew he mustn't say anything. If he did, he and his family would suffer. He was a man back in training. It started at daybreak.

He was just about to push open his front door when there was a roar overhead and then an almighty explosion outside. He fell to the floor as the building shook.

Looking outside he could see the hospital had taken a direct hit. How could this be? He ran out on to the street to see what he could do.

As he stepped onto the dusty street, he felt he had been transported back to the road when once before a bomber had come overhead, when his father had run out into the dusty street to be with him, and there he had died, shot before Ali's eyes. The moment came back, a bright and vivid flashback that paralysed him. He shook himself to bring himself to his senses. His mind turned to Mo and Ahmed. I must find them, he told himself running into the dust.

Bedraggled, shocked and bleeding figures approached him. Mo's wife Sara was among them, blood running down her face. Soon he learned the awful truth – Mo and his five-year-old son Ahmed, along with everyone else on the ward, had died. All were dead. Sara had only survived because she had gone outside to get bread, but she too had been knocked down in the street by the blast. He walked her back to his uncle and mother who had also stepped out on the street like himself. Then he ran to the hospital to see what else he could do.

Ali knew as he ran they were really after him and he felt vulnerable and unsafe again. He asked himself how anyone could do this to a child unless they were as desperate as IS were themselves? The thought gave him fresh resolve. He reminded himself he was a Jihadi warrior called to fight for a noble cause. There was nothing left for him here in Mosul and the sooner he left for Turkey to take the fight to the enemy the better. First, though, he must attend to the necessary preparations: more hastily arranged funerals and then carefully laid plans that had to be made.

8

The last part of his journey was tedious. Adam never enjoyed cycling in London traffic much, especially late on a Friday afternoon, and it was a hard final uphill drag to reach Muswell Hill with all his loaded panniers slowing him down. It had taken him an hour's effort from Waterloo and he was perspiring and weary. When he pushed open his grey-green front door to wheel his bike into the hallway he was immediately greeted by his parents, obviously and overwhelmingly delighted to have him back home.

Adam found the next month boring in the extreme, being away from student life, many of his London friends away and no holiday job to fill his free time. Facebook was a lifesaver as he amused himself by keeping up to date with everyone's summer exploits. He couldn't wait for the middle of August, whilst at the same time feeling a growing apprehension as their time for departure to Istanbul drew ever closer. The intervening weeks passed all too slowly. However, he consoled himself in thinking that his travelling companions would be here soon.

The plane for Istanbul left after a weekend, on Monday morning, 15th August, from London Heathrow. His three friends were arriving the day before, the Sunday, to stay over, his father having agreed to chauffeur them all to the airport, but that was ages yet.

He knew his parents had been looking forward to him coming home, and since his return they hadn't given him space to breathe. He'd often used his bike in the past few weeks to enjoy the summer sun and to take himself out of the house and find some space. They couldn't help themselves, he concluded. They were as much damaged by the trauma of last year as anyone.

A few weeks into his time back at home, his mum, Sue announced that there would be something of a dinner party the next day, Friday evening, where he would be the star guest. Adam had had ideas of his own and his heart sank. He tried not to show it, but his mum immediately chipped in.

'People aren't round until eight, so feel free to go and see your friends beforehand. Your aunt Ruth and uncle Phil won't stay long, so you'll be able to get out later too if you want. Ruth really wanted to catch up with you. She's got her own story to tell about last year. We thought you'd be interested.'

Adam had mixed feelings about hearing what Ruth would say. He had no doubt he'd be interested in knowing more about what had happened he didn't see, but he dreaded being brought near to the climax of Ali's attack in London – he didn't feel ready to talk about that with her.

'There'll be just the five of us. Like old times. Summer is always a good time to catch up. Mum and I are on holiday and it's easier for Ruth in August. Her Edmonton parish seems to chill-out in the summer, though I haven't seen her let up much,' his dad, Jim added.

Adam made his excuses to escape to his room, take a shower and change. He suddenly felt the pressure of being with parents again, his style cramped, his mood swinging. Picking up his mobile he found he'd got a list of messages and missed calls.

'Mum, that's great about tomorrow. I'm just going to take a shower and answer some of these calls.'

Friday 8pm arrived all too quickly. It was warm enough for T-shirt and shorts as far as Adam was concerned, and he flopped into the kitchen chair waiting for his aunt and uncle, Ruth and Phil, wondering whether to volunteer to help in the kitchen, but in the end deciding it was best to let his parents get on with the last minute preparations. The weather promised thundery showers, so there was no question of eating outside. Adam grabbed a lager from the fridge. It was reassuring to see it well-stocked.

His aunt was the vicar of a challenging Church of England parish in Edmonton, a quarter of an hour away, his uncle Phil an accountant. Adam liked them for their social commitment and they were always good to have an argument with, whether about God or politics. When they started talking about education, then his parents always had the advantage.

The doorbell went and after the customary greetings they all wandered through to the dining room and fell into their usual places. Funny that, always the same places, thought Adam, no reason for it, it's just what people do.

A Waldorf salad appeared for starters, white wine poured out to all except Ruth, who claimed to have drawn the short straw and was tasked with driving Phil home. Just for a moment Adam felt nothing had changed. The people, the room, his small Muswell Hill world, were just as cosily middle-class as ever. Meaningless polite conversations lasted until after the main course, and what little remained of the Boeuf Bourguignon was being removed to the kitchen. It was only then Adam really engaged. Ruth was sitting opposite him.

'Tell us Adam, how have you been since last summer and autumn's adventure. Is it, er, behind you, or does it still live with you?' she asked with a genuine warm concern on her face.

'Bit of both really, I suppose. Sometimes I think it's all a distant dream. Other times, sometimes when I'm not expecting it, I end up drawn back into it. Strange really. Sometimes I still wake in the night, but the year at Exeter has been great. I feel like a regular student. Life's been good actually,' reflected Adam.

'I don't suppose you got to hear how it worked out for us. You see, the Drop In Centre was where Ali established himself. I was plain naive. I had no idea and was so busy, I missed all the warning signs until it was too late. That Ali, he was a manipulative schemer, a very clever man. He took advantage of me as well as the student we had from Southgate College, young Kaylah Kone. A bright girl, but even she fell under his spell,' said Ruth.

'I know Kaylah. We've kept in touch a bit, what with the enquiry and so on,' said Adam.

'Did you know she's just had a baby? I saw her this week pushing her baby-buggy. She looked well. A lovely baby boy too. I don't know whether I should say this, but word on the street is that Ali is the father.'

'No, I didn't know. Just goes to show how life moves on. That's going to make life complicated for her,' said Adam.

'What is? Having a baby to look after, or Ali being the Dad?' said Ruth.

'Both, I suppose,' said Adam.

Ruth wanted to tell Adam her story. He sat back munching on a bread stick no-one else wanted, swigging his lager straight from the bottle at regular intervals.

'I've been working under a cloud since last autumn. It was me who let Ali sleep in the church when he had nowhere else to go. It was me who gave all of you tickets to watch the Armistice Day parade. I even gave Ali his ticket! Yes, I gave them to Kaylah, but indirectly I supplied Ali with the ticket he needed to commit an atrocity. It makes me shudder to even think about it.' Ruth paused, lost in her own thoughts for a moment.

'There was an enquiry, it's still running, nothing is done quickly in the Church of England, led by one of the assistant bishops, Bishop Stanley Chapel, from the other side of London. Between ourselves, it's been like the inquisition. Even elderly parishioners like Sid and Flo who put Ali up for us have been cross-examined. It'll be a whitewash of course, I know it will. No-one wants to accept responsibility. They'll look for a scapegoat to get them off the hook, and we all know who that will be, don't we? Everyone has wonderful ideas about checks and bureaucracy after the event, but it's hell to explain how you did things for what you thought was the best and with only limited resources to meet such a huge human need,' Ruth said.

She paused to pour some water from the jug into her glass before continuing. Adam thought she looked careworn and older than he remembered. It wasn't surprising really.

'You see, Ali would never have got near the Prime Minister otherwise, he'd have been caught! I've just felt so responsible, so guilty; I've had the Archdeacon of Hampstead watching and scrutinising everything I do ever since. You know we don't have any Muslims coming to the Drop In any more since it happened. It's not my doing. Everyone's welcome as far as I'm concerned. It's just they haven't been coming. I don't know why. Yes, we do get more police interest now, but it is as if the place has become tainted for everyone. The Muslims I've talked to don't want to be associated with a place of terrorism. That's what they say in private. Hardly surprising I suppose, that must be the reason.'

Adam realised the experience had taken its toll on his aunt and he felt sorry for her. She'd always been someone whose social conscience was well-intentioned and the Ali incident had knocked some of the stuffing out of her. She was scarred too, he thought.

'You shouldn't be too hard on yourself, aunt; Ali was a determined, ruthless guy. The media say he's back in Mosul, made it home to a hero's welcome. I saw a film clip IS had put out. It was him alright. They were treating him as a celebrity, guns firing in the air, crowds applauding. You can bet there'll be a price on his head for what he's done. He'll be living on borrowed time, always looking over his shoulder, nowhere to run. Reality is, he'll be hiding in some hole in the ground. Sooner or later he'll get what's coming to him. Those guys don't have a future. He'll be betrayed, a drone will get him or some of his own vicious colleagues will finish him off, you just wait. Ali's history, aunt,' Adam added.

Adam's phone rang. He half apologised and rose to leave the table to take the call, not recognising the number. He put the phone to his ear out in the hallway.

'Hi Adam, Krish Patel here.'

'Who?'

'Krish, you remember.'

The name rang a bell somewhere in Adam's memory. No, not a friend exactly, and then he had it.

'You're not Krish, the guy who picked me up when I arrived back in London?'

'The very same.'

'What are you ringing me for?' asked Adam.

'Heard you were going to Istanbul on Monday.'

'You're well informed,' Adam chirped back, trying to hide his surprise.

'We keep an eye on you. You know how easily you get yourself into trouble,' he laughed.

'OK, I'm going there. What about it? I'm not an idiot. I'm not cycling on my own this time, but I guess you know that too, don't you?'

'It's fine that you go. No problem at all. Do go and enjoy it. Istanbul's a great city. You'll have a wonderful experience. Just wanted to let you know, if you needed us at any point while you're there I'm texting you a number you can call any time.'

'That's too kind,' Adam replied a little sarcastically, 'but I intend it to be a fun trip with three friends from uni and we've got things we have to do for an assignment we have to write.'

'Oh, I'm sure it will be all of a fun trip, as you say. However, not to alarm you, Turkey is a bit of a focus for us right now. You've seen the news. You know what I mean, and we wouldn't want you to feel, well, vulnerable whilst you're there. Not after all you went through last time, and the trouble we went to to bring you back at government expense!' Krish laughed again. Adam couldn't help but warm to the guy. He said it all with such a carefree, light-hearted touch.

'OK. I'll log the number when it comes. Thanks Krish.'

He rejoined the dinner table. Ruth was lost in thought, looking down into her lap, whilst everyone else was talking enthusiastically about their summer. Adam thought further about the call he'd just taken. The trouble was, he knew full well Krish's department didn't do social calls. There had to be more to it than he'd said. He'd got absolutely nothing to go on, he told himself, but made a mental note to do a Twitter and Blog search later, before he went to bed, to check if something might be brewing in Istanbul he ought to be aware of. For now, he certainly didn't want to alarm family or friends, or indeed to start unduly scaring himself, so there was nothing for it, he decided, but to keep quiet.

As the evening wore on slowly, the trip to Istanbul was increasingly beginning to play on Adam's mind. He went into the kitchen to help himself to another lager before rejoining the family group still at the table, now on teas and coffees. He planned on going out sooner rather than later – he would make his excuses and meet up with friends for a drink somewhere.

Adam began texting to see who was around and within ten minutes learned that a number of his friends from schooldays were up at the pub on Muswell Hill Broadway. Pippa, Sian and Alex were already there, Matt on his way. As he set off up St James's Lane towards the pub, leaning into the rising hill, a thought struck him. How, he wondered, could he just have a normal time, a regular conversation with these friends, most of whom were also back from uni for the summer. No way did he want to talk any more about what happened last year, those terrible months culminating on Armistice Day. Krish's call had unsettled him, put his nerves on edge. He realised, since his call, the idea of going to Istanbul had stopped being fun.

As he wandered and mingled into the warm conversations and relaxed crowds filling the pub, he knew he needn't have worried. Students, he told himself, were the same everywhere. They'd already had more than a few drinks judging by the empty glasses and he could see his friends were already well-oiled; conversation was reduced to the usual chat about who had seen whom, what relationships were happening, and how the long summer was being spent. No-one wanted to mention what was happening at home and Adam was spared anyone asking him directly how things had been since 'it' happened. Nonetheless, he knew they saw him differently now. He was Adam Taylor: the only one whose name and story had been splashed across all the media, the only one whose name would appear in history for inadvertently killing a serving British Prime Minister. He shuddered at the very thought, then ordered a pint of lager.

He was a new Adam: the Adam who had been at the centre of every table talk ethical discussion. No longer Adam the ordinary lad who'd recently finished school, but some monstrous hybrid of ultra-ordinary and dangerous celebrity. He recalled how, in instinctively acting to save his friends, he'd thrown Ali's grenade meant for his group of viewing guests, out of the open window and had inadvertently killed the PM. He knew and felt the guilt from having ended up doing the terrorist's work for them. That the official enquiry had excused him of all blame, didn't mean he had entirely excused himself.

The conversations he had had endlessly with himself had lent him a special empathy for Joe Simpson, the mountain climber, who starred in the film, 'Touching the Void.' Not knowing what would happen, Joe had cut the rope supporting his friend, to save his own life. Adam suspected his friends saw him like Joe, as a tainted man. Inside, he often thought he understood Joe. Tonight he simply didn't want to talk about all this. But he needn't have worried, everyone was too glad just to meet up on a summer's evening and have a good time and drink. Finally, around 1am, people began to drift away. Adam smiled, the evening was better than he'd anticipated. He'd been spared. It was only then Adam remembered he had come out without a front door key.

'Fuck,' he said, as he pushed open the pub door.

The thought crossed his mind to ring the number Krish had given him to say he was in a fix, just to see what would happen. He began laughing and found it hard to stop as he set off alone on the ten minute walk back home. And then he thought, it's not home anymore. I've moved on. Home is where I am with my friends.

As he walked, he spotted 'bag lady Lil', one of Muswell Hill's 'characters'. Some things don't change round here, he mused. She was pushing her trolley on the other side of the street. Adam was glad there was room in life for people like her, sad and lonely people with nowhere to go home. He wondered what had happened to the other person he remembered. Everyone referred to him as Jim. Maybe he hadn't been so lucky, or maybe he'd gone back to his native Scotland. He didn't see Jim.

Ten uneventful minutes later he was outside his front door. His heart sank as he saw the downstairs light was on. It could mean only one thing, his mum or dad had waited up all this time. He'd stressed them again and then he thought of Istanbul and dark thoughts brooded in his mind, not leaving him alone. Would it really be OK, would he cope? He shook as he didn't know the answer. His mum let him in after he'd tapped the front window.

The boring days rolled into weeks. He read books, spent more in the pub than he'd intended or could afford and watched films with friends. All the while he was thinking of his trip to Istanbul and Krish's call. He scoured the media for news of the city and, not finding anything of interest, he gave up looking in the end.

When Sunday morning of the 14th August eventually arrived, Raqiyah was the first to appear, a large suitcase in trail. She'd pulled it from Highgate tube station having given up waiting for a Sunday bus. It was a half-hour effort, at the end of which her right arm was aching; on arrival Adam had to help her pull her case into the hallway. He was pleased to see her and his spirits immediately lifted. The others, Bilal and Sophie, arrived together by taxi around 4pm. All were excited about their journey tomorrow.

Adam's dad popped out to clean and fill the car at the local garage in preparation. Then his parents went off to the cinema with tickets they had got some time back and this gave the four friends chance to be on their own together. A film was chosen and called up on the TV, but in the end they didn't really watch it, only wanting to chat about what it had been like returning home, what friends were doing and to share their excitement, thoughts and hopes on going to Istanbul.

In the evening they sent for a takeaway and by then the normally immaculate lounge was looking like any student accommodation with takeaway cartons, mugs, glasses, bottles and snack-packets scattered around. Shoes had been cast off and feet were on furniture. Adam felt his friends were enjoying the experience of being at his home and for that he was pleased.

As to his own apprehension about what lay ahead he kept that to himself, and he made a conscious effort to join in the jollity as far as he could. Only Raqiyah who kept glancing at him seemed to notice that all was not what it seemed. She cast a knowing look, Adam took comfort from it and from the fact she chose not to say anything. He thought again that he liked her and found himself looking at her and into her eyes as she glanced at him.

Throughout the evening Adam kept thinking of Krish's call, made to him now over two weeks ago. It had to mean more than was said at face value. It weighed heavily on his mind, disturbing his concentration. British Intelligence didn't run a student baby-minding service, they were driven by risk assessments and national interest. That must mean they knew of some risk in Istanbul that he, Adam, might end up exposed to, a risk that had wider ramifications, even a national or international impact.

He looked at Krish's number on his phone and had half a mind to call it. But Krish had said, if while he was in Istanbul he needed to, he was to use it. Should he then phone the number now or not? In the end and not for the first time in the long run-up to going to Istanbul, he put his phone back in his pocket.

So did that mean they actually wanted him there in Istanbul? Well, they certainly didn't try to dissuade him from going, he reasoned. And why him, he thought, why me? He concluded it could only be because of the experience he'd had last year, either travelling in and being taken hostage whilst in Turkey or because he had seen the inside of Islamic State.

As he reflected and turned over and over his ideas, seemingly getting nowhere, it suddenly dawned on him, the point of connection had to be that maybe British Intelligence might think Ali would be in Istanbul whilst he was there and that they had a use for him, a purpose in him being there too.

68

What that might be he just couldn't imagine when all he really wanted to do was to have fun with his friends.

The thought of what might be, frightened him. Feeling too uncertain to know what to do, a kind of creeping paralysis of body and mind enveloped him. From that point on the Sunday evening got worse for Adam. In his mind's eye, at any lull in the conversation, he kept seeing Ali's face smiling at him, haunting him. Late that evening as he laid his things out in neat order ready to put in his rucksack to take to the airport in the morning, the ritual packing took him straight back to the night before his epic bike ride east, a journey that began with exhilaration and ended in, well, tragedy and trauma.

Finally, having set his alarm, he lay down, but he just couldn't sleep. His mind drifted, sometimes he could almost feel red desert sand between his toes and could hear distant Arabic voices whispering, taunting him. Shadowy figures in black robes came to look at him and then disappeared. He began to wonder if he'd made a terrible mistake in agreeing to go to Istanbul, but at the eleventh hour he couldn't cry off. There was no escape.

The alarm to get up and go to the airport went off unnecessarily, Adam was staring at the ceiling, eyes wide-open, having slept but fitfully, wondering what he had let himself in for. He could hear other people in the house stirring. Soon they'd all be on their way to the airport. Steeling himself, he sat up and tried to put on a brave face as he entered the day.

9

College had long since finished, Kaylah's diary was empty. She had only been out of the hospital a couple of weeks and her days now centred solely on Jacob and meeting his needs. Kaylah's life back at home was but a short honeymoon. She knew the parental sweetness wouldn't last. It never did. A small terraced house in Edmonton, North London, was too small to contain the pressure-cooker of Kone family life.

Predictably, everything exploded after Jacob wouldn't stop crying one night at the end of July. That night there was no escape for anyone from the incessant noise, maybe the neighbours heard it too and, no matter what Kaylah did, extra feeds, walking around, rocking him, in fact nothing she tried worked. Everyone had been kept awake. By breakfast time exhaustion and tension combined in equal measure to make a volatile mix. She felt the air was so thick it could be cut with a knife.

This morning, it was Wednesday, even her mum in her sagging dressing gown looked dreadful, bags under eyes, a slouching step to her movement, rabbit slippers flip-flopping as she joined Kaylah at the small table.

'Coffee, black, please,' she murmured. Kaylah passed her Jacob, now sleeping peacefully in her arms and went to boil the kettle. Minutes later she reappeared clutching the steaming brew. Shazee Kone took the coffee eagerly, Kaylah apprehensive as to what might follow.

'Thanks. I feel so bad, not as young as I was. Can't handle it. Can't cope. What can we do?' She paused before adding, 'Don't you think you ought to have your own place now you have a baby?'

'Oh yeah! How's that going to happen then?'

A silence followed, Kaylah grabbed a bagel from the packet and began to spread peanut butter thickly and roughly.

She knew there was no quick fix to finding somewhere to live and money, well, there wasn't any, and her Mum well knew it. Anger boiled over.

'Fuck Ali,' she shouted out, her knife clattering on her plate.

'Now dear, not in this house,' her Mum said, lifting the coffee mug to her lips in one hand and trying to keep Jacob steady in the other. She kept her tired eyes fixed on her daughter's face.

'It's not you in this mess. It's not you who's been trying to keep Jacob quiet all night. Huh!'

'It takes two.'

'What you say? Bit late for the morals, innit? Hold his head up more, think he might have been feeling a bit sick.'

'Don't tell me how to hold a baby. He's fine.'

'OK, give him back.'

Shazee passed Jacob over and a frosty quietness enveloped the space between them. Her mum had been brilliant up to now, but a corner had been turned, today everything was going wrong.

Her brother Clive would normally still be asleep at such an hour. He had nothing to get up for in the mornings and Sam, her dad, he was usually up by now; he too hadn't yet come downstairs.

In fact Sam Kone didn't appear until nearly ten when Kaylah was beginning to put breakfast things away. With a hard stare, first at Jacob and then at Kaylah he went straight to the point.

'Got to find some way of him sleeping. Can't you give him something? They got medicines for insomnia.'

'Try taking something yourself if that's all you got to say,' Kaylah fired back.

'Just remember who provides you with a roof over your head my girl.'

Her mum and dad were both against her now. There was nothing to be gained by trying to reason with either of them when they were like this. She got up and retreated clutching Jacob and climbed the stairs to their bedroom. As the sunlight

71

came in through the window, her next thought was that as it was a nice summer's day she would get out of the house, escape for a bit, maybe go to Edmonton Green or Wood Green Shopping City. She would go anywhere rather than stay indoors waiting for the next round of argument.

Her phone rang. It was Lena Bloom. Now that's unexpected, what might she want? she asked herself as she lifted the mobile to her ear.

'Hi Kaylah. How are you?' asked Lena cheerily.

Glad for someone to talk to, Kaylah decided to tell her just how things were.

'Well it's not so easy with a baby just a couple of weeks old and with a set of healthy lungs to boot. I've just had an awful night up and Jacob's kept everyone in the house awake too. I'm not exactly the most popular person with my family at this moment. So, guess today I'd say I was struggling a bit.'

'Sorry to hear that. How's young Jacob doing?' Lena said.

'Just fine. Health Visitor's pleased. He feeds, he poos, he sleeps, he cries and, well, he's adorable. I'm sure you didn't just call to see how I was. Any news?'

'Well, not exactly, but I have been told by people here to keep in with you, because "we never know when she might be useful to us again." Well that's what they tell me here. So that's why I made the call, but to be honest it's no problem for me. I've always enjoyed our chats, and truly, I was wondering how you were doing.'

Kaylah listened to the sarcastic put-on voice Lena used to quote her boss, feeling that here was a kindred spirit, someone who knew what it felt like to be on the receiving end of pressure like herself. She got the impression Lena was being honest with her, and so the conversation continued on. Lena was a good listener. She seemed genuinely interested and when told how hard it was for someone in Kaylah's situation to find somewhere independent to live, her sympathy extended to a promise to have a word with friends to sound out possibilities. Kaylah expressed her gratitude,

72

not thinking anything would ever come of what she took to be merely kind platitudes.

'You did so much to help earlier,' she told Kaylah before signing off. 'I really do appreciate it, and it is so good to chat with you again. Look I'll call you soon and see what my friends say about independent living. Have a nice day!' With that, she had gone, but Kaylah felt all the better for having had the conversation. The day was brightening up.

Kaylah realised that in recent days she'd been so absorbed in looking after Jacob, she hadn't chatted to someone like she'd just talked to Lena for ages. Even her friend Melissa from college seemed to have disappeared somewhere for the summer, and her usual circle of friends had gone unusually quiet. Yes, Facebook contact was something, but with a baby to look after now, her life seemed to have drifted apart from that of many of her friends. Her new life as a mum of two weeks ran in a clockwork around Jacob and his unrelenting needs.

Standing at the window she was gazing into the blue sky, there was the promise of a good day, so she began the task of preparing Jacob for going out. She changed him, gathered things together he'd need for later, then put on his warm clothes, realising as she did so that her life had changed more than she knew. No longer could she simply get up, grab a coat and bag and walk out of the door. Her life was two lives.

Once downstairs again, she placed Jacob in his baby-buggy, the baby-bag installed in the rack beneath. She glanced briefly around and called out loudly to her Mum, 'I'm off out to get some things. See you later,' trying to sound relaxed and cheerful.

Out of the corner of her eye she could see her Mum washing up in the kitchen, face fixed as she gazed down at the dishes in the sink. There was no reply. With that Kaylah slammed the door shut behind her and headed towards Edmonton Green, knowing she'd be less likely to spend money she hadn't got if she went there rather than Wood Green Shopping City.

10

A few houses on, Kaylah turned her head as she heard what she rightly guessed to be her own front door open behind her. It was Clive.

'Hey, Sis, mind if I come with you?' he said, pulling the door shut and his hood up over his head.

'No, but what gets you up so early?'

'The house is no place to be with those two grumping and complaining like bears with sore heads. They'll be having a go at me again if you're not there to take the flack.' He laughed, lifting her mood as he did so.

'I'm just wandering up to the Green. Need a bit of space. Jacob needs a sleep and the buggy will do it. How's that mate of yours, Winston? He was so good to me when Ali betrayed us. He picked me up and took me home. You were good to me that day too. I was, well, I was in total shock. Who'd have thought? Those people and the Prime Minister, all dead, and Ali the one who did it. How's Winston? Is he going to college like you in the autumn?'

'Winston's cool. Saw him yesterday. Replaced his car again. He likes BMWs, got one in Alpine White now. We went down to Cliff's Cafe in Tottenham in it yesterday. He loves his cars. He drifts along and gets by. Can't see him going to college, no way.' He laughed again at the very thought of it.

'I often wonder how he affords it all. I'm struggling. How does he do it? Or is it best I don't know?' She smiled knowingly, her brother taking the baby-buggy from her.

'That's it exactly Sis, best not to ask,' he whispered in her ear.

'Do you think the only way to get by is to work round the system, join the black economy? It's well, so normal round here to do that,' Kaylah quipped.

'Hey! What's my business studies goody-two-shoes Sis saying there? You really don't want to know what happens on the dark side. I won't hear of it.'

'But you know something about it, don't you Clive? I mean you're close to what Winston is into, you must have some idea?'

'Look I'm no innocent, I admit it. Me and Winston have been wayward in the past, but you get forced into these things. You end up not having a choice. But for the grace of God anyone can end up a criminal, a dealer, whatever. Me, I'm off to college September, got my place, following in my good sister's footsteps, my wayward youth all behind me.' He laughed again.

She seemed happy with that, though she wasn't sure she believed him entirely. After their conversation she didn't want to push Clive to tell her more, reasoning to herself that it was probably for the best; as Clive said, she didn't know what Winston was up to.

By this point they were passing The Latymer School in Haselbury Road, with its redbrick education buildings and sweeping sports fields surrounding it. It sat somewhat incongruously squashed between the A10 Great Cambridge Road and the densely built housing estates of urban Edmonton. The culture of the school and that of the people living around it couldn't be more different. The pupils, almost all from well outside the area were bussed in or dropped at the gate by doting affluent parents.

'That's a selective school. Whenever I walk past it I think of the divide between the haves and the have nots. It just makes me want to shout, "it's so unfair!" Only the best kids get there. The dice are loaded from early on and life's not fair is it? Jacob, could he get there one day, Clive? Do you have to be white and Asian and middle-class to get by? Life's not fair is it? How do they pay for those blue uniforms, their music lessons and fancy cars? Those like us living on the street have to find ways to get by. I tell you, having a kid makes you stop and think,' said Kaylah seemingly unstoppable.

Clive didn't reply. She couldn't tell what he was thinking. He was having one of his daydream moments. Suddenly something stirred within and called him out of it.

'Hey, over there, that's Winston's car. Coming towards us. What's he doing round here?' said Clive, his raised arm pointing towards the approaching car.

The shiny white car pulled up alongside them and Winston's window wound down with a quiet electronic buzz.

'What's up with your parents, you two? When I called they looked like they'd got the hump. Never seen them so miserable. How yer doing? Exercising baby, eh?' said Winston, a cheery smile on his face.

'Going up to The Green. Not much happening. Were you looking for me?' asked Clive.

'Yes, need to call over to Muswell Hill. Will's asked us to pop in on Dillon. Will's not heard from him for a few days, not answering his phone. Thought you'd fancy the ride. Sorry Kaylah, would offer you a lift, but no baby-seat yet. Anyway I've heard babies throw up!' he laughed.

'See you later Clive, I'm fine. Bye!' she said to her brother, pointedly ignoring Winston's friendly wind-up remarks.

With that, Clive and Winston left Kaylah wheeling her buggy on towards Church Street and The Green. Once in the car, Clive immediately asked Winston what this was all about. Something must be up. Will wouldn't ask a personal call be made simply because Dillon wasn't answering his phone.

'Well bro, Dillon has been out of touch with everyone nearly a week. Will says it's on his mind and he needs to know what's up. Perhaps Dillon has got himself picked up, but no-one's heard anything. Then again for all I know he's overdosed or spaced out after trying some new stuff. It's in all our interest, especially since the Post Office job, to make sure he's OK. Know what I mean? And, no way was I going on my own.'

Clive recalled how, after the Post Office job last November when they had divided the spoils, Winston and he had lain low, but Will couldn't help but keep his drugs

76

business turning over. His reasoning was there was good money to be had filling the vacuum left after Abu's unexpected death, and it was Will's name alone that everyone now knew as boss-man in Tottenham, Edmonton and across North London, he knew they'd come to him for their stuff and he'd been right.

No longer Will, his name on the street was 'Wicked' and to those closest to him, 'Wicked Will'. He had to instil fear, what he called 'respect'. The nickname helped. Strange business that, thought Clive, Abu dead in his flat and his dying nothing to do with any turf-war anyone knew about. A mystery. Perhaps he did die of a heart attack like they said. Whatever happened, Abu's demise did Will a big favour. His mind turned back to Dillon. Dillon was always the weak-link, unreliable, half out of his head on this and that. Will was right, it made sense to check him out.

It took a quarter of an hour before they were approaching Muswell Hill and Dillon's flat. Winston had taken to driving more carefully since a series of past parking tickets had caught up with him and he could do without the aggro or added expense of any more. Today he was in luck and pulled up right outside Dillon's flat.

'I want you to come with me,' Winston said, opening the door to let Clive out. Winston looked left and right, before beckoning Clive to join him.

Clive climbed out the car, moved to the flat entrance and pressed the door buzzer. He pressed again, and it was soon clear that either Dillon was out or was not going to answer his door. Clive looked round at Winston. They were left standing on the street wondering, what next?

'What we do now?' said Clive.

Winston shrugged and again looked left and right.

'Hang on a minute. Just popping back to the car. Keep watch a moment will you,' said Winston leaving Clive alone.

Seconds later he reappeared with a sports bag and pulled out a crowbar.

'No choice. Will says we must do what must be done. Stand there, give me some cover and keep an eye out. It's not a burglary, Dillon's our friend isn't he?' explained Winston to an anxious-looking Clive.

As Clive moved to cover as best he could any possible viewing of what his friend was about, he heard a splintering crack. Turning his head, he could see the front door had swung open. That's right, can't call this burglary, he told himself, it's our mate Dillon's flat. Dillon would never grass us up, but he might want some money for the damage.

'Come on,' said Winston, quickly pushing his jemmy back in his bag, 'we don't have long.' Inside, Winston pulled the jemmy out again to ease open the inner door to Dillon's flat.

Clive hadn't got fully inside the room when the powerful smell hit him. He put his sleeve to his mouth and nose, swallowing and gagging with revulsion and nausea. He saw Winston doing the same. Then he saw it, the shape of a man's body on the leather settee, stretched out, one leg down to the floor, the other leg crooked high with the foot resting on the seat.

No doubt, it was Dillon, it wasn't hard to tell, though his blotched and pasty-grey face clung more tightly now against his bony skull. His stomach was bloated and his hands claw-like. Nearby, a dirty spoon and foil, lots of pieces of foil, every one stained with brown residues. Clive was finding it hard to breathe and was feeling light-headed. Winston who'd stopped them both in their tracks with a raised and outstretched arm prevented Clive moving any further into the room.

'OK. This is bad. Now we know why Dillon's quiet. He's bloody dead! Looks like he overdid it once too often. Shit! Shit! Shit! Don't move. Don't bloody move,' said Winston, trying hard to take control of the situation, creases of concentration appearing across his brow.

Clive began to fear they were in a trap. Panic began to rise inside him, tentacles of paralysis were beginning to seize his limbs. His mind raced. He wondered whether Dillon had been killed and whether the attackers were still around. He looked round anxiously before dismissing those particular fears. The smell was so bad, his stomach was retching. He fought back the urge to be sick, swallowing saliva hard. Winston grabbed his arm to get his attention. It felt real and solid, somehow reassuring. He nodded in acknowledgement.

'Look we need to search this place before we leave. Anything, anything that might link Dillon with the Post Office job, or with Will, or us, must be removed. Get it? And, while we're at it, anything of value put in this holdall. Dillon can't use it anymore. You take over there, I'll search close to Dillon. I think he popped one too many, he regularly overdosed, even mixed and experimented, he had it coming, an accident waiting to happen. Don't feel too bad, he did it to himself. Look, he's been dead days. Don't think anyone else has been in. We need to be quick, but must be thorough. That's what Will would want. We're protecting ourselves. Wait. We've got to be careful. Don't touch anything. If you need to, use these to cover your hands. Mustn't leave prints, no DNA no nothing. OK? The pigs will have their noses in this trough soon enough.'

'OK,' Clive replied. His biggest fear was being caught for the Post Office robbery last November, and what Winston said about searching made sense. Steeling himself to the task, he was desperate not to get caught now he was trying to get his life on track. Winston grabbed some used plastic orange Sainsbury's bags.

'Use these as gloves if you need to touch anything, and make sure we take them with us.'

They hurriedly and methodically began their search. Clive began in the kitchen. There wasn't much to examine. Hardly any food or containers, nothing in the cupboards, a microwave with a meal still inside. Dillon lived frugally, mainly on takeaways by the look of the bin. The kitchen sink was filthy; dirty mugs and plates lay chaotically on every surface. Dillon's life had clearly taken a downward spiral right to the bottom. Clive opened the fridge using the plastic bag to avoid touching the handle. It was well-stocked with lagers on the upper shelves. He was in two minds whether to take them, but decided against it. In the door was a long carving knife. Dillon must have put it there for self-protection, Clive concluded. He bent down to peer below the lagers and into the bottom of the fridge. There was something in the frosted vegetable box. He pulled out the drawer.

'Bingo! Winston, I've got something. You don't keep a box of Weetabix in the bottom of your fridge, now do you?'

Winston joined him in the kitchen as Clive lifted the yellow box on to the windowsill, the only clear space. The yellow Weetabix box was full of wrapped foil packages, whether for Dillon's personal consumption or for selling on, who knows. There was certainly more than enough for many weeks of personal use. But underneath the yellow box in the base of the plastic vegetable box, was a clear plastic folder bag, the very same they had taken from the Post Office. Inside it was what was left of Dillon's share from the robbery. It was stuffed with a wad of notes. Winston flicked them through his fingers making a quick reckoning. Clive's visual impression was Dillon still had at least half his share from the robbery unspent. He whistled quietly at the lucky find.

'Put the whole yellow box and the folder in my sports bag. We'll check it out again later,' said Winston.

Clive did as instructed. Another five minutes and they'd found nothing more. Standing with their backs to the door where they had come in they decided to survey the scene one last time.

'Anything we've overlooked?' asked Winston.

'Nothing, 'cept we must be careful leaving,' said Clive, having cast his eyes round as best he could, though he could not help but look once again at the shocking grey-moulded mask that was now Dillon's face, the half closed dead eyelids threatening to open and look at him.

Moving to make an exit, Winston pulled the front door open a fraction. The coast was clear. They pulled the door shut using one of the plastic bags and tried pressing the splintered wood flat on both doors to make them less obvious. Clive pulled his hood tighter over his head, and even though they were out in clean air he couldn't lose the smell. They were careful timing their exit, pausing before entering the

80

street. When they did step out, it was to quickly climb into the car and pull away.

Unknown to them, Martha Jones from the flat opposite had been waiting in her old Ford estate, driving up and down for several minutes looking for somewhere to park. She really needed a place soon so that she could collect her elderly mother to take her shopping. Every Friday was the same. It was always busier and harder to park on Fridays, but that was when her mother wanted food in for the weekend. She observed the two as they left, black guys carrying orange bags and a sports bag to a shiny white BMW. They looked anxious and didn't notice her move across to take their parking place. As she watched them leave she was grateful for the space they had so timely provided.

Later that morning when she was dropping her mother back she wondered why there were police over the road and people in white plastic forensic overalls. She phoned Caroline, her neighbour opposite. Caroline worked in one of the nearby Muswell Hill nursing homes. She told Martha she'd called the police because of the bad smell in the hallway. She just knew it would be a dead body. It was only after she'd made the call she had noticed the front door to the block had been forced. As Martha crossed the road to go and see her friend, the police were reluctant to let her through at first, but Martha was not to be stopped.

The second officer in the hallway showed her to Caroline's door. She told him her mother lived opposite and wanted to see her friend. PC Bob Steer from the Edmonton station was a kindly policeman. He had been sent across as extra manpower. An experienced beat officer he knew the value in never missing an opportunity when it presented itself, however unlikely.

As Martha was about to disappear behind a closed door it occurred to him to ask her if she had seen anything suspicious. He discovered Martha was very willing to help and had an excellent memory for detail. He took out his notebook as she began to describe for him the two black men and their white BMW. It could be nothing, after all the guy inside had been dead a while, but somewhere in his head a connection was being made. As he thanked Martha for her invaluable help and for being an example of concerned citizenship, he slipped his notebook back into his top pocket. As to the identity of the two men, he knew, given time, it would come to him later.

11

Winston drove them back to his flat in Crouch End. The traffic was slow and they hardly spoke, each absorbed in his own thoughts. It was different once they were inside. They both grabbed cans of Diet Coke, the bad taste lingering in their mouths needed to be got rid of. Clive put the orange plastic bags on the coffee table and they both stood back looking at them.

'What do we do now?' asked Clive.

'Guess we've got to decide what to tell Wicked Will. He'll need to be told, but not everything and only what we want to tell him. Look, he doesn't need to know about the money. He wouldn't expect us to find money, or even if we did, to hand any over to him. I think we divide that between us,' said Winston.

'OK, but what about the drugs?' asked Clive.

'I'll deliver them to Will later. He'll be glad to sell them on. That way he'll be happy. He gets something. It's worth a few hundred. I'll tell him we searched Dillon's place thoroughly and left it clean. He needn't have any worries on that score,' said Winston.

'We'll need to get rid of that Post Office wallet. The idiot, fancy hanging on to that. It's as if he didn't care. Also the orange bags,' Clive said as he gathered the incriminating items together.

'I'll dump them on the way over to Will's place. It's best I talk to him face to face. I'll drop you off first, it's on the way,' said Winston.

Kneeling on the floor, side by side, they began to count out the money, putting the notes into two equal piles.

'There's less than I thought, just under two thousand each. You OK with that?' asked Winston.

'Yeh! Yeh! More than happy. I need to think about where to put it. Think I'll use the larger half to pay off my credit card. The rest will see me right until I start college. I spent what we got before on clothes mainly; and bought my new nephew a baby-buggy. This'll mean I have to plead for money off mum and dad less often – they make me feel like I'm getting charity. Tell you the truth, I need out from home, someday soon, I'll get my chance. Can't come soon enough. You saw how they were this morning. Does getting old make you miserable and grumpy?' Clive laughed.

Job done, Winston scooped up his wad of notes and waved them.

'This will see me through the summer. A nice cushion. Nice of Dillon to leave us a small bequest. It's good to get hold of cash. Nothing traceable, no complications. What do they say, every cloud has a silver-lining. Dillon's dying has done us a favour.'

The humour fell flat. Both felt shaken, though neither wanted to admit it. Realising his comment was inappropriate, Winston made a suggestion.

'Tell you what, we'll call into Cliff's Cafe on the way back to yours. Chill out a while. Then I'll go over to Will's. I'll send him a text now to alert him I'm coming. It'll keep him off my back.'

Clive nodded in agreement. He was glad not to be going to see Will. He was a little frightened of what Will had become. Wicked Will's new name and growing reputation on the street said it all. He wasn't particularly bothered about trying to keep a low profile, for increasingly he believed himself to be totally invincible. It would seem no-one could touch him.

Winston grabbed his phone and tapped out a message. Meanwhile Clive stood listlessly gazing over the Crouch End rooftops, looking into the distance out of the window, a vacant expression on his face. He couldn't get the image of Dillon's putrid body out of his mind. It did make you stop and think, he told himself. Life's raw edge, one minute safe, next over the edge, dead, oblivion. What did it all mean? Life's got to be better than that dealt to Dillon. He couldn't help feeling a little sorry for him, dying on his own like that, spaced-out on drugs. He wondered if he'd suffered, but thought he probably hadn't. A mercy really.

Slipping on a pair of leather gloves he used for driving, Winston carefully transferred the plastic container of Dillon's drugs into a new bin bag fresh off the roll, carefully keeping everything fingerprint free. Even a hair could give him away, and he kept telling himself he couldn't be too fastidious. Particularly since the Post Office robbery last November he'd had this fear that his way of life would one day meet a day of reckoning, but he didn't want it to be quite just yet.

Winston saw himself as one of life's lucky guys and he wanted to keep it that way. There was luck, but there was also luck that came by being careful. Another bin bag was torn off and the orange Sainsbury bags and empty Post Office wallet then disappeared deep inside. He screwed the bag small and stuffed it in his jacket pocket. Later they'd discreetly drop it in a street bin, somewhere there were no cctv cameras to observe them. The final link with the Post Office robbery last November would, they both hoped, simply disappear with the bin bag. Before leaving, Winston split his cash, half went straight in his pocket, the remainder he stuffed in the top drawer of the TV cabinet.

'Let's go,' he said, grabbing his jacket. Clive moved quickly, following him outside. They tumbled out into the street where it looked like just another summer's day. He took a deep breath of welcome fresh air. Climbing into Winston's wheels and putting on some music, they began to feel everything was under control again. What had happened to Dillon got pushed to the back of their minds. These things simply happened on the street if you were young and black in North London.

As the white BMW pulled smartly away, both thought they'd got away without being discovered, that Winston's charmed life continued to roll forward and life had already moved on.

12

Before going inside, Winston threw his bin bag into the large commercial rubbish container at the back of the café in Bruce Grove. He could see it was instantly lost in a mountain of used paper coffee cups and mounds of other waste from Cliff's café. Job done, they went inside.

Cliff was pleased to see them both, standing in a bouncer pose in his barrista suit in front of the shiny-chrome coffee machine stacking cups. Hissing steam, the gadget held a glamorous aromatic mystique. His better half, Tracy was busying herself with a tray clearing tables. She gave them a nod and then came over.

'The usual is it?' she asked. 'You boys keeping out of mischief these days?' she added with a twinkle in her eye.

Clive was too embarrassed to answer, but Winston quickly countered.

'Mischief, that's your middle name isn't it? We're a pair of clean-living dudes. Did we ever cause you any trouble? We're both Mr Nice Guys, but we're thirsty, we've been busy all morning. So one double-shot Americano and one Diet Coke if you don't mind,' said Winston, as irrepressibly cheerful as ever.

She rocked his head playfully with her hand and then shot off to get their drinks. They both began to feel better, but only briefly.

'I've never seen anyone dead before,' said Clive quietly. 'It kind of makes you think.'

'I suppose,' said Winston looking down at the tabletop.

'It's that smell. It's like it's still in the air, hanging round me. Can you smell it? Do you think anyone else can?' said Clive.

'Know what you mean. No, no way. It's us, the mind playing tricks, don't think our minds want to let us forget it. But we will.'

86

'Do you think someone will do a funeral for Dillon? I mean someone ought to. Has he got any family you know of? Will anyone be there?' asked Clive, realising that these things mattered to him at least.

'That's a lot of questions. Can't think anything will happen quickly. He'll be looked at by the police, kept chilled in a mortuary for ages. An unexpected death like that, the Coroner will be involved. Don't expect his body will be released for a funeral for months, maybe years. Not our problem now, Clive, think about it,' said Winston.

'But has he got family? Friends?' Clive asked, wondering if Winston knew any more about Dillon.

'Dunno. I only met him for the first time last summer. Wicked Will got me to call round. Never seen anyone with him except dealers. Someone will know him. Someone will come out the woodwork when the police start looking, you wait. As I said before, not our problem now.'

'Do you think the police will make any links?' Clive said, trying not to sound anxious.

'When a death happens, things get looked at, it ups the ante. Will won't like it. Everyone tries harder to get the drug dealer when someone dies, the police included. There's nothing for us to worry about. His body will get discovered. Someone will say there was an attempted break in. They'll conclude it was by another drug user, they'll find Dillon overdid it, end of. No way can anything stick to us,' said Winston, opening his palms in a display of innocence.

Their drinks arrived. Winston remembered which pocket had his small change in and covered the bill. They drank mainly in silence. It was hard to convince oneself that what had happened wouldn't jump up and bite them at some future point, but they both tried to suppress such a thought and neither dared say so.

After half an hour at Cliff's, the ride back to Edmonton didn't take long and Clive walked the last few yards home just as Kaylah and Jacob were returning from the Green. They all arrived at the front door together.

'Well,' inquired Kaylah, 'what was all that about? You look like you've seen a ghost or something.'

'Oh, nothing really. All a waste of time. Went over to a mate's. Knocked on his door. He was out. Went for coffee to chill out and then he drove me back here. Guess he likes some company, and to show off his new car! If I'm a bit off-colour, guess I'm not used to being got up so early,' he jested.

Kaylah was getting Jacob out of the buggy, her mind on the feed now due. Her breasts were uncomfortably full and Jacob was stirring. Time was pressing in her life of new routines.

'Can you bring the buggy in. Got to feed him,' she said, leaving him to it. With that she disappeared upstairs clutching Jacob in one arm and undoing her blouse with the other.

Clive left the buggy in the hallway and made for his own room. He had money in his pocket he needed to hide. He chose to put some in the Children's Bible his parents had given him when he started Sunday School, the rest he spread around. Some went in his jeans, the rest in the envelope with his latest credit card statement. Finally, a couple of hundred went in his back pocket. He made a mental note to pay off his credit card at the bank later. It would mean a trip up to Edmonton Green.

Music, that was what was needed now. It usually kept him in a good place, soothed his mind, shut out the world. He threw himself on his bed, pulled his earphones on, but was unable to relax into his favourite hip hop, his mind repeatedly returning to the image of Dillon, lying out on his sofa, a wasted life. Winston and I are safer now he's gone, he thought. He was always a liability, off his head, unpredictable. But what a waste, his life spent on drugs.

Then he thought about his life in a 'Christian' home. His parents' life in the church where all was good and evil, black and white. Maybe his parents knew more about good living than he'd given them credit for, he thought. Dillon's life was shit. Kaylah and himself, well, they were different, and a new nephew needs a decent uncle, and don't we both want something better, deserve something better in life?

His mind turned to the opportunity going to college in the autumn presented. Deciding to go had been a turning point after more than a year of drifting and arguing with his parents and getting sucked into trouble. He'd just about done well enough at school to get there but, much to his parents' annoyance, he'd never really worked whilst at school. What if he really worked? What could he achieve if he turned his mind to it? Then he remembered the conversation Kaylah and he had had earlier about getting by in a divided world, the haves and have-nots, and he felt uncertain again whether it would all be worth it. The odds were against him. His mind relaxed and drifted, the music beat more in tune with his mood and he finally slipped into the pleasure of it.

Kaylah had just finished feeding Jacob and after winding him to produce a climactic burp, she laid him down, his eyes already shut in contentment. She thought she might have a few minutes to herself, and lay back on her bed. She could hear her parents talking downstairs and the conflict over breakfast came back to her and weighed her down. She decided to stay in her room for now. Sitting up she absentmindedly began folding baby clothes to put away when her phone vibrated into life. It was Lena again.

'Hi Kaylah, are you having a better day?'

'So-so. It started badly, then got better. Jacob's happily asleep right now, probably saving his waking time for tonight.'

'Well, you remember you said you thought it was difficult to find somewhere to live independently. I'm ringing because I think I might have come up with something. I really have. My friend at the embassy, Sharon, she's going home to Israel at the weekend. Won't be back for a long time. Thing is, she has a flat in Hornsey. She posted a note in the staff-room asking if anyone knew someone who wouldn't mind flat-sitting for her whilst she was away. I thought of you,' Lena said.

89

'That's nice of you, but I really don't think so. She'll need it back soon enough. I'll cope. Thanks all the same,' Kaylah replied, not wanting to be dragged into something so big and uncertain.

'Have a think about it. She won't be back here for the rest of this year at least. It could be longer. You see, she's having a baby and is taking maternity leave. She's going to be back home with her family in Jerusalem. The earliest she'll return will be next summer. Have a think. I know she just needs someone trustworthy to live in it, to keep an eye on it. She doesn't want rent or anything. Her family are loaded. If you like, on my day off, I'll borrow the key and take you to have a look at it. If it were me, I'd leap at it. Chances like this in life don't come along very often. Then you can make your mind up. What do you say? You've got nothing to lose by having a look. I'm off on Sunday. Can you make it if I pick you up about 10am? It'll be a fun outing if nothing else,' said Lena making it difficult for Kaylah to refuse without appearing churlish.

Kaylah was confused, it was all too sudden and quick, but in the end she agreed with Lena it was reasonable to just have a look. After all it would get her out of the house.

Sunday morning came soon enough and Lena's smart little Citroen took them both down to Hornsey. The flat was on the ground floor, easy access off the street, handy for the shops and bus. It was simple inside, with none of the girlie things, the pastel shades that Kaylah had half-expected to see. Two bedrooms, all the pots, pans and furniture, including a cinema-size TV and broadband router, all staying. It looked too good to be true, a nice place.

'Would you really mind all that much looking after it for Sharon? You can see why she didn't want just anyone moving in. You'd be doing her a big favour,' Lena said appealingly. 'There's no paperwork, you can have the key now.'

To Kaylah's surprise, Lena held the shiny silver key out and Kaylah took it in her hand. It was attached to a star of David fob, spiky and sharp to the touch.

'She's taken her things, flies tomorrow from Heathrow. I'd love to be able to tell her her flat is being looked after. In fact, she said to me, "I'm prepared to pay £50 a week for someone doing this for me", and she left me this as a down payment.'

She opened her bag, pulled out some rolled notes held in a rubber band. She relaxed them from the band, straightened them as Kaylah watched, before pressing in turn, ten £20 notes into her open hand. That £200 made Kaylah's jaw drop. It was followed by a smile.

'Don't you think this kind of makes it manageable?' said Lena. 'If you change your mind, just let me know. We're so grateful for all the help you've given us. Just think of this as one way we can say thank you to you. See this place as an opportunity. It'll give you a start, at least until your own business career gets under way. You can move in as soon as you're ready. No pressure.'

It was done. By the end of the week, she'd moved in. It was Friday 12 August. Winston helped with the move, cardboard boxes filling his car, for after all he only lived round the corner. He seemed more than happy to help his new neighbour.

Her parents were surprisingly happy too, even admiring of her good fortune and what they saw as her growing independence. The place was near enough to give her accessibility to everywhere she needed to go and to keep in touch with her friends. It was but a short bus ride back to her parents. Alternatively, Winston seemed very ready to give her a lift once she'd persuaded him that the buggy top also served as a portable baby carseat that both secured Jacob and prevented any risk of dirt contaminating his immaculate car.

Clive wasn't so sure about the arrangement. He felt uneasy. It wasn't that he was jealous, maybe only a little, no it was more than that. The flat didn't feel right and it had all happened that bit too quickly. He sensed something, and he knew all too well from his own experience that such big favours never came without some comeback later. He screwed up his face. All this he would keep to himself for now. He wouldn't be the first one to spoil what seemed like Kaylah's stroke of good fortune. Instinctively, though, he could feel something wasn't quite right and there would one day be a reckoning. With that he grabbed his music and raised the volume.

13

Ruth opened the door. It was Kaylah with a baby-buggy.

'Hello Kaylah. Would you like to come in? It's such a nice day, we could go through to the garden if you wish,' said Ruth greeting her warmly.

'Yes, yes, I wanted to ask you something. It may take a bit of explaining.'

'But first, can I offer you something. Phil made some home-made lemonade which is rather good. Like some?' offered Ruth.

'That would be nice,' said Kaylah.

She manoeuvred the buggy up into the house, then followed Ruth leading the way to the back door, taking them back outside again. Kaylah was directed towards the garden furniture, wooden chairs around a circular table sitting in the middle of the large lawn, an open green parasol above casting a welcome shade. Jacob was sleeping, the short ride in the buggy from the bus stop having finally sent him off. She pushed him into the shade. It was late morning, the sun high and the temperature rising. It would be another of those sultry hot days London gets in summer, maybe there'll be a thunderstorm in the afternoon, she wondered.

A couple of minutes later Ruth re-appeared, carrying a tray, two glasses and a carafe of chilled cloudy lemonade already misting in the warm air, the ice clinking as she walked. There were several large cookies on a plate too. A missed breakfast meant these were a welcome sight. Hunger winning, Kaylah didn't wait to be asked, she leant forward and took one, the sweet delicious chocolate taste immediately kicking in as it was quickly devoured.

'So nice to see you Kaylah. Neither of us have had chance to catch up since last year. I've spotted you about, pushing the buggy, but not for a week or two. How old is the little fellow now?' Ruth inquired.

'Four weeks in a few days. His name's Jacob.'

'He's adorable. I bet he doesn't sleep like this all the time,' Ruth said, bending over him to take a closer look.

'He's not so bad, but doesn't yet know the difference between night and day. I hope he will soon, it gets wearing at times. He does all the things he's supposed to, and don't get me wrong, I love him to bits. Oh you won't see me around so much now because I've just moved. Since yesterday, I'm in a flat in Crouch End. Don't know how long for exactly, but it's working out well. A friend asked me to mind it while she's abroad. My parents, well, it wasn't ideal coming home from hospital with a little one. As you know our house is small, so the flat came along just right,' said Kaylah telling more than she had really intended.

'How's your dad, Sam, busy as ever with his Church and broadcasts, I expect?' asked Ruth.

Kaylah nodded, her mouth full with the second cookie.

'And your mum, is she enjoying being a granny?'

'Yes, she sure is and very proud of her little grandson. It hasn't been easy, but she's helped pave the way for me. I'm going straight from here to see her. Then I expect we'll go shopping, nothing's planned. Why I called was to ask you about getting Jacob christened,' said Kaylah, trying to bring the conversation round to the reason for the visit.

'That's nice. Tell me what you're thinking,' said Ruth.

Kaylah took a deep breath. This wasn't going to be easy. She wasn't so sure of her ground for asking, and she knew that conflicts with her parents over the subject were bound to follow. Ruth looked at her in an understanding way and Kaylah instinctively felt she could trust her and tell her how it was.

'When you have a baby, your world changes. I've had to stop thinking of myself as number one. Like it or not, it's Jacob and what he needs that directs my day from dawn to dusk, and beyond. When I first held him in my arms and he clasped my little finger in his hand, I was astonished by him. Lost in wonder you might say, but then I soon realised that I was responsible for this little person, to see he got fed and changed, but also had a future, and what I want, I totally want, is what's best for him and what will give him a good life.' She paused wondering if she was getting too passionate. Ruth was sitting quietly in the warm sun, listening attentively, waiting for her to continue.

'I want him to know he's loved, cared for and in my tradition that means a christening to start him off in life in the right way. It's funny, but though I've grown up in a Christian home, very much so, there's much of what my parent's believe I just can't get my head around, they just take things so very literally. Everything for them is in black and white. Nevertheless I have to say, they've given my brother Clive and me a good life. I've had a good home. I'd like Jacob to have that too, though not exactly the same. I know it would please them too. I thought it might be easiest if I asked you to do it, a christening that is,' said Kaylah, pausing this time to see what Ruth would say.

'That's lovely. Of course I'd love to help,' said a relaxed Ruth.

Then Ruth went quiet. All of a sudden all kinds of complications started running through her mind and she didn't really know where to start. Kaylah sensed her hesitation and cut in.

'I know there are some issues in my case, me being a single mum...' said Kaylah.

'No, no that's no problem. I'm baptising the babies of single mums all the time,' said Ruth.

'Then what is it?' asked Kaylah

'Well two things crossed my mind straight away, and we need to talk about them. Best clear the air from the start. First, your father being the Bishop of the Edmonton Green Holy Tabernacle Church, just how will he feel if you don't go to his church? Why come to me? Won't he be upset? Have you talked to him about it?' enquired Ruth.

'I thought about that. My dad is a good man, but he and I don't agree on everything. He's very dogmatic about things. What I mean is he sees everything as straight from the pages of the Bible. He doesn't give me room to think or find my own faith with all the questions I have. Any of my questions are like a personal attack on him. He's also so patriarchal, so man-in-charge, it's not where I am. Anyway, the biggest problem is, he sees me as being immoral, a stain on his reputation, so without even talking to him I know he wouldn't want to do it. Besides, he wouldn't do a christening, he thinks it's all wrong. He says people can only come to the church through repentance and believer's baptism as adults. He wouldn't baptise a baby because they can't say they believe,' Kaylah explained.

'Forgive me for asking, because I just don't know. Does your father's church have any service for new babies?' asked Ruth.

'No, none that I know of.'

'But you'd like Jacob baptised, and baptised in the Church of England?' continued Ruth; Kaylah wondered where this was all leading.

'Yes. When I was on my business studies course placement with your church last year, helping out at the Drop In Centre, I got to see a different kind of Christianity than I'd met with before. It was a pleasant surprise to me to find I was just accepted. You made a point of including anyone, even me. You welcomed everyone to the Drop In and I sensed you and the team really cared for all who came through your door. I liked that. You never quizzed me about what I thought about God, about women vicars or whether a church should only look after its own members. No, you accepted me, and I guess looking back I feel grateful and OK with what you do. But there is still something else on your mind, isn't there? Is it Ali?' Kaylah asked.

'You can read my mind,' Ruth said trying to be light-hearted about it, 'I don't mean to intrude on something personal to you, but Ali is the father isn't he?'

'Yes,' said Kaylah apprehensively.

'Would you mind if we talked about that, confidentially, just today, and then we can forget it?' said Ruth.

'No I don't mind, that's OK. I feel happier talking to you. I've not actually talked to anyone else about him. I guess

96

I owe you an apology, a big apology. When I was here on placement in the autumn you tried to talk to me about proper boundaries and I just wasn't listening. I just went on doing what I thought was best. I just want to say it was all down to me, you tried to warn me and I didn't listen,' said Kaylah.

'It's me who owes you the apology!' interrupted Ruth.

'How come?' said Kaylah.

'I was too preoccupied, too busy, to give you the time I should have. I have kicked myself so many times since. I saw Ali manipulating you, steering you, taking advantage of you and I didn't intervene until, until it was too late. I am so sorry. I was the person responsible for your placement at the end of the day, so responsibility lies with us both I guess,' Ruth said.

'But, you needn't feel any blame. I was responsible for my actions. I helped Ali. At the time he really was charming and good company to begin with. I was completely fooled, taken in. I had no idea what he was up to. I couldn't see for a moment what was coming. But I see him now as a chameleon. One side of him he kept hidden, the side bent on doing great evil, the other side of him was a lonely guy, steered and pressurised to do something I still can't understand. There was a side to him I saw and liked.' She thought for a moment and then asked what was on Ruth's mind.

'Tell me Ruth, what makes someone do what he did? When I met him he was on his own. He needed a friend. I was the one person in this country who knew this terrorist better than anyone. The media and the inquiry made him just look evil, a determined, ruthless, extremist killer. Looking back I see him as little more than a young, lonely man who yes, could be great fun to be with. Trouble is, with hindsight, I feel he abused my trust in him, I feel betrayed, angry, bitter, and that doesn't start to describe it. There were two sides to him. One side dark and evil, the other innocent and fun. Is that how we all are, a mix of good and evil, or was Ali somehow different, someone who gave himself over completely to the dark side, a guy dominated by evil?'

'I don't know, but I do know he's still Jacob's father,' said Ruth.

'That's really weird. I see Ali in him. It scares me sometimes. I think, what am I going to tell Jacob about his dad? And how's Jacob going to turn out?'

'And Ali was a Muslim,' said Ruth.

'Yes. But what are you saying? That Ali has a say in what religion Jacob is brought up in?' asked Kaylah in alarm.

'Ali's Islam, and the theology of Islamic State is not the Islam of most Muslims. Just think about it for a moment, Jacob probably has many Muslim relatives. One day he might just meet them. It's something we have to think about,' said Ruth.

'I hadn't thought of that,' said Kaylah, taken off guard by the realisation of what Ruth said. Something which had never crossed her mind and now left her feeling somewhat unnerved.

'You may need to tell Jacob at some future time, when he's older, when he's ready, about that side of his family, what they believe and why. In the meantime, I think you have the sole responsibility for bringing Jacob up and I think you have made a good choice to ask to have him baptised. Of course we will support you in bringing up Jacob as a Christian,' Ruth explained.

'Thanks,' Kaylah replied genuinely and with some relief.

'In this church we offer parents like yourself a choice of services. There is baptism, which is, if you like, the welcoming of a child into the church community where parents and godparents make promises about bringing Jacob up as a Christian. The other service we offer is a thanksgiving service. This is where we simply give thanks for Jacob's safe arrival in the world, thank God for him, pray for him and, in due course, when he is ready himself, he comes to baptism later in life.'

'I'm confused. Have I got it right? Either he can be baptised, that's with the water, yes; which is like he takes on the full Christian thing now or, we have a thanksgiving and he makes his own mind up later? But will he be accepted by God if he dies without being baptised? What about the water, that's what everyone expects isn't it?' asked Kaylah feeling the whole thing was getting overly complicated.

'God loves little children. There are different traditions. One Christian tradition states, as you say, that baptism is the gateway to salvation. But increasingly, there is a tradition which recognises God as more gracious and loving, and this tradition involving a service of thanksgiving, no water I'm afraid, argues that God receives little children whether or not they have been baptised,' said Ruth.

'That one makes more sense to me. I was just imagining you could have a crazy situation where Christians rush to baptise babies as soon as they are born, otherwise, just in case... And what about those who have babies too early to survive? No, I go with your second tradition. Sounds fine by me,' said Kaylah.

'We have a lot of thanksgiving services these days.'

'I think I'd rather go with that. I grew up in a family where there was a lot of religious pressure. I don't want that for Jacob. I want him to be able to choose for himself, when he's older,' said Kaylah.

'When were you thinking you might like us to do this?' asked Ruth.

'I need to talk to my family. They need to accept this is what I want, and I really want them to be here for this. Let me go and talk to them and come back to you. Is that OK?' asked Kaylah.

'That's absolutely fine by me. Come back to me whenever you want. It really is nice to see you and catch up with you and Jacob is a delightful little baby. Look, I think he's beginning to stir.' Ruth leant over to watch, Jacob shaking his head and screwing his eyes.

'Thanks for the lemonade. I need to be on my way. He'll need a change and a feed,' said Kaylah getting up from her garden chair ready to make a move.

As Kaylah left the vicarage and pushed her buggy towards her parents' home, she realised that the future looked more complicated than she'd thought, though she was more than happy with what Ruth had offered her in the way of a service. Ali was always going to pop up in conversation now and again and she had better get used to it.

What if, she asked herself again, Jacob became interested in knowing about Ali's side of the family? It's only natural. It'll happen one day. What if he asked about Islam? What do I tell him? What if, what if he wants to meet Ali? She shook at the thought. No way, not if I have anything to do with it.

14

PC Bob Steer was having one of those mornings when everything was proving very frustrating. Each time he tried to get on top of his paperwork, to clear up a case, a call would come in from switchboard to give him more to do. Police work felt like it was all paperwork these days.

Beth, on switchboard, knew he was struggling and for his part he could tell that each time she called him she did so with a heavy heart. Everyone at the station liked Bob. He was straightforward, a good, experienced, beat PC and happy with his lot, except when bureaucracy and paperwork got on top of him. There was yet another call.

'Sorry, Bob, but this lady has called me four times already about her neighbouring flat. I get the impression she's an older person living on her own. This time she's insistent there is something going on we ought to know about. She only lives over the road from the police station, in Shrubbery Road, N9. Hers is the first house. Her name's Daisy Randall. The flat upstairs is known to us. Drug users have squatted there in the past. We think it's empty, but the lady is hearing noises upstairs and she says they're coming from that flat. Someone needs to take a look, if only to put Daisy's mind at rest,' said Beth apologetically.

'I know the lady. She's OK. I'll go over there right now,' Bob replied.

'Thanks, Bob. I'll call her back and say you're on your way,' said Beth cutting the call.

Bob was glad to be able to close down his computer and walk away from his desk and the paperwork. He thought paperwork would be the death of him. He didn't mind what he encountered on the street, the people, the challenges but the bureaucracy that went with modern policing, the cuts to the police budget and the effort that had to go into getting the Crown Prosecution Service to prosecute a case meant he was

101

losing the will. When the admin got to him he felt he'd had enough; he didn't like the way policing was going. He grabbed his helmet and began walking, leaving the pressure cooker of low police morale that was today's Edmonton Police HQ behind him.

As he stepped out onto the street, the July sunshine was hot and the air humid, but he immediately felt a load had been lifted. He knew if he walked too quickly he would sweat, besides he had no wish to hurry back to the station. Under his breath he cursed at all the paraphernalia today's police had to carry with them. He told himself they tested each piece separately but never added up how much all the items together weighed by the time they were strapped on the officer's body. Gone were the days when only a solid truncheon, Metropolitan police whistle and notebook were all that was required. To keep cool he slowed his pace still further.

It was then, as his hand was raised and his finger poised to ring Daisy Randall's bell, he remembered something. He couldn't immediately place it, but he knew it was important, so he stood like a statue, his finger frozen in mid-air. Then in a flash it was clear. The drug dealer's den in Muswell Hill, the guy Dillon Williams who'd overdosed, the description the woman gave of the two men who left in the white car.

He suddenly remembered where he'd seen them before – in Edmonton, fairly recently, maybe a week ago. They were outside the Kone house. It was the way the witness who lived next door, Martha her name was, how the two were described to him, it had to be them.

He took his notebook out of his pocket and made a note to self to call round there. He was certain Kaylah and her brother Clive would be able to throw some light on this. That lad Clive has been on the edge of trouble for ages, he just knew it. Maybe, he thought, calling once again on a lady living next door to a drug den had triggered something deep in his brain, brought the memory back. It was a useful knack he possessed, having a good recall of seemingly unconnected

102

things, it had served him well many times before. The retrieval made him feel good about himself, being a beat policeman. Details, he told himself, came back if you waited, not always when you expected them. With a smile of self-satisfaction, he rang Daisy's bell.

'I thought you were going to stand out there all day,' she said from behind a half-closed front door. 'I saw you coming. I was keeping an eye out. Come on in, officer.' The door was opened just wide enough to let him in.

Bob showed Daisy his police ID and explained why he'd been sent over.

'Put it away. No need for that. Seen you before,' she said.

Daisy shuffled into the front room, using a Zimmer frame to help her move the short distance between door and raised chair. She called Bob to follow her. Daisy only told him the full story when she'd got him sitting down.

Finally, after much more time than Bob felt he really had to give to his visit, he said that he'd go and ring the bell for upstairs, but if there was no reply, no-one there, there was little more he could do. He couldn't enter without a warrant, he told her.

'Well just get yourself a warrant then. The place is supposed to be empty, but I am telling you someone has been moving around up there. It could be burglars, it could be those drug-dealers back again. But until my mind is at rest, believe me you'll be getting more calls from me,' bossed Daisy.

Bob had a thought.

'Tell me, Daisy, is the landlord for upstairs the same as yours?' he asked her.

'Of course.'

'Well, why don't you just give me their contact details, I'll phone them and I'll get them to come and check their property over.'

'Look, can you reach it. It's on that letter over there,' she said pointing towards a pile of correspondence.

Bob got out of the chair and soon picked out the right letter from the shelf underneath the TV stand. He made a quick call to the landlord while he was still with Daisy, and once the call had been made and the visit concluded, Bob left knowing Daisy was one more satisfied customer. This was policing at its most basic and it made him feel he'd done something intrinsically worthwhile.

As he said his goodbyes, Bob didn't want to go straight back to his desk at the station. It was a lovely day, so he called in on his radio and left a message saying that he would be following up one of his old cases with a visit to Cheddington Road. He'd be back by the end of the afternoon. Beth was still on switchboard. She said that since he'd left it was turning out to be a very quiet afternoon, perhaps the warm sunshine was making everyone agreeable. She hoped it would stay that way.

Bob walked slowly, not really observing things as he should; he'd allowed himself to get lost in his own thoughts. He turned right into Park Road and then into Pymme's Park, familiar places each with memories for him of people he recalled from past cases. Being the school holidays and a sunny day, the Victorian park with its lake, playground, shady trees and welcome green expanse of grass, was crowded.

There were ball-players, mums with babies in buggies and the occasional yellow-vested security guys keeping an eye on everything. They exchanged a friendly wave as he passed. Bob left the path and strode out across the mown grass taking the most direct route to the exit gate to the street opposite. He quickened his pace and it didn't take long to cross to the other side. Minutes later he was in Haselbury Road and approaching Cheddington Road and the Kone house fast, but he still hadn't decided how he would play this.

In fact he got to the door with only one thing clear in his head. He was going to adopt a full-on brazen approach. He instinctively felt that the Kone family were malleable and this would get him a quick result. Unlike experienced

104

criminals, they would give way when direct pressure was applied. That's where he pinned his instinctive hope.

The door opened and Shazee Kone was standing there, her eyes wide-open, a shocked expression on her face. She was clearly wondering what the latest disaster was to have befallen her family and she looked at Bob, her jaw agape. He introduced himself, showed her his ID and asked if he might come in a moment. This wasn't how he had anticipated the visit going. For some reason he'd assumed Clive or Kaylah would have opened the door. Now another approach was called for, and he took a conversational line to see where things would lead.

'It's nice to see you, Mrs Kone. Lovely day isn't it?' he offered.

She nodded apprehensively wondering what was to come.

'I think we were all glad to see the events of last autumn become history,' Bob continued. He soon learned his comment was ill-judged.

'What do you mean? The events of last autumn become history! Our family has never been the same since then,' Shazee countered.

'Well, what I mean, what I mean is...' and he paused, for much to his surprise, he was momentarily lost for words. Shazee Kone took her chance and seized the initiative.

'And what brings you round here? What is it you want den?' she asked, looking straight into his eyes.

'Well, I was hoping to have a word with your Clive, or maybe, Kaylah. Are they in?' he asked, his eyes looking around.

'Kaylah, no, she don't live here no more,' said Shazee.

'Oh,' said Bob, a quizzical expression on his face. She was not going to enlighten him further. Instead, Shazee looked to the ceiling and yelled out.

'Clive, Clive, come down here. You're needed.' She shouted in a voice that must have carried through the party-walls to either side, her eyes fixed, boring a hole in the ceiling above.

She explained the volume was needed because Clive probably had his earphones on listening to his music. Moving to the foot of the staircase, she began ascending, calling his name ever more loudly. She got a result, Bob heard movement upstairs.

'Clive, you have a visitor. Come down here, dis instant,' she said.

First, Bob saw smart, pointed tan shoes, followed by clean-pressed, dark-blue jeans, then a designer-label, grey-hooded, sweater top before Clive's face finally came into view. He knew that Clive's facial expression when he first saw a policeman facing him in his lounge would betray whether there was something or nothing in the visit. Over many years he had become something of an expert in reading faces and he was rarely wrong these days. As Clive's face came into view, he knew instantly he was right in his decision to call round.

Shazee asked him if he would like tea, to which Bob agreed – she quickly disappeared into the back kitchen pulling the door shut behind her. Whether she didn't want to hear what her son was up to or was just being polite Bob could only guess, but he had the feeling it was more likely to be the former. What parent really wanted to know what trouble their son was into? Whatever the reason, he was glad he could speak to Clive alone.

'Hello, Clive.' He stood up to shake his hand and make his presence felt. Sitting down he had felt at a disadvantage. Standing up kept the pressure on.

'Please sit down,' he added. With slow deliberation he took out his notebook from his top pocket and slowly flipped the pages until he came to a fresh blank page. He could tell Clive was feeling anxious. He would go straight to the point.

'Now tell me, what had you been doing immediately prior to when you left Dillon Williams' flat in Muswell Hill around lunchtime last Wednesday?' Bob said, making an assumption and giving the impression he was less interested in getting Clive to actually admit he was at the flat, rather he wanted him to focus on saying something about while he was there inside. It was a tactic he found often got results.

Bob watched Clive's face. It was fascinating. First, the silence, the quiver in the lips, the loss for words, the startled look of panic in the eyes and behind the eyes, a brain desperately trying hard to find something to say. Bob watched and waited. Clive's face was in shock; his body uncomfortably shuffling in the chair. Then, Clive cleared his throat to speak.

'I'm trying to sort my life out, honest I am. I've got a place at college in September and please believe me when I tell you I had nothing to do with how Dillon was. I was only there to check he was all right.'

With Clive's admission, which sounded plausible, Bob immediately knew he was getting somewhere. He felt sorry for the lad.

'But he wasn't alright, he was dead, very dead, wasn't he?' followed up Bob.

'Yes. But I had nothing to do with that. That was how we, I, found him. Dead, and he'd been dead a while, I guess. That's why it was necessary to check up on him. We had to force open his door. Then when we found him like that, the stench, we thought he'd taken an overdose or something, but we couldn't be sure. We left, we just left.'

Bob knew Clive was spilling the beans. He'd now implicated his accomplice.

'But you didn't call us? You and...' said Bob, leaving his sentence hanging inviting its completion.

'Winston, my friend.' Clive couldn't see any point in keeping Winston's name out of it. He was so scared he'd get accused of killing Dillon or something, he thought it best to appear to be open about things. Bob heard the name Winston and knew progress was being made. He decided to keep the pressure on whilst it was getting results.

'But you're not telling me everything, are you Clive?' asked Bob, relentlessly and firmly prodding him for answers once again.

Unfortunately for Bob, before Clive could answer, Shazee arrived from the kitchen with the tea and asked him if he took sugar. Pointedly, thought Bob, she didn't bring anything for Clive. She looked as if she was about to settle herself down in the front room with them.

'Mum, do you mind giving me and the policeman...' began Clive.

'Bob,' said Bob, thinking he would switch to a more collaborative approach to questioning now.

'A bit of space. He's asking me about something important,' said Clive.

She shrugged her shoulders dismissively and disappeared back into the kitchen without uttering a word, closing the door behind her. Bob could hear her tidying up. He decided to adopt a more gentle tone.

'Now, as I was saying Clive, you're not telling me everything, are you?'

'What do you mean?'

'Well, I want you to start from the beginning and tell me the story, how you ended up at Dillon's last Wednesday. Take your time. What made you go there?' said Bob, sitting back and sipping his hot tea.

Clive thought it was always easiest to try and tell a story as near to the truth as possible. He'd learned that as a boy, when his parents had cross-examined him for childhood misdemeanours. Telling lies was harder work and he'd never been any good at it. So, he began describing the walk up towards Edmonton Green that Kaylah, his new nephew Jacob in the buggy and himself were making that Wednesday morning when quite unexpectedly his friend Winston had pulled up beside them in Haselbury Road.

'You can ask Kaylah. It was just as I said,' he said plaintively.

Bob knew it to be true and just nodded, waiting for Clive to continue, slowly sipping at his tea.

Then Clive told him that Winston had said he wanted him to come with him to check how Dillon was because no-one had seen him about. Clive had no intention revealing it was Wicked Will who had sent them.

'So Winston drove us over there. We parked right outside. We couldn't get an answer and knew that something was wrong. We had no choice. We forced the doors to get in, but it was only to check on him. He would have wanted us to. We weren't doing anything wrong.'

'That's domestic burglary as I see it,' Bob said, keeping up the pressure, but not really believing such a charge would stick. He had to press Clive, put the pressure on again, keep him talking, spilling the beans. He didn't think it worth adding the two could have called the police.

'What did you find?'

For just a second, Clive's face betrayed something else, something he wasn't prepared to admit. The momentary hesitation and accompanying look were enough for Bob to register that rather more lay behind it than Clive was prepared to say. Clive described Dillon just how the police had found him and he knew that part be to be true, but he also knew that Clive and Winston had been up to something, there was more to tell, but for now Clive wasn't saying.

'Are you quite sure there isn't something else you want to tell me?' asked Bob.

Clive wasn't forthcoming. The story went on for another ten minutes and Bob dutifully scribbled in his notebook, taking contact details for Winston, before flipping it shut and pushing it into his top pocket.

'What's going to happen to me?' asked Clive, his head down in his hands.

Bob knew this was not one of the worst lads he'd met. Unlike many young men, Clive had the advantage of a home and a family behind him too. For some reason Bob felt he needed to leave on a kindly note. He stood up.

'I'll need to talk to Winston. And this will need to be reported back to my superiors at Edmonton Police Station. It will be up to them what happens next. I'm afraid at the very least they will need you to come in and give a full written statement. There's also the matter of the Coroner looking into

Dillon's death. You'll be hearing from us soon enough. Now, be a good fellow, and thank your mother for the tea will you. I'll show myself out,' said Bob getting up from his chair.

Bob stepped onto the street, pulling the front door firmly shut so that it clicked behind him. It was still sunny, but a bit of a breeze had got up which made the conditions much more pleasant for the walk back to the station. All in all he told himself, not a bad afternoon's work.

Then as he began walking, a thought crossed his mind. Two apparently quite separate cases involving drugs. The Daisy Randall visit and now Dillon Williams. What if there was more of a connection? The supply of drugs right across North London was getting a lot worse, it was all the station talked about. Talk on the street was of a Mr Big who was running everything in North London now.

Perhaps, he thought, there was a way ahead to be found somewhere in all this? And, what were Clive and Winston up to in Dillon's flat, there was something more that Clive didn't tell. Was it drugs, money, or something else? And what about that drug-dealing fraternity, who was behind it all? There was still much that needed to come to light, he was sure of it. When they questioned Winston, they would send in the blues and twos and get a warrant to search his place. He just knew he was on to something, call it policeman's nose, intuition, whatever you like, it was what made him an excellent beat officer.

As he strode towards the familiar doors of Edmonton Police Station, he thought that after an oppressive beginning, the afternoon had, in the end, looked up and he noticed it had put a spring back in his step.

15

Clive didn't want to be cross examined by his mum and ran straight up to his room. He picked up his mobile and called Winston.

'Winston, we may have a problem,' Clive began.

'What you mean?' said Winston.

'I just had a visit from the police. A PC Bob came knocking on our front door. No messing. Wanted to know what you and me were doing breaking into Dillon's flat?' said Clive trying not to sound too anxious.

'What! How do they know that?' said a startled Winston.

'I didn't ask, but I guess we were seen,' replied Clive.

'So what's the police officer gone away thinking then? What'd you tell him, eh?' quizzed Winston.

'Only what he knew already. That we had to go there; we were worried about Dillon. We only broke in because we couldn't get a response and we were concerned about our friend,' said Clive.

'And did he believe that?'

'Yes, I think so. He threatened me, said it was domestic burglary, but come to think he didn't take it any further. He's just left, but I've called you because he's bound to come and ask you the same. He insisted on me giving him your address and phone number. Best you have a tidy round before they come a-calling. And be careful, he's sharp, I could tell,' reported Clive, trying to sound confident.

'Thanks for the call. I'd better get straight on to things right away. But I'm clean, man. Nothing to pin on Winston. Teflon, that's me – nothing sticks!' He laughed and Clive felt some of his own tension evaporate. Winston was always one of life's cheerful souls, even when under pressure.

'We need to be careful bro. Very careful,' he said quietly.

'Sure, and Winston, I never mentioned Will's name, but don't you think you had better tell Wicked Will what's up. Just so he knows. As for me, I just want to keep out of things, lie low for a bit until it all passes over,' said Clive.

'Me too. Thanks for the heads-up. Speak to you soon. I'll keep you posted. Bye,' said Winston and he had gone.

Clive didn't know what to do next. Winston never picked up his suggestion to alert Will, probably because he wouldn't. Then, he thought, he ought to go and explain to his mum, at least tell her something. If he didn't, it would only put tension between them and it would get worse when his dad came home. He went downstairs and strolled into the kitchen.

'He's gone,' he said, as if everything were over with.

'I know, I heard the front door,' said Shazee frostily.

'He said, thanks for the tea. He wanted to ask me about Winston's friend Dillon. I guess now's the time to tell you what happened,' Clive said, facing his mum.

He turned and leaned on the kitchen worktop as she rinsed a saucepan with her hands in the sink. He told her how last Wednesday Winston and he had gone to see how Dillon was in Muswell Hill, only to find him dead.

'Why didn't you call the police? Why didn't you tell me?' she asked enquiringly.

'Because he's a drug user and he'd overdosed. Not something I think you'd want to know about. You worry enough about who I'm with and what I do,' said Clive.

'Was that why you didn't call the police too?' she asked.

'That's partly it. We didn't want to get caught up in it either. You know what it's like. Young black lads, drugs, gangs, there's no knowing what the police might have tried to put on Winston and me,' Clive explained, wondering whether he was convincing her or not.

'Is it over now? Will the police come back?' she said, her eyes searching his.

'They want me to make a statement and they'll want to see Winston too, ask him the same questions. The Coroner is looking into it,' Clive told her.

Then it was over. Shazee seemed to relax. Maybe she wanted to believe the best of her son, but the questioning was done with for now.

'Thanks for telling me, Clive. You know your father and I, we only want the best for you. Just be careful, will you, my boy,' she said pleadingly.

At that, her hands dripping with water, her eyes streaming with tears, she flung her arms around him, and he found himself sobbing too. Extricating himself from her clinging embrace, he went back up to his room, threw himself down on his bed and picked up his headphones and resumed listening to his music.

Later in the afternoon when Kaylah called round, she could immediately tell her mum had been crying and it wasn't long before she had heard the story from her. She desperately hoped that what her mum had said, that it was the end of the matter, was true, but she had a deep sense of uncertainty about that and said she wanted to go and chat with Clive. Her mum nodded understandingly and she bounded upstairs to speak to her brother.

When Kaylah came into his room, Clive took off his earphones and placed them on the bedclothes. She could hear the tinny rhythm still playing somewhere in the duvet.

'Clive, mum's just told me. You had a visitor,' she said.

'Yes, but it's sorted. Nothing for you to worry about,' he told her.

His phone went. It was Winston.

'Just a tick Sis, it's Winston. Hi, Winston,' said Clive.

'They came, soon as you were off the phone. They turned me over, they searched this place from top to bottom. Found nothing – there was nothing to find. Asked me much the same as they asked you, about Dillon, why we went. I had to tell them I had a call from a friend who hadn't heard from him, but I couldn't mention Will's name. I'd be dead. I think that's it. It's over with. But like you say, stay quiet until the heat has passed. Can't stop, bye,' and with that Winston had gone.

Clive turned his attention back to Kaylah with a smile on his face.

'It's over,' he told her.

Clive still had to tell her all. Kaylah heard the full story of last Wednesday. It left her worried, if not alarmed. This wasn't over, she thought to herself. Her brother hadn't told her about this. Finding Dillon's dead body! He hadn't told her. There's more going on. There's drugs behind all this and where's Clive been getting all his money? She didn't trust her brother any more. He'd been caught up in something bad, so much so she thought she could even smell it or touch it. As she went downstairs Clive knew for his part he hadn't satisfied his sister. He felt the pain of the gulf between them as he knew she would. His hand reached for his music again, it was what he did to lose himself.

Meanwhile, PC Bob Steer thought he was coming to the end of a long day. He'd written up his reports on his findings earlier in the day and had been pleased to get the warrant and expedite the raid on Winston's flat so quickly. He was finishing a coffee chatting with April Cooper, a young woman recruit who had shadowed him on the beat. He thought highly of her and was pleased to hear she was now assigned to the local Prevent Counter Extremism Team.

April was telling him that Martins in the Met's Gangs Team had made a breakthrough earlier in the day, placing a guy called Wicked Will at the centre of the North London drugs trade. He's supposed to be hanging out in our patch, she told Bob.

It was good to catch up with April, she'd been good to walk the beat with and he wished her well in her new posting as he got up from his seat ready to finish his shift and leave for home. It was now early evening and he should have signed-off two hours ago. Switchboard reached him as he was about to change out of his uniform.

'It's Daisy again in Shrubbery Road. There are people there right now in the upstairs flat, she says. She thought you'd sorted it earlier and now she sounds in quite a state.

Can you possibly call back before you go?' asked Elsie, just on duty since Beth had left at 5pm.

Bob knew he had to go. It was what police work was all about, keeping the peace, keeping the good people in the community, like Daisy, feeling safe. It wasn't worth taking a car, it was just over the road. Tired, ready to go off-duty, he resigned himself to what had to be done and told himself that was the way it was. He told the desk sergeant where he was going as he strode out of the door.

As he approached, in the dimming light of a warm summer's evening, he could see that this time there were indeed lights on upstairs above Daisy's flat. Just as well he didn't leave it, he told himself. Got them red-handed this time.

He got nearer and he thought, rather than call Daisy, he'd go straight up to the neighbour's and then fill her in after. The door to the street was ajar and he walked briskly in, climbing the stairs swiftly to the flat above. He knocked on the door and the voices behind it, he'd heard as he'd ascended, went quiet.

The door opened quickly. He saw the surprise in their eyes. They were clearly expecting someone else. His eyes saw immediately what was going on. Drugs on the table. There were too many of them if it came to it, four, with maybe more in the kitchen, but most of them were little more than kids. He remained in the doorway facing them, his mind racing. Police training only went so far in preparing one for this, he thought as he analysed his options. He spoke a hasty emergency message into his lapel microphone calling for back-up.

His adrenaline was kicking in. He wondered why they hadn't tried to hide anything? Then he realised why the front door had been left ajar. People were still arriving.

He heard someone else coming up the stairs behind him. He should have seen that sooner. His options were closing down. He probably ought to turn round and try backing out – the narrow stair-well, even the street would be safer than in here. Even before he turned someone in the room shouted a warning over his shoulder to the person approaching slowly on the stairs.

'Will,' the warning voice called out.

That was the last word Bob heard, the final thing a cornered Bob Steer knew. Fear welled up inside as he realised this time, there was no way out. He sensed his own mortality worn naked on his blue sleeve.

Those in the room heard the deafening shot. Will had quickly raised a pistol and without hesitation fired into the back of Bob's head. Blood and bits exploded from his forehead on to the others and across the room as Bob's body fell forward, knees hitting hard on the floor, then head crashing down. With the shot fired up into the back of his head, Bob's blue helmet of red blood and white brain spun forward spilling the gore everywhere as it rolled across the worn carpet.

A kind of paralysis affected them. Then slowly one by one they climbed over Bob's prone form and dashed down the stairs to make their escape. When they'd all gone, Will stepped into the room, looked round, pushed his gun back under his jacket and wrapped his hands round the drugs left on the table, then after carefully side-stepping around the PC's now still helmet, slowly walked back down the stairs.

Daisy heard the shot. She knew what it was. Agitated and frightened she was calling the police whilst watching through her front window at everyone running away. Her one hand held her phone, the other gripping her Zimmer frame for support to stop herself falling. She was so very frightened.

When she got through, she had to halt her call, one last man was leaving, but he wasn't running like all the others. He just stood and looked round. It was his face that really scared her. This one was in no hurry, his manner ruthless and dominant. He swaggered as if invincible. She felt his piercing gaze in her direction. Perhaps he could see her behind her blinds, but then she told herself, that wasn't possible.

It was taking ages to speak to someone at the station. They seemed preoccupied. The person on the switchboard kept asking her to hold.

Daisy wasn't to know everyone in the police station was occupied, hurried calls being made, every available officer being gathered to come to her street. Bob's call had come through and everyone pulled together to respond quickly to a lone officer in distress calling for urgent help. The fact they couldn't get back to him only added to their sense of desperation to go and help their colleague.

After a long pause, and in response to the encouragement given by the lady on the switchboard on the other end of the line, Daisy finally took a deep breath and finished making her call, telling of the gunshot she had heard. She said how many people she had seen run from the flat, how the one she had seen leave last, the man who seemed above it all and quite unafraid, had been slow to leave, but thankfully by now he too had also disappeared from sight. And yes, she was able to assist in giving an accurate description of him.

The help, when it arrived in Shrubbery Road from Edmonton Police Station, an armed response unit of four men in two cars, came less than two minutes later, but it was too late to save Bob. It was 6.15pm on Saturday 13 August.

Bob hadn't moved from where he fell. His face, or what was left of it, was bleeding out into the grey-white Ikea rug. A major scene of crime investigation swung into action, blue and white tape quarantined the block as a call was put through to the Chief Constable saying simply, 'Man down.'

Will, for all his swagger and feeling of invincibility, had pushed things too far this time. He didn't realise it, but now both he and his drugs empire were about to feel the full force of the Metropolitan Police bearing down on them and even he, for all his bravado, decided it was time to seek the shadows.

16

It was just a short journey home, but as Kaylah pushed Jacob along, her mind flipped to thinking about Clive. Instinctively, Kaylah couldn't help but worry about him. Her younger brother's association with Winston and through him with a wider dubious group was a subject Clive never ventured to discuss with her, which raised her suspicions. This led her to conclude he was on the edge of some shady business or much worse.

Her fears had substance, not only because Clive didn't share anything, but also because sometimes he seemed shaken by his time with these so-called friends. She knew this because he was in her view an innocent abroad. Now and again he was out of his depth, and his face just said that was exactly where he was, in deep shit. It was the same when he was a boy at primary school.

Occasionally, when young, Clive mixed it with the rougher kids to try and prove he was one of them, but he never was one of them and it shook him up then as it shook him up now. More than this, Clive had stopped asking her mum and dad for money like he used to and she knew full well he had no job or source of income. So she asked herself where he got the money from, and whichever which way she reasoned, she concluded it had to be bad.

She made her mind up to confront him about it. Just when he was about to start college in the coming autumn, it would be a disaster if it were all to go wrong at this point. She told herself she was behaving like their parents and maybe she was, but she just wanted Clive to stay safe and happy. And if he asked her, yes, she wanted him to be a model uncle for her little Jacob too. Was that so bad, was that too much to expect? By the time she'd made her mind up that she was definitely going to talk to Clive, she was closing fast on her parents' front door and pulled out her key to let herself in.

'Huh! This is no welcome,' she called out aloud, sensing no-one to be in, 'Anyone at home?' Then she realised, it being Sunday morning, her parents would be at the Tabernacle Church.

There was no reply, but she thought she could hear a noise in Clive's room. Maybe he had his earphones on, as ever. First, Jacob was desperate for a feed and she had to change him too. She'd soon learned the first lesson of motherhood, that to feed first and try and change after, never worked. This time he needed a complete change; the most smelly nappy yet, had leaked. The delay caused Jacob to cry ever more loudly and not even Clive's headphones could keep that noise out. Clive pushed his head out of his bedroom door to say, 'Hello.'

'A piercing noise and a terrible smell. How do you cope? Hi, Sis,' he teased.

'Gimme a minute. Nearly there. She swept Jacob up into the air, and as he began to feed, the noise instantly abated. What you sayin' Clive?' Kaylah asked.

'Just said, Hi. Mum and dad have gone to Wembley for a church conference, won't be back until late. It's just us. Want a drink?' asked Clive.

'Just some water please. Thanks.'

They both made their way downstairs, Kaylah rather awkwardly, Jacob still happily sucking away. A few minutes later both were in comfy chairs. Clive had a designer label T-shirt to match his tight jeans. She gazed at his clothes.

'I just don't know how you afford all the stuff you wear, and that buggy you bought for Jacob, it cost hundreds. I'm amazed, puzzled even. How do you afford to live the way you do?' Kaylah said, going straight to the point.

'Oh, I get by, do bit of this, bit of that. Help Winston out sometimes. The other day, Winston and I both got given some money by a friend who didn't need it anymore. Mix with the right people, you get by,' Clive said, light-heartedly trying to fob her off.

119

'I worry about you Clive. I know you and it isn't all like you say. I see through you. Mum and dad might not, but I do. I was thinking about you on my way over. You worry me. Winston and your so-called friends are trouble. There's nothing open or above board about what is going on. You remember when I went for an evening out with you and them last summer. Ended having a police raid we did. You're Jacob's uncle and I want him to grow up proud of you, like I am, really I am.' She smiled at him.

'Don't you worry about me, Sis. I can look out for myself. College beckons soon and I won't have time to keep up with Winston and his mates. Anyway, what have you been up to since you moved into your flat? We don't keep up like we used to.'

'Melissa called to see me yesterday which was nice. Winston's got me some things in from the shops a couple of times which was a help.'

'Don't tell me you're sweet on him, Sis?' Clive teased.

'No way. You know that, you, you...' and despite holding Jacob, she managed to throw a cushion at him.

Just then the front door bell went.

'You expecting someone?' asked Clive with a dead straight face.

'Nope.'

Clive got up and peered through the net curtain.

He opened the door, a uniformed UPS delivery man stood as if to attention, peaked hat on in spite of the hot day. He held a machine in one hand and a shoebox-sized parcel in the other.

'Looks like a delivery,' Clive announced to his sister.

'Parcel for Kone,' the delivery man said in a routine monotone voice.

'Which one? enquired Clive.

He looked down at his machine.

'Machine here says, Kaylah Kone,' he replied, 'that you or the lady?' He smiled cheekily.

'Sign for me will you,' said Kaylah.

In an instant he'd gone, his brown van vibrating the sash window as he accelerated away. Clive turned the brown package over in his hand.

'It's from Germany. Looks like Berlin. Another home shopping order?' asked Clive glancing over to Kaylah.

'No, not me. I ain't ordered nothing. Might be something for Jacob. Someone might have sent him a present. Some of my friends, and you know what, some of the people who've known us all our lives in the church, they've knitted things or sent him things. So, could be for Jacob. Reckon so. Can you open it for me please?' she asked seeing it was securely bound with parcel tape.

Clive dropped it on the chair and went into the kitchen to find a knife. Kaylah put the now sleeping and contented Jacob down in his buggy. He'd be asleep for a couple of hours now, she hoped. Looking across at the mystery parcel, for a moment she quite irrationally began thinking it might be a bomb – shoebox size, bomb-size. Her heart fluttered, missed a beat. She told herself not to be so silly. Even so when Clive came back she voiced her fears and eyed the object suspiciously.

'Just be careful opening it, would you,' she said.

'Why? You think it might be fragile? You've got some idea what it might be haven't you,' he jested.

Kaylah felt foolish and stayed quiet, watching with apprehension as Clive slowly unwrapped the strong outer paper wrapper, cutting through the tape with the bread knife. Inside there was indeed what looked like a shoebox. He put his hand on the end of the lid, then stopped. Clive felt he should pass it over to Kaylah.

'It's your present,' he said. 'Go on, open it.'

After a moment's hesitation whilst she calmed her anxiety, she swiftly lifted the lid. Fortunately, nothing went bang, but there was still more wrapping to remove. There was tissue paper wrapped around three separate parcels. One looked and felt like a book. She picked it up, pulled off the tissue. It was a book, unlike any she had seen before. Her eyes searched quickly for clues, for meaning, but found none.

She opened it and flicked the pages. It looked like the pages were handwritten in fading ink with beautiful patterns. It was old, some kind of antique. Wrong person, wrong address, she thought. She'd seen writing like this before and suddenly panicked, throwing it on to the floor.

'It's, it's Arabic. An old Arabic book. I don't want it,' she blurted out.

Curious, Clive reached down and picked it up and turned it over in his hand.

'This could be worth something. I guess it's a collector's piece. It would raise a few bob. I'll find out what it's worth for you if you want. Anything's better than nothing. You need some money, don't you? But who sent it? You'd better see what else you've got,' he said.

Kaylah felt less worried there might be a bomb, but a sinking feeling was coming over her as to who might have sent the parcel. Instinctively she now knew it was definitely sent to her and not someone else. She chose the next largest package and again pulled off the tissue paper. Inside was a brown envelope. On the outside, there was was some neat writing in English.

'For Jacob, it says, that's nice,' Kaylah said, feeling reassured it was for them.

She began opening the envelope and pulled out what looked and felt like a wad of banknotes.

'Christ! U.S. dollars,' exclaimed Clive, immediately recognising their familiarity. 'How much is there, Sis? How much you got there?'

Kaylah was dumbstruck. She passed them over to Clive to count. Kaylah looked on, as Clive flicked them through his fingers, her mind racing.

'Two thousand five hundred dollars,' he said after counting them out on the floor twice to be sure, 'Two thousand five hundred and you ask me what I'm doing with myself. Just what are you up to, Sis? Are you money laundering or something?'

'For Jacob, it says,' said Kaylah, under her breath.

'What's that then, in the last one, a gold bar or something? Quick, come on, open it,' instructed Clive.

Kaylah picked up the remaining postcard-sized parcel.

'No gold here, it's too light,' she said, weighing it in her hand.

She unwrapped the tissue to find a smiling picture of Ali. It caught her by surprise, though her growing apprehension at what the parcel might actually be should have alerted her to its source. She looked at him, and for some inexplicable reason she remembered the time they'd gone to the fireworks at Alexander Palace and the fun they'd had, felt guilty at the thought, recalling next his subsequent betrayal and cruel act of terror. She didn't want to look at his picture and turned it over in her hand. It didn't end there, there was a handwritten message on the reverse. She hesitated.

'Read it out, Sis, read it. It's from him, isn't it, from Ali?' said Clive.

'OK, OK.' She took a deep breath before reading. 'Hi Kaylah, I have a friend who drives a van to Berlin. He's only a driver, not a fighter. He promised to post this for me. I trusted him before with my life, so a small parcel should reach you with the money and book intact. There's no other way of getting things through. It may surprise you but I found out about Jacob through Facebook. They have ways of finding out these things here too! I know he is my son and I like the name. I don't have long for this life, but I want you to give him what's in this box. The book is a precious old holy book, a Qur'an. It was recently given to me as a gift, but I have one already. He must know his father was a Muslim. You will tell him please. I am not all bad. I have to do what a man has to do. The book is good. The money is for you to use as you think best. I know you want to start up in business. My friend the van driver delivers traditional rugs and carpets to Germany where they sell well. He could supply you too and there is money to be made. Text me. You have my number. I have one final request to make. I want to see my son one time before I die. I will be in Istanbul this summer. Text me a yes or no, to say you will bring him. I promise no harm will come to either of you. I long to see him before martyrdom, Ali. PS. My life depends on you not sharing this with anyone.'

'Hell! Some parcel,' said Clive breaking the heavy silence that had fallen between them.

'I don't want anyone to know about this Clive. Can you wrap it all up again for me and put it in a plastic bag under the buggy. Do not, do not tell mum and dad,' Kaylah pleaded. She was feeling upset and struggling not to show it.

'And you think I'm the one with dodgy friends,' chided Clive gently, before disappearing into the kitchen.

Kaylah was shaking. It was as if she had seen a ghost. Clive continued speaking.

'Like I said, he wasn't all bad, Ali wasn't, Kaylah. I got on with him, so did you. Admit it. I reckon that's a pretty decent letter and a thoughtful gift to you. He didn't have to do anything and he's put himself at risk and to no small expense, I guess, to send these things. OK. OK, I know he deceived us both big time, but he had a job to do, bit like an undercover policeman. You can't trust them either. There's stuff to think about there and at the end of the day, he wants Jacob to know that in spite of everything he's his dad, he cares.'

Kaylah was confused again. She seemed to get confused a lot these days.

'Shut up, Clive. What, you think, he's all of a sudden a decent dad, some kind of nice policeman? No way! He's history, a terrorist and a bastard, that's all there is to it,' she said her voice full of emotion.

'Just think on it, Sis. One man's terrorist is another man's freedom fighter. We might not agree with him or his methods, but love him or loathe him he's quite some guy, you've got to admit,' said Clive.

'I hate his guts,' she said slowly, trying to have the last word on the matter.

Kaylah then remembered that she'd visited Ruth earlier and wanted to share her plans with Clive. It seemed a good moment to move the conversation on.

124

'I called in on Ruth Churchill at Holy Trinity earlier. I wanted to talk about a christening for Jacob. She was very kind and understanding, and offered me a service of thanksgiving. It's something I want for Jacob,' she said.

Clive wasn't really interested, but thought he ought to hear Kaylah out.

'I just think it would be the right thing to do. I can't ask dad and his church. You know why. Anyway, I don't think like he does,' she continued.

'Mum and dad won't like it. Then again, I think they'll be relieved. It spares them embarrassment, to have it there I mean. Do you want me to tell them or will you?' Clive offered.

'You can if you like. Sound it out with them and let me know. There's no date or anything yet. But it's what I want, a thanksgiving service for Jacob.'

With that Kaylah thought she ought to be going, to get back in time for the next feed. She gathered her things, roughly wrapped up Ali's parcel with its contents, thrusting everything in a plastic shopping bag under the buggy and opened the door, Clive kissed her and Jacob goodbye.

'Good to see you, Sis. I appreciate your concern, what you said earlier. Don't worry about me. You've got your own worries. And look, if it helps, I'll come with you as chaperone to Istanbul, can't think of anywhere better for a week away,' he jested.

Kaylah gave him a smile and a scowl. He always teased her. The door clicked shut. As she walked, she thought about Clive. They'd always been pretty close and he'd been an absolute brick when she needed him this afternoon. The buggy picked up speed, click-clicking as it rode the paved slabs beneath her feet on their way to the bus stop. Underneath the buggy, she couldn't help but glance down to see the corner of the plastic bag containing the gifts from Ali poking out.

No way was she going to Istanbul, in spite of Clive's offer. Ali was history, dead and buried already as far as she was concerned. She was lucky, there was the bus – a red

London Routemaster arrived at the bus stop just as she did and she manoeuvred the buggy on board. She always travelled on the lower deck now, never used to. Being a mother makes all kinds of unexpected changes in your life, she mused.

It was only a short walk at the other end to her flat. What a stroke of good fortune. Such a nice place to start her off. The thought that she needed to get some business going soon was now pressing. Money would soon become an issue. While it lasted this flat-minding was a good interim arrangement. Pushing open her front door, the cool interior was welcome after the hot air of the street.

It was now late afternoon. After the next feed she thought she'd take Jacob out again and explore the local shops. It soothed him to be in the buggy and she liked to be outside. Might even see another young mum to talk to. Warm August days get people out. The change and feed were becoming second nature and she was back in the street within the hour. She left the plastic bag and its contents in a drawer in the bedroom she and Jacob were sharing, pushing it firmly shut before leaving.

There was another mum, a white woman with long blonde hair and twin boys of about six months. They'd got talking outside the corner shop. She knew of a mothers and toddlers group nearby. Both seemed needful of a conversation. They'd recently exchanged addresses and mobile numbers, agreeing to look out for each other. Kaylah gave her a call and moments later they were walking to the corner shop deep in conversation. She bought herself a magazine for later before they went their separate ways and she headed back. In all she had only been out fifteen, maybe twenty minutes, but it had been nice.

It was when she pushed open the front door she sensed something wasn't right. Could someone have been inside whilst she was out? But she was certain she'd checked she'd locked up before going out. The last thing she wanted was to leave Sharon's flat unlocked whilst she was responsible for it. She felt unnerved. Her eyes scanned the floor and corridor for

126

any clues. Was it her imagination, or was there a lingering unfamiliar smell? The thought of a burglar and maybe one still in the flat began to terrify her. She paused, listened, then thinking of Jacob backed slowly out of the door again. No way was she going in there. She called Winston on his mobile.

'How are you doing Kaylah?' he cheerily asked.

'Are you nearby?' she said.

'Where?' he said, detecting the anxiety in her voice.

'Home.'

'Yes. Why? Need some help?' he offered.

'Yes. Just worried about someone who shouldn't be there, being in my flat. Can you come over?'

Moments later he was there, white plastic bag in his hand.

'Got my tools,' he pulled out a claw hammer, 'just in case,' and smiled cheekily at her before putting on a macho-man look as he gazed towards her front door.

Even Winston was cautious. He called out first before entering, but there was no-one, and nothing obvious was missing. He felt he had done the brave, tough-guy thing and that was enough, so he wasn't overly disappointed his time had been wasted. In any case he'd grown quite fond of Kaylah. Helping her move in had placed her in his debt, he thought, as had this little incident. Before leaving he double-checked she was alright and told her not to hesitate if she was ever worried again. He wasn't too sure about leaving her on her own, but she insisted and he left after a few minutes.

It was only later in the evening when she began putting Jacob's clean clothes away in the bedroom drawers Kaylah noticed it. The corner of the plastic bag containing the things from Ali was protruding out of the drawer, not much, not more than the size of a postage stamp, but enough to terrify Kaylah. There had definitely been someone there. Someone had looked at those things from Ali. She frantically checked round every last detail to see if there was any other clue to her intruder's presence. There was none. That night, feeling very alone and scared, she didn't sleep for listening out for every noise and in fear her mysterious intruder might come back again.

17

Ali wondered whether his parcel had made it. There was no way of knowing. He dare not risk calling to find out, certain that all his calls were listened to, and since his return to Mosul the monthly calls to Kaylah had had to end. His reverie was interrupted as a messenger came in and whispered in his ear that one of the guys detailed to go to Istanbul as part of Ali's new unit had admitted to being a spy. Apparently the man's brother was in Turkey and the man had been communicating with him, telling him he was coming and worse.

Ali's mind immediately went back to the risks he himself had taken in sending the parcel. No-one was safe. It was too late to do anything about either his own calls or the parcel he'd sent now. He had no regrets and he knew that his life was short anyway given the direction things were taking.

Salim Ismat, his CO, had ordered everyone under Ali's command to come to the nearby Victory Square to see justice done, the man added, and to do so now. Ali nodded to show he had understood and followed the man downstairs from his family's new apartment and headed into the street. The man hurried off, summoning others noisily as he went. Ali hated the thought as to what this meant. He'd seen summary justice done too many times before.

Ali scanned the sky. He always did. Fear of another drone attack, one sent for him, scared him. There could be little doubt the bomb killing Mo and Ahmed had been meant for him. He knew they'd try again and again until they'd got him for what he'd done. He walked more quickly despite the blazing heat. He found he wasn't the first to arrive. The CO and seven others, all of whom he recognised, were already standing in a line waiting. Ali pulled his black robes tighter and joined them. He wondered which man had been the unlucky one this time. There was a small crowd of curious onlookers beginning to drift into Victory Square.

A quick scan of the faces gathered and he knew. Then he heard him, not his voice, just the sound of a man being dragged across the ground, the toes of his boots leaving two parallel wavy lines in the red sand. Blindfolded, he was made to kneel before the CO.

Terror is generated slowly. Fear, a carefully administered poison, whose deadly weighted dose was best only gradually administered, as much to terrify the victim as to inculcate obedient fear in those assembled to watch and learn. This, Ali calculated was an orchestrated exercise so that his new team would unquestioningly do everything asked of them. The man's head was tilted up towards Salim Ismat who then started walking round him.

A lengthy talk followed, and each time Salim turned to approach the man, all watched and wondered whether this time the speech was about to finish. The man was told in a one-sided conversation that he had collaborated with the infidel unbelievers, he had betrayed Allah, he had betrayed the greatest and most honoured warriors of the Caliphate. For this he would die and his family be made destitute. His name would be wiped from the face of the earth. He knew what was coming, everyone did, and the man could be seen trembling as he tried to hold his kneeling position with what dignity he could muster.

His CO produced an automatic pistol from within his robes. He clicked the safety catch off right next to the man. The man flinched at the sound. Then Salim walked along in front of the lined assembly, gathered wraith-like in their black warrior robes. He looked each one in the eyes, pausing, letting each know he had the power of life over them too and each in turn wondering whether they would be the one to be commanded to shoot dead their disgraced comrade.

Ali knew what was coming. He was right. The pistol was placed firmly in his hand. Of course the CO was too clever to be the one who would do this. It was part of his CO's initiation of him, an insurance put in place so he knew there would be no turning back. It was too late for any way out. Ali felt another part of him die somewhere deep inside.

The man was just five paces away. Ali briskly walked up to stand behind him. He knew the man could hear him coming. Maybe it was kinder this way, to make it quick. He placed the gun at the back of the man's skull, looked his CO in eye as if to say one for you and squeezed the trigger. The noise, brains and bits of bone flew everywhere, the man's body slumping forward onto the ground. Ali walked back to the CO, spun the gun in his hand, his CO grasping the offered handle to take it back. Ali tried to make it as commanding and convincing a performance as he could muster.

Ali knew he would need to change. With the noise of the shot still ringing in his ears, he turned and walked from the square. They could think what they liked. The CO could think him insubordinate, but he didn't care. The others would just think he was a strong warrior. Not for the first time, Ali told himself, he was a dead man walking. He pushed open his front door, desperate to dispose of the wet and contaminated garment clinging to him.

He spent the rest of the day indoors. Soon, very soon he'd be told he would be leaving for Istanbul. The final escorting arrangements for the journey were being made and the international group at Ali's command were almost ready to move, the last pieces of operational military equipment currently being sourced and put in place.

He received one caller that evening, Syed, one of his CO's close team, who reported that word had finally just come back from one of the Kurd groups. For so long IS and the Kurds had been their sworn battlefield enemies in Syria and Iraq, but this splinter group wanted to collaborate. More than this, they would actively support a joint venture in the heart of Turkey. The Kurds came round to IS's way of thinking in return for a promise made by the IS leadership to respect this Kurdish group's claims for sovereignty. As part of the deal, the Kurds agreed even to facilitate the safe passage of Ali's IS fighters across the Iraq/Turkey border and into south-eastern Turkey.

131

A further significant verbal condition was tied to the deal which stated that although this joint enterprise was known to senior Kurdish officers and those directly involved in helping the campaign along, no public mention of it would ever be made. Both sides had much to lose if this was to be the case. So far as the rest of the world was concerned, Kurds and IS remained sworn enemies and evermore would be so. Secretly however, depending on how well this pilot initiative went, the promise of further future co-operation to mutual benefit was held out as a distinct possibility. Syed gave his report in an encouraging way and expressed the belief that all their joint plans were coming together to allow for a successful mission. Ali thanked him. He quite liked Syed, one of the more friendly members of his team.

To Ali's surprise the order to move off came through that Thursday evening. They were to leave at dawn on Friday and to meet their Kurdish guide, Nebez, north of Akre, before sunset on Saturday. It had started. Ali lay on his bed, his face to the wall. He had been on dangerous missions before, and knew that the experience was not conducive to a good night's sleep.

A hasty pre-dawn breakfast, a sad goodbye to his diminished and traumatised family and by daybreak he was leading a group of nine men racing north in a group of four vehicles, each laden with equipment. High above, as Ali well knew, a satellite recorded and reported their moving vehicles.

When the report duly came in at the US monitoring centre in the USA it was logged and reported, but before pre-emptive action was decided upon, the small convoy had driven into the Kurdish area and were thereby assumed to have been IS defectors or Kurds returning from a mission. The watching man was finishing his long shift and thought no more of it.

The information was nonetheless routinely shared between allies, and in an office in Tel Aviv, one person was thinking this small convoy worthy of further enquiry, just as she had identified a solitary cyclist from England morphing into an IS lone-wolf terrorist the previous summer. Anna Simonsson had a gift for spotting the significance of the abnormal in the normal. No list of figures, no apparently chaotic picture, no streaming image, was too demanding for her insatiable curiosity and compulsive need to find order in everything she looked at.

It was Anna who looked at and scrutinised the four vehicles' separate points of departure in Mosul, watching their trails merge and head north. One had begun its journey only after pulling up adjacent to the hospital where an unsuccessful attempt had been made to kill Ali Muhammed. Unlike her now off-duty US counterpart, she spotted more than a coincidence here and immediately shared her suspicions with her Israeli boss who knew to treat everything Anna sent him with the utmost regard and respect.

In response, a number of key individuals were then hastily mobilised for a security briefing to try and assess what might be happening, at the conclusion of which, as those attending began to file out of the Tel Aviv Security HQ conference room, an immediate report was sent to Washington, Jerusalem and London. It said simply, 'Ali Muhammed is on the move, heading for Turkey.'

18

Fortunately, there was no room in the car for Adam's tearful mum to come to the airport. He was much relieved. He felt stressed enough at the impending trip and to have his mum clinging on to him, metaphorically if not literally, would have been just too much. As it was, his dad hardly said a word as he drove them all to the Departures drop-off point at Heathrow. On arrival, they quickly unloaded. Predictably, he pushed an envelope in Adam's hand. He knew it would be some money and without opening it pushed it in his inside pocket with a simple, 'Thanks,' adding, 'I shall make sure I spend it this time! Thanks as well for the chauffeuring, dad.'

'Let me know what time you get back and I'll be here,' he said. Adam thanked him again. There was just the briefest of hugs and he had gone. Adam knew that he was putting his parents through another anxious time and until his dad had disappeared from view, it screwed him up inside.

Passing through the Departure Gates at Terminal One, the four of them deposited their cases and rucksacks to go into the luggage hold. They then headed through customs without difficulty and into the lounge to wait for their British Airways flight to be called up for boarding. Everyone was in high spirits, except Adam. This hadn't gone entirely unnoticed.

'Adam, you're not your usual cheerful self,' said Raqiyah. 'It'll be fine. My uncle will meet us. He's just texted to say he's got the use of a university minibus plus driver and he will be coming to meet us at the airport. Just you wait, you'll find he's really nice. He left our home village in Oman as a young man to teach Anthropology in Istanbul. He's very western, just like our lecturers in Exeter, well the best ones! Sometimes he comes back to Oman to see us. I remember him as always bringing us presents when I was younger. You'll like him. He'll make sure we have a good time, you'll see.'

Adam felt comforted by her reassuring words and the softness of her voice. She gently put her hand on his arm as she spoke and they moved towards some empty seats to while away the remaining time. Idle chatter helped and he was feeling much more relaxed when twenty minutes later they were back on their feet making their way forward with a motley assortment of Western and Middle Eastern passengers all heading in the same direction. Once on the plane, Adam was in a window seat with Raqiyah sitting beside him. It was as if she had chosen to be with him and Adam didn't mind. In fact he realised he was really glad of her company.

'You know, last time I was in a plane was when the military brought me back to London. There was hardly a single passenger on board, just military equipment and there were no customs and immigration, no check ups of any kind,' he told her. She understood his mind was locked into his past traumas and was happy to be next to him. She thought he needed her and she liked to be with him.

In the final preparations before take off, a stewardess broke into their conversation to ask him to lift his arms so she could see his seat belt was fastened. Moments later they were away. It was a direct flight, the journey no more than four hours. It soon passed.

In the bright sunlight, a blue sea sparkled below and then Adam could see the coast of Turkey appearing. Suddenly they were descending from the west into Istanbul's Ataturk Airport, the flight ending with a disconcerting but gentle double-bump judder as the plane touched down and rapidly decelerated. Adam spotted rows of parked planes outside shimmering in the heat.

The airport's busy International Terminal 2 was like any other modern airport and this reassured him. He realised that arriving in Istanbul by bike and by plane were two entirely different experiences, and with that thought he tried to put some confidence back into his stride as they stepped off the plane.

Once reunited with their baggage in the air-conditioned baggage hall, they walked out into the bright sun and the

135

searing summer heat, to see Raqiyah's uncle standing next to a young man holding a sign with their four names printed on.

The clean-shaven, balding, older man had spotted them before they saw him and in his white shirt and dark glasses Adam saw a kindly man. He was wearing his identity badge from the University of Istanbul. 'Prof Abdul Zayed, Business & Social Sciences,' it said in blue lettering. Raqiyah bounded up to him and they embraced warmly, faces relaxed and smiling, happy at seeing one another again. They broke away and Abdul turned his attention to his niece's travelling companions.

'Welcome to Turkey! I trust you had a good flight. This is Mustafa, who kindly brought the minibus over and will be taking us to where you will be staying.'

Mustafa did an awkward bow, his cigarettes falling from his shirt pocket as he did so, items which he hastily retrieved. Adam watched him. He asked himself whether Mustafa was someone they could trust. Abdul was straightforward, open and looked genuine. Mustafa was an unknown and only because Abdul was so obviously in charge of proceedings did Adam feel he would be able to step into the minibus. He tried to tell himself not to be so stupid and he wondered whether his sense of rising panic so early in the trip would ruin it for everybody. He tried to pull himself together as Abdul called them to be ready to move.

'Have you all got everything, your bags? Then follow me. Airports are no places to hang around. Let's go!'

Mustafa led the way, jangling the minibus keys in his hand, immediately followed by Raqiyah now walking alongside her uncle Abdul, the two busily engaged in conversation. Adam imagined they were catching up on family news, it was all so good-humoured and flowing, there could be no sinister planning going on there. He wondered whether she was telling him about her three travelling companions, and what, if anything, she might be saying about him. At that thought he laughed at himself for taking himself too seriously or maybe simply being too paranoid. It didn't

136

take long to get to the modern white minibus, to climb inside and for the welcome air-conditioning to begin to take effect.

Mustafa soon had them away from the airport, heading east. Abdul, sitting in the front passenger seat swung round and began giving a running commentary, rather like a tourist guide. Adam thought this might be helpful and gave him his full attention. He could have done with a bit more local knowledge last time he came to Istanbul, he thought.

'Istanbul's centre is about sixteen miles from the airport, it's a big city, maybe as many as fifteen million people live here. It's the meeting place of east and west. It straddles the Bosphorus Straits, a busy shipping thoroughfare. So, a big city has many universities. Tell me, how old is your University of Exeter?'

'Oh I know that. It was founded in 1855, in Queen Victoria's reign,' chipped in Bilal, 'I saw it somewhere.'

'It's modern then. So what would be an old university in the UK? Cambridge? Cambridge is the 4th oldest university in the world, founded in the early thirteenth century I think, and my university, the University of Istanbul was founded in the fourteenth century. So it too is one of the oldest and we can trace our beginnings back to the 1320s. Personally, I don't go back that far,' he laughed at himself before continuing.

'You'd be interested to know that Muslim rulers have at different times given the development of this university much encouragement. In the west, Muslims are so often portrayed as backward, conservative, religious fundamentalists. Lesson one, Istanbul has an academic record second to none. And this, my university, has given rise to no less than thirty other universities and colleges across this city. Today, we have around 300,000 students at this university alone. I do wonder why you've come here when so many Turkish people are living in the UK. Last figure I heard, there were over 100,000,' he jested. Abdul turned round to face forward again and the next few miles passed in silence.

A few minutes later, beaming with pride, he paused to look around. They were approaching the older city, and his bright eyes gazed round looking for something to fix upon.

On his instruction and after a word in Mustafa's ear, they turned right leaving the main D100 from the airport to the city after less than a quarter of an hour and swung into the Fatih district and into the heart of the old city. Adam was the only one wondering why indeed they hadn't stayed in the UK and found some local Turks there, but then again, they were such a low profile group, where were they? Maybe in London?

'We have five main campus locations and some fine university buildings. We're just coming up to Beyazit Square and a splendid building. You can see the university's Beyazit Tower over there. It is in the university grounds. This side of the Bosphorus we call the European side. The popular Sultanahmet district is nearby, lots of places for you to explore whilst you're here. Now, we're going to head a little way north where there are some student apartments I have arranged for your use.'

They followed a road beside the shining blue Bosphorus, before turning left away from the water into a side street and towards their apartment block for the remaining few hundred metres of their journey. On first sight the accommodation looked every bit as good as the latest student halls they had just left in Exeter. It was modern and bright and Adam's spirits lifted. Another fear was dispelled.

'You should have everything you need here. There's good Wifi, and several cafes and student restaurants you can use without needing to go anywhere. A good bus service operates between here and the old city and the concierge and security people speak English and will help you I know. Raqiyah has my mobile and will give it you, so any problems you can just give me a call.'

The minibus had come to a halt and they stepped out into the hot sunshine. Abdul raced into the building and came out with a young woman in a blue suit. 'Martina will show you to your rooms,' he announced. They said their brief goodbyes and thanked Mustafa, before the four of them, lugging their bags along, followed Martina to the reception desk.

Passport details taken, room cards issued, they made their way up to the first floor by way of the lift, to find they each had a room along the same landing with a common room at the end. By now they had learned that there was no accommodation fee, Abdul having arranged things through his department. The place seemed very quiet and Martina said the number of summer vacation bookings was lower than they had expected so they were staying at a quiet time. Disappearing into their rooms having agreed to meet up in the common room in thirty minutes, Adam surveyed the scene.

It was a typical student room, but better equipped than most and clean. It still smelled new, the dry hint of plaster dust just catching the back of his throat. Nice, he thought, better than anywhere I stayed last time. He threw his things into the wardrobe and hung his rucksack on a hook on the back of the door. The air-conditioning was hissing quietly, almost imperceptibly in the background. Being on the first floor felt somehow safer. No-one could get to him from outside and he was reassured that his friends were nearby in neighbouring rooms along a short corridor. It'll be fine, he told himself, trying to dispel the fears that kept rising from somewhere deep inside. He grabbed a glass tumbler and tried the local water in the manner of a wine connoisseur. Hmm, he thought, a bit chlorinated for my taste, but passable.

His mind wandered back to Mustafa, the minibus driver. That was the one person he didn't trust, he told himself. It was just instinct, nothing he could pin down. Evening was drawing in, the shadows lengthening. Then he heard it. The echoing, haunting adhan, called by the muezzin at a nearby mosque. He hadn't anticipated it, and should have done – the Muslim call to prayer. It shook and unnerved him. He felt at once in an alien place, transported back to Mosul and he felt his heart pounding in his chest. Glancing at his watch he knew it was not long before they had all agreed to meet in the common room. So he set off and found he was the first to arrive. He looked round anxiously, he didn't want to be alone for too long.

139

That evening, Raqiyah talked them all through a programme her uncle had put together to give them an introductory tour of the must-see tourist sights of Istanbul. They downloaded it to their phones. She announced that her uncle had laid on the minibus for them and Mustafa would be their tour-guide the following day. Tomorrow, Abdul himself had commitments at the university and wouldn't be able to join them. Mustafa would be calling for them at 09:30 which she thought was early for students on holiday and with lost sleep to make up. Nonetheless, all agreed it was a good start and generous of Abdul to have arranged it for them.

They then made their way downstairs to explore the extensive university rooms of the Ataturk Academic Apartments or 'AAA' site as it was abbreviated to everywhere they looked. A convenient ground floor café seemed an easy option for somewhere to eat. Alcohol was conspicuous by its absence, a compromise Adam was happy to make for a few weeks, but this absence of alcohol was another reminding resonance of being back in an alien territory from which he had not so long ago escaped.

Later, back in his room, he sent a text home to his parents. Just a brief message to say they'd all arrived safely after an uneventful flight and, in a moment of thoughtfulness, he gave them the address where he was staying. He knew they'd be doing an internet search the moment they got it. It'll keep them happy and off my back, he thought. He'd downloaded a Kurt Wallander crime thriller, the e-book 'Faceless Killers' – something to read when he couldn't sleep, he'd reasoned, though once he started reading he wondered if he'd made a good choice; the opening pages described a violent killing in a rural Swedish farmhouse.

While he was reading, his phone buzzed. Expecting just to see an acknowledgement message from his parents, he was surprised to see a message from Krish Patel. Now what did he want? He opened the message. It read simply, 'Trust you had a good flight. Remember, if you need us, we can come and help.'

Adam tried to get his mind to think what this meant. Why had he been sent a second call from Krish? The first had been strange enough and had left him thinking there was no smoke without fire. There had to be a solid reason why British Intelligence wanted to keep in contact whilst he was in Istanbul. They definitely knew something was afoot. What could it be?

This second contact unnerved him more than he was prepared to admit to himself. They had him on the end of a piece of string, he thought. They know something is going to kick off and they wanted him to be ready to call them. Of course, it could all be innocent support, he tried to tell himself, but what little experience he already had of the security services quickly told him that was just not being realistic.

Much as he'd like to, he couldn't accept these calls were just for his well-being. He knew these people to be hard-headed pragmatists. Krish was a man under orders. He told himself he had got to keep his eyes wide-open and his ears to the ground every minute he was here. Something nasty was about to happen, he could feel it. As if to tell Krish he knew what was implied by his message, he decided to compose a carefully coded reply. He simply wrote, 'Krish, thanks, will call when temperature here rises.'

Lying on his bed, he began reading his novel. It was better than he thought, it was just right, so violently absorbing it took him away from Istanbul to the countryside of Sweden and into a distracting thriller. Without noticing he drifted into a land of deep and dreamless sleep.

19

The air-conditioning in the cramped conference room in the Tel Aviv Israeli security service office was never designed to cope with this number of people. It was midday on Monday 15 August. All those present had had messages sent to them two days earlier, late on the Jewish Sabbath, instructing them to attend. There were no absentees. Eight people in a room meant for four in the height of summer could only mean one thing. The subject was important.

Standing room only, Anna Simonsson held her report close to her chest waiting for the moment when she should speak. Her new superior, Elias didn't seem so sure of himself as her previous boss of last year. Everyone was looking round at each other wondering when the meeting would eventually get under way. Feet were beginning to shuffle. Finally, Elias himself pushed in through the door. That was as far into the room as he could go.

Elias was an able guy. The sort you imagine teaching maths, thought Anna. However it was almost embarrassing when he spoke, his voice invariably little more than a whisper. For a man of such ability, Anna wondered what sapped his public confidence. For her part, her own confidence had grown no end since a year ago and she was no longer the junior in the team. Elias began apologetically.

'Sorry to keep you all waiting. It's the early hours of the morning in the States and it took longer than I anticipated to get the replies I needed. As you know we have seen increased IS messaging and military activity both in the Middle East and in Europe as they try and take their war abroad to create internal instability and muster indigenous support in the West wherever they can do so. Anna, can you give us your report please.'

He waved his hand in her direction, the signal for her to share her findings.

'I'm Anna Simonsson, from LISP, the Listening and Interpretation Services Programme. What I have to say is classified Top Secret, not a word goes to anyone outside this room.'

'That needs to be stressed. You are only here on a need to know basis and the most serious disciplinary kickback will follow if a word of this leaks anywhere,' added Elias. 'Carry on Anna.'

She looked up. There were understanding nods. She knew that since her work identifying Ali Muhammed the previous summer, her new professional reputation overrode the earlier view people had held of her as a geeky, raw intern. All eyes were on her as she held their attention.

'Since last November, Ali Muhammed, the number one most wanted IS terrorist, has been on the run. Somehow he made his way back from London to Mosul where we have all seen the propaganda footage showing him on the receiving end of a hero's welcome. The lesson from his return is, firstly, he is a resourceful individual operative, supremely capable of conducting operations outside IS territory and secondly, he had help in his travels and there are IS sympathisers everywhere – indeed some of them have been brought to light as we have traced Ali's movements.' Anna paused to look up and to gauge their level of attentiveness before continuing.

'Though we didn't catch up with Ali himself, I am able to tell you that one of Ali's contacts in North London, Abu Nazir, a major IS fundraiser, died and for now IS funding from his outfit has dried up. I am also able to tell you that with Allied support we have degraded the Ali Muhammed family home complex. It is no more. There has just been a drone attack to try and get Ali himself, though early intelligence analysis suggests that although this failed, two male members of Ali's family are now deceased.'

Anna looked up from her notes again. Everyone was still looking at her intently.

'The question that concerns us now is this: What is Ali up to and where will he strike next? A person in Ali's position is on a one way ticket. He thinks it is taking him to paradise, but the reality is, his commanders see him as a useful tool and there will be no let up by them in the pressure to get him to lead a further terrorist activity. My work these past eight months, since Ali's return to Mosul, has been to use whatever means I have available to me, be it local sympathisers able to get a message out, escaping refugee stories, mobile phone eavesdropping and tracking, drone surveillance, IS personnel movement analysis and the use of the latest predictive software – all have contributed to what I am going to tell you now.'

One of the group, a woman in military uniform was called out of the room to take an urgent call. The trouble was, she was the furthest person from the door, so for a minute or so, Anna was on hold, until the door had been shut and her boss, Elias, nodded for her to continue. Her mind told her that now the number in the room was seven people, things were perfect. With her in the centre, those remaining formed a balanced strong hexagon shape of six points around her. She felt much more comfortable with that. She continued to address the matter in hand, her index finger moving line by line on her referenced notepad.

'Ali Muhammed has left Mosul. He's travelling in a small group of four vehicles and they have moved very quickly north from Mosul and into Kurdish territory,' Anna said, hearing the intake of breath around her.

'That will be the end of him then,' said one of the regular office comedians, but when no-one smiled, he quickly added, 'The Kurds and IS are at war with each other, unless you know different, that is.'

'No, it won't be the end of him, and yes I do know different,' Anna stated boldly.

There was an audible gasp somewhere to her right.

'IS have somehow come to an understanding, an accommodation, with elements within the Kurdish leadership. Only by permission from the highest Kurdish level, have Ali and this small group been allowed to make their way into north-eastern Turkey. Yes, the Kurds have until now been fighting IS and there is no love lost between them, but in recent weeks things are perceptively quieter on that front. A couple of us have been having a go at working out what possible scenarios might emerge from what we know. Let me take these one at a time,' Anna said, flipping over her notes to the next page.

'The first is this. Let us assume IS have somehow persuaded the Kurds, or more likely come to a subterfuge deal with the Kurds which could never be publicly acknowledged, to work together for mutually beneficial ends. Currently, we know the Kurds are losing political support in Turkey and are increasingly on the receiving end of Turkish military attention and their campaign of many decades to build a nation is, to all intents and purposes, stalling. The Kurds need to see Turkey destabilised enough to give them some leverage to gain autonomy, and ultimately gain the prize of a national Kurdistan,' said Anna.

'But IS would never agree to that, surely not?' said the Jerusalem military representative present.

'We think they might. IS might promise to recognise Kurdistan, because it is expedient for them. To break up Turkey and see a new Kurdistan emerge side by side with the Caliphate, which they can then claim to have helped establish has some big plusses for them. We think IS are prepared to play a longer term game on this one. Remember, almost all Kurds are Sunni Muslims, so there is a huge potential, at any later time they choose, for IS to turn their attention back to Kurdistan.' She could tell this was something no-one had really thought of as possible before. They were all ears.

'Looking from where we sit in Israel, the idea of IS and Kurdistan finding common cause one day is an entirely reasonable view to take. Muslim joins Muslim against a common enemy. It is a case of the enemy of my enemy is my friend. If IS can forge a strategic partnership with the Kurds, and in our view, no-one is going to either agree to or have the capacity to plan more than a short term initiative at this point, then that's what we need to be giving our attention to and decide how best to meet this new double threat. It is our considered view that such an agreement is already in place. It

145

is not one that will be made public, but it is there, because there is absolutely no other way, Ali and his co-conspirators could have made their way into Turkey without Kurdish help on Friday last,' she said driving her point home.

'OK,' said Elias, 'any questions at this point?'

'How do you know he hasn't tried to defect instead? That could be the reason he headed north couldn't it? The scenario you've painted assumes an awful lot if you don't mind me saying so?' asked the lead political office spokesperson.

'Good question, but for a number of good reasons what you suggest isn't plausible. The most compelling reason is that there has not been a squeak from Ali or anyone that that might have happened. Precisely the opposite seems to be the case. The fact that since entering Turkey, Ali and his co-conspirators, including Omar al Britani, have gone to considerable lengths to try and make themselves invisible in the suburbs of Istanbul, just adds more weight to what I have already surmised,' replied Anna.

There was a silence and Elias invited Anna to take their thinking forward.

'Anna, could you go through some of the possible courses of action now open to Ali, his team and his Kurdish allies,' invited Elias.

'Sure. The level of certainty with which we are working drops quite markedly at this point. Personally, this isn't my territory. I don't do guesswork, but I have been asked to list some ideas to put before you. If the first point is well made, that IS are opening up a joint front with the Kurds, the second point is speculative, and I'm doing no more than second-guess how things might play out. I don't need to outline the particular vulnerabilities Turkey faces at the current time. It has seen some individual IS and Kurd terrorist initiatives in recent times, none of which to date have made a significant impact, not least because they were poorly directed. But what if, between them, IS terrorists and a Kurdish campaign choose targets more carefully and attack in a coordinated way, and do so simultaneously over a short period of time?' There were shuffles and grunts as people were digesting and assessing what she had to say.

'Might it be possible to destabilise Turkey sufficiently to give IS a window of opportunity in the doorway to Europe? Might they disable Turkey as an effective base to launch Western attacks on IS? Might the neutralising of Turkey leave us in Israel more dangerously exposed to the enemies surrounding us? All this might not be beyond the realms of possibility and imagine what follows. Turkey's large Muslim population with divided loyalties disintegrates; the country's large resources falling into IS, providing fertile recruiting grounds in its large and unstable migrant population who have fled Syria, Iraq and elsewhere. Then there is the loss of US access to airfields and the defeat of a NATO member. Do I need to say more? The potential prize from an IS perspective is huge, and you know what? It might not take much to tip Turkey over. The scary thing is they might just succeed,' concluded Anna as she closed her notes, pulling them once again close to her chest.

There was a thoughtful silence all round before Elias stepped in.

'This is where we have got to. IS can't afford to hang around given their limited military options. Ali will act soon, certainly in weeks rather than months. What we need is for each of you in your various departments to come up with possibilities and feed them in to Anna here. We need them asap, and that means by 8am Wednesday at the latest. I also want to know what leads any of you have as to how we might successfully disable the Ali initiative and how that might be expedited. Just so you know, the usual liaisons with the US and Britain will happen on this, but for obvious reasons we cannot talk to Turkish or other NATO allies at this stage. The Turkish military are so frightened, desperate to keep control, with information like this who knows what unpredictable overkill reprisals they might put in hand. So we keep this to ourselves. Thank you for your attendance. This meeting is now concluded.'

147

20

Kaylah no longer liked the flat she had been given. There were unsolved mysteries that troubled her. Nothing would shake her conviction someone had been in while she was out. The intruder had gone through her things. She had half a mind to phone and ask Lena about it. Perhaps one of Sharon's friends had a key and was also keeping an eye on things. That might be it. A moment's reflection and Kaylah thought it unlikely. She resolved to ring Lena soon.

August was proving a humid, hot and uncomfortable month to be in London. Some years it seemed to be like that. The air didn't move and she thought a thunderstorm would be a good thing. She'd been in the flat nearly two weeks and each day the weather had been predictably more of the same.

It was easy to get out with Jacob, fewer things to put on him, more people on the street. She'd already met up again with Lottie, the young woman with the twins who lived nearby. They'd been down to the local park together. Through her she was now on nodding acquaintance terms with three or four other local mums, most on their own like herself and glad for company.

Knowing a few people to say 'Hello' to didn't help her overcome her fears of being in her new flat. Every time she came back she was scared as she went in, screwing up her courage to go through her own front door, though she hadn't had the sense anyone had been inside her home again since the night Winston had come to her assistance. She wondered what it might have been about. It couldn't simply have been someone looking to see if the place was secure for Sharon. People didn't check through personal drawers doing that, no, there had to be more to it.

Today, Jacob had gone straight back to sleep after his morning feed; unusually she decided to leave him in bed and watch some morning TV. About 10.30, just as she thought it was about time to check Jacob, her mobile went. To her surprise it was Lena.

'Hi Lena,' she greeted.

'Hi Kaylah, just ringing to see things are alright with you. How's it going?'

'Well, glad you called actually as I was thinking of calling you. I think someone has been in the flat whilst I was out,' Kaylah said, hoping that Lena might just be able to put an end to the worrying mystery.

'Are you sure?' said Lena.

'Certain of it. Things had been moved. I was wondering, does anyone else have a key?' asked Kaylah.

'Not that I know of, but I'll check with Sharon. She doesn't tell me everything,' said Lena defensively.

'Thanks. It would put my mind at rest,' said Kaylah appreciatively.

'Do you mind me asking you something?' said Lena.

'What?' replied Kaylah.

'Have you heard anything more from Ali?' inquired Lena.

Kaylah paused. She looked over to the drawer where she had put the things away, not touching them since then. She wasn't going to tell anyone about Ali's parcel, not even Lena. She quickly responded.

'No, not a thing,' she said dismissively.

'OK, just thought I'd ask, because my boss will ask me, you know how it is. If you do hear anything please let me know. His name keeps cropping up in conversations here. People are very worried about what he'll get up to next. It's for all our sakes we keep an eye out. It's one of those things today, no-one can feel safe. I'm sure you of all people understand,' said Lena seeking Kaylah's understanding.

'I do, believe me,' she replied.

'Kaylah, can you hold just a minute, my boss has come in the room. Won't be a minute,' said Lena.

'OK, but why don't you call me back?' suggested Kaylah.

'Fine, will do,' and with that Lena hung up.

149

Kaylah was left worried by the call. Lena had asked if she had heard anything further from Ali, yet surely she would trust me to ring her if I had, as I always have. There was this uncomfortable nagging feeling more was going on behind her back than she realised and she didn't like it. She had half a mind to go out and simply not answer Lena's return call, but then she thought of the flat. It was too soon to risk losing it despite her worries about an intruder.

Her parents had made it very clear she was now out of their house and had to stand on her own two feet. She couldn't risk losing this flat, not just yet anyway. Her mind had often turned over how she might use her business studies course to her practical advantage, to turn a profit. She really needed to as she couldn't see how she could survive without some income by the autumn. Ali's offer of the oriental carpet and rug business contact in Berlin crossed her mind, but that was too complicated and she didn't want to have anything to do with something that had links with Ali. She wanted him put into history. It was then Lena returned her call.

'Hi Kaylah, I've got some news and a big favour to ask. Are you ready for this? My boss came in with some hot news about Ali Muhammed he needed to pass on and I'm more than happy to tell you what he said, though he did say we must keep it between ourselves, as it is, let's say, sensitive information,' Lena confided.

Kaylah didn't like the sound of this. As she listened to Lena she felt she was sinking back into the nightmare of the previous summer and autumn. Feeling trapped, she meekly responded like a child in a classroom with her teacher. For some reason that she couldn't explain to herself, she felt any fight she might have had, had gone out of her, leaving her flat and deflated. She had to go along with Lena, hear her out at the very least.

'Something's come up then? What is it?' quizzed Kaylah wanting to know more.

'From where I'm sitting it's not that bad really. In fact you might find it pleasurable,' said Lena trying to lift the conversation.

Kaylah didn't know what to make of the remark, what to think or what to believe, but wanted to know more.

'Just tell me Lena, what's on your mind, then I can make up my own mind,' said Kaylah.

'Tell you what, I'd rather come over and talk to you, face to face. I can be over to yours within the hour,' Lena said, surprising Kaylah once again. Kaylah could think of no reason to say no, it wasn't as if she had anything in her diary.

Lena arrived by taxi exactly an hour later in an, as ever, smart outfit. Kaylah tried to be hospitable. Too late, she realised, she only had tea without milk to offer her unexpected guest. Lena chose water, helping herself to a glass and running the tap for ages to make sure it was cold. Making herself comfortable, Lena explained that her office in London had received a news message to say Ali was definitely heading for Istanbul in Turkey. In fact they thought he was in all probability there already. It was precisely at that moment, Kaylah noticed Lena's gaze drift and linger a little too long on the closed drawer where Ali's things had been put away and suddenly Kaylah knew. She knew Lena had been to the house. She was the mystery intruder. Her mind was racing.

Alerted to the subterfuge game she was now certain Lena was playing, she tried to listen to the story she was telling her about Ali. She kept saying to herself, she should have guessed. Look how she guessed straight away where to find a glass just now. As Lena's story went on, Kaylah knew she was being dragged ever more deeply back into things way above her head whether she wanted to be part of it or not. Every few minutes Lena would say, 'I shouldn't really tell you. You won't tell anyone will you. This is our little secret.' And with every word Lena uttered, Kaylah felt she was caught by a spider weaving a verbal web around her prey, from which there was just no possibility of escape. She was trapped.

Lena made it clear that Ali and his other friends were located in Istanbul, because at some stage soon they would plan some kind of terrorist attack. No-one yet knew exactly what they had in mind, though guesses were being made.

What Lena seemed to be saying, and in the complexity of it Kaylah wasn't certain she was hearing it correctly, was that Kaylah and Jacob, with Clive as chaperone, should go on an all expenses paid holiday to Istanbul for a few weeks in the hope that Ali might be lured to meet them and then somehow a terrible IS attack could, simply by her being there, well, be stopped in its tracks. It sounded fanciful and far-fetched, yet Lena was apparently sincere, her face showing she was believing absolutely every word as it came out of her mouth. There were moments when Kaylah thought Lena was a mouthpiece of those standing behind her as the line of conversation flowed all in one direction sweeping Kaylah onwards and downwards.

'We might together be able to talk him out of it this time and just think of the innocent lives that you and I could save. We think you and your baby, together with Clive, might be able to win him round, give him an exit route. The thing is, to save all those lives, it's got to be worth a try, hasn't it? What else can we do? I can't think of anything, can you?' she said, as a stunned Kaylah could only merely nod her head up and down in agreement.

'Look, if it's any help, money isn't an issue here. We will make all your arrangements, pay all your bills, give you a great time, even provide you all a generous holiday spending allowance and in return all you have to do is help us arrange a conversation with Ali. And don't worry about security. We won't let you be exposed to any harm, we'll lay on some top class protection believe me. Our world-class guys are so good you won't even know security is there. I'm not one to pressurise anyone. I'll let you sleep on it until tomorrow, but promise me this, you will talk it over with someone you trust. What I mean is, this can't simply be talked about with just anyone, so I suggest talk to Clive, he'll know what to do. That would be the thing to do, wouldn't it?' Lena proposed.

Kaylah nodded meekly, and with that Lena got up as if to leave, no doubt to rejoin the taxi waiting outside, ready to return her to Kensington. She paused at the door.

'Kaylah, would you mind if I had a picture of you and your lovely boy?' she asked, with a cheerful smile. And without waiting for a reply, she held up her mobile phone, moved across the room to frame her shot, the light grey wall behind to frame her subjects and clicked.

'That's really lovely. I'll take a couple then at least one will look good! I'll text you the pictures later. Little ones change so much when they are babies,' said Lena as she slid her phone back into her pocket.

She turned on her heels and when she had finally gone, Kaylah was completely disoriented and now Jacob was beginning to stir after a very long sleep. She couldn't concentrate on what Lena had said if she tried. It was time for Jacob's next change and feed. First, she picked up her mobile, but Clive didn't answer. So, she sent a text message instruction, 'Please ring we have to talk.'

Clive didn't notice the text until early afternoon when he promptly called his sister.

'Where the hell have you been?' she shouted, her anxiety getting the better of her.

'Having a bad time, Sis?' he replied cheerfully.

She immediately felt guilty and recognised how much she had been wanting him to call for the past few hours.

'You could say that. We need to have a conversation. Something big has come up and I need your advice. Can't really talk about it over the phone,' she told him.

'OK Sis, I'll come over now. I'll get a minicab, won't be long,' said Clive.

Clive rang Gus' Taxis in Fore Street and waited downstairs for a car to arrive. Then his phone went. He didn't recognise the number and was in two minds whether to answer, but he knew Gus' Taxis would take a few minutes, he took the call.

'Clive Kone?' said a male voice.

'Who wants to know?' asked Clive, suspecting a cold caller – some annoying call centre offering useless services.

'The name's Stephens, Dave Stephens. You don't need to know any more about me, but you do need to listen very carefully to what I'm going to say. I work for the government. I'm on your side! You need to know your sister is in danger and so are you.'

'Who is this?' demanded Clive, realising he needed to give this call his full attention.

'Call me Dave. Just listen and then work things out for yourself. Your sister Kaylah is living in an Israeli-provided safe-house in Crouch End. She thinks she's just looking after it for someone who's gone abroad. You might think to get a flat like that for free is too good to be true. Well, think about it, it is is!' Dave paused. Clive didn't respond. He'd had thoughts along these lines.

'They're wanting to use her as bait to reach Ali Muhammed. Just to alert you, her house will have been regularly searched by the Israelis since Kaylah moved in and we can assume it is bugged, so the Israelis know everything going on there. Let's just say they also know, for example, that although she has denied it, she has received artefacts from IS. These include extremist literature and terrorist funding from a known terrorist. Surely you know what Ali sent her, don't you Clive?' Dave said very directly.

Clive didn't respond. He thought about what Dave had just said, and just how bad the box Ali had sent could play out for her. The government had draconian powers up its sleeve it could no doubt use. This was turning bad. Dave started talking again, not waiting for Clive to reply.

'Do you want your sister to end up being separated from her child and imprisoned under the Terrorism Legislation? Because, believe you me, Clive, she will go down and they will throw away the key.'

There was a longer pause as Dave let his message sink home. Clive was in shock. This was turning into a very unpleasant day. He couldn't think of anything to say.

'You still there Clive?' Dave asked.

'Yes.'

'I want to be helpful here, believe me. Your sister's predicament is your opportunity. What I am saying is, there is a way you can help her,' Dave said.

154

'There is? How?' he said compliantly.

'That's the spirit. You can help her by sticking close to her and making sure she doesn't get drawn into things she shouldn't, that OK with you?' he asked.

'I'll do anything,' Clive offered. No-one was going to lock away his sister if he had anything to do with it.

'There is one thing, and you will do this for your sister because it is also good for you,' said Dave sounding forceful again.

'How come?' He wondered what was coming next. Was this a threat? He couldn't be sure, but Dave, whatever his real name was, seemed to have some call on him, some hold, but what did he know?

'Your own personal affairs don't bear close inspection, now do they? We know the friends you keep are into crime, drugs, and the like. We can trace you back to Wicked Will. We could also let the police know there is more to Dillon Williams' death than they know and where would that leave you? A word from us and like your sister, you could be locked away for a very long time,' threatened Dave. Clive was feeling pretty vulnerable now, like a desperate fish being steadily reeled in, but on a hook of his own making.

Clive didn't know whether he was bluffing or really knew something, he thought the latter had to be the case. There was no way of testing this guy out. He was totally in his power and he was feeling increasingly terrified. He desperately wanted to find a way out.

'Dillon died from a drug overdose,' he protested lamely, before adding, 'you said there was something I could do. What is it? What have you got in mind?'

'When you next meet your sister, she will tell you that her Israeli contact wants her to go to Istanbul to help bring the terrorist Ali Muhammed out of hiding so that a suspected terror plot can be averted and innocent lives saved,' said Dave.

'Istanbul?' Clive repeated.

'Yes, Istanbul. The Israelis simply want to get her there, to be bait, to expose Ali. They are quite the international

155

experts in personnel protection issues, so the trip should be safe and secure for her. She will have nothing to fear from Ali. He won't be allowed to get to her. I'm sure Kaylah will explain everything to you. The Israelis have put the idea into her head that you are to go as her chaperone and to help with Jacob. We cooperate with the Israelis and they with us when matters like this come to light. But we also take our own decisions in the UK, and it is our decision that this is something we want you to do, to go to Istanbul with your sister. OK?' asked Dave.

'OK. I suppose,' murmured Clive, trying to take it all in. He felt he was into things way over his head. It was all too much.

'When we end this call I'm going to text you a number you can reach me on, day or night. All I can say is that in working with me you are helping your country and I can assure you at the end of this, if all goes according to plan, you and Kaylah will not be brought before any courts. Let's say it will be so out of recognition for the loyal service you will have provided for your country in its time of need. For you two, there will then be an end to all of this, a line drawn in the sand. You'd want that, wouldn't you Clive? You would want to come back from Istanbul knowing that Kaylah, her baby and yourself will never have to face any serious criminal charges. You'd all have a clean sheet, a fresh start. How does that sound then?'

There was a pause whilst Dave let the weight of his bargain sink home.

'I won't be making this offer to you again and you are not to say a word of our conversation to anyone, not even Kaylah. We don't want the Israelis getting any wrong messages here. So we keep it simple – you talk only to me. All you have to do is go along with the proposed trip to Istanbul. Everything will then just happen to get you there, the Israelis will fix it, pay for it and it will all come off very quickly. You will need to forget everything else you might have planned over the next couple of weeks, possibly until the end of August. Any questions?'

'No.' Clive said meekly. He could think of nothing more to say and someone was ringing persistently at the front doorbell. He hung up, grabbed his jacket and went out to take his taxi, his head spinning from what he had just been told to do. He had a terrible, sinking feeling in the pit of his stomach, aware his past misdeeds were no longer a secret, they were catching up with him and his life felt like it was disastrously spiralling out of his control.

21

Ali's group was only allowed to stay in the Kurdish south-east of Turkey the Saturday they arrived. Nebez, their accompanying Kurdish guide from Akre, had been hard pressed en route. He'd been questioned time and again by fellow Kurds. He seemed relieved to leave his charges on arrival. The Kurds saw them as hugely risky, highly suspect and wanted to see them on their way as soon as possible. Never left alone, minders gathered round them making the stay feel incredibly oppressive, likely to break down at any point. They even went to great lengths to ensure they left quickly.

Ali felt their very presence was an awkward embarrassment and they were treated with puzzled looks by most Kurds who saw them, who could have no idea why they were there. Their allocated senior Kurd link-officers took great care to avoid provoking any attention to the group from the Turkish military, who could be seen passing by from time to time on nearby roads, only a short distance away.

Early the following morning, Sunday, the four old Toyota Hiluxes they'd arrived in were hurriedly exchanged for more discreet vehicles, a white Mercedes C-class saloon, a flat backed tip-up truck and a food delivery van. Ali couldn't help but feel the exchange had been in their favour, their new vehicles shiny, clean inside, more modern and with no apparent dents! Equipment they had brought with them, including weapons, ammunition and high explosives were carefully but hastily relocated and hidden in the Mercedes boot, under tarpaulins on the flatbed truck and in small compartments elsewhere in their new vehicles. Most of the explosives were placed in the van, much to the relief of Ali. Smaller items, like automatic pistols, they kept handy on their person.

They never saw what happened to their unloaded Toyotas. Kurdish helpers drove them off and they disappeared from sight. Their Kurdish hosts provided each vehicle's crew with a basket of bread, bottles of water and enough other food to see them through the next day until they got to their destination. Ali was also pleased to see the fuel gauges at full. So far so good. He had to admit he still didn't trust the Kurds. There was no love lost between them, too many old scores, too little trust in return. At any moment one of their number might decide to have a go at them. It put everyone on edge and feeling wary.

Ali naturally got to drive the prize Mercedes and took three men with him. Omar al Britani and two other men went in the flatbed truck and the remaining two in the van. Others would join them once they got to Istanbul to complete their complement. The three vehicles left separately and discreetly, with departure times half an hour or so between each one. Ali saw off the truck, then the van, wishing the guys inside a safe trip. The Mercedes was the last to leave; being the quickest vehicle it would soon make up time on the others. It was a great relief to Ali to have all his men on the road again and heading west. He had no doubt the Kurds were equally glad to see the back of them too.

One of Ali's companions knew Turkey well and acted as his navigator. He sat beside Ali in the front passenger seat. Besides finding their way, his other job was to keep a watchful eye for Turkish road blocks and patrols. They headed west and Ali was glad to have the bright morning sun to his rear and not glaring in his face. It was good to be on the road and he was gradually getting to know his team.

The two men in the back of the car were two brothers he'd known at a distance since childhood, though no-one would have thought they were brothers by looking at them. Like himself they were from Mosul and had lived about fifteen minutes away from Ali's family compound. Whether they still lived to the north of him as he remembered, he'd check out with them later. Both brothers had full dark brown beards, but there the resemblance ended.

Yazen was tall and slim, Jahmir, his younger brother, was much shorter. Each had useful technical skills, Yazen was an expert in explosives and Jahmir, apparently the brighter of the two, seemed knowledgeable about almost anything Ali cared to ask of him. They'd both served in Raqqa for years, fighting close-fought bitter campaigns and were highly regarded for their courage by Ali's CO. Kemal in the front seat beside him was still somewhat of an enigma to Ali. He had joined IS recently from Turkey. He was the link-man between sympathisers in Turkey and IS back in the Caliphate.

Ali knew he was going to have to rely on Kemal's local knowledge to keep them all safe and get them around. He didn't like dependency, especially when he was supposed to be the one in charge. There was also something about the man sitting beside him he didn't like. It wasn't simply the body odour from a man who wasn't particular about personal hygiene and cleanliness, it was his surliness, almost insubordination, each time he spoke. Maybe Kemal was thinking he ought to be the one in charge, Ali thought. One thing was already clear, he didn't like Ali and was not holding back in letting his resentment show. At some stage he could imagine the two were going to end up having a serious falling out. He'd need to be ready for it.

The drive towards Istanbul was long and the roads to begin with, not especially good. But as they travelled ever further west the threat of being stopped lessened as the Kurdish area was left well behind. It was at this point his front seat companion, having issued instructions as to the roads to take, promptly fell asleep and began snoring. The two brothers in the rear were chatting about their family they'd left behind. It was nice to listen in on, and their normal chatter reminded him of happier times with his own family.

He wondered how, back in the Mosul apartment, his sister-in-law Sara was coping, having so recently been left a widow and without her son. He couldn't think his elderly uncle and sorrowful mother would be much help to her for they in turn really needed looking after themselves. He

160

concluded that compared to his happy companions he didn't think of himself as having much family any more and the thought filled him with a deep sense of sadness and loss.

Then for some reason he thought of Jacob. After all, he did now have a son and he wondered how his new baby son was developing. From somewhere deep inside himself he drew comfort from the knowledge he had a fine son living in safety well away from the hellhole that was his own world. The brothers in the back were still talking away, they had a large extended family by the sound of it. Ali turned his concentration back to the road, and the long drive ahead.

Kemal had said they would be driving for up to eighteen, maybe even twenty hours and Ali was to wake him after four hours when they would take a break. The first break was on the outskirts of a dusty village, a chance to stretch their legs, drink in and pass water out. Ali breathed in the hot midday air, before all too quickly climbing back inside the car, the welcome air-conditioning soon making him and everyone else feel comfortable again. Ali was relieved the journey was, so far, proceeding smoothly.

Kemal had chosen a route that took a sweeping arc to the north, keeping them away from the Syrian border where there would be less chance of their being discovered and stopped. Their next rest break would be near Kayseri, or just beyond the city, but it was still some hours away.

By now the sun had moved ahead of them and was descending low in an orange sky, dazzling Ali as he concentrated his eyes on the dusty landscape ahead. The August heat shimmered on everything around them. Even his dark shades didn't help that much. Ali looked down at the car radio and pressed the button bringing it to life. There was western music playing and his companions immediately started making disapproving noises. Ali had forgotten how much he'd taken music for granted whilst in England, but hastily apologised to his fellow travellers and instantly switched the radio off. He wondered whether IS were intent on creating a gloomy, musically silent, future world and he

161

wriggled uncomfortably thinking about what he was committed to.

The suburbs and outskirts of Kayseri were upon them; it was a modern and industrial city, so different to the run-down cities they had left. It took a while to get near the centre, where they passed a large square with what looked like a fort with a mosque to its side. Buses, cars, lorries and heavy traffic at the end of the day moved in every direction. Ali kept his eye out for direction signs for Ankara, the Turkish capital. Soon they were heading out of the urban sprawl and once more into the quiet of the countryside.

Kemal said he knew a place in Ankara where they could park up awhile, maybe have some sleep and then make an early start next day for the remaining leg of the journey to Istanbul. All were feeling relaxed. The trip so far had been tedious and uneventful. For that they were relieved.

As they drove into Ankara in the early hours Ali spotted something going on up ahead. There were blue lights flashing on several vehicles as if there was a road block. There was nowhere to turn off and they had little choice but close in on the roadside incident. The tension and sweat levels in the car rose. In the dark of night it was hard to make things out, but Kemal saw it first. Their two team mates who had travelled in the van, who had left a good hour ahead of them, had obviously been pulled over and were now lying spread-eagled, face down on the road, surrounded by armed police.

Ali slowed. Yazen leant forward to speak to Ali.

'Is there anything we can do?' he asked.

'No. There are too many of them. Ignore them, chill,' Ali ordered. 'We have to get through this. I think we'll be OK, look, the officer up ahead is simply waving traffic past. Have your pistols ready, but out of sight. We're going to a family wedding if he stops and asks, right?' said Ali, looking round to ensure everyone had understood.

In a matter of moments they were there. The police were all too preoccupied with handcuffing the two men and dragging them to separate vehicles to pay attention to the

162

passing traffic. They were waved through without a second glance, the police not wanting any of the passing cars to slow too much and stare. Accelerating away, with the blue flashes now but pinpricks in the rear view mirror, all began to breathe sighs of relief, but anxious questions remained unanswered.

'How come they got stopped?' asked Yazen. Ali hadn't a clue.

'Maybe, the vehicle had come up as suspicious. Maybe they drove badly. Who knows? We'll never know, that's for certain. Where does that leave us, Ali?' followed up Jahmir.

'I'm not sure. We may have to find two more guys when we get to Istanbul or the rest of us will have to work harder. I'll think on it. To be sure though, we press on. It doesn't change anything. I think they would have stopped us too if they had been looking for us, so we can assume we are OK for now,' said Ali.

'What if they talk?' asked Kemal.

'They won't, but even if they say anything, only I know our targets,' Ali told them.

'But they do know us and the vehicles we are using,' replied Kemal.

'OK, so we make a change of plan. We don't stop. We keep driving overnight, pass through Ankara in the early hours and on to Istanbul. We'll ditch the cars with our friends there and find new wheels with local and clean registrations. Now I'm going to need to concentrate and I want one of you to watch the road behind, another the road ahead. We can't risk our mission getting compromised now,' Ali commanded.

Many hours later Ali was very tired as Kemal guided them into Istanbul. This great metropolis seemed vast. Sprawling urban development stretched as far as the eye could see. For Ali it felt like sanctuary. Here were millions of people, the perfect place to hide. He made a call on his mobile to alert his local contact to their arrival. Some directions were given, an address provided. Then he slipped the mobile away again.

'Nearly there. Our friends are expecting us. Food, fresh water to drink, beds await us,' he said.

There wasn't much response. His passengers were tired and spaced-out from so long in the car, and the relief of getting to their destination seemed to have made them even more lethargic. Ali joined the line of traffic crossing the Bosphorus and then they were in Istanbul proper and into a distinctly European world. Following the road hugging the coast they passed signs for Yildiz Park and then Macka Park as his local contact had indicated. Ali looked for a right turn, heading towards Taksim in the busy modern Beyoglu district. A road sign for Galatasaray reminded him of football, a sport IS never allowed back home. No sport, no music, how have we come to this? he mused silently, keeping his thoughts to himself.

Ali was surprised to see where they were to stay. The building advertised itself as an apartment hotel. He circled the block a couple of times to cast his eye over it and make sure it was the right place and safe. It was small, unpretentious, anonymous and with rear access to the garages and open-air parking on the ground floor level. He'd been told to drive in through the rear gates and towards the parking area where he would be met by a young boy who would direct them where to park.

Ali saw the boy before he saw them. He was sitting on the low wall opposite. He looked up at the white Mercedes and when Ali looked back he leapt off the wall and began gesticulating for him to follow, waving his arm and running as he did so. Ali followed him into the darkness of the garage and was directed to a vacant spot in the corner next to a closed entrance door for the apartment hotel. Once parked, the boy had a key, opened a green door, and waved again, indicating that they were to follow him inside. It was innocent enough and Ali, always mindful of a trap, thought how clever his contact was to use a lone child. No-one would suspect him and no-one could prosecute a child.

Once inside, the boy lit the passageway by pressing the light's timer-switch and a low-level light just about lit the

164

corridor. They went up one flight of steps to a door Ali guessed led to an apartment which overlooked the rear of the complex. There was a key in the door. The boy waved them on towards the door, ensured they were entering and then ran off, his job done, no doubt to be amply rewarded by someone later.

Ali pulled the key out of the door and they all explored the accommodation they had been provided with. It was a three-bedroomed flat, clean, modern and furnished, the bedrooms with made-up beds. In the small kitchen was a Formica-top table on which stood bags of food, clearly left there for them. Ali took charge.

'This looks fine. Kemal, I want you to go down to the car. Collect what we might need for the night. Make sure nothing is on show that shouldn't be and make sure it is locked and secure. Yazen, can you and your brother get that food sorted. Put together something for us to eat now and then put the rest away. You two brothers can take that room, Kemal and I the other.' He was tired and sat down. He'd done all the driving as he preferred it that way. He pulled out his phone and sent a text to Omar al Britani in the flat-back truck.

'Arrived Istanbul. Lost two in van,' Ali wrote and pressed send.

An instant reply came back. 'Pulling in now. With you in five minutes. You should see the truck in the car park next to the Merc.'

After acknowledging the message and telling Omar and his two men to come and join them, he then sent a text to his CO in Mosul. It might be getting late, but he'd be waiting to hear from them.

'Two out of three arrived safely, lost the two in the van,' he said.

A message came back almost immediately.

'Link up with locals and recruit two replacements. We will be victorious, enshallah.' Ali noticed, not for the first time, that among the IS leadership any setbacks were never voiced. Only talk of continuing jihad and victory was permitted.

With everyone together, Ali announced there would be a formal briefing at 8am the next morning. They ate together, some hot, mint tea proved a refreshing last course. When guys get thrown together it takes a while for the group to find its level. Ali worked hard to make his disparate group talk, they needed to bond, they needed to be united and looking out for one another from now on. He still wondered about Kemal, a man who kept his thoughts to himself. Ali still didn't fully trust him, but there was nothing that he could put his finger on.

The two brothers offered to clear up after the meal and Ali and Kemal made use of the bathroom, then disappeared into their room. A few minutes later Ali heard the brothers shutting their bedroom door. Omar al Britani and the other two guys disappeared into the third bedroom soon after.

Lying on his back, the room in darkness, Ali knew it would take him a while before he drifted off. Kemal was already snoring, the stale body aroma he gave off already permeating their room. That was my first mistake, he thought. I should have made one of the brothers share with this guy. At the same time, his instinct, which usually proved right, told him he needed to keep an eye on him.

He began thinking of Kaylah again, the fun they'd had together in London and he began to feel guilty about the way he had coerced her into helping him. She was an innocent abroad, putty in his hands. It made him feel dirty inside even though he had been taught that she didn't count for anything. It had been so easy. But in some deep place inside he called his conscience, he felt like an abuser, a bully, and that didn't sit with anything worth the dignity to be called faith. The thoughts troubled him. He wished he had someone trustworthy he could talk to, but it was too late for all of that now, he concluded. She'd had their baby, now a month old. It filled him with a deep sadness at what might have been and a great weight knowing that he could never really be Jacob's father. If only the world were different.

He thought of his new surroundings in Istanbul. Once more, unlike back home, he was in a city of relative peace, in a very European world where a secular state pushed Muslims into private space. Here faith without shariah was an abomination. This peace will soon be shattered he told himself, their complacency shaken to the core. The true followers of Allah, the Ummah will unite when the yoke oppressing them is lifted. Given the opportunity this will provide, there will soon be millions ready to join the new and true Caliphate. The Turks once knew what a great empire was, they will recognise it's time for a new one to arise, he reasoned. What we are doing will reawaken things long suppressed.

Then, as Ali thought of the violence of the struggle ahead, he knew more people had to die and, as he so often did these days, he recalled the moment when his own father had been shot before his very eyes, running across a dusty city street in the hot sun. As the image repeated itself before his closed eyes, he realised it was then, as that bullet flew all those years ago, his own life had changed for ever. His hands became sweaty and his pulse raced. He rolled on his side and tried to make the terrifying image go away. It was to be a disturbed night when Ali drifted in and out of a fitful sleep.

That Sunday night, the Turkish police interrogators were getting information out of the two men they had picked up in a van on the main road through Kayseri. The local police inspector congratulated his patrol car officers on their excellent powers of observation. He had been longing to get at least one result to brighten his day and this was as good as it got. It transpired that a van, stolen in the city centre six months earlier had come to light on the main road and the culprits had been caught red-handed. The watching, stationary patrol car beside the main road didn't like the way the front passenger had eyeballed them as they passed, so they pulled in behind and then checked out the registration.

Half a mile on, blue lights flashing, they'd pulled them over. The van driver had hesitated a little too long before slowing and the experienced pair in the police car were alerted to exercise due caution. Once stopped, a knowing look to each other and they both understood. Drawing their weapons they flanked either side of the van. It was just as well; one of the occupants in the car pulled a gun, but found his door kicked against his extended arm before he had time to use it, the weapon dropping from his reach. Both men were then thrown unceremoniously onto the ground.

A few minutes more and it was clear this was more than a simple case of van theft. Backup had been called and, in the end, six cars were at the scene. The two men remained lying on the road for an hour in the blazing sun whilst the first careful fingertip search was made of their van. To their surprise it wasn't supplies of food they found inside when they opened up the back.

Agricultural sacking was found to contain a veritable arsenal of high explosives and detonators. It was then the inspector had been called out and his driver had raced him to the scene. The inspector was no expert, but from his time seconded to the military police he knew a serious consignment of high explosive when he saw one. The technical analysis on their find would be done later. He thought to himself that such a significant arrest would go well with his superiors and build his case for further promotion. That in turn would go down well with his wife, who had pushed him to get on since the day of their marriage sixteen years previously.

Once he got to see the two men lying on the ground, he was initially puzzled. He had thought these men might be Kurdish sympathisers, but clearly they were not. Possibly IS, but they weren't yet saying anything as to who they were, where they had come from or what their intentions were. In frustration, the inspector ordered the two be taken back to the police headquarters where he would see that the right kind of interrogation would yield some much-needed answers. What were these guys up to, he thought; he needed to know and quickly. Too many terrorist incidents had recently occurred.

As the inspector was driven back to the city centre headquarters, he wondered when to put in a call to his superiors at HQ in Ankara. This was a very significant weapons find. Possibly these two might prove to be terrorists, but organised by whom? Then he thought, he could easily delay the call to them a little, at least a few hours until he knew more. He didn't want anyone else claiming jurisdiction over his prisoners before he had got some sensible answers from them. He decided, judging by past experience in such matters, that he would have the information he required from them during the night and his Ankara Chief Inspector would be happy to have what intelligence he had gained so long as he got it by daybreak – at least by when the Ankara police station morning shift arrived for duty.

The inspector was right. He got his information. Within six hours of questioning in the police station by his most experienced interrogator, who never messed around, never had any scruples about methods employed, the answers were extracted. The interrogator, sleeves rolled up, his forehead perspiring, personally and proudly placed a sheet of paper on the waiting inspector's desk. One quick glance and he realised it told him everything he wanted.

The men they had picked up on the road were as he'd suspected, two IS terrorists from Iraq. Their names were Ishmael Suleman and Ahmed Muhammed and they had left south-east Turkey early that morning. They were unable to say from where precisely, but had provided some general indication of the place. It was likely they didn't know the village's name. It was a Kurdish area and it was there they had picked up the van, moving the explosives and equipment they had brought from Mosul into their new vehicle with Turkish plates. They confessed they were part of a group of three vehicles heading for Istanbul.

The descriptions of the other two vehicles had been provided, a white Mercedes saloon and a white flatbed truck. In all there were seven remaining IS terrorists still on their way to Istanbul led by Ali Muhammed. He was the only name they said they knew. Much as the two men were pressed, they neither claimed to know who their Istanbul contacts were, nor what their mission was about. No doubt analysis of their mobile phones would provide some further leads, but that would have to be done in Ankara. They tried to argue they were simply drivers. The inspector smiled as he looked up. He knew that no court would ever accept such an implausible story.

The inspector put the information into a typed report which he emailed straight to his superior at police headquarters, following it up with a phone message. It was now 3am. Not everyone was asleep. He was totally unaware that his call to Ankara's police headquarters was intercepted by Israeli intelligence.

Even before the Ankara morning shift picked up the inspector's news, Israeli intelligence had already acted and passed the information on from Tel Aviv to Jerusalem and from there to New York and London. Next day there would be a flurry of activity to see what must be done now that Ali had a heavily armed terrorist team in place in Istanbul. Whereas there had once been a small group of eight summonsed to the conference room in Tel Aviv just days ago, security forces across four continents were now massing their personnel to avert a probable imminent major incident in Istanbul.

Meanwhile, before going home to sleep off a busy shift, the inspector ordered that in the light of the seriousness of his interrogator's findings and the probability the two prisoners would be shipped out to Ankara very soon, all possible medical help should be immediately provided to ensure there were no questions asked later about the police methods used to get the information everyone concerned with national security needed him to provide. He told his deputy that he wanted the men's resistance to arrest stressed in the follow-up reports he was busy typing. Awkward questions about police methods, torture and needless brutality all too often got asked these days. Once he was sure everything that could be done that night had been set in motion, the inspector rose and set off for home. It was going to be a short night and he desperately wanted some sleep before his all too soon 8am start.

22

Ali was feeling anxious and restless. It had not been a good night. He'd made a mistake. Having Kemal bunked up with him was a disaster. He snored, he washed badly, his clothes smelled of body odour and he constantly tossed and turned in the night, noisily grunting as he did so. It didn't help that the poor quality divan bed, just a metre away from his own bed, squeaked on the tile floor as if to complain at the treatment it received from its occupant. Too late to change things. He resigned himself to further miserable nights awake. Maybe, Ali thought, he wouldn't have slept much anyway.

Somehow, as the first light of day was penetrating the edges of the window blinds that Monday morning, he knew he had to pull everything together, it was up to his leadership skills to make his motley group of companions into an effective military outfit. He cajoled his sluggish body into life.

Their commitment he didn't doubt, but their expertise to undertake the mission in hand was something else and now there were the gaps left by losing the two guys in the van, Ishmael and Ahmed. People talk, but thankfully the two had no real information of any use to give to their captors. He wondered at their fate. His own night was bad, but he knew from stories he had heard about Turkish police, their night would have been a lot worse.

Nevertheless, he thought he ought to conduct a mental checklist of what they did know just to be on the safe side. Well, they knew Ali's name, but then everyone did. However, now they knew he was here in person he'd have to be doubly careful. The Turks would be on their guard and looking for him here in Istanbul. But, the two didn't know the address of the flat they'd been heading to. This base remained secure. They didn't know of the secret arrangement with the Kurds.

Hmm, he thought, they knew about our other two vehicles. He'd need to see someone got rid of those and soon. It was a shame, the Mercedes was comfortable and nice to drive, but it had served its purpose now. The loss of all the equipment carried in the van was a blow, but that could be replaced. He'd need to get on to it, it would take time, a few days at least to get fresh explosives and munitions sourced and then shipped in from the Caliphate. Kemal was still sleeping, but Ali sensed it would not be for much longer.

Silently Ali got himself out of bed and went and splashed water on his face, followed by a more thorough wash. He felt better, and gulped some of the cold tap water. He pulled on clothes, his blue jeans, tied the laces of his trainers, clothes that would allow him to pass anonymously as just another young person in the city. As he sat on his bed, feet square on the floor, contemplating the day, he pulled his rucksack towards him and undid the top to check through his things. Then he picked up his mobile, and called his Istanbul contact.

'We're meeting here at 8am,' he ordered. 'Oh, and just so you know, what we will need to do will take most of the day.'

The call finally brought Kemal to life. As Kemal knew the city, Ali told him to get up, go out and get them all some breakfast. He would see the others were up and ready by the time he got back.

'You'll need to shop for an extra one joining us, our local man, so don't skimp. Come on, get to it. He'll be here by the time you're back. I need to go and get the others up,' said Ali.

Kemal obediently followed orders and a short while later he'd returned laden with plastic bags full of bread, fruit, drink bottles and goodness knows what else. Ali almost drew his gun when he let Kemal back in through the front door. He was being followed up the stairs, but Ali quickly returned it to his pocket when he saw it was only their expected contact who had coincidentally arrived at the same time. They greeted each other with an embrace and Ali welcomed him, inviting him to join them for breakfast. He told them all to eat and be ready for work in fifteen minutes, grabbing something for himself and taking it to the bedroom to allow himself time to collect his final thoughts for the meeting to come.

Once the breakfast was eaten and the leftovers cleared away to the kitchen area, Ali rejoined them, instructing that the main room in the apartment be made ready for a makeshift council of war. A framed religious calligraphy was taken down from the main wall so that Ali could write on it with his black marker pen.

When the fifteen minutes were up, Ali told everyone to drop whatever else they were doing and called them together. The first thing he did was explain that the most urgent matter was to see that their vehicles were safely disposed of. They were now a big liability threatening to expose them if discovered and Ali knew the police would even now be searching for them.

Their local contact, Zaid, said there was a lockable store that went with the flat at the end of the car park. If they were to give him the vehicle keys he would see his man moved everything from their vehicles into the store, cleaned the car and truck of any forensic evidence and then saw that they were driven to the outskirts of the city where he had a contact who would see they were never traced. Ali placed the Mercedes's keys into the guy's hand and told Omar to do the same with his keys.

'I left them in the ignition like I always do, unless either of you two picked them up,' said Omar, looking round at Fazil and JJ, who had travelled with him. They shrugged their shoulders. Ali saw red, his mind going straight back to the time his brother's carelessness had let Adam Taylor escape in his own vehicle because the keys had been left in it. He exploded.

'You idiot! If anything's missing you'll pay for it Omar,' Ali barked. He wasn't feeling in the best of moods after a bad night and he didn't want to be dealing with stupid risky behaviour by those whom he was going to have to rely on later. He told Omar to go down to the truck to check nothing was missing, hand over the keys, then come straight back. Their Istanbul contact, Zaid, stepped forward and made a suggestion.

'I'll go with Omar and get things moving. We can't have these vehicles hanging around here any longer. They should be disposed of now, whilst the rush-hour traffic is still filling the streets, when no-one will notice as they are driven off,' their contact said.

'How long will you be?' questioned Ali.

'Give me ten minutes to empty the cars. I'll get my boy to help. Both vehicles will have left here in fifteen. Then I'll be back. It's not a problem,' Zaid said.

He turned smartly and disappeared out of the door. This man was proving useful, thought Ali. Once the door had shut behind him, Ali took the opportunity, in the light of the key incident, to give his team some timely advice, more like an all round security monologue. He made it quite clear that one more act of carelessness like that and their cover could be blown and their mission over.

Omar returned as Ali was warming to his theme, thankfully reporting that the truck had not been touched overnight. Ali signalled where Omar was to sit, then repeated what he had already told the others about attending to security. He'd pretty well finished by the time Zaid also returned, fifteen minutes later. Ali hadn't held back in laying into his men. He'd told them if they didn't pay attention to every detail of their behaviour from here on in, that would be it, their lives forever tainted by failure and disgrace. The same applied to the day's briefing. It required 110% attention, nothing less.

They all seemed subdued as Ali moved to stand before the white wall. Taking his black marker pen he began marking out a grid. Having an engineering background, he liked to break complicated tasks into their constituent parts; what better way to do this than put it all up in front of them as if on graph paper. He marked the targets along the vertical axis, which for now he simply marked as A-D, with the horizontal axis serving as his timeline left to right.

When it was done, the ordered, yet incomplete fretwork already gave him the impression the task ahead was organised rather more than in actuality it was. The others watched, no-one daring to interrupt or ask him what he was doing. He placed the pen on the windowsill when he had finished and rubbed his hands together. He looked round at his motley team and wondered if they were capable of pulling off the audacious mission prepared for them. They were looking his way and it was time to begin the detailed briefing.

'What you will learn now must remain within these four walls. You tell anyone,' Ali looked at the local contact, 'even the boy, then we risk everything.' He had absolutely no means of knowing whether the man could be counted on, but he had no choice but to proceed on the basis of mutual trust until any subsequent events indicated otherwise.

'We're going to need to work together. We're going to need to be working so hard today you will all wish you were back in the frontline in Mosul. And, let me make this clear, I want to hear you asking questions, clarifying our mission, being hungry to have one-hundred percent understanding of what each and every person has to do. This is a collaborative exercise, if you think I've not covered something, you need to say. Got it?' Ali said taking control.

'Yes, sir,' they all replied, apart from their local contact who said nothing.

'You,' Ali looked the local man in the eye. 'Tell the men your name?'

'Zaid, that's all you need to know,' he replied.

'Are you with us, Zaid, or a hanger-on?' asked Ali.

'With you, completely with you. But as I made clear to your CO Salim six months ago when we met here in Istanbul, this is my city and you are the visitors,' Zaid replied.

'Thank you Zaid. We are counting on you in so many ways.' Ali then addressed the team as a whole once more.

'Now listen carefully. There are a number of targets we are to hit simultaneously which I have listed here, down the side, as A-D.' Ali pointed them out one by one.

'The Kurds have responsibility for several further targets in the capital Ankara. What the Kurds are doing is something no-one here knows anything about, and it's best that way. What we do know is the Kurds will be attacking the head of the snake; they will go for key parliament, police and military buildings in Ankara. We don't know which ones. All we know is that when everything kicks off, it all kicks off at the same time and Turkey will be changed for ever. The Kurds will deliver their attacks as we deliver ours. In the ensuing fear and chaos, there will be a breakdown of society. Then in the coming days we shall see the real Muslims, the true followers of Allah, stepping out of the shadows, helping us build the greater Caliphate. Then this decadent sick man of Europe we call Turkey will be no more.'

Ali went over and asked Zaid if the flat screen TV on the opposite wall was working. A nod was given to indicate that it was and Ali passed him a USB stick. Moments later all were watching a message from their CO, Salim Ismat. The video was part selling the ideal of the Caliphate, part action shots and part lecture. Ali recognised pieces he had seen before.

It began with a utopian vision of what the Caliphate offered. This introduction was a well-made, no expense spared, professional piece of fieldwork that had been edited in as an introduction. Then a momentary black screen and a different clip – he personally found the beheadings and shootings crude and distasteful, but knew they served their purpose in instilling fear and loyalty. Maybe the more he saw, one day he would become anaesthetised to it. After another edit transition marked by two seconds of black screen, there was a moving speech directly addressed to the team gathered in Istanbul whom the CO called 'his noble Jihadi Warriors'.

In the respectful silence which concluded the clip's showing, Ali went to retrieve his USB – something he knew that many people failed to do. In spite of its shortcomings, the film had left them all feeling quite moved. They were recognised by their leaders as being part of a worthy and praiseworthy cause, soldiers of the Caliphate, a looked-up-to band of brothers.

'Back to work,' Ali said, picking up his pen again. 'Pay attention.' He began writing.

'Target A is the main University of Istanbul building, there will be a degree congregation taking place, a big opportunity for us. Target B, this may surprise you, is the Blue Mosque itself and we'll strike whilst they are in the busiest period of the summer tourist season. Target C is the U.S.A. Consulate, the corrupted Americans will have another reminder we can reach them wherever they are, and finally, Target D, the Galatasaray Stadium football ground where our attack will occur precisely when a pre-season friendly international match is being played between Turkey and England. All these targets have been carefully chosen for their combined impact and a warrior group of four men will be assigned to each one. Together with the Kurdish targets, our combined attacks will destabilise the evil secularist government of Turkey and it will fall,' summarised Ali, lowering his pen and looking at his men.

There was silence around the room. Kemal wanted to say something.

'Yes, Kemal,' said Ali.

'This is very ambitious. But would it not be better to go for one target at a time and incrementally build up the attacks over the coming months? And who will bring about the new government?'

'A good question,' Ali replied, whilst thinking privately that Kemal might not be making a full commitment. 'Our illustrious leadership have of course considered these very points. Now is the time for a maximum effort, something to shake their very foundations and terrify them. If more attacks are still needed later, then I'm sure our leaders will order them. Establishing new political leadership is not up to us. It is a matter for the religious and political cadres who are working, even as we speak, to get sympathetic religious and political figures here to mobilise the people and bring the military and civil authorities into line. On the military

178

warrior front, we focus on our task and we do what we are told to do. Are you OK with that?'

'Of course,' his tone betrayed a less than convinced Kemal.

Ali moved on and spent some minutes putting up the timeline for the coming week, the attacks scheduled to happen in five days, on the following Friday. He ascertained from Zaid that there were six local Jihadi warriors ready to join them; that would be seven men including Zaid himself, assigned from today and under Ali's command. Ali asked for another two to be added to their number to make up for the loss of Ishmael and Ahmed in the van. Nine men to add to his own seven, sixteen in total. Zaid seemed unfazed by the request. Maybe he had anticipated it.

'It will be arranged as you wish, enshallah,' said Zaid.

Turning again to his wall-chart plan of campaign, Ali began listing what needed to be put in place for each target – the resources of weaponry and the men to be deployed, but for the present he refused to be drawn into allocating named men to targets until he had assessed what the local fighters were like and which skills they brought to the scenario. He also wanted to think very carefully who was paired with whom. It would be quite a task to decide the right combination of skills, personalities and local knowledge that would work best.

At lunchtime they took a refreshment break and this time Ali instructed Zaid to leave and fetch in fresh supplies of food and drink. After a twenty minute break, Ali ordered the detritus of fast-food trays and polystyrene drink-cups to be bagged away and the lounge cleared, ready for the next session. In all the small tasks Ali had given him, Zaid was proving himself to be every bit the competent local leader.

It was hot and humid in the flat. The air-conditioning didn't seem to work particularly well, if at all. As the afternoon wore on they began thinking through what needed to be done day by day by way of preparation. In the end when Ali turned to look at his wall, it looked a mass of black scribble, a reflection of the intense effort all had put in and the enormous amount of work still to be done.

By 6pm the team was showing it was time to take another break, Ali thinking they weren't going to take any more in, so he stood the meeting down. He allowed his men to leave the flat in intervals, to take short walks in small groups. It wasn't good for them to be caged in this flat without a break.

Before they finally broke up, Ali agreed they would gather that evening as a full team, including the local jihadis, for an initial meeting. He knew he had but an hour until these fighters would be arriving. It would be a crucial meeting and Ali thought he would need to prepare carefully for it.

It was then he recognised something. The feeling he had before had returned, once again the adrenaline surging as it had in London the previous year, the incredible buzz combined with over-tiredness that came with a live mission. The fear of being caught, the drive to stay one step ahead, the stretching commitment to achieve the mission that no mental or bodily weakness could be allowed to compete with. All these things made him feel so very alive.

Ali knew he was committed, focussed, a man in total command. Nothing would be too great an obstacle. Everything would come together – the graph laying bare their detailed plans showing it was so. There might be nightmares, the distraction of flashback images of horror, the anxiety in being betrayed or discovered, the guilt he felt about his family and Kaylah and Jacob, but this, all this, he told himself, made him purposeful and powerful. For a moment he felt like a god, a man able to change the world.

23

Adam and his friends got up early next morning to find the café area downstairs had an open buffet-style breakfast available for a very reasonable set price. It all looked fresh and appetising with a range of cold meats, cereals, fresh fruit, dried apricots, nuts and yoghurts as well as local bread. It was reassuringly European, mirroring the best of university hall-style facilities back in Exeter and yet it was all done with a noticeable oriental flavour.

However, breakfast was, for all its promise, cut short and over-rushed, as Mustafa was calling for them with the minibus. So hastily gathering their things, they grabbed some yet untried breakfast items – bread rolls and pieces of fruit. These were carried out in clutched hands to finish en route.

Mustafa, or someone else, had cleaned the minibus since yesterday and it was standing there white and shiny with the University of Istanbul emblem on the side door looking pristine. Mustafa had his one hand on the sliding side door, with information sheets in the other, ready to give them out as they climbed on board.

A hasty discussion and they had agreed on travelling in the back together, leaving Mustafa with an empty front passenger seat next to him. After a perfunctory 'good morning,' he didn't say much else to them, but seemed happy to listen to the radio as he navigated his way through the morning traffic. The four turned as one to the sheets Raqiyah's uncle Abdul had provided to discover what their programme for the day had in store for them.

No sooner had the minibus slid into the traffic than they were once more conscious what a vast city Istanbul was, with busy roads, and a mix of elegant commercial buildings together with a sprawling mass of modern buildings as far as the eye could see. But here and there were some amazing cultural gems that Abdul had arranged for them to see. Adam wondered just how they were going to get around so many places in one day, his eyes glancing through the six sides of typed A4 paper which made up their itinerary.

They learned that the area of Beyoglu itself where they were staying, had been the home to foreigners arriving in Istanbul for centuries. They were just the most recent, albeit temporary, inbound travellers to do so. Then, before they knew it, Mustafa had pulled up and told them they were to get out and walk the length of the district's main street, the Istiklal Caddesi. Being pedestrianised, he would drive round to the southern end and pick them up in one hour outside the Mevlevi Lodge.

'You should allow yourself time there,' he advised. 'You will learn something very interesting about the Muslim sufi tradition. It's more than just whirling dervishes you know.'

He pointed out the destination on Abdul's note, before handing them a map they could use as they walked. He couldn't help but add that he hardly felt the map was necessary, but if it made them feel more comfortable they could take it.

Whilst this was going on, Adam looked out of the van windows. Somewhere in his head he had a faint recollection of passing through this very district the previous summer as he had cycled north and east out of the city. He remembered how he had already been identified and targeted by IS and a plan of action to take him hostage had evolved even before he had arrived at this point. It was indeed somewhere just round here, he recalled, he had put on a cycling spurt, believing himself to have been followed, vainly trying to put safe distance between himself and his – at the time anonymous – pursuers.

The recollection sent a shiver down his spine, leaving him feeling somewhat of an outsider in contrast to the excitement his companions were now showing at the thought of some sightseeing and window shopping. He was reluctant to step out of the safety he felt whilst in the minibus and into the vulnerability of the open street. Not for the first time he had to tell himself to pull himself together and get on with his life.

Out on the street he caught himself looking round at everyone suspiciously. As the four began to amble slowly downhill and past the fine facades of the buildings, Adam found himself using the shop windows as mirrors to see who was around them in the street. He kept telling himself it could never happen twice and that he should enjoy the sights and experience, and forget his wild imaginings. There were bars aplenty, but, having just had breakfast and with a tight schedule to keep, they pressed on.

They caught sight of the British Consulate up a side street to the right. They approached until they saw its metal gates facing them, before turning and rejoining the main thoroughfare. Bilal was the first to point it out and Adam felt his spirits immediately lifted. An accessible bastion of safety was how he saw it. Soon there was evidence of other consular buildings. By then it was only around four hundred metres to the Mevlevi Lodge at the end of the street. A small peaceful terrace garden surrounded this quiet building set slightly back in a quiet garden off the busy shopping street. They joined a small group of other visitors making their way inside.

'We haven't done much about Sufism in our Islam course yet. Does anyone know what it's about?' Sophie asked, a genuinely puzzled look on her face.

'It's a bit of an anachronism really. It's controversial too. At one time it was banned here,' added Bilal.

'I thought Sufism is what the Pakistani Muslims followed. It must be what the majority go with in the UK,' said Raqiyah.

As they approached the front door to the Mevlevi building, it became clear it was multi-purpose, a museum, a tourist centre and a lodge for Sufi visitors. They made their way inside and tagged on to a group of German and Swedish visitors. Their guide was talking in English, introducing himself and telling them they would all be leaving enlightened by what he would tell them and by the things they would see. Adam thought he was over-egging it, but nonetheless got himself in close enough to make sure he would hear everything being said. As a historic building, the Lodge felt quite cosy, small, informal and homely.

'Sufism is about the heart of Islam,' he began, 'it's not political, it doesn't align itself with national or local politics. It is primarily about a spiritual and mystical way of life and worship. Extremists have no time for us, so you are all safe here!' He laughed out loud and suddenly Adam was finding this promising.

'That's not to say there hasn't been a long argument within Sufism between the Barelwi and Deobandi traditions. The Barelwi argue for love and spirituality, whilst the Deobandi, though definitely wanting the same thing, see it being achieved through a devotional adherence to holy texts and having a right knowledge of Islam. I think of it like this – the Barelwi bare all there is in their hearts before God and just let go; the Deobandi are all bound up by rules and you can tell them by their strict austerity and miserable faces – but don't tell them I said so!' He laughed again, and this time his audience joined in. This guide had a sense of fun and freedom which Adam was curious to know more about.

'Let me tell you about Sufi Islam as we know it here in Istanbul,' he continued.

'But first,' called out Adam, 'tell us whether Deobandi are more likely to end up radicalised than Barelwi, because of their hardline approach to Islam?'

'A good question. You're probably right there, young man, but then some young people have got disillusioned with their Barelwi mosques. Tell me where you are from?' the guide asked.

'London, but we,' he used his waving arm to point out his three friends, 'are all students from Exeter University in the south-west of England,' said Adam.

'Oh, well then, you'll understand Sufism very quickly. Just think of it as a kind of Muslim Church of England! It's very significant in Islam. It has room within it for those who are devoutly religious in a mystical sense and room too for

184

those who like Islamic prescriptions and legal requirements. Yet still others are what you in the church might call liberal Muslims who don't particularly display their faith but still carry a loose association with it,' said the guide happy to engage.

'So it's full of contradictions?' challenged Adam.

'Yes, just like your Church of England!' was the reply, and laughter rang out again. 'But what I will say is that Sufism plays an important role in helping Muslims accommodate what it means to live at ease with a modern society. In your country Sufism is most closely aligned with the Barelwi tradition. Sufism's less radical, more mystical, which is why sometimes governments, including yours in the UK, like to seize on those westernised Sufi individuals and associations as friendly faces to talk to. The trouble is they sometimes forget that Sufism is not just one face, it has many faces. But I don't want to give you a wrong impression, the image of Sufism I want you to take away today is one of a rich and peaceful tradition which above others might just hold a key to help unlock the door for Islam to move forward into the modern world. Now come with me into the museum. There's much more to see in the short time we have available.'

Adam found his arm pulled by Raqiyah who whispered in his ear, 'Your question got to the heart of the matter there Adam. I guess I'm like most Muslims, there's a lot I don't know, there's a lot I take for granted and there's simply loads I've been taught never to question. As a woman, it is doubly hard, and being here in a Muslim city again, I tend to revert to default position: a lowly, pious, unquestioning female – it's what is expected.'

'You, lowly and pious, not asking questions? That's three things new I've learned. But in your case, I find it hard to believe,' Adam replied with a smile. They hurried to follow the group disappearing into a large adjoining room, a kind of ceremonial hall.

Adam thought what beautiful dark eyes Raqiyah had. They had seemed so intense when she spoke to him just now.

She was really attractive, and not for the first time, he began wondering whether mixed faith relationships were a 'no' in her case. But how do I find that out, he wondered, and seeing Sophie chatting to Bilal, an idea began to form in his mind.

The guide was busy talking with great enthusiasm about the founding mystic poet of Sufism, 'Jal al Din, or as he is more usually called, Mevlana Rumi. This man,' he said, 'lived in the thirteenth century, and in his day did much to try and reconcile Muslims, Christians and Jews who all lived here in Turkey. Let me tell you one of Rumi's stories.'

Adam listened intently; this too was something new to him. Clearly inter-faith dialogue and a quest for peaceful and harmonious co-existence was not just a recent enthusiasm of desperate western faith leaders wanting to avoid conflict. He wondered what this guy Rumi had to offer, and sidled forward to the front of the group to be sure he heard every word. He noticed Raqiyah following him.

'Rumi,' he voiced his name affectionately, before beginning his story. 'Now tell me, how do all the best stories begin?' The guide played to his audience.

'Once upon a time,' everyone dutifully intoned.

'Once upon a time, in a far country, there was a city where all the inhabitants were blind. One day they were told an elephant was passing by. So, they sent a three-man delegation to find it and report back what on earth this creature was. Being blind, they all felt the elephant when they found it and on return gave their reports. The first said, "it's like a vast snake that stands vertically in the air." The second said, "Nonsense. It is like a pillar, firm and solid." And the third said, "the two others were liars, for the creature, was like a large fan, wide, flat and leathery." The truth is, one felt the trunk, another a leg and the third an ear. All had a partial grasp of the truth. Just think what they might have understood if they had listened to each other, said Rumi, reflecting on what each had said, instead of being so arrogant and proud with their half-truths. So it is, said Rumi, with our three great faiths, we are like blind men stumbling around in the dark until we talk with each other. The end.'

There was a round of polite applause. Before their guide could continue his carefully polished talk, an attendant came in from the side door to the hall and whispered in his ear. Such things made Adam anxious. However, his suspicious nature and rising fears were soon quelled when it was announced that they were fortunate indeed this Tuesday to be present when there was to be a rehearsal in preparation for the following Sunday's performance by none other than the Whirling Dervishes. Their guide immediately began to give a hurried explanation of what they were about to see.

'The Whirling Dervishes in residence here perform their sema ceremonies at 5pm each Sunday in this very hall. This particular group, from Istanbul itself, is one of the very best! Let's move to the side of the hall and give them space.'

Adam watched as the half-dozen men, each with a matching beige fez on their head, placed their black cloaks to one side to reveal their matching white outfits, to all intents and purposes a loose-fitting shirt with a full-length skirt. Quirky black leather shoes completed the attire. They began to spin in synchrony, making repetitive circles as if mimicking the planets in a solar system of their own making. Faster and faster they went, trance-like, in some kind of religious stupor, their left hands facing down to the floor, their rights to the ceiling above. The only noise was some kind of prayer recitation masked by the soft rustling of their skirts and the smooth brushing of their feet on the polished floor.

Adam tried to interpret this bizarre expression of Islam, seeing performed some kind of spiritual ecstasy experience. He saw a sign on the wall in English and Arabic quoting the great Rumi, 'All loves are a bridge to the Divine love. Yet those who have not had a taste of it do not know.' Somehow he understood that what he was seeing was what Rumi believed – that in losing oneself in the religious ecstasy of dance, the participant discovered and knew god.

Adam and Bilal began a quiet conversation trying to weigh up the significance of Sufism in the Islamic world. At one level it offered variety, inclusion, spirituality and for those who wanted it, a more rigorous programme of teaching

187

and liturgy. But it was Bilal who pointed out that it could only be counted as a side act on the wider Muslim stage.

'Why's that then?' asked Adam.

'Well, look around, it has no structure, it has no leadership, it has no power in the real world. Even in the UK it doesn't run the Muslim schools or training establishments. It doesn't move or shake anything. Sufism looks great, offers a place for all, and threatens no-one. As I say, a bit-player, interesting to note, no doubt great in terms of individual religious fervour if one's into this kind of thing, but Sufism has no influence in the Islamic world,' was Bilal's summary.

Then there was a nudge from Bilal. It was time to move. By now Mustafa would be waiting outside in the minibus. Waving apologetically to their guide, the four made their way out of the portico doorway and into the hedonistic noise of the street. They soon saw him, talking to a policeman who was trying to get him to move his minibus.

Their arrival was timely and in a moment they were moving away towards the distinctive Galata tower and the road-bridge over the Golden Horn waterway into the very heart of the old city. They swung passed the impressive New Mosque before heading away from the waterfront.

Mustafa had not been idle and had provided takeaway wraps and cans of drink for lunch. He explained that Abdul had paid for them and that now they were headed to Sultanahmet Square. As they ate, Mustafa drove. First he pointed out the dome of the Hagia Sophia, a fourteen hundred year old legacy of old Byzantium. Once Christian, it became a mosque in the fifteenth century with the coming of the Ottoman Empire and today stood primarily as an historic building and tourist site. Mustafa told them they must see inside the vast interior space and then make their way to the Blue Mosque at the other end of the Square where he would once again meet up with them at the end of the afternoon.

Stepping out of the minibus once more, Adam and his companions mingled with the many tourists, the hot summer day sapping everyone's energy. They clutched the plastic water bottles Abdul had also provided for them, glad to have them. Time moved quickly and Adam felt more secure, his fears subsiding. Everything seemed very orderly and relaxed.

Even at the Blue Mosque with its five soaring minarets – a building evidently still very much in use as a place of prayer for Muslims, the areas for ritual wudu ablutions being well used by the faithful – he wasn't fazed. He was impressed by the blue Iznic tiles, absorbed by their intricate patterns and lit by the hundreds of windows. No matter where he looked there were no images, paintings or statues, a familiar characteristic of Islam. The four felt happy exploring and chatting together. Many photos were taken, and the two girls gave time to attend to their Facebook pages, both changing their profiles.

It was a rich experience. As they left the Blue Mosque, it was getting late in the afternoon. Adam scanned the streets for any sign of the minibus. Then Raqiyah announced she had had a text from Mustafa via her Uncle Abdul. They were to make their way to the Faros Hotel nearby where Mustafa had parked up and refreshment in the Faros's restaurant would be awaiting them.

Adam soon found it on the map, just a block away. It was hot walking and he noticed they weren't the only ones on the street. Very quickly they found they were part of a large group, in fact inadvertently they were caught up in some kind of procession. No, it felt more like a demonstration.

Looking around him, Adam could see there were maybe eighty or even a hundred, mainly young people. Some had banners with the letters 'HDP' emblazoned and others with the words, 'Justice, Democracy and Freedom'. He still had no idea what it meant, except he was now clear they were caught up in some kind of protest. This was something over which he had no control and he felt panic begin to rise up inside him. He knew he must get out of the crowd, then felt bad for thinking about himself first, his attention turning next to the safety of the foursome they had very much become.

They nodded to one another indicating a direction out which they should take. As they tried to move out of the now pressing crowd towards what they knew was the front

189

entrance of the hotel, there was yet more noise. Police vehicles, sirens blaring, were heading their way. The hotel door was now just yards away and Adam had one objective in mind, to reach its sanctuary as quickly as he could.

'Let's get inside,' yelled out Adam and without thinking he grabbed Raqiyah by the hand and pulled her towards the safety the modern hotel promised. Bilal and Sophie were just ahead breaking into a run. With Adam pulling her along, Raqiyah and he caught them up, as sinister-looking, black-armoured riot police, faces hidden, were diving into the crowd causing pandemonium.

Then they were inside. Mustafa was standing next to the security man barring the front door, yelling at him that he was to let the four in. For once Adam's regard for their driver lifted. Once in, the doors were pushed closed, the security man turning his key and leaning hard against them to ease the crowd's pressure.

Safely locked in, sounds outside instantly became muffled and distant, but nonetheless disturbing. There were screams and hisses, bangs and shouts, as police started laying into everyone with little regard to restraint. People were falling to the pavement, others were trying to run for their lives. Gas canisters were discharged, people began to try and flee.

'They're Kurd supporters,' offered Mustafa calmly, 'nothing to worry about. Always causing trouble. Our Prime Minister will soon have them put in their place. Sorry about that. Come inside. Forget that little bother, it was soon dealt with, come, follow me, have some tea.' He led the way into the comfort of the hotel's interior.

Shaken, none of them felt like refreshments, but felt obliged to show politeness at the generous hospitality of their host. Adam reached down to massage his leg. The bullet wound he had taken escaping from Mosul last summer was hurting. Just some adhesions, he told himself. In the desperate run to seek sanctuary he'd probably strained the muscle. A bit of his past catching up with him unexpectedly, was how he read it, nothing serious.

190

It had been quite a day. Their introduction to Turkish society had been more of an education than they had anticipated and their view of Turkey as a safe and secure tourist destination had been irrevocably shaken. Only Bilal seemed to be able to make light of it.

'Just like home,' he joked, 'you'd think that group could just as easily have been after student fee reductions, don't you think?'

Later, the refreshment break extended until Mustafa was quite certain all was quiet outside, they went to rejoin their minibus to be taken back to their AAA residence.

As they crossed the street Adam watched as local government workers were busy trying to wash the blood off the pavement. He couldn't so easily erase the images etched into his memory that afternoon. His mind was troubled. His body too. He rubbed his hurting leg once again. He tried to reflect on what the day had brought.

The Islam he had come to Turkey to try and learn about had offered him new insights into a Sufi world he hadn't imagined. What was it the guide had said, 'an Islam just like the Church of England'? He'd liked that and found it comforting. Then they'd done the ordinary tourist visits and seen amazing sights, but then, bang, they'd been caught up in a protest which brought a Turkish conflict right upon them. Weren't Kurds Muslim too? he wondered. Just when he thought he was putting things in their place, bang, it all exploded and he was back at the beginning.

Adam needed to understand more and thinking ahead about how they might spend tomorrow, he considered that maybe some prior internet searches and reading could be useful. He realised his own resurgent fears were driving him into a hunker-down mode, a self-preservation move to keep him back in the apartment out of the way of any possible hint of trouble.

His instinct told him that not only would his friends not allow it, but like it or not he was going to have to face his old demons out and about in the city. Just maybe he could take the odd day on his own to stay behind in safety and write up some notes for the university assignment required after their placement visit. That would enable him to recharge his batteries, take the pressure off being so exposed.

For the first time since they'd arrived, he wasn't sure he was going to get through this visit. He started wondering if it were possible for him to change his flight ticket to an earlier one in the next day or two. Coming to Istanbul had been a bad idea after all.

24

Gus' taxi made short work of the ride to Kaylah's flat and Clive handed him ten pounds and watched him make a u-turn to head promptly back. He paused before pressing on the front door bell to be let inside the Crouch End flat, the all too difficult conversations of earlier still coursing through his mind. Just let it happen, he told himself. Kaylah will tell all. Looking at her front door and the smart flat, he couldn't help but already notice he was viewing it with distrustful eyes.

Kaylah was holding Jacob as she opened the door.

'Hi, Sis, Hi, little fella,' said Clive.

He kissed them both before they retreated inside to the lounge. She offered him a drink. He grabbed a Diet Coke off the coffee table. His eyes looked round the room. It was modern, clean and bright, painted greys and purples, with a smart, clean wooden floor.

'Thanks for coming over. I wouldn't have asked, except it's important,' she said.

'I know, it's not a problem, not exactly busy, me,' he countered.

'This flat, I realise it now, has come with a hidden price. No such thing as a free ride in life is there Clive?' Kaylah said.

'No, probably not,' Clive acknowledged.

'It's like this. Ali has come up in conversation again. It wasn't of my doing. It was Lena Bloom from the Israeli Embassy. She was here earlier and like, she sees me as the key to stopping Ali commit another atrocity, another terrorist attack,' said Kaylah.

'How's that then? Oh yeah! How can you possibly do that? What did she say exactly?' said Clive.

'She says, they know Ali is going to Istanbul. In fact he might be there already. They don't know why, but something

193

big is planned to happen soon and they want to stop it before it's too late,' said Kaylah.

'They sound really desperate if they are asking an unarmed lone mum with a baby just over a month old to help them,' said Clive.

'Well they are. And, Clive, I don't feel I can say no to her,' whispered Kaylah.

'What do they want you to do, Kaylah? Is it something you can do, Sis?' asked Clive, remembering he had to support this.

'They want me to go to Istanbul to get Ali to come out into the open, to talk to him, to head him off, I don't know. They think I might be the one person he would listen to. But I hate him, I hate him. I don't want to bloody well ever see him again.' She began to cry and grabbed a tissue from a box on the coffee table.

'There, there. I'm sure we can work something out. You know I'm there for you, Sis, I'll help you,' said Clive comfortingly.

'Well that's it. They say they want me to take Jacob and you as well. You'd be like my friend and what did they call you, yes – chaperone. They'd put us up in a nice hotel, all expenses paid, and have absolutely promised total security for us. Apparently the Israeli security is world-class. But we'd have to go soon, very soon. Could you come? Could you come with me if we have to go? I couldn't go without you,' she said imploringly.

'It's your call, Sis, but if you must go, of course I'll come with you. It could be fun as well. Thing is, I think they could call the shots about you keeping this flat if you don't listen to what they say. That's the bottom line isn't it?' he asked.

'I'll call her and say OK, then. I'd like her to come too. I wouldn't feel safe if she wasn't there. Is that reasonable?' said Kaylah.

'You can ask and see what happens. I take it they'd get all the tickets, make all the bookings for flights and hotel?

And I suppose we have no idea how long this is for? There's a lot we need to ask her,' said Clive.

'It can't be for very long, I guess a couple of weeks. Will you explain to mum and dad? Tell them something, anything. That we've won a prize-draw holiday, anything. Can I leave that to you?' she pleaded.

'Sure. Will do. Fancy a walk up to the park? It's a nice day. It'll do us both good. Then I ought to head back,' Clive suggested.

'You're such a good brother, Clive. I worry about you lots, but you've a heart of gold and it's at times like this your true colours come out,' she said.

'Now, now, then, let's get out to the park while it's nice,' said Clive, knowing he didn't fully deserve the affection, his own secret deal being the prime reason he was helping this time.

It took a few minutes until they closed the front door behind them. Clive felt relieved, the whole thing had proved easy in the end. Kaylah had indeed led the way. Even so he felt uneasy. All this was taking him deep, way out of his depth. The sinking feeling made him worry that tragedy might not be far away. Morbid thoughts didn't usually come to mind, for he was a carefree kind of guy, though not, as he recalled, as laid back as his best friend Winston. One thing was certain, he told himself, in all of this, Kaylah will have me watching over her. Nothing harmful will happen to her or Jacob on my watch, even if my life depends on it, he told himself. Kaylah interrupted his thoughts.

'Clive, I want to introduce you to a friend of mine. This is Lottie. It's just that we've got to know each other a bit. She lives locally and we often bump into each other.' A young woman in jeans, with two blond-haired twins stepped up to say hello.

'I'm Lottie. These boys are Benjamin and Ollie.' She said, extending a hand for Clive to shake.

'Nice to meet you Lottie. I'm Clive, Kaylah's brother. Just popped over to see how she was doing.'

'Thought we might head off towards Alexandra Palace, bit of a walk, but there's loads of space for them to run around, want to come?' said Lottie.

'Look I'll leave you and Kaylah to it. I really ought to be getting back. OK, Sis?' asked Clive.

'Yes. But you will tell mum and dad what we discussed?' she reminded him.

'Sure. Will ring you later,' he said as he waved a cheery goodbye, knowing Kaylah would enjoy her walk with Lottie.

Kaylah watched Clive head off towards the bus stop, disappearing round the corner just in time as a red London bus drew up to the stop.

'He's always lucky,' Kaylah told Lottie. 'A real help to me too.'

'Wish I had someone like him,' Lottie replied, as they headed off towards Alexandra Palace. It was as they approached the gates, Kaylah suddenly remembered going there with Ali for the fireworks the previous November. The memories came flooding back and unable to prevent herself, she began to cry.

'Now what's got into you, Kaylah?' asked Lottie. 'It's hard being a mum, I should know. Had two at once! Come on, I know where we can get some ice creams. They're on me.'

When Kaylah got back it was dusk. The time out with Lottie had extended into buying fish and chips. It had been really nice, almost taking her mind off all the big things earlier in the day. But as soon as she stepped inside her door, as if Lena knew her every movement, her mobile went.

'Tell me,' she said, 'what does Clive say? Will he come with you to Istanbul?'

'Yes, he's been very understanding. But will you come too? I'd feel more secure if you were there, we both would,' Kaylah pleaded.

'I'd have to ask permission. But I do cultural and tourism work, so I might be able to. I've more news for you. Everything is happening so quickly. There are spare seats on a plane tomorrow night. All you need do is pack your stuff. We'll have a car come to pick you all up and a courier to take you onto the plane. It'll be hassle free I assure you. I've asked for a generous holiday spending package, so you can have some fun whilst you're there too. You've got my number, call me any time, day or night. It's all arranged. We're so very, very grateful, so indebted to you. I'll ring in the morning to run through final details. Must go. Bye,' and Lena had cut short a call that Kaylah had wanted to use to ask so much more. Looking at her silent phone, Kaylah realised that Lena had raced ahead quickly with arrangements.

She was actually going to Istanbul. It was all too sudden and she wasn't at all ready. She went into the back room to get the big suitcase she'd used only recently to carry Jacob's things when she moved in. Then she stopped in her tracks, pushed the case back into the wardrobe. It can't happen, she said to herself. Jacob doesn't have a passport, so it can't happen. She supposed she had better let Lena know it was off. The minute she got through she knew she'd made a mistake.

'Hi Lena, just thought I'd say the trip is off I'm afraid. Although I have a passport, Jacob doesn't, and I'm not going without him,' she said.

'No problem with the passport,' Lena said cheerily. 'It's already sorted. I told you we'd help. No problem is too great. I've got tickets, taxi and some money sorted too. You remember when I came to see you, I took some pictures before I left? Well I asked our guys here, they spoke to your guys, and I'll bring the passport over with me tomorrow. Everyone wants to help, Kaylah. They really do. And yes, they say I can come with you, so an extra pair of hands. Should be fun. I take it Clive's on board?' She didn't wait for a reply before continuing.

'And Kaylah, I'm so excited. It's the trip of a lifetime. I don't get to travel nearly enough. We're going to have a great time. Now look, I need to go. I need to pack my own things. Expect you're busy packing too. Your Taxi will be round about 3pm tomorrow, Monday. I'll meet you, Jacob and Clive at Heathrow. Don't worry about a thing.'

197

'Yes, thanks for the passport,' Kaylah meekly answered. She hadn't really taken in a lot of what Lena had been telling her; she was still not quite believing that she was going to Istanbul tomorrow afternoon. It was all so unreal. Lena had fixed a passport for Jacob just like that, all done for me and I haven't had to sign anything. She couldn't believe it. How could that be? It must have been done with the British Passport Office's help. They must get last minute requests and Lena fixed it for us.

Kaylah busily gathered things for Jacob and herself, mentally noting what she still needed to buy at the corner shop first thing in the morning. As she filled her large suitcase on automatic pilot, she suddenly stopped as she reflected further on the call she'd just received in which she had just stepped into the unknown without a word of protest. She remembered feeling that way once before.

When she was eight or nine years old and at primary school, one of the older boys had persuaded her to step into the classroom store-cupboard. When she did as he said, he'd slammed the door shut and turned the key, then turned off the outside light switch, leaving her in total darkness. She'd heard him run away laughing. She'd cried and screamed until eventually her teacher came and found her and rescued her. The same feeling she had then had just returned. She felt she had entered a trap, a door had been slammed shut on her and there was no way out. Like it or not she was going to Istanbul. She was left powerless, totally in the dark and all she wanted to do was scream but the noise wouldn't come out.

25

It was another fine and sunny August day when Clive returned to Kaylah's flat around noon. Gus had been called into service again with his minicab. Clive had two bags, a small black rucksack slung over his left shoulder and a small hand-luggage case. Kaylah was looking at what she thought was a minimal amount of stuff.

'You got enough there, Clive? Don't look much to me,' she said.

'Sure,' he said. 'By the way, mum and dad have been trying to ring you all morning.'

'I know, I've been too busy to take their call,' Kaylah said none too convincingly.

'Yeah! Know what you mean. They've given me an ear-bashing. Think we're mad, even though I told them we really didn't have any choice and that we were going to save lives. I thought they might warm to that bit,' he said smiling.

'It wouldn't be like them if they didn't tell it how they saw it. I think I'll speak to them when we get out of the country, I'll find it easier that way,' decided Kaylah.

'You all packed up? Can I do anything?' offered Clive.

'You couldn't keep an eye on Jacob? I wouldn't mind taking a quick shower. He hasn't let up today, not given me a chance. I'd feel better for it,' she said.

'Sure. I'll put on your luxury TV!' he smiled again.

Kaylah left him to it and disappeared into the bathroom. Clive could hear the hiss of the power-shower kicking in as he tuned in the TV and flopped on the leather sofa. Jacob seemed content enough gurgling away, lying on his back in the buggy. Guess we need to take your transport little fella, he told himself.

'You and me will be getting to know each other somewhat over the next week or two,' he found himself saying out loud.

'You big enough yet to give your uncle Clive a high five?' he added.

He lifted Jacob's flexible arm, opened his clenched tight fingers and pressed his tiny hand against his. He marvelled at his small hand against the size of his own.

'You got some growing to do little fella. In the meantime I keep my eye on you,' he said with all seriousness.

When Kaylah returned smelling all fresh, rubbing dry her still wet and dripping hair in a large white towel, they both came out with the same words simultaneously.

'Be great to spend some more time with you.'

They burst into laughter, a fleeting moment of much-needed relief. The laughter made it seem that bit easier. They both knew in that instant they be together as they faced the daunting and uncertain journey awaiting them that very afternoon.

'I'll just get dressed, then we'd better double-check we've got everything, and it won't do any harm to think through what's ahead of us. We need to second-guess what's in store. They can't just make us do anything they want,' said Kaylah not really believing what she was saying.

'OK Sis. We've got a couple of hours, that's all, then they'll be coming to pick us up.' Clive fingered his watch trying not to look as anxious as he was feeling. Kaylah disappeared again. Jacob seemed just as placidly content.

When Kaylah returned, wearing pressed jeans again, the first time in ages since the baby, she felt better in herself. They were tight round the middle but that was the least of her worries.

'Come on Clive. Tell me, just tell me, how you see all this playing out? I've no doubt these Israelis are going to watch over us, they are so cool. You know I thought we weren't going to go as there was no way I could get a passport for Jacob in less than a day, but blow me, Lena had got it sourced. She has one, is bringing it with her. It's so well organised it's really scary. They seem one step ahead of us every bit of the way,' she said, only adding to Clive's sense of concern.

200

'I've been thinking that too. They are so slick. But you know what, when we get there, to Istanbul, they can't make us do anything we don't want to do, anything we think will be too risky. We just have to put our foot down, support each other and say, "no",' he said with conviction.

'Easier said than done. They're very persuasive. I feel they've got a hold over us. They are the puppet-masters and we are the puppets,' she said.

'Muppets more like. But if we know that, we can let them think they're in control and then when we have to, say "no". I mean, what can they do? As last resort they would have to put us on a plane and send us home. They can't do anything else now can they?' Clive replied, trying to feel more in control.

Their conversation dried up. Neither of them was convinced by what was being said. They felt a growing sense of apprehension as time seemed to slow while they awaited their taxi. Kaylah picked up a magazine Lottie had finished with and passed over to her. Clive switched his attention back to the TV. Unusually, the highlights of a baseball match were being shown on terrestrial TV.

A car-horn sounded outside and Clive split the closed blind with his fingers to see if it was for them. A smart black people carrier with darkened windows and an airport taxi sign on the side had pulled up, the driver impatient having nowhere to park.

'Yes, it's ours, let's grab our things. Time to go,' said Clive.

Within five minutes they were inside and on their way.

'Lady called, name of Lena, said she'd meet you at Heathrow Departures. Traffic's not so bad this time of day on a Monday, but can't say it's a drive I like to do too often from North London,' their driver said. 'All set? Let's get going then.' He peered at them quizzically in the rear-view mirror.

Kaylah and Clive looked at each other, then both nodded to the driver who was already moving away.

'Going anywhere nice?' said the cheerful driver, 'weather's so nice here, don't know why more people don't stay at home, I say. But there's no adventure in that, now is there? Come on, where you going? Somewhere sunny?'

'Turkey,' said Clive not really wanting to engage in a conversation.

'Turkey, you say, well that's a bit different. It'll be hot there this time of the year. Took some smart businessmen to Heathrow bound for Turkey, only last week. Don't mind me saying it, but you're not business people, not the types. Having a holiday? Hope you got your suncream, especially for the little one. I have to be very careful with mine, being fair-skinned,' he rabbited on.

'We'll get some there if we need to. My baby's still very small, so we won't be out in the sun too much,' answered Kaylah with a look of concern on her face. She looked at Clive who was in no mood for a chat.

'I hadn't thought of suncream,' she told him, 'You're right, it will be hot. I wonder what else I haven't thought of. It's been so rushed.'

'Don't worry. Anything we've forgotten we can get when we're there,' Clive added.

It took them an hour and a half to get to Heathrow. When they asked the driver about the fare, he told them he had been contracted to take them and he would send an invoice later in the usual way. He didn't want to hang around, but helped them unload to the pavement outside Departures Terminal 2 and wished them a – 'great holiday. I'm sure you'll enjoy it.'

They stood together in a huddle round the buggy not knowing what to do next. This felt so unreal.

'Suppose we had better head inside the terminal building, wait near the entrance. What do you suggest?' offered Clive.

'Yeah, let's go,' said Kaylah.

They moved inside and were immediately joined by Lena sporting what could only be described as smart-casual. Kaylah couldn't work out whether her outfit was work or play and concluded it could suit both. She felt she had to comment on her clothes.

'You look nice,' she told Lena.

'Thank you, Kaylah. Looks like all went well with the journey here.'

'Young Jacob, this is for you.' She thrust a red British Passport into Kaylah's hand. 'Let's go and check in your baggage and get moving. I've already done mine. Follow me.'

Clive took the buggy and steered it through the pressing crowd, many of whom were clearly people leaving for their summer holidays, excited children running round everywhere, worried parents trying not to lose them.

An hour later they were boarding the afternoon flight for Istanbul. With a small baby, they were let through ahead of the other passengers and ended up in the front row on the plane, sitting in a line across the width of the British Airways Boeing. Kaylah sat by the door, then Jacob had a seat for his things, then Lena. Clive was just the other side of the aisle, giving him some space to himself, which suited him fine.

Before take-off, he took out his mobile, was about to switch it to flight mode and put it away when he saw Winston had been trying to reach him and had left him a text.

'Hi bro, sudden trip to Istanbul, hey! Lucky fella. Saw WW who called me. He wants you to meet a friend of his there. I'll text you details when have them. Better do what he asks, know what I mean,' it read. Winston's message was the last kind of complication Clive wanted just now. He thrust his mobile back in his pocket despondently.

Clive's heart sank. He felt so trapped between what felt like a rock and a hard place. He had Dave Stephens, no doubt after conniving with the Police first, pushing him to go; and now, Wicked Will was sinking his talons into him, what else but to get him to fix up some drugs deal. At least for the next few hours on the plane, he had his own company, his own space. As the plane took off he leant back, closed his eyes and so far as anyone else was concerned he was fast asleep.

Only he wasn't. His mind fully alert, turning over the desperate situation his sister, little innocent Jacob and himself were getting into. He wondered what possible use he could be when it came down to it. There was no way he could protect

Kaylah or Jacob if things turned ugly. He hadn't a weapon, not even the slightest local knowledge of where they were going. The only thing that was positive was he could support Kaylah and be there for her so she wasn't so on her own. And yes, they could dig their heels in if they thought something was too risky. But how would he know whether anything was too risky until it was too late? He wondered just what they were getting themselves into and the more he pondered the less he liked it.

'Would you like some lunch, sir?' the smiling stewardess asked.

'Oh, thank you,' he replied, taking the plastic tray of plastic boxes. He looked across to Kaylah who was busy trying to feed Jacob, Lena chatting away to her. He wasn't sure about Lena. She struck him as clever, highly organised, a real fixer and he had to admit hard-nosed. He thought she was a strong personality, someone who was ambitious, thorough, and accomplished. She'd seen so much more of life and the world than Kaylah and himself, he thought. But then, by the look of her, she had never had to survive on the street. That's a whole different education. Maybe knowledge of the street is what would help Kaylah and himself survive when they got to Istanbul.

He thought it strange they were flying somewhere not knowing when they would come back. They'd been over to Kingston, Jamaica three years ago, travelling as a family, mum and dad returning them to their own roots, to meet extended family, people they didn't know and whose world was so very different to their London life. Clive wondered what they'd find in Istanbul. Then Lena passed across a brochure she had been showing Kaylah.

'It's where we're staying. Hope you like it,' she said confidently.

Clive's very first impression before opening the booklet was that this felt like five star quality, the glossy weight, the handsome hotel picture, the guys in their concierge uniform, Turkish style, standing by the grand entrance door just waiting to offer their assistance. The All Seasons Luxury

Hotel was located in Sultanahmet in the tourist heart of the city. On looking inside, he was entranced by the photos of the rooms, the facilities – so much so he forgot about all the things that had filled his mind earlier. He flipped through the pages, skim-reading and letting the glossy images work their magic.

If he had read more closely he would have noticed the hotel was a former Ottoman Prison. The brochure performed its magic, selling him the perfect venue for his Istanbul break, with its acclaimed perfumed garden and its massage services providing relaxation for its guests, and before he closed the last page ready to pass it back, he realised he was smiling again. This was something he hadn't done since he'd left his home early that morning. Can't be that bad, he thought, closing his eyes and this time falling asleep.

Whilst Kaylah was busy again with Jacob, Lena was working on her Tablet, typing away. Despite the appearance of being a relaxed holidaymaker with her friends, in her head she was working, planning ahead, lining up the emails to those who needed to know the state of the mission. As the plane began its long descent, she saw she could press send, and she knew back in London, her controller could not be more pleased with the way things were turning out.

As Kaylah changed Jacob, he began to grizzle and then cry. She noticed the changing pressure in her ears and wondered whether it was affecting him too. She picked him up and cuddled him and he was soothed. Minutes later the plane was down, moving to its holding location. Another half hour and they were passing through customs and into the baggage hall. When they might have been delayed by the customs and immigration official, Lena showed some badge she had, upon sight of which they were granted their visas and then simply hurried through.

'Diplomatic status helps sometimes,' she beamed.

Wondering what would happen next, as they were reunited with buggy and baggage, Kaylah looked up to see Lena had dashed across to a man holding a white sign with a blue flag insignia. After she'd spoken to him, he put the board back in his briefcase and Lena looked across and called out to her fellow travellers. 'Follow me.'

They were led to a waiting taxi. Speeding east in the hot evening on the main airport arterial road, it wasn't long before they were slowing as they approached the heart of the city. Neither Kaylah nor Clive had ever been anywhere like this before. On the approach road there had been many resonances with modern metropolitan city life, but once in the old city, they had stepped back in time to a bygone era. Old buildings, the shapes of minarets and domes, the crowds of strangers on the street, not one black person like themselves, all combined to make them feel instantly out of their comfort zone. Only once inside their modern hotel, which offered all the promised amenities and more, did they begin to relax. Lena, as ever, led the way.

'We're the Kone party from London. Kone with a 'K' that is. The name's Lena Bloom. I was the one who called and made the late bookings yesterday.' Leaning over and peering at the receptionist's monitor, she pointed.

'That's us, right there,' Lena said, indicating their names on the reservation list, having read it upside down.

'Oh yes, Miss Bloom. We spoke. I have the rooms you asked for, they're all together on the third floor, 308, 309 and 310. I take it the baby cot you ordered goes with the lady holding the baby. They are both in 309. What time would you all like dinner, we like to take a time from our guests, it gets so busy? How about eight-thirty and I recommend the quiet window table in the Iznik Restaurant, our blue room?' said the smiling receptionist.

After checking with a tired Kaylah and a curious Clive who, mobile in hand, was checking out the wifi facilities so that he could connect, Lena replied, 'That sounds just fine. Thank you so much.'

'Is there anything else I can do for you?' asked the receptionist.

Lena said, 'No.'

Clive had a thought and asked, 'How long do you have us booked in for, Miss?'

206

'Oh, no worry there, sir, it's an open booking. By all means stay as long as you need to. Enjoy!' the receptionist said.

She handed back their passports, hotel registration complete, then passed over their room keycards and gave them each a colourful printed map of the old city.

Two young men in matching smart navy-blue uniforms were then summonsed to help them to their rooms. It was so unreal, such a luxury treat, but neither Kaylah nor Clive could bring themselves to think in terms of their being on holiday. How long do we wait, wondered Kaylah, until the first of the unpleasant requests arrives? In her fearful heart, she knew that they would come soon enough.

Clive was still thinking about the open booking. This Lena would not be letting them leave until her mission, her goal, had been completed. He'd seen enough of Lena Bloom to know here was a feisty, determined woman who both of them would find it very hard to deal with. She seemed to get her own way every time.

As both of them entered their rooms, stacked luxury cushions piled on their silk beds and swans made from folded white napkins on their coffee tables, Clive glanced at the copy of the hotel brochure lying open on his dressing table; it was then he read what he had missed earlier, that this was a former Ottoman prison. In that moment he felt that in spite of all its excess and luxury, it was still the same as it used to be, a place of bondage and captivity with no possible means of escape.

26

In the modern office block which served as police HQ in the capital city Ankara, Chief Inspector Kizilay switched on his desk fan. It was the first thing he did on entering his office in the morning. A click of the switch, then a soft accelerating whirr as the four curved aluminised blades behind their protective wire-mesh guard spun ever faster. He glanced at the outstanding paperwork in his pending tray. It never seemed to get any less. Yesterday, Monday, he'd simply added to the growing pile. After a cursory glance, today's messages and reports would also no doubt have to wait until he was ready to look at them later. He'd learned through experience that eventually most things just kept going down the pile, never causing a problem until eventually they became history and could be forgotten about completely.

He reached over, switched on his computer and logged in to see what was happening. First he checked his diary and his heart sank as he saw he had a series of political meetings with different elected councillors all wanting him to deliver a greater police street presence in their wards.

He then checked his inbox, and amongst the routine dross spotted Inspector Celik's report marked urgent and important. He speed-read it and quickly grasped the significance of the arrests made on the main road the previous afternoon. Before doing anything further he immediately rang the local area police inspector to congratulate him and praise him for the comprehensiveness of the report on his desk. He'd learned that it was always better to do this verbally, it went down well with the men. Not leaving a paper message trail meant that he had more flexible options later when the matter was seen in the full light of day. That kind of thing only came with experience. It was a brief call and his subordinate seemed pleased to receive it.

He didn't expect much more from a local inspector who was never going to reach the level of Chief Inspector. He knew as he ended the brief call that rather more would need to be known about the two men picked up, Ishmael Suleman and Ahmed Muhammed, than the inspector had managed to provide. He therefore immediately put through the written command ordering the two prisoners be moved to the central police station ready for further questioning under his direction. He was troubled and these were troubling times when an ever-increasing number of terrorist attacks were happening, several major incidents in the past few months alone. Where exactly he wondered had these two come from? Who had sent them? They certainly hadn't arrived with such a vast supply of high explosives without backing.

Also, these two guys weren't the complete group. They had to be part of something bigger. So what was their mission, their target and who were their accomplices? They seemed to be passing by Ankara, so were they going to Istanbul, or maybe into Europe? The questions kept coming and he knew a busy day lay ahead of him if he was to get the answers he needed.

He put an intercom call through to his secretary to arrange for strong coffee to be sent in and when he had done that, the secretary was to clear his diary for the day, sending apologies through to all the councillors whose appointments and meetings had had to be cancelled. It was much more satisfying to be doing this than the political stuff, he told himself, sitting down again on his green leather executive chair facing his desk.

He knew that when something as potentially serious as this cropped up there were police protocols to be followed and he called up the rule book on his computer and began working his way down the list. This took a while.

Around 10 a.m. Kizilay called in the uniformed subaltern from his desk situated immediately outside his office door and, after explaining briefly the substance of the latest events, ordered him to make a series of urgent calls to convene the necessary officials in one of the station's meeting rooms. Gazing down the room bookings page his subaltern looked up shaking his head.

'They're all booked already, chief,' he said.

'Well clear the biggest one on my orders,' Kizilay requested.

'Yes, Sir,' he replied, and smartly turned to get on with it. The Chief Inspector was pleased that after many years he'd found someone he could actually delegate work to without having to worry or check it was being done properly.

He then returned to his desk and shut his door. He needed time to think. Too many policemen don't give themselves time to think and let the subconscious do vital work, he reminded himself. Over the years he had learned that important things, details so easily overlooked, coincidences to be spotted, only came to light when he sat in the quiet with his door firmly shut against any distraction.

He realised that a pending terrorist attack was the last thing Turkey needed right now. One could only assume the detention of these two young men from Iraq with such an enormous load of high explosives strongly indicated Turkey was meant for another round of troubling IS terrorist attacks. He knew that, though some might see this as a lucky break, there were dozens more terrorists hidden out there, undetected. And the more he thought about it, the more worried a man he became.

His instinct was that something really big was pending this time and the chance discovery of these two with their explosives was just the tip of the iceberg. There was a knock at his door which he acknowledged and his coffee arrived, thick, sweet and strong, the aroma scenting the air. He picked up the small cup carefully eyeing its promise, got up from his desk and stood looking out of the window over the capital city. It was a view he never tired of. He took a swig and sighed. It would be a long day, and this would be but the first of many coffees he would need to ensure he'd get through it.

Sitting down again at his desk, he thought it would be useful to know what the intelligence goons were on to, if anything. He phoned the national internal security chief,

210

Hakan Turan, whom he knew well and respected. The man had been in his post many years and came from the same area of rural Turkey as himself. They'd always got on. He had found his calls to Hakan were always put through with minimal delay and this morning was no exception. Very quickly he filled Hakan in on the latest news and asked whether he had missed anything in the recent intelligence briefings.

'Is there anything going on? Any electronic eavesdropping news I should know about?' asked Kizilay.

Kizilay hadn't picked up that Hakan was now a man on the brink of retirement, the end of August marking his final day. Nor that his hope was that the holiday month of August would prove to be a lightly loaded run-in to his final day on the 31st. Hakan was working on the assumption he could fill his remaining time quietly – he'd clear his desk and shred old files before departure. More importantly for him, diary days were already being allocated to 'time to be taken in lieu', extra days off to give him time to get his yacht equipped and prepared for the Mediterranean sailing holiday he had promised himself in September. To be frank, it was all he could think about. Kizilay's call was, though he didn't show it, a major irritation, threatening to derail his personal plans and bring him back in the office.

With Hakan's energy for addressing anything at work rapidly evaporating, recent weeks had seen him stop providing the full security briefings for senior police he had done in the past, and his first thoughts now were how to defuse the call he had just taken and how to let matters raised run on beyond his final working day, so that someone else had to carry the can.

He knew he was failing in his duty, but he was a beaten man. He just didn't have the will to do the job properly any more. Though Kizilay didn't know it, the police appointing minister knew Hakan was beginning to slip, but he owed him for helping him to political office in the last elections, and so he had privately decided the best thing was just to let Hakan remain where he was, in his post, untroubled for just a few more weeks, to serve out his few remaining days of service. It was a judgement worth the risk, so he thought, and a decision he would later regret.

Hakan's decision not to place in police reports the message that he had received a few days earlier saying Ali Muhammed was probably in Turkey was excusable and justified in his mind because it had its origin in Israel. He had a deep mistrust of the Israelis, never knowing whether their information was really misinformation, a cover for some action or cause that suited them. Personally, he took the view that there was a strong government in Turkey that was ruthless enough to stamp hard on any potential trouble makers, whether or not people like Amnesty International or other 'lefties' bleated on about human rights. He thought IS were glorified hoodlums, a gang of thugs, of no significant threat to Turkey, though it troubled him that so many million refugees had infiltrated the country and there was no way of knowing just how many dangerous extremists had slipped in with them. Things were getting more complicated out there, he was losing track of it, he wanted out.

To his mind, belonging to NATO and Europe meant Turkey had powerful friends, people they could count on if they were ever in serious times of trouble. If he'd had a call from NATO, the British or Americans, then he'd be more concerned, but as it was information from Israel, he didn't see the Ali information as a problem, and if it ever came to it, a need for the cavalry to come charging over the hill to Turkey's rescue, then that was exactly what would happen, he was sure of it.

In his thirty years in security, Hakan had seen threat levels change from low to high more times than he'd had sailing holidays, and he'd had many of those. By the time this latest episode came to anything, even if it did, which was unlikely, he'd be somewhere out at sea on his yacht again, this time without having to think for one moment that he would ever have to come back.

So, Chief Inspector Kizilay was much flattered to be told by Hakan that he'd done well in his urgent handling of this new matter so far and that he would personally be given the necessary delegated authority to convene a meeting of security leads. Hakan said he was rather busy with matters of state and would be delighted if Kizilay would step up for him, and act as chair for the Security Task Group standing in his place and, yes, of course he could count on full support from the security and intelligence HQ office to get everyone on board. Kizilay knew Hakan gave each Security Task Group a new name, working his way through the alphabet, and so he asked Hakan what he would like this new group called.

'Kizilay, this will be called Security Group Delta. I suggest you convene the group's meetings in your own offices rather than over here. It will be more convenient for you. Are you happy with that?' asked Hakan.

'That's fine. I'll keep you posted with regular update reports.' With that, their conversation was over. Chief Inspector Kizilay settled back down to work. He flipped through the protocols once again and decided to call a meeting at 2pm that very day, Tuesday. It was the earliest he could expect everyone to be there, and he could not delay matters until later even though he knew some would express inconvenience at being called so urgently.

For now he decided to circulate an abbreviated version of Inspector Celik's report to all those invited, the one he'd already sent to Chief Inspector Hakan. He reasoned that it would serve as a good basis to start from. One of his email invites went to Dale Winton at the US Consulate in Istanbul.

Little did Kizilay know that Dale immediately copied in his Israeli Consulate counterpart, also in Istanbul and she, in turn, sent it on as a security service encrypted message to Tel Aviv. There it was instantly picked up by Anna Simonsson who immediately passed it to her supervisor, who forwarded it on to Jerusalem and from there it went to Washington.

London also knew, even before Kizilay had finished writing all his email invites. In fact, by the time Chief Inspector Kizilay was having his second sweet Turkish coffee of the morning, NATO were taking their positions on this latest piece of intelligence and their consensus was that this was to be treated as a very serious potential threat.

At the British SIS, the Security and Intelligence Services HQ in Vauxhall overlooking the River Thames, the morning sun was just rising. It was the hush before rush hour, with the promise of another hot sunny day. The post-modern building, now a generation old, was itself quiet, though it never slept day or night, even with many staff away, being the height of the school summer holidays.

Deep inside the building, it was the links between the latest emails coming in that were especially of interest. The new messages just received from GCHQ, the Government Communications HQ listening centre near Cheltenham, resonating with those from other allied sources, made the duty team leap into action. Data was hastily collated into a short briefing summary for the aptly but vaguely named 'Considerations Meeting' already being assembled.

Once convened, the meeting recognised that something major was about to kick-off in Istanbul under Ali Muhammed's lead. As a significant footnote to the briefing, someone had also picked up, in the way that sifting through endless lists sometimes does, the fact that Adam Taylor and Kaylah Kone were both currently present in Istanbul. Bullet point (f) on the list of decisions to be taken, asked what was to be done in relation to these particular 'additional British assets on location' and a meeting decision would be required for action.

Unaware of all the wider activity elsewhere in the world, at precisely 2pm in Ankara, Chief Inspector Kizilay took the chair and began addressing his meeting of eight internal security heads. Those gathered from the various police, military, political, security, media and communications offices across Ankara together with three anti-terrorist heads who had dashed across by police helicopter from Istanbul, were astonished at the size of the high-explosive haul.

Kizilay was able to add a few more details for those assembled before him that had emerged from the morning's interrogation of the two prisoners. Those apprehended had confessed to being part of a larger IS terrorist group who had infiltrated the country from Iraq. It was believed they were to be met and assisted by others once in Istanbul, but as yet they had not been forthcoming as to by whom.

What was especially alarming to those gathered was that it was clear there had been some significant collaboration with the Kurdish Peshmergars. With a hardline political position taken by the government towards the Kurds, at one level such a response was hardly unexpected, but it was clear it took the whole meeting by surprise. No-one could believe it. Hitherto there had not been any common ground, and definitely no love lost between the Kurds and IS. An entirely new and worrying dimension as to what might be happening was being voiced around the room; the size of the threat they were considering had grown significantly and those present were scared.

Meanwhile, Hakan Turay had decided it was too nice a day to stay in the office. He decided to take another day in lieu and went off to find an old sailing friend to discuss his forthcoming plans and see if he could persuade him to come with him on the Mediterranean trip in September.

27

As Kizilay's Ankara meeting was drawing to a close, Krish Patel from MI6, the British Secret Intelligence Service, was sitting in a parallel, rather larger meeting in the basement of SIS HQ, Vauxhall, London. It was a windowless room and thought to be especially secure from listening ears or watching cameras. There was no sight from down here of the summer sunshine above, glinting on the plate-size green leaves of the plane trees on the River Thames embankment. Krish turned his attention to the business-like discussion going on around him.

He didn't know it yet, but by the end of the meeting it would be decided he'd be on the next plane to Istanbul. He might still be a relative junior in the ranks, but behind his obvious social charm, he was increasingly perceived as talented, loyal and trustworthy, and most importantly concerning the task in hand, he was the one person thought to have built a special relationship with Adam Taylor, something those at the meeting saw as having 'potential to exploit' and it had occurred to them that Krish could develop further. The only way to know whether this was possible was to get him to Adam as soon as possible.

Hurriedly packing a travel bag he was whisked by car from the underground carpark straight to the Departure Gate at Terminal 2, Heathrow. A wave of his pass and he was escorted straight through to Boarding. Things then slowed down, and after boarding the plane, the long flight to Istanbul did not prove to be as easy a journey for him as he had anticipated.

A dozen or so seats on the British Airways plane were taken up by excited football supporters who had come from South West, England – all heading for the following day's, Friday's, pre-season friendly international match between England and Turkey. Most were in jeans and T-shirts and had been drinking, something that Krish never did. Wearing a dark-blue sports jacket and white business shirt, Krish with his dark skin stood out. For a man who was supposed to work in the shadows, today he felt uncomfortably exposed as the group surrounded him, jostling to find their allocated seats.

Earlier, as Krish had walked to board the plane he had found the jovial banter innocuous and good humoured and had replied in kind. He wore the usual innocent smile and broad grin on his face that had always served him well. He learned from one of their number that they were a vanguard group of supporters travelling over a day early because one of them had made the mistake of arranging to get married, so he'd chosen to come with his true mates for a bit of a party before the match.

It was only when Krish found himself in his window seat he realised he was about to be trapped in his place and in an awkward situation. To begin with none of the group of England supporters wanted to sit next to him. They argued amongst themselves as to who should take the still vacant seat. Eventually the person with his name formally allocated to the seat gave in and threw himself down in his place in abject defeat, bowing to the decision and derision of his friends. He pointedly ignored Krish next to him, swinging his back towards him.

Krish wasn't alone in picking up the unruly nature of the passengers; the plane's preparation for take-off was delayed because the cabin crew wanted the noise amongst the passengers, meaning the disruption emanating from those sitting in the rows around Krish, to quieten down. The captain insisted he wasn't going to fly his plane with an unruly crowd of passengers and if things didn't improve he would order the plane cleared. There was some 'tut-tutting' from an older man at the back of the plane. He got the predictable response of, 'We know where you're from mate,' and a round of raucous drunken laughter by way of reply. When everyone realised the pilot wasn't joking and was taking charge of his domain, one of the group of football supporters who seemed to carry some authority, a guy they were calling Big Harry, stood up and addressed everyone.

'Now come on boys, behave for our captain please. We don't want any trouble here, now do we? We've a match to see. Enjoy the flight boys, stay cool,' Harry said, his eyes flashing round to make sure all his group understood him.

It was enough to calm things, the noise levels subsided and the usual take-off safety announcements were then delivered by the steward as they taxied towards the take-off holding area. There was no loss of flight slot and the plane left London on time.

Krish knew that sometimes it was best when in a minority position to say and do nothing to provoke the majority. It was something his parents had told him from a young age and, squeezed in his seat with no room to wriggle, he soon gave up any idea of getting his tablet out to work on. He looked out of the window at the receding English landscape bathed in sunshine below, but when the plane swung to the east and the glare of the sun became too bright, his attention moved to the plane's interior and he began seeing what he could make of his fellow passengers. He was one of those people with a good memory for faces coupled with an extraordinary ability to read their characters, a skill that had served him well in life.

His exercise came to a halt when meals were passed along the row. It was only at the stewardess' request that his tray of food made it to him, the football supporter beside him initially refusing to pass the food on along the row, as if Krish didn't exist.

As he waited for the detritus to be gathered in the black rubbish bags after the meal, he resumed his profiling of fellow passengers. His eyes stopped at the guy calling himself Big Harry, sitting just one row in front. Big Harry had stood up to walk down towards the toilet, quietly speaking, whispering conspiratorially into the ears of other fans as he made his way forward. Krish had no way of overhearing, but he knew a leader when he saw one.

218

On the back of Big Harry's white shirt was written 'England's Glory' and beneath that, 'Plymouth's Finest – Ocean City'. Krish didn't know whether the word finest referred to Big Harry or Plymouth or both. He certainly wasn't going to ask to find out. Big Harry was built so differently from himself, strong arms covered with dark-blue swirling tattoos, tall too. Krish wondered whether he had a job and what it might be, after all a trip like this didn't come cheap. When Big Harry came out of the toilet, just for an instant his eyes met Krish's – eyes that hunted and sought out everybody, analysing and taking in everything he surveyed. Krish was fascinated. In that fraction of a second when he met big Harry's gaze, Krish turned away – keen to avoid provocation.

Fortunately the next four hours passed without incident and it was with much relief he was finally able to move towards the exit at their destination. He did his best to keep his distance from the potential sources of trouble. The smell of stale alcohol from the football supporters tainted the air.

Once in the Arrivals area, he picked up his phone and called his link at the Istanbul Consulate to check in and was told a car had been sent to pick him up. Stepping outside he saw it straight away, no doubting its distinctive presence. He thought the football supporters would have been pleased as well as surprised to see the Union Jack flying from the Range Rover bonnet, but probably puzzled to see him stepping into it.

Less than half an hour after landing he was being driven into the seclusion of the Consulate building. He was welcomed and shown to a guest suite where he would be staying – it was comfortable and looked out on the manicured garden to the rear.

Tomorrow he would decide what to do about Adam. He thought he probably ought to just meet him first, assess his personality and temperament, only then come to a decision how useful he might be.

The trouble with Adam is, he thought, the guy is so fragile he could easily just fall apart and be more liability than asset. Finally, tablet in hand, he was able to pick up his unopened mail and catch up on his day job. These days, ninety-nine percent of his time working for the intelligence services seemed to be spent handling emails, writing reports and attending endless meetings. This trip to Istanbul promised a few minutes' relief from such tedium. It would be nice to see Adam and with that he decided there was no time like the present for making the call.

'Hi Adam, Krish here. How are you finding Istanbul?' he asked cheerfully.

'Uh. Hmm. OK, nice of you to ask. How's things with you? Just got back from a sightseeing day. Really rather more enjoyable than I'd expected, except that is for a spot of bother at the end of the afternoon,' said Adam in a more sombre mood.

'What was that then?' inquired Krish.

'Some demonstration or other, pro-Kurdish. We got caught up in it, had to dive into a hotel for safety. The riot police waded into them, broke it up,' said Adam.

'You'll have another story to tell when you get back home then,' said Krish.

'Sure will. But you didn't call just to pass the time of day, Krish, you guys don't. What's up?' asked Adam.

'You won't believe this, but I'm in Istanbul as I talk to you. I'm here at the British Consulate for a few days. Tell you what, why don't you pop over and pay me a visit? They offer good hospitality here. Why don't you come round for breakfast tomorrow, Wednesday morning? I'd love to hear how things have worked out for you since all the excitement of last summer and autumn,' said Krish.

'Breakfast! As soon as that? Well, I suppose I could. OK then, we saw the Consulate earlier, just off the main thoroughfare,' said Adam reluctantly, not feeling entirely comfortable with this unexpected change of routine.

'Well, breakfast suits me best. It'll leave me free the rest of the day to get down to the things I have to do in the office whilst I'm here,' Krish hurriedly explained, thinking fast. He needed to see Adam sooner rather than later and was reassured that Adam was happy enough to come to him. He reasoned that Adam would feel safe at the Consulate, and hopefully it would feed his ego to have had the invite.

'OK then. The Consulate. I'm sure I can get there. How do I get in?' asked a hesitant Adam.

Krish gave directions, but then recalled the less than confident tone in Adam's voice, so Krish spoke up, thinking on his feet of a way to make things easier for Adam.

'Tell you what, I can borrow a car here and come and pick you up. It'll be just like old times, me as your friendly driver,' he joked.

Adam, much relieved, quickly agreed, but Krish wished he hadn't mentioned old times. He shouldn't have run the risk of reawakening past memories of when Adam was flown back to London with the help of the military last autumn, when Krish had met him at the military airfield and taken him back to a North London safe house.

Anyway, it was settled. Krish would call at around 9am and Adam would be waiting at the main entrance to Ataturk Academic Apartments. As soon as the call had ended, Krish dialled his superior in London, explaining that he had arrived at the Consulate, he had already had a conversation with Adam and that they were meeting up for breakfast first thing. His boss, Sharon Armstrong had had some thoughts of her own as to what should go into the forthcoming conversation. More intelligence had come to light and Adam might need to be carefully prepared to help bring Ali's latest escapade to a satisfactory and early termination.

Krish was good, but didn't think himself that good. He was aware he'd made a basic error mentioning the past, possibly leaving Adam feeling less secure than he'd intended. He realised he'd made another mistake – not once had Adam told Krish where he was staying, yet Krish had shown his hand, he knew already.

After the call Adam was feeling very unsettled by the fact he was clearly being spied upon and actively drawn into things he had no wish to be. Nonetheless, he knew he'd still be keeping the breakfast appointment, but he was nobody's fool and he was not going to be played for one. He'd take the breakfast and the visit to the Consulate, enjoy the social chat; as to anything else Krish might have in mind, Adam was resolved to play hard-ball. It was a matter of self-preservation.

28

Yesterday, Monday, had concluded with the first gathering of the full team. Ali, if he were being honest, was not much impressed by the Turkish fighters Zaid had brought along that evening to join his own men. They were all so young and inexperienced. They made a lot of noise, said the right things, but they were just full of radical fervour, talked the talk rather than knew battle experience. He wondered whether any one of them was really up to what lay ahead.

Reluctantly, and in the light of such obvious weakness, he decided he would have to split his own guys up, so that each team of four took a couple of these local guys. He himself decided he would take Zaid and two locals. It would be useful for Zaid to be close to him and he'd already decided privately that his group would be the one to take on the Galatasaray stadium.

His Mosul guys weren't going to like being in mixed teams and with such young novices, but he admitted his men needed their local knowledge; the experienced ones would need to exercise the attack leadership and, Ali concluded, he had no other option left to him.

Often in the course of a mission things had a habit of going this way, starting with high expectations at the outset, but as the days went by all too often the cumulative effect of little knock-backs along the way had the result of diminishing mission objectives and dashing hopes and outcomes. Still, there was a chance he could pull this attack off. After all, he told himself, he had no choice but to press on.

Today would start with another briefing for everyone cramped into the flat again. As the local men arrived in their ones and twos, there were soon sixteen men squashed together in the main room. The risk of such a gathering being noticed and discovered was something that troubled Ali, but it was something he could do little about.

Ali was shortly going to send them out to recce the targets he had assigned for them. They would go out in pairs, two pairs to each target, but not as a group of four because that would be more likely to attract unwelcome attention. His Mosul men were to go as tourists, to try and blend in, look relaxed, the local guys acting as their hosts and guides, charged with getting them there and back safely. He'd send them out from the flat at intervals so as not to attract suspicion. Ali didn't want to take any unnecessary risks; they would, he'd insist, go out sporadically.

All this shouldn't be too hard to organise, he thought. Just in case any were going to treat the exercise too casually, he was going to tell them they were going to have to report back to everyone what they'd found when they all reassembled at 8pm. He was going to impress upon them to be thorough, careful, and to observe every last detail, for the very success of the whole enterprise depended on it.

On return he would expect them to provide a considered impact assessment of their planned attack target. He expected this to be well thought out and he would question them thoroughly at the evening de-brief. If their work wasn't good enough they would be out again tomorrow doing exactly the same thing. Thinking how they would receive this, he decided he had to deliver a boost to their morale in his address to them, something to lift their spirits before they went out.

This time, as he briefed his men, he felt they were more attentive and respectful. His commanding style was getting the right response. After he'd briefed them, he began putting them into their pairs, noting, on his improvised whiteboard, names against target for the first time. He sent them out in ten minute intervals until just Zaid and himself were left. Zaid told him the neighbours were no worry and people were used to a constant coming a going in these apartments. He wondered if any threat had been used to get them to turn a blind eye. He thought the two of them could have a private conversation before setting out themselves to look at the Galatasaray stadium, the target he had allocated to Zaid, himself and what he judged to be the two least experienced local fighters. It was preferable that he personally kept a close supervisory eye on the weakest men.

His mind briefly went back to the two guys he had lost in the van, Ishmael and Ahmed. He asked Zaid if there had been any news of them, only to be told not, but then he wouldn't have expected any. Ali thought the two faced a difficult time with the prospect of a long prison sentence ahead of them when eventually they were brought to court. Just maybe, if we triumph, we will meet again, he hoped. He didn't know whether to discuss his fears for their mission with Zaid, now the security forces knew something was coming, but decided against doing so. Zaid knew Ali's men had failed in getting caught, risking the safety of his own men in doing so. Such organisational carelessness, thought Ali, was best not paraded by bringing it up again.

'OK Zaid, let's just go over things together, shall we – check we've not overlooked anything. What is your assessment of the warriors we have?' asked Ali.

'Hmm. Some I'd rely on, others are weak links,' Zaid ventured. 'My guys will need your guys to lead them, no doubt about that. They'll expect that. They look up to your men, I can see that already. Have no worries, they have been well prepared to do what is expected, but for all of them this will be their first time.'

'That's exactly my impression too. And the targets we have to attack, what's your assessment of them?' said Ali.

'All of them are difficult. All are risky and with challenging security measures to reckon with. Together they make up Istanbul's crown jewels. They are hardly likely to leave them unattended so we can do with them just what we please. What did you expect?' Zaid said, as he shrugged his shoulders.

'OK. I want you to take me round to all the targets, every one, in the course of today. I want to see them first-hand and have your take on them. We'll need to make sure we look especially carefully at our own target, the Galatasaray stadium, and we must be there around 3pm – the time of day we intend to attack. We need to know exactly what things will be like there at that precise time,' commanded Ali.

'That's fine by me. We won't go to them as you've listed them – alphabetically, it's not so easy to get round that way. I suggest I take you on my motor bike. We'll get to each target quickly and we can see our guys without them necessarily seeing us. With the bike it is easier to park and if trouble comes I can get us both away. I know this, my city, like the back of my hand, you'll see. OK with that?' Zaid said, moving towards the door.

'Fine. A nice way to travel on a hot day, the wind in our faces,' said Ali approvingly.

'I want you to wear a helmet. Your picture is in the papers and there's a price on your head, so best hide your face. I've got one for you,' said Zaid.

This was unexpected news and Ali felt a thump in his chest. It brought home to him that the enemies of the Caliphate were indeed on to him and closing in. London all over again, he thought, just the same as before with me keeping one step ahead of those chasing me.

Ali decided he would take his handgun with him, retrieving it from under his pillow before leaving. He double-checked it was loaded and that he had enough spare ammunition. Both were well hidden inside his jacket as he and Zaid went out of the door to leave the now empty flat.

'Bike's in the car park out the back,' said Zaid.

Within five minutes, Zaid was proving what a skilled biker he was, weaving the powerful machine in and out of the traffic going into the city. Even now, as they sped along, passing slower traffic, the morning air conveyed the discernible charcoal smoke mix of kebabs and street-food. With the hot street air blasting his face, Ali had a thought. This bike could give them the edge if they were to use it on the coming Friday.

It was a long day for all of them. Zaid wanted to take Ali to a restaurant run by some friends at lunchtime, but Ali said no and they picked up a lamb kebab and salad from a roadside vendor. Ali felt obsessed by the task he had been

226

given as they hurried between targets. As they rode, whenever he could he talked to Zaid, quizzing him continuously. His quest for local knowledge was insatiable, as if his very life depended on it.

At each target he spotted his men lounging or walking around, eyeing up their targets, familiarising themselves with their surroundings, the entrances and exits, the layout of the buildings, the level and pattern of security cover. He was relieved to see they were mingling unhindered. If only it was all going to be as easy on Friday, in just two days' time, he reminded himself.

By five, Ali had seen enough and ordered Zaid to return him to the apartment. Zaid said he needed an hour, and this suited Ali as he himself wanted some time alone to prepare carefully for the 8pm debrief. Consequently, on arrival outside the flat he ordered Zaid, to get food and refreshment for the soon-to-be-returning men, a request to which Zaid quickly assented and he sped off, leaving Ali alone.

Once inside the flat again, he opened the windows to refresh the still stale air his men had left behind many hours before. He went and sat on his bed, carefully rehearsing in his mind what he had seen during the day, until he was quite sure he had it all at his fingertips. He concluded that all the targets were pregnable, none would escape what they had in mind for them.

Making a couple of aides-mémoire notes, he then remembered it was about time he checked his phone. It had been tucked away in his jacket whilst he'd been out and he realised that he wouldn't have noticed it ringing whilst he was on the bike. He flicked open the cover and saw he had a message. He cursed himself at not having picked up on it earlier.

His CO in Mosul had sent a message of encouragement, and said he, Ali, was to expect an imminent delivery to be made in Istanbul to replace what had been lost in transit. Ali knew Zaid would get on to these explosives as soon as they appeared. At least this was some positive news to tell the men later that evening before he'd finished with them and they crashed out.

There was noise at the front door – the first of his men were returning.

29

Adam had no time to reflect further on Krish's call, since the four students had been hastily summoned to be ready for Mustafa. He was picking them up for an evening out which Raqiyah's uncle Abdul had arranged. They all agreed Abdul really was taking his role as host very seriously indeed. Mustafa would be round at their apartments with the minibus to collect them soon. Bilal told Adam that apparently Abdul wanted to introduce them to some of his friends in what he called the Gulen Movement. Having no idea what Gulen was, Adam asked Raqiyah if she'd heard of it.

'Well, all I know is that lots of moderate Muslims, academics and businessmen are attracted to it. It's a bit elitist if you ask me. The Gulen Movement began here in Turkey and is now all over the world, and in the UK too, so it's more westernised. I think it's where my uncle has found his spiritual home here in Turkey. Being away from Oman which has a very tolerant, relaxed Muslim tradition, for him Gulen is the next best thing. We'll find out more soon. It'll be fun, you'll see. Nothing to look so worried about. I hope I haven't got it wrong,' she said.

'Sounds interesting. We met the Sufis yesterday. Plenty to write up in our summer assignment in all this,' Adam added. He wondered if he was permanently wearing a worried look these days.

'My uncle will lay on good refreshments, you'll see. We're going to where he works at the university for this, the Arts and Sciences Faculty. It'll be just like going to a seminar in Exeter!' said Raqiyah.

Adam felt calmer, but wanted to tell, or rather share with Raqiyah, the news of Krish's breakfast invitation to the British Consulate. Perhaps the right moment to do so had just arrived.

'Raqiyah, I took a call just now. I've been invited to have breakfast at the British Consulate here tomorrow. They're sending someone round to pick me up around 9am. I'll come back to the apartments afterwards and catch up with you three when you get back from your next round of mosque visits!' said Adam.

'You lucky thing. How did you land that one? Is there someone you know there? Did you pull some strings?' asked Raqiyah.

'Well, there's a guy called Krish I've kept in touch with since the events of last year. He happens to be there at the moment and it was Krish who gave me a call.' Adam knew he wasn't fully telling it exactly how it was and went quiet, knowing he perhaps shouldn't disclose more.

'Well, I know last year was bad for you, but apart from the run-in with the ugly scenes at the demo yesterday, this has been a pretty good trip,' she cheerfully stated.

'We're only a couple of days in,' said a more cautious Adam.

It wasn't long before Mustafa had swept up his passengers and was driving them the short distance to the University's Faculty of Arts and Sciences Building in the Laleli district. It wasn't so very far from the Sultanahmet area they had visited the previous day. The imposing building came into view. Why, thought Adam, are universities obsessed with classical buildings complete with stonework, Greek-style colonnades and arcades? They were the same at home. Maybe it was all about creating authority, exercising influence, making a mark.

Job done, Mustafa disappeared with the minibus, saying he'd return to deliver them back to their apartments afterwards. A smiling Abdul, impeccably dressed in dark-blue trousers and white shirt, stood impassively framed in the Faculty entrance. He greeted them warmly and invited them in.

'Welcome to my second home, though my wife thinks I really live here,' he laughed.

'Tonight I want you to come and sit in on a lecture by a fellow academic, a dear friend of mine. Don't worry, it'll be delivered in English and she never goes on too long. I thought that whilst you're here you need to hear from and experience some of the aspects of Islam you might not have come across before. She's a great speaker, lectures in the Faculty of Communication. You know there is no one thing called Islam. Your visit to the Sufis yesterday will have illustrated the point I'm sure. But first, come through for something to eat and drink. Meet some of my friends. You'll find quite a number of our students have come in this evening for this. I spread the word we had some visiting students from England here and I'm sure they'll be most interested to meet you and hear more about the UK and Exeter. Some of them are planning on going to the UK,' said Abdul.

They followed Abdul as he led them into the welcoming cool of the building's interior. Adam was impressed by the man's unassuming and gracious manner. Nothing was too much trouble. He was quiet, urbane, engaging and not arrogant like some university staff could be. A moderate, was his assessment, a man to be trusted, a man to feel quite at ease with, someone who didn't push his Muslim identity. Being in the confines of the university felt reassuringly safe to Adam, certainly far more preferable to being out on the street.

As he helped himself to something to eat, with a soft drink in his other hand, he was aware that he really needed a session with his psychotherapist Inger Walker and was missing the meetings that had been so much a regular part of his first year at Exeter. Right now, he was missing that reflective space, the room she gave him to express himself, to talk out his anxieties.

He was realising that after only two days in Istanbul his inner equilibrium had been really unsettled. He'd noticed it every time yesterday's demo came to mind, as it frequently did. The very remembrance brought on fits of shaking which he tried hard to hide. He preferred to think it was more in his mind than apparent, hoping none of his shaking showed and that he could hold things together long enough to get back home without falling completely apart.

Dr Meryem Akalin was introduced by Abdul. She was younger than Adam had anticipated, maybe only in her early thirties. Every bit a western-looking lecturer with long hair, make-up and attractive fashionable clothes, yet still a Muslim. He learned she held a senior lecturer position in the Faculty of Communication, her specialist field being contemporary social media. This evening though, she wanted to talk about the Gulen Movement and the means the movement used, past and present, to spread its message. She had clearly been briefed beforehand, probably by Abdul, to give some background to the Gulen Movement before addressing the particular theme of communication.

'The Gulen Movement is recent, our founder Fethullah Gulen was only born in 1941, though that's still well before my time,' she laughed.

'It was in the 1960s that he began attracting followers and not long after that he came to the attention of the Turkish authorities. His teaching, in offering an alternative Islam, meant that in 1999 the Turkish Government's on-off persecution of him as a perceived threat forced him to flee and make his home in the United States. This is ironic because Fethullah's message is one of tolerance and engagement with other faiths.' That was as much as she was going to say about the movement's history.

'A strong believer in education, he has been the inspiration behind the Gulen Schools in this country and across the world. Today over 800 Gulen Schools offer a modern alternative to the failing madrassa system of education which has so held back millions of Turkish Muslims in ignorance and conservatism. Our schools are beacons of academic success and more and more parents want their children to go to them. For this reason the state sees Gulen as a threat to the historic accommodation that has existed here between secular state and Islam because its enemies see Gulen Islam as a threat to both. We are no small movement here in

Turkey, some five million people sympathise with our way, we are gaining influence all the time.'

'Yes, but there are over 70 million Turks,' called out one student, abrasively interrupting her.

'True, but a poll showed that over 83% of Turks are supportive of us even if they haven't signed up with Gulen, and don't forget the 5 million who are located where the important thinking and learning is taking place in our country. We are in science, business, education, media and communication, even the police. Gulen is where it counts. Some say we are the most powerful movement in the country, and most importantly we are where the thinking is done,' she countered.

'But you are a political, power-hungry, factional Islamist group. You are elitist, you want to undermine our secular state, stirring revolution and revolt. You are making your religion a threat to Turkey by forcing it onto the agenda.' The young student had now interrupted the speaker twice. He clearly had another pro-secular or pro-state agenda, but this was becoming more than a student asking a question of a lecturer. Adam could tell from watching Abdul, the student was being viewed with suspicion by him as well as much of the audience present. He was overstepping the mark. Then Abdul stood up.

'I wonder if we might take comments and questions after our guest has finished giving her lecture. We have a proud tradition of good manners here in this Faculty. Let us see that we show proper respect for our distinguished speaker,' said Abdul, being gracious enough not to single out the troublesome student in person. The majority of students then applauded his intervention.

The lecturer, Meryem Akalin, then put up some PowerPoint slides on the big screen behind her. She was particularly keen to promote what she called the movement's core values: love, tolerance, hope, dialogue, activism, mutual acceptance and respect. She went on to describe how the movement had successfully utilised media and communication to expand its ideas, organisation and influence. It seemed to Adam that Gulen had created its own TV, newspaper and media organisations to put out its teaching, backed up by humanitarian charity organisations and vocal professional organisations.

Adam could not doubt this was a slick, market-friendly, and openly promoted lecture, to be followed by debate and dialogue. At the same time he wondered whether Gulen was rather like Freemasonry, albeit without Freemasonry's secrecy, in that it promoted an alternative system within the system. In spite of its urbane, intellectual and apparent openness, such a body could be seen by some as deeply counter-cultural and threatening, even a recipe for conflict and trouble. Perhaps that was why one of the students had spoken out earlier as he did. The lecture drew to a close with polite if not enthusiastic applause and with Abdul resuming the chair, Meryem Akalin took questions.

'Yes,' Abdul pointed to a young woman on the front row. 'Questions in English please, for the benefit of our visitors from England. Please keep questions brief and to the point.'

'Dr Akalin, thank you for your lecture. Why do you think our government has recently become so hostile to us in Gulen and what can we do about that?' asked the young woman.

'You are right to raise this important point. There have always been incidents, but it has only been since 2011 that we have been on the receiving end of politically motivated mischief-making and oppression. In 2011 Gulen journalists were arrested. In 2013 we were said to have bribed ministers, influenced the police and the courts and were said to be responsible for attempting to overthrow the government. We were branded terrorists. In 2014 the government made more arrests of Gulen supporters, and then in 2015 they attacked the media again because it was critical of the Turkish Government. Since then it has got steadily worse. I fear we are lurching towards an ever more polarised Turkish State where power is concentrated and increasingly tightly grasped by the nationalists with their one-size-fits-all accommodation

234

of Islam. Everyone else is seen as a threat. These are difficult times for openness and dialogue in this country. My own Faculty of Communication has never been so scrutinised and intimidated by government. Indeed I am fearful for our very freedom. And what was the second part of your question?' Meryem Akalin asked.

'And what can we do about it?'

'President Kennedy once said, "The only thing necessary for the triumph of evil is that good men do nothing".'

Several more questions were asked, by the end of which Adam thought he understood that the Gulen Movement was based on a reformist Sufi ideology; that it was collaborative and respectful towards other faiths; it had a strong education/self-advancement ethos and it was in favour of the European Union and generally held a strong pro-western bias. It was the latter, including having an exiled leader in America, which seemed to be giving it such a hard time with the current political leadership of Turkey.

Adam was beginning to think he'd had enough education for one day and was wondering how long it would be before Mustafa came to collect them to return them to their apartment. He looked back over his shoulder towards the glass doors where they had come in, only to see there was a bit of a commotion going on just outside. He leaned across Raqiyah to get a better view.

There were police standing outside the lecture theatre looking in, one of the University security personnel standing between them and the door trying, with plaintive apologetic gestures to tell them something. Spreading himself across the doorway it was as if he were preventing the police from entering. Adam felt his pulse racing. What was going to happen next? He turned to look at Abdul who was getting up from his seat and looking past Adam at the unfolding scene. Taking the initiative, Abdul gave a beckoning wave to invite the police in and the security officer gave way.

Eight policemen moved in and formed a line across the back of the lecture hall. None of those present dared move.

One of the policemen, with more gold braid on his sleeve, moved forward down to the front, all eyes in the now silent hall fixed upon him.

'Welcome to this evening's lecture. I'm afraid you've just missed it. Professor Abdul Zayed, Business and Social Sciences at your service. I'm professor here at this faculty and responsible for this evening's lecture programme.'

'We had a report of subversive activity, Professor. Can you ask everyone to remain seated for now please,' the policeman in charge ordered.

'Certainly. Incidentally, we have four visiting students from the United Kingdom for the lecture this evening, from the University of Exeter, our specially invited international guests,' said Abdul, waving his arms in the direction of the four students sitting at the front.

The police officer seemed surprised and looked across towards the group, eyed them carefully, and dismissed them as unimportant, but then had second thoughts. He knew their presence limited his options for further action without creating a risk of unwelcome publicity. That was, thought Adam, exactly why Abdul had deliberately pointed the four of them out.

'Can you assure me, Professor, that everything is in order here tonight?' he asked, now standing right in front of Abdul.

'Absolutely,' the professor beamed, knowing the threat of police action had in that moment passed. 'Our students and visitors are about to leave. Would it be in order that they do so now?'

'Go ahead,' and with that the officer brusquely turned on his heels, stepped briskly to the exit doors of the hall, and with an almost imperceptible hand-signal told his men to follow him outside.

As people filed out of the lecture hall into the night, Raqiyah turned to Adam. He seemed to be having some kind of turn. His head was down and he was shaking. She was worried.

'Adam, Adam, are you alright?' she asked.

Adam lifted his head.

'Have they gone? Have they gone?' he said, fear written across his face.

'Yes, they've gone. It's alright now. She put her arm over his shoulder. Come on, Mustafa's waiting. Let's get you back. Are you feeling unwell? What is it?' said Raqiyah with confusion and concern in equal measure.

Bilal and Sophie came over to them and Raqiyah said she thought Adam was feeling unwell. She alone knew that it was more in his mind than anything physical. All the while she kept hold of him, leading, comforting, supporting, speaking, doing anything she thought might lift him from the place of hurt and anxiety into which he had so evidently descended.

She sat next to him on the minibus. He wasn't saying anything and she didn't know whether they might need to get him a doctor, even send him back to England. As Mustafa drove them back to the apartment, his shaking gradually subsided, but leaning against her she could still feel his trembling in pulsing waves, and she just knew, in spite of his brave protestations to the contrary, Adam was in a dark place and would need help.

30

In Istanbul's All Seasons Luxury Hotel, Kaylah, Jacob and Clive had been left to their own devices for the day. Lena had disappeared. A message had been sent to her to report for duty to the Israeli Consulate that very morning. Kaylah thought Lena was genuinely surprised at this development, but Clive was more circumspect.

'To be expected,' Lena said with resignation as she made her apologies. 'I thought I'd be left to my own devices, able to spend my time with you guys. They should have been told that by London. Let's hope they only want me in today.'

Before disappearing, she went off to change her clothes and smarten herself up. She said she wasn't going to go in until she was ready. They would just have to wait. Lena recommended that, in her absence, they take a walk around the nearby square, look in on the Hagia Sophia and the Blue Mosque like everyone else who came to Istanbul. Taking Clive's tourist map from his hand, she pointed out the square and the key places to visit. She claimed to have seen them before on an earlier visit and said they were well worth a look and she was only too disappointed not to be seeing them again.

Having already handed out some spending money to them after breakfast, she promised to meet them back at their hotel at 4pm. They had no better options and Kaylah and Clive nodded a thank you before Lena made a hasty departure. She was every bit the successful professional executive; Kaylah still nurtured hopes of being one herself, one day. The thought was soon dismissed, as she gazed at Jacob's innocent face and felt a strong pull of motherly love and affection for the young life who was now and would always be the centre of her world.

The sun was already fierce as they went out of the front door, powerfully hot after the air-conditioned cool of the hotel. It took only five minutes before they saw the complex of the Hagia Sophia before them. Joining the crowds of tourists moving towards it they enjoyed wandering round sightseeing rather more than they had thought they would and felt quite safe as they ambled round, taking it in turns to push the buggy or carry Jacob.

'This ain't so bad, Sis,' said Clive pausing to take yet another picture. He actually believed Kaylah was giving him genuine smiles now. 'Let's wander down towards the Blue Mosque after we've had a drink, it's so hot.'

'OK, I'm just a bit worried about Jacob. I might take off his top so he doesn't overheat. I must keep him covered though,' said Kaylah.

'He seems happy enough,' observed Clive wanting to move on.

'That building was amazing. I feel as if I've been transported to a different planet. This place is so different to London, a real collision of East meets West. The summer heat makes you feel so relaxed and seems to slow everyone down. Not felt anything like it since we went to Jamaica. You know what, I haven't seen anyone on the street who looks like trouble either. The whole city feels chilled out,' said Clive, looking every bit the relaxed tourist on holiday.

'Don't speak too soon,' Kaylah chirped. 'Look, if we set off now, cross the square to the Blue Mosque, there's every chance we'll get round before Lena finishes at four. She did recommend we see it.'

They braved the bright light and searing heat, and moved steadily, rather than quickly, to join other tourists milling outside the Blue Mosque. Clothes were beginning to stick to bodies in the inescapable heat. To their relief it didn't take more than a few minutes to get there.

'Looks like they seem quite relaxed about who goes in, though make sure you keep your shoulders covered, Sis. We need to show respect,' suggested Clive.

'Glad you're not in shorts, otherwise you might be the one waiting outside!' she teased.

They looked round the mosque and were amazed. There was a clear expectation of respect, but it didn't need to be requested, somehow the building itself just spoke of beauty and holiness. It permeated their inner beings, very obviously leaving all its visitors awestruck. Kalyah and Clive both fell under its magical influence. It was a living faith building not just a tourist heritage site. Not for the first time they heard the call to prayer through loudspeakers and for ten minutes or so the noisy intoned liturgy in Arabic filled the air with incantations.

'Bit like being in dad's church if you ask me,' said Clive, bringing them back to earth.

'That reminds me, I called home first thing this morning to tell them we'd arrived safely. How about you? Called home yet?' asked Kaylah.

'No, reckon your call will do for us both. How did you think they were?' he said.

'Easier than before. It always takes them time to come round to anything a bit different. I told Mum we were staying in a very nice place. They asked what we were doing for money and found it hard to accept it was all paid for. They couldn't understand that bit. I said it was best to see it as a kind of thank you from the Israelis, but I don't think they fully believed me. Be a good idea if you send them a couple of sightseeing pictures from today to reassure them. Do it when we get back to the hotel's wifi,' she suggested.

'Oh well, sounds like life goes on just the same back home in London town. I'm beginning to think, if you ask me, we've done alright coming here, Sis. I'm not one for old buildings, but this place takes some beating,' said Clive with genuine admiration.

As the afternoon wore on, Jacob became irritable and began crying, refusing to be comforted. They decided he might be uncomfortable in the heat. It was time to head back. Once back in the cool of the air-conditioned hotel, a change of nappy and a bottle of feed later, he was content. Clive suggested the three of them go downstairs into the hotel lounge and await Lena's return there. They took the lift downstairs and whilst they waited, Clive ordered them a fruit based cocktail each from the bar and Kaylah picked up a glossy magazine to look at.

It wasn't long before Lena showed up. Something wasn't right, thought Kaylah. She and Clive both knew it and exchanged knowing glances as Lena came in through the front door, so far away in her own thoughts totally ignoring the helpful concierge.

Lena glanced at them, then looked away, her face a picture of concentration as if she had something important to say. She waved a greeting in their direction and before joining them went to the bar and ordered herself a drink which she carried over to join them. By now she seemed to have regained her composure.

'How have you been today? Did you see any of the local sights, like the ones I suggested?' Lena said calmly.

'We've been fine. Went to the Hagia Sophia this morning and the Blue Mosque this afternoon. Crossed the square in the heat of the midday sun and survived! Not long been back. When you came through the door I wondered whether you had had a bad day at the office for a minute. How was it for you?' asked Clive.

'There have been developments. Nothing stands still for long and it's good we came here when we did. Bear me out while I tell you some news. Ali Muhammed is definitely here in Istanbul. I don't know where he is exactly, but he came here a couple of days ago. Two of his team were arrested on the way, not here, near Ankara, the Turkish capital. Ali and the other terrorists with him are believed to have made it and are thought to be planning something big. We don't know what, but it doesn't look good. We don't know when either, but all the signs are they intend to act soon, maybe in the next few days, maybe in a week or so. Who knows?' said a concerned Lena.

'The two guys who were arrested. Surely they will lead the police to Ali?' said Clive.

'I hope so, but nothing like that has been reported. In fact, between ourselves, our people don't put a lot of store by the Turkish police being able to pick up Ali quickly enough. Ali is an experienced operative. He can lie low when he has to, he's proved that before in London. Our people think we need to try and expose him, get him out in the open, and they asked me to suggest that you help us with this,' said Lena.

Lena then looked Kaylah in the eye, almost pleading with her.

'No,' said Clive, 'it is just too risky.'

'Needn't be actually. Could be as simple as only making one phone call. The rest you can leave to us. How about it Kaylah, one brief phone call? I'll tell you exactly what to say. How about it?' Lena addressed Kaylah, leaving Clive feeling sidelined.

Kaylah just knew that she would have to make the call, Lena needed her to. She felt somehow she was in Lena's debt, she owed her that much and much more. Clive felt his stomach turn as he saw Lena had his sister eating out of her hand.

Just then, Clive felt his phone vibrate in his pocket and retrieved it to find Dave Stephens calling him from London. Suddenly another security world came crashing in. Clive knew he had to take it.

'Excuse me a minute, a mate from London's calling. Back in five,' he said, moving away from them.

Out in the hotel lobby, once Dave Stephens had checked it was Clive on the other end of the line, he continued speaking with a real urgency in his voice.

'I don't care what that Israeli woman is saying to you both, but we in the UK need help on this one. News today is that Ali is in Istanbul and poses a major threat.'

'I've just been told that much,' said Clive.

'OK, that much you also know, but he's a threat not only to Turkey, but also indirectly to us here at home. I have to ask you Clive, to do what you can to see that Ali is apprehended before it's too late. I don't mean you to do anything dangerous, but just provide some help as if you are one of our own on the ground, understand me?' said Dave Stephens forcefully.

'Yes. Sure. Just now the Israeli woman, Lena, has got my sister round her little finger, wants Kaylah to call Ali, to flush him out,' said Clive.

'Get her to do it. That's not a lot to ask, a phone call and remember the deal we have Clive. We do so want it all to work out for you when you get back, we really do. Just support your sister Kaylah in exposing Ali. Others will do the rest,' and then the call went dead.

Clive didn't like this Dave Stephens fellow. He was another bullish man. For some reason he thought of his father as he pushed his phone back in his pocket and rejoined the others. He felt like a trapped animal and he didn't like it.

On return, Clive found that thankfully he didn't actually have to do anything. Kaylah had already said she was OK about making the call to Ali. Lena, satisfied, had disappeared upstairs to work on what needed to be said. She wanted to get the message to Ali exactly right, and they both wanted it done, over with, before supper. All Clive did was to tell Kaylah he thought she had done the right thing. Yet even saying that left the nasty taste of insincerity in his mouth. All the while he was keeping things from his sister, and it was happening more and more, but he felt powerless to do anything about it. He tried to tell himself it would all work out one day soon. A future still beckoned when all their problems would be behind them. Well, maybe. His wistful thoughts were interrupted.

'Who was it who called?' Kaylah asked.

'Oh, the mobile, just a friend,' he replied. That was enough to tell Kaylah that Clive was keeping things from her. She wondered whether it was one of Winston's dodgy friends. Just at the moment one more insecurity was not what she needed. Clive then had an idea, something to change the conversation.

'How about tomorrow I take you out to do something I know you like – shopping. I saw a leaflet promoting a trip to the Grand Bazaar. It's a must for tourists, nothing like anything we've ever seen before. It's not so far from here and we can keep Jacob out of the sun. How about it?' he said.

'Think we have to wait and see how this telephone call to Ali works out first. But, yeah! Sounds good to me,' she said, happy at the prospect. Things eased between them.

Kaylah turned round as someone approached. It was Lena.

'All sorted. Clive, how about you sorting us some drinks from the bar whilst I help Kaylah make this call? Mine's a G&T.'

But even after several attempts, much to Lena's frustration and Kaylah's relief, Ali did not pick up.

31

When Krish called for Adam just before 9am that Wednesday morning he had little idea he would find him in such a state. He saw him scrunched up in a foetal position, head down, arms crossed in front of him. A young woman was at his side, another student, he surmised. Raqiyah introduced herself and then bent down, arm over Adam's shoulder to tell him that Krish was here. Adam let out a little whimper.

Krish and Raqiyah exchanged worried glances. With their help Adam was raised to his feet and led outside, a withdrawn shadow of himself, to the waiting white BMW Mini Pacman Krish had driven over in to pick him up. Raqiyah whispered into Krish's ear that she didn't think Adam had been fully well for some hours. He had been shaking and trembling since the previous night when the police had come into the university lecture hall. She didn't really understand it, it hadn't been that bad last night. She could only think Adam was maybe having some kind of breakdown.

'Is this something the Consulate might help with? We just don't know what to do,' she pleaded.

'Don't worry. I'll see someone sees him when we get to the Consulate. Can I have your number to let you know what happens, to keep you up to speed?' said Krish taking charge.

They exchanged numbers and then Krish drove off with a silent Adam in the front passenger seat. For Krish, this was an unexpected turn of events that was not going to be helpful. First though, he needed to see if he could get Adam seen by the Consulate doctor. Having initially thought he would take Adam out for breakfast in the city, he now revised his plan and drove straight back to the parking lot at the Consulate he'd left less than an hour previously. As he drove, he'd tried speaking to Adam on the journey back but got very little response, a few, barely audible, single words. Krish thought

Raqiyah's reading of the situation was probably accurate, Adam was seriously unwell. Once he'd parked up, he walked round to the passenger door and opened it.

'Come on Adam, we're here, at the Consulate. You're safe here. We'll see you're alright. Let's go and get that breakfast I promised you and then we'll get someone to see you. You're just not your usual self today. Are you up to eating something?' he asked.

Adam didn't speak, but got out of the car, following Krish through the exits from the car park and into the Consulate building.

'Think we need to get you seen by the doc before anything else. Sit yourself down here whilst I make a call,' Krish said, in as kindly a voice as he could muster. He was lucky, with the help of reception the doctor was reached and promised to be over in about an hour. As they had time to wait and he himself was hungry, he thought no harm would be done if he tried to get Adam to have some breakfast in the Consulate kitchen area.

'Come on, let's see what we can find for breakfast,' Krish said, leading Adam into the back of the building.

'No thanks, not hungry,' he heard Adam say.

'Well, we'll go into the kitchen out of the way. I could do with some coffee and toast,' Krish explained.

He led the way and in fact, with persuasion, Adam took a fruit juice and yoghurt, but he was still no more able to hold a conversation than earlier.

Dr Denver Arnold arrived in less than an hour and a side-room was found for him to see Adam. Krish was allowed to be present as his 'friend'. Adam didn't object, so the three squeezed into the tiny interview room.

Dr Arnold recognised the symptoms quickly, but was thorough in conducting a complete battery of physical as well as mental checks before coming to his diagnosis. Krish was surprised at how successful he was in getting Adam to give information. He could work for us, he thought. Dr Arnold had begun with simple things, the data he needed, name, age, address and so on. Then he moved on to stages that required more from Adam.

Krish added some background to what had happened in London the previous summer and autumn, Adam being taken and held hostage, escaping only to find himself caught up in the Armistice Day terrorism attack the previous November in London. Adam told Dr Arnold in brief about his recent bout of shaking beginning when they had been caught up in a Kurd demonstration violently broken up by the Turkish police on Tuesday afternoon. Then, when he was at a University of Istanbul lecture later in the evening, the police had raided and his shaking and trembling had become worse. Adam also confessed he hadn't been able to sleep since he'd arrived in Istanbul and had been getting increasingly anxious since the idea of coming back to Istanbul had first been discussed.

After half an hour the doctor asked Adam if he wanted to return home. Krish understood the question, but privately hoped it wouldn't come to that. He was much relieved when Adam answered.

'No,' Adam said, 'I want to stay with my friends, finish my summer placement here, but can you help me? I'm so very afraid and my body is doing things I can't control.' There were tears in Adam's eyes as he spoke. Krish thought it a pitiful scene.

'Sure, sure. If you want to stay, you must assure me you'll get some help through your GP when you get back home. I can give you something for now to cope with the anxiety and something to help you sleep, but you really must listen to your body and ensure you don't get into stressful situations in your remaining time here. I can see you again, here would be best, in a week from now, just to check how things are, but if things are no better then I will be suggesting an early flight home,' said Dr Denver Arnold.

'OK. Thanks,' said Adam as Dr Arnold was writing out a prescription.

'Can you go and get him these and make sure he knows how to take them? There's Lorazepam 2mg he's to take three times a day, and some 5mg he can take if he finds himself in times of heightened anxiety. They work pretty well in my experience, but call me again if you need to. Oh, the other medication is for him to take at night only. That's the Quetiapine.' said Dr Arnold handing Krish the prescription.

'Sure, no problem. We'll keep an eye on him and I'll make sure he understands the medication he's to take. It all goes with being a consular official,' Krish said with a smile.

'One final thing Adam, I think you would benefit from some therapy, someone to talk to when you get back to England. You'll need to see your GP to tell them what has happened anyway, but ask them about counselling services. Tell them what has happened here and what medication I put you on. While you're here in Turkey, is there anyone else who might keep a close eye on you over the coming days? I don't suppose Krish can be at your beck and call with his duties here at the Consulate. Do you have someone else here who will listen to you, someone you can talk to?' asked Dr Arnold.

Adam nodded to both enquiries. Krish explained Adam was with a small student group. After the doctor had left, Adam found he was to have been left in the interview room whilst Krish went to get the prescription, but the thought of staying in the enclosed space any longer brought on a wave of panic.

'I can't stay in here. It's too, too small. I can feel my chest tightening. I won't find it easy to breathe,' he explained. He realised he was gabbling, speaking too quickly.

'Tell you what,' said Krish, 'I'll put you outside in the garden. It's a delight, so restful and shady. Come on. I'll even see if we can lay on something for you to drink. I won't be gone long. Let me just show the doctor out and I'll be straight back, just two ticks.'

He was gone briefly. On his return Adam got up from the chair. The doctor had lifted his spirits a little and he followed Krish out into the Consul's garden. It was as Krish had described, a veritable oasis in the sapping heat of the city, with a fountain playing into the water of a small fish pond beside which he found a cushioned wooden chair where he was left to his own thoughts.

The doctor had suggested going home to England. In the present chaos of his mind, Adam definitely knew he didn't want to do that. It would be like admitting defeat. He wondered if he did go back whether they would expect him to repeat his summer placement again. No, he didn't want that and resolved come what may, he was going to stay. He became fearful about what his parents needed to be told and what effect this episode might have on them. It would be easier to keep it from them for now, he thought, but deceiving them made him feel more anxious again. He couldn't decide what to do. He was confused and knew it.

As he'd talked to the doctor something of the reality of his fragile mental health had dawned upon his consciousness. He knew from his conversations with his Exeter University psychotherapist Inger Walker that, much as he'd scorned the idea at first, there had been a real and damaging legacy from the trauma of the previous year; demons waiting to come up from below given the slightest encouragement.

Her counselling had done more good than he'd realised at the time. She had heard his anger, listened to his anxieties, calmed his fears, and visits to see her had helped keep him focussed and able to live with himself. He recalled the last meeting they had had when he had asked her whether she thought he ought to go to Istanbul, and remembered how he had, despite his fears, decided that was exactly what he wanted to do.

Thinking about the drugs Krish had gone out to get for him, he knew he had never taken drugs to help his state of mind before and the thought worried him, but he didn't have any choice, did he? Either he had to manage his uncontrolled state of mind or he'd have to go back. Besides, many students used drugs as legal highs or of an illicit kind, and they remained students. He then thought of his own drug of choice, alcohol, and how big a part it had played in his student life so far. Maybe the relative absence of it here whilst he was in Istanbul had meant his demons had been able to get back in. He knew he would now be using prescribed drugs – no real difference, some normality in it, he supposed. He started to feel tremors and shaking and wondered how much longer Krish would be. Could he hold on and see off this latest wave of panic?

Then Krish was back, a white bag of boxed tablets in hand. He handed them over to Adam who checked them out. He knew what to take, and Krish knew Adam had taken in every word the doctor said.

'I'll take one of these now. You'd better get me back before they do something strange to me. Can you get me a glass of water, please?' Adam asked.

Krish took the comment to be a good sign. He'd wondered whether he'd come back to find Adam unwilling or unable to take his medication, then what would he do? He quickly agreed to fetch some water for Adam and went to the cooler dispenser in the foyer, taking a blue plastic cup. His own agenda, to work Adam as his minders in London had required, would have to wait for a better time than today. He wondered if a better time would ever come. Probably not soon enough for them. He needed to hear what other ideas they'd come up with in London. He knew he had work to do and time was moving on. Making the most of having Adam in Istanbul was looking right now like a lost cause.

As he drove Adam back, Krish thought through the call he would have to make to London as soon as he got back to the Consulate. Play it by ear, tell them how it is, he told himself. They always trust the judgement of the man on the ground, they've no choice at the end of the day.

Unfortunately for them and for him, Adam didn't look much use in the quest to track down Ali Muhammed. Gazing across at him, he saw Adam locked in his own thoughts again, vacantly gazing out of the car's passenger window. He would have to see if they had any other strings to their bow.

From the UK end, there didn't seem much to be done there in Istanbul to prevent an attack in Turkey. He hoped that perhaps GCHQ, SIS or one of their allies had picked up something new. He'd ask them directly presently. Always one of life's optimists, Krish would make enquiries and work away until some kind of solution could be found.

In the meantime, he was arriving back at Ataturk Apartments where he knew Raqiyah was waiting to receive Adam. He'd speak to her about taking time out to look after him, make sure she'd call him if necessary and then check back on Adam later when the medication had had chance to take effect. Hopefully he would get away without having to say too much to the other students about his role at the Consulate or how he knew Adam. He decided to play the part of a lowly consular official simply assisting with a hospitality invitation to one of the UK's young citizens, whose dramatic escape as an IS hostage the previous year demanded every consideration to be given to him by Her Majesty's Government.

In the event, he needn't have worried. Raqiyah was too interested in finding out how Adam was and in looking after him to pay any attention to Krish. After just a few words of explanation about Adam, the doctor and his medication, he was able to speed away, his mind focussing on how best to pick up the pieces and formulate some form of Plan B.

32

Adam found the medication had a helpful effect and much sooner than anticipated. Very soon after taking those first tablets at midday on Wednesday, he found he was calmer and able to hold proper conversations again. He took the rest of the day quietly, watching online TV, a film about the making of the early Wild West. Taking Lorazepam and Quentiapine was something he didn't want to do for long, but that night, having taken them, he slept like a baby, his first unbroken sleep since arriving in Istanbul.

On Thursday morning he found yesterday's feelings of anxiety had subsided, and at first wondered whether to drop his medication altogether. Maybe the sleep and the drugs had combined to give him the noticeable uplift. His trembling had also stopped, and feeling better seemed to add to the momentum in returning to a general state of well-being.

For some unknown reason he'd counted the days out since they'd left London. Four – then counted the number until their flight back, which came to eleven. This changed his perspective of his time in Istanbul. He was in a place that had an end, eleven days away. All of a sudden it seemed to make staying on to see it through an achievable ambition. If he took one day at a time, it wasn't long, he told himself. A feeling of some contentment and calm washed over him. He hoped the feeling would last. He then decided he would keep taking the medication, at least until he got back to London. He needed all the help he could get to manage the next eleven days. The risks in not taking the tablets whilst in Istanbul, which medically subdued the causes of his increased anxiety as he understood it, were just too great. He just had to get through his time here.

The others expressed their delight at seeing a much restored Adam when he was the last to show for breakfast. No-one was more pleased than Raqiyah who had taken

Krish's request to watch over Adam very much to heart. Now she hardly left his side for a moment.

Today, they had no fixed programme, Abdul having decided to leave them to explore the city by themselves. He'd phoned through to Raqiyah and shared a few ideas and then excused himself, pleading that he was overworked at the university. Students got time off in the summer, not so the staff like himself, he complained wearily.

The foursome wanted very much to include Adam and not have to leave him behind on his own. Splitting the group into two didn't appeal either, Bilal and Sophie going off leaving Raqiyah to be with Adam. All voiced the wish they stay together and quickly agreed that after breakfast they would go and find the Grand Bazaar, with its labyrinth of alley streets and thousands of booth-like shops. It wasn't so far from Beyoglu where they were staying. They just had to drop down across the Galata Bridge and into the Bazaar Quarter of Beyazit. It looked easy enough on the map.

As they talked over the idea, Adam kept insisting he was fine and he'd be happy to go out and stroll round with them. What he was saying was something everyone wanted to believe and to make it easier still they agreed they'd call a taxi for 10am to take them down into the city to what their smart phones quickly informed them was Istanbul's biggest and busiest bazaar, a tourist sight not to be missed. Sophie was particularly excited as it meant she could shop. Adam and Bilal took the girls' shared enthusiasm in their stride. An air of holiday relaxation had at last come over them.

In the quarter of an hour they had before the taxi arrived, Adam decided to put a few posts up on Facebook. He knew his parents would be following him and he wanted to make sure they weren't going to worry. Looking through his phone photo album, he chose and posted the best of the many pictures he'd already taken over the past few days – Sufi Dervishes spinning, the Blue Mosque and Hagia Sophia, shots of the university where they'd gone to the Gulen lecture. Some were silly shots of him and the others larking around by shop windows. When he had finished, he realised he had actually done something positive and this further lifted his spirits. Likes and replies from friends came in even as he added the last of the uploads. It more than filled the waiting time before their bright yellow Hyundai 'TAKSI' arrived.

Grabbing his phone and wallet, Adam rejoined the others and they headed off. Raqiyah seemed to have taken his care very much to heart and to be frank he had to admit he was rather enjoying her attention. He sensed a reciprocal pleasure in her.

Bilal paid the taxi driver when he dropped them off by the Oracular Gate, saying the three could settle up with him later. The taxi driver helpfully signposted them which way to walk and pointed out a place where they could get a taxi back. Then he sped off leaving the four in the sun, before heading slowly into the busy shadows of the Grand Bazaar. As ever the air was filled with the now familiar sounds and smells of the city, loudspeaker calls to the faithful, street hawkers seeking customers, kebabs smoking as they cooked in the open air.

They passed some secluded courtyards called Hans, enclosed two or even three-storey areas, each dedicated to the production and trade of one particular commodity, be it brightly coloured carpets and rugs, pottery, birdcages, leatherwear or metalworking. Everywhere they went people pressed in on them. Soon they were lost in the Grand Bazaar, its labyrinth of narrow streets and souks. For an hour they wandered in and out of shops. Raqiyah sometimes grabbed Adam's hand and pulled him over towards her, ensuring, so he thought, that he wouldn't get detached from the others.

An hour of strolling and yet they knew there was still so much more to explore. Raqiyah had bought her uncle Abdul a traditional brass coffee pot as a thank-you present, something everyone said they would chip in on. They'd arrived at one of the Han courtyards where jewellery was made, the Zincirli Han. It was a beautiful cool space with white stone and orange brick arches surrounding them on two levels. Carefully placed plants and a character tree added to the special atmosphere.

Sophie was entranced and ordered some earrings. Whilst they were being made, they decided not to wander off too far for fear of not finding their way back to the jeweller. They settled on a traditional Turkish coffee shop and found a corner table to while away the next half hour. Adam was taking it all very much in his stride, much to his and everyone else's continued sense of relief.

Adam decided to try the local, strong and sweet coffee. The others settled for mint teas. They were laughing and joking about students they knew in Exeter and thinking that those who had stayed at home really had missed out. As they chatted their attention switched to people-watching. There were so many people moving across their vision just outside. It seemed that in the heat, everyone chose to live out their lives on the street, making the whole scene one big theatrical pageant.

Groups of young men in jeans and light shirts ambled by, a couple of women in long skirts, who could have been sisters, also passed by, lost in conversation. Children ran, street-hawkers plied their wares, cleaning shoes or selling items from trays. Within minutes hundreds of people had passed their window. Sophie then spoke up.

'You don't see so many black people, but look, there's one family out enjoying themselves.'

Adam had already seen them. He wasn't sure, told himself it couldn't be; then got up, pushing back his chair recklessly so that it toppled over backwards, and ran quickly to the café entrance.

'Kaylah, can it be you?' Adam yelled.

He moved in closer and knew immediately it was. It wasn't a trick of the medication. She didn't twitch a muscle in her face, yet instinctively he knew that in that first glance and turn of the head she had recognised him too. He looked back at his astonished friends who were clearly thinking he had flipped.

'Adam?' was all she could say, disbelievingly.

One of the other tables was pulled across by the waiter and Adam's chair righted, ready for their enlarged group, and the buggy with a sleeping Jacob was wedged in. It took a few minutes to order more drinks and to make all the necessary introductions, and to begin to try and explain why they were all there in Istanbul.

Adam said that the university required them to undertake a summer placement in a Muslim context and his companions were fellow students here with him. He knew it didn't look like they were working, he jested, but that really was why they were here.

Kaylah said Clive, Jacob and herself had been given an expenses-paid holiday in the city and were making the most of it. She omitted mentioning Lena or the news Ali was in Istanbul and that she was there to help expose him. It was too difficult to explain, she was scared by the information anyway. Thankfully, the need to mention Ali Muhammed never arose.

When they had established where each was staying and compared sightseeing notes, Sophie realised that half an hour had passed and it was time to collect her new jewellery. Kaylah liked the idea of visiting the jewellery Han courtyard and they all set off together. Adam liked being part of this unexpectedly larger group and walked beside Kaylah asking her how she was doing.

'Well, I'm juggling looking after Jacob, looking after a flat for someone whilst they're abroad and thinking just how I'm to put to use the business skills I'm supposed to be good at now I've finished college,' said Kaylah.

'There must be a market for some of this stuff in London,' suggested Adam, waving his arms to point out the colourful array of items on sale around them.

'I've thought about that, Maybe, if I had the right contacts, got to know my product, found a supplier, something like these oriental rugs and carpets...' She got distracted and her words trailed off as she remembered Ali's offer of help.

'I don't know what I'll do when I finish at uni, but I've got two more years before I have to cross that particular bridge. But what a coincidence, you being here, unbelievable.'

He paused before adding, 'Kaylah, do you mind me talking about Ali?'

'No, go ahead,' she said, all too guardedly.

'Oh, it was nothing really,' said Adam, sensing that he should back off. 'Coming into somewhere like this has brought a lot of things back for me. Hasn't been easy.'

'I can understand that. Nor for me. I have to say, I wouldn't have come without Clive coming along too. He's such a help. You wouldn't believe how much your life changes when you have a little one to look after,' said Kaylah.

The group were at the Mahmut Pasha Gate leading out of the Bazaar. It was then Kaylah and Clive excused themselves saying they needed to get back to their hotel, Jacob needing his next change and feed. Adam and Kaylah exchanged mobile numbers, but the rushed parting didn't allow for making any concrete follow-up arrangements. Adam felt they were parting with a half-begun conversation left hanging between them.

'Great to see you again,' Adam called out, as his friends were leading the way back into the still unexplored areas of this vast market place. As soon as they were out of earshot, Adam turned back to Raqiyah.

'That's too much of a coincidence, don't you think? The two people closest to the Ali Muhammed attack last November, end up unexpectedly in Istanbul at the same time and in the same place. Can I tell you something in confidence, Raqiyah? I need someone I can trust to talk to.'

They walked on together, moving a little away from Bilal and Sophie who were still talking about the jewellery Sophie had bought, Bilal telling her she had been ripped off, she should have bartered more, held out for a better deal.

'What is it, Adam? Something on your mind?' asked Raqiyah, moving close.

'This has to stay between us, only us, right?' said Adam.

'OK. Tell me,' she said with a look of seriousness Adam had not seen before.

'Since last November, the British Security and Intelligence Services have kept in touch with me off and on. The strange thing is, the security guy who drove me back to North London when I escaped from IS, nice bloke actually, well, he contacted me again just before we left London for Istanbul last weekend. Then he simply said he knew I was going to Istanbul and he wanted to give me his contact number should I ever need it. He made it sound like some kind of continuing support. At the time I didn't believe that was all it was,' Adam paused.

'And you know what, he called me again when we arrived here. Then, you'll never guess what happened next. I get a second call from, yes Krish, to say he's also in Istanbul. I didn't tell you that my invitation to have breakfast at the Consulate was to have breakfast with Krish, did I,' said Adam.

'Wow! This is sounding more and more like a spy thriller movie. You must be joking?'

'Absolutely no joking,' he responded, his face a study in seriousness and he knew from one look at Raqiyah's face that she now knew he wasn't messing about.

'So, did he say any more when you went to have breakfast?' she enquired.

'Well, I think things took an unexpected turn so far as he was concerned. You see he really did have to look after me. He got a doctor in to see me and all I can say is that he was really helpful. Not once did he say anything or ask anything of me. Then, when he brought me back here, that's when you saw him, that was Krish,' explained Adam.

'The guy who asked me to keep an eye out for you?' asked Raqiyah.

'The very same. But since seeing Kaylah just now, it's got me thinking. I don't know whether my mind is playing tricks again, but I think we're both in Istanbul for a reason. Something's going on here, and my guess is that it's to do with Ali Muhammed. These people aren't just being nice to people like Kaylah and me, they want to use us to reach people, to do things,' said Adam.

258

'That sounds a very reasonable conclusion to me,' she said, 'maybe Krish backed off telling you everything when he saw what state you were in. You were a different guy yesterday,' said Raqiyah thoughtfully.

'Could be, but I'll only know what's going on if I get talking to Krish again. Do you think I should?' he asked.

'You need to be sure you can handle what he tells you. You are in a bit of a fragile state at the moment. But it's your call. If you want to leave it until you're certain you're up for it, a day or two, why not?' she said.

'But with your help, if you were willing that is, I reckon I could call him. You see I can't handle not knowing what's really going on. I think it would help me, knowing a bit more, instead of all this guessing in the dark like a blind man groping around not being able to tell what's what. I know I'll feel better knowing than not knowing, dealing with some certainties,' he explained.

'But what if it's bad stuff. I mean, if Krish said Ali was here in Istanbul and that he was here because things were going to kick-off, like they did in London? That's what you have to consider Adam. If it was that, and I hope it isn't, are you ready for that?' she asked.

'I'd still do it, call him, only it would make a difference to me if you're with me, when I make the call. They say a problem shared is a problem halved, and that's how I am feeling about it now. But I feel bad bringing you into this,' he said, only not really believing what he was saying. In truth he desperately wanted Raqiyah in it with him. He didn't feel bad at all.

'No, I'm in Adam, I'm in. Call him,' she told him.

They decided to make the call to Krish when they got back to their AAA Apartments later. They'd find somewhere quiet in the apartments where they were less likely to be disturbed. It was agreed.

33

When Kaylah, Clive and Jacob got back to the All Seasons Luxury Hotel early on Thursday afternoon, Kaylah was tired and just wanted to rest. It was still early weeks since Jacob was born and some days she felt more tired than others and this hot afternoon was one of them. After a change and feed Jacob was content sleeping in her arms as she sat in the upholstered easy chair. She kicked off her shoes and settled into the comfortable chair, gazing fondly at Jacob's relaxed and satisfied face. Such innocence, she thought. The distinct smell of a small baby was something intimate and she drew him closer still.

It hadn't been such a bad thing coming to Istanbul, she thought. The city was amazing, quite unlike London, but still possessing all the similar energy and life of a major metropolis which kind of made it begin to feel like home. The morning in the Grand Bazaar outstripped Edmonton Market any time.

She'd been amazed at the chance meeting with Adam Taylor. How extraordinary he should be here with his university friends. She thought she might go back to the Bazaar again. On the one hand she quite liked the jewellery courtyard Sophie had been to and on the other, she wanted to see what kind of prices carpets and rugs were, just to check out whether there might be a business idea worth exploring further in the future.

Clive announced he was going down to the bar where he had seen some football supporters from England and thought he'd hang around in the public area where there was a widescreen TV and see what was going on. Kaylah was happy to be given a few minutes in her own space. She thought how the now familiar surroundings of her hotel room made her feel safe and, instead of picking up her half-finished magazine, she began to think she might fall asleep where she sat. The white net curtain let in a soft light, the slightly open window moving the net back and forth with the light following in shifting mesmeric patterns on the wall in front of her. She felt herself drifting off.

Rather than come with them to the Bazaar, Lena had, at the last minute, gone off to the Consulate again to work. Kaylah was all alone in the quiet with Jacob. Just as her eyelids were falling shut, she suddenly thought she ought to put Jacob into his buggy to sleep, fearing she might drop him if she dozed off holding him.

Settling back into the chair, her eyes once more feeling heavy, the world of her room becoming ever more distant, it was then her mobile rang quietly, insistently, somewhere under the buggy. She had to get it or Jacob might wake.

Once the phone was in her hand she was wide awake and alert in an instant. The screen said it was Ali. She tried to collect her thoughts and rehearse what she was supposed to say, using the lines Lena had given her, but in the crisis of the moment her mind remained obstinately blank. For the life of her she couldn't think what on earth she was supposed to say. For fear of waking Jacob, she couldn't let it ring any longer and she clicked on the green answer button, getting up from her chair and moving away from the still sleeping Jacob.

'Hello,' she ventured cautiously.

'Hi Kaylah. You tried to reach me. Sorry I couldn't take it earlier. I just can't answer calls when other people are around. You understand.'

'Yes,' she said.

'Wondered what you wanted. Is everything alright? How's Jacob doing? Is he well?' He couldn't stop the questions tumbling out.

'I'm in Istanbul, Ali,' she told him.

'What? What do you mean?' He was thrown, disorientated. Had he misheard? The conversation paused.

'I'm in Istanbul on holiday with Clive, you know, my brother.'

'Yes, but I can't believe it.' Ali didn't know whether to mention he was here too. It would create a huge risk, and not

261

knowing what to do, he decided he had to play safe and stay silent as to his own whereabouts. He never liked betraying where he was anyway, not since the drone attacks that had been meant for him back home.

'Are you enjoying it?' he asked.

'Yes, we went round the Grand Bazaar this morning. I'm having a rest now,' said Kaylah.

Kaylah didn't feel she could say anything about meeting up. She couldn't betray the fact she knew he was there, and had forgotten what Lena had suggested she should say in the eventuality that Ali didn't disclose his location.

'Have you any other plans for sightseeing?' he asked.

'I'd like to go back to the bazaar. There was some jewellery I liked,' she said.

'Well, you have a good time, and look after Jacob. I was in Istanbul once, I'm sure you'll enjoy it. Good to hear from you,' said Ali.

Kaylah didn't want the conversation to end without feeling she had found out more.

'What are you doing now?' she said.

'I've had time off, I needed a few months, but I'm serving my people again now. They've put me in charge of a group of men on a mission. Expect you'll get to hear what I've been up to one day. I'm a man under orders, that's the way it is.' Ali didn't feel he could say any more and the conversation stalled again. Then he started worrying in case Kaylah took Jacob to any of the targets identified for the coming Friday. He didn't know what to say without sounding like he was giving something away.

Kaylah remembered that Lena wanted her to get Ali to meet her, to bring him out into the open. She broke the silence first.

'You still there Ali?'

'Yes, just thinking, that's all,' he said.

'Do you get to travel around at all? I mean do you ever get chance to travel abroad yourself?' she asked.

Ali's instinct for self-preservation was instantly aroused. He knew Kaylah was now someone else's puppet, and some hidden strings were being pulled behind the scenes.

'No, can't say I do. Look, it's been good to hear from you again. Don't leave it so long before you call again. Until next time. Got to go.' He ended the call, his sense of alarm telling him his enemies were getting near. It could be the only reason why she was here. They brought her!

Kaylah immediately called Lena who picked up straight away.

'Lena, Ali called me back. He caught me unawares. I told him I was in Istanbul, but he never said where he was and when I tried to push him he ended the call,' she said.

'That's OK. The good thing is you re-established contact. We can build on that. Some of our technical guys might be able to locate where he actually phoned you from, so the call will have been a great help. I think you did really well. Did he say anything else?' asked Lena.

'Yes, he said he'd had some time off, but was now in charge of a group of men again. On a mission he called it. He reckoned I'd hear about it some day when it went in the news. But he seemed reluctant to say any more. He described himself as a man under orders, and I think he was keeping his cards close to his chest because of his duty, his loyalty to IS,' Kaylah reported.

'Did he ask who you were with? And what about Jacob? Did he ask after him?' Lena quizzed.

'I told him Clive was here with me. I didn't tell him where we were staying and he never asked, thank goodness. Having spoken to him, he seemed, well, so very near. I don't feel safe knowing he's nearby. I'm glad you're here. The state I was in, I might well have inadvertently told him where I was, but I didn't. Yeah, he asked after Jacob. I think he's fond of him, I could sense it in the way he spoke.'

'Look, when I get back, around 5pm I hope, we'll talk further about what to do next. I'd imagine we'll need to think about making a follow-up call, but let's talk it through carefully first. Have you any plans for the rest of the afternoon?' Lena inquired.

'No, Clive's gone down to the bar and I was about to get a few minutes shut-eye. I've been feeling so tired. I blame Jacob, but he's adorable, so can't be too hard on the little fellow. I'll see you later then,' and with that Kaylah ended the call.

Ali, meanwhile, decided he needed a few more minutes on his own before going back to rejoin his men. He was once again in the crowds outside the Blue Mosque, waiting until 3pm to see if each day's routines were exactly the same. He had insisted that this time he had to come down to observe on his own. As he leaned against a wall in the shade, his mobile still in the open palm of his hand, he had to think fast. He had a mission to lead with a countdown now in hours, rather than days, requiring his concentrated preparation, until all hell broke loose.

Kaylah's call had thrown a cat amongst the pigeons. In the minutes since the call had ended he felt certain she knew he was in Istanbul and equally certain she had been brought there to track him down. He had to be doubly on his guard. The infidels knew something was afoot and they knew he was here.

At the same time, he couldn't help but explore the idea that he might, just once, be able to see his new son. All he needed to do was exercise some cunning. She would call him again, of that he was certain, but next time it wouldn't be him who would be lured into a trap: he would set one of his own making. But how was he going to make sure Jacob was kept safe from the chaos that would hit Istanbul on Friday afternoon? He needed a plan and soon.

34

Anna Simonsson never liked Thursdays. The end of the week in Tel Aviv in the nondescript office of the Israeli Security Service meant for most people that their thoughts were turning elsewhere, to the coming weekend, anywhere but the job in hand. By Thursday, the meetings that kick-started each week were over, and people's minds would be thinking about the coming Sabbath preparations on Friday, getting home and meeting up with family, taking some time off for sport or culture or whatever. Not so for Anna.

She simply didn't understand her colleagues' lack of focus. Disregarding her colleagues' pre-weekend conversations and the office banter filling the air, she applied herself with unceasing commitment to the task of spotting the anomaly, the unique traces and markers that others, who had different minds, would miss.

Making sense, finding the picture, these were the only things that would make her weekend. Her colleagues had submitted their reports as to possible Ali scenarios the previous day. She'd read them all in minutes and decided they didn't possess one imaginative idea between them. She could have written them herself. They were a waste of time, containing nothing new.

Ever since that first report had come in on Tuesday saying that two men and a vanload of explosives had been picked up on the main road near Ankara, bound for Istanbul, she knew that somehow, someone, somewhere, would be trying to replace those losses and send in another load of explosives. They had to be found and time was running out.

She worked as if the safety of many depended solely on her efforts and she ruthlessly drove herself on. With the agreement of her new boss Elias, she hadn't left her workstation for forty-eight hours. She knew that she needed to freshen herself up, but there wasn't time for that, not yet.

She liked Elias, he appreciated her skills and gave her space to do what she did best. She knew in her head there was a fine line between working at her limit and tipping over the edge, though she wasn't always very good at reading the signs. Right now all she knew was that she didn't have many more hours left to give.

In front of her, the satellite imagery of lined dots on the screen, representing thousands of moving vehicles, were beginning to dance before her eyes again and reluctantly she knew it was time to pull herself away from her screen, get off her chair and take a break. She went out of her room to the staff vending machine to take yet another chocolate confectionary snack and a coffee.

Guilt about the calories played with her mind. She knew she must have put on another 3-4 kilos since the beginning of the week. Waiting for the coffee machine to grind the beans, ever so slowly, and discharge the boiling water into the cup beneath, she wondered whether this time IS would get away from her, keeping always one step ahead. She was running out of avenues to explore. The thought was too painful to think about.

Returning to her desk ten minutes later, able to focus again, she went through in her head once more all the intelligence she had been given, what was known about the van and the two other IS vehicles she herself had traced leaving the Mosul area. If only they had had time to get an attack to them earlier. They'd since moved on and she'd gone over the route they'd taken time and again. She could see where the van had been apprehended, and how the two other vehicles had gone on to Istanbul and once there they had disappeared, lost in the city traffic.

In spite of enquiries her colleagues had made of the Turkish authorities to be given access to on-street CCTV of traffic entering the city, nothing had yet been forthcoming. Turkey wasn't always helpful in such matters and she discounted ever getting anything now that 24 hours had passed and she'd heard not a word back let alone a set of images to work with.

She'd calculated that it would take a day at least for IS to prepare another vehicle to send to Istanbul and that it only had a limited number of routes it could safely use to get it into Turkey undetected. Each and every vehicle she'd watched and followed so far had taken her to a dead end. She had just one final string to her bow, one last road to check out.

This was a much longer route circling in a great arc anti-clockwise from Mosul, heading east, then north on quiet roads, eventually hitting the main road west at Agri, before passing through the ancient city of Erzurum and on to the west and Istanbul. It was an unlikely route because normally it meant the Kurds would stop any suspicious IS transport, but it had to be checked out, for she believed IS and the Kurds were cooperating this time, and if so, the replacement explosives could be let through.

It was late on Thursday afternoon, when colleagues were beginning to leave for the day, that Anna first thought she might be onto something. She zoomed in using maximum magnification on the satellite imagery and spotted it, an articulated lorry with a single container on the back.

It took a further three hours of non-stop concentration to track its entire journey. By that time she had followed the truck from where it was loaded near a Mosul warehouse to its final Istanbul destination. This time the satellite imagery allowed her to follow it right into Istanbul itself and into the Beyoglu district before it disappeared near some apartment buildings. She immediately called her boss Elias to share her news.

'I'm coming through,' Elias told her and hung up.

She pointed out the articulated lorry with its single container load, jumping the frames so that he didn't have to watch the whole thing. She froze the picture at the last shot she had.

'What is that Elias? What is that?' she exclaimed like the excited child who'd just found the hidden matzo bread at the Passover seder.

'That's got to be it. You're a genius Anna, a bloody marvel. What time was that taken, Istanbul time?' he quizzed, as his index finger excitedly jabbed at the lorry in the city on her screen.

'Just a moment, I need to work that out. The satellite time clock and the local time are different.' She flicked to another screen to do the calculations.

'It arrived today late afternoon Istanbul time and has been parked up by those apartments since then,' she said.

'Anna, send me a report, and then get yourself off home. You're so tired, you need a break now you've done all that is required for the present. Let me have your report and then go,' ordered Elias, seeing in her face the all too evident stress from overwork.

With that, each hurried to their respective tasks, Anna to furnish Elias with his report, Elias to ring Jerusalem. He knew as soon as he put his phone down, swift action would follow before the lorry with its load had a chance to disappear or, worse still, detonate its deadly cargo.

Within Israeli Intelligence a crisis conversation took place between the Prime Minister and the Head of Mossad. They went back a long way and usually the Prime Minister just nodded through any actions placed before him, trusting that his old friend always delivered what was required, observing the political sensitivities involved.

This time however, the action Mossad proposed to take place in Turkey was so full of risk, the conversation between the two became heated. However, in the end, the Head of Mossad got his way and immediately phoned through to authorise what he ironically called, 'Operation Turkish Delight'.

35

Whilst Clive was in the hotel foyer his phone rang. He was surprised to see that not Winston, but Wicked Will himself was calling him. He didn't dare not answer. Will didn't wait to check who he was talking to, he was so cocksure of himself, he waded straight in.

'Now listen here Clive, bro, I'm so glad you've had a lucky break, landed on your feet, a holiday in Istanbul and all that. Now I know how you is spending your ill-gotten gains. But let's put all that to one side. Me, I'm just looking after the business that still needs to be run back home. Things are tighter on the profit margins lately. People don't realise how hard it is for those running a business and I need you to take care of something for me at your end. It's not a lot to ask of a loyal friend. Are you hearing me Clive?' checked Will.

'Yes, Will. I is listening real careful,' said Clive, feeling Will's intimidating presence reaching across two thousand miles.

'As good fortune would have it, you are the one person well placed to help me with a delivery. You have always been so good at that kind of thing in the past. Deliveries, drops, pickup, I know I can rely on you to do it properly. This time. I've a lot riding on a package I need, Clive, you follow?' said Will.

'Yes, I understand.'

Clive's mind went back to the way he'd been drawn into the gangs and drugs delivery world in North London. The first time, it was his friend Winston asking for his help. He didn't know then he was stepping into the drug gang's world. He had no idea it was so close, so easy a line to cross and that was it, he'd unwittingly crossed it. Since then he'd been trapped, sucked down into a world he now desperately wanted to escape, a hell with no way back. He felt his heart sinking lower as he recalled the Post Office robbery last November.

He remembered the promises Dave Stephens had made about granting him a clean sheet from all this when he got back. It all sounded such an impossible dream now that Will was on the other end of the line. He couldn't see how any free pardon could ever happen. Will had got his hand round his throat. He was so choked up, he could hardly speak. Will meantime spoke on, giving instructions he wanted followed.

'Now, take this down, Clive, no messing. This has got to be done exactly as I say. Listen carefully. Get it down right, do it right and you get a big reward. Follow my meaning?' said Will, hissing.

'Yes, I understand. Take it down. Big reward,' he intoned.

'A special parcel of precious items is arriving in Istanbul from Afghanistan on Thursday afternoon. Delivered by courier driver. You don't need to know any more about it than that. I want to make it easy for you. Now, tell me where you're staying. I'll see it's delivered there, directly to you personally. You see I need to let him know right now where to take it. I've paid for it and I want to be sure I get all of it, so I'm calling someone I can trust. See!' said Will. Clive felt he had no choice but to do everything Will asked of him, sensing a harassed tone of desperation in Will's voice he'd not heard before.

'A delivery. Thursday afternoon, first thing, you say.' Clive proceeded to read out the hotel's address from a card he'd picked up from reception when they'd first arrived. He'd slipped it into his pocket just to be sure they never got totally lost when they went sightseeing, so they could always get back.

'I'll text you with the time he'll be arriving. Now Clive, you have to do this for me. I trust you on this. Listen here. My usual delivery man from Turkey to London has been taking a cut of what's mine and sending it to Amsterdam or somewhere. I'll sort him, you'll see, double-crossing bastard! He doesn't know it yet, but he's out of a job from now, he'll never work, let alone walk again when I've finished with him. No-one cuts out Will without getting cut up themself. He'll find out there is nowhere beyond my reach,' said an increasingly incoherent Will.

'What do I do with it when it comes?' Clive suddenly thought to ask, interrupting Will's flow of vitriol.

'I want you to simply send it on by regular courier. Easiest job you've ever had. It's the safest way for all of us. The delivery firm will simply ask you what it is, what address it's to go to, if you packed it yourself, what its value is, that kind of thing. The usual boring crap. I'm getting someone to forward on all that kind of stuff you'll need. Keep an eye on your phone messages. All you have to do is copy it down. A bright lad like you won't find that too difficult will he?' said Will.

'In a text message to me,' said Clive.

'You just need to wrap it up securely, tape it up, leave it at hotel reception, they'll collect and do the rest. Simple innit? A piece of cake. Then you can carry on with your little holiday in the sun. Let me know when you get back Clive, I can always use a good delivery boy.'

'Do I pay anything?' asked Clive.

'Yeah! Forgot to mention that. It will cost you around fifty quid. Don't you worry, you'll more than get your money back!' said Will with a laugh.

'That's about two hundred Turkish Lira, Will. OK, I'll wait to hear then, Will,' Clive meekly answered before Will signed off.

What did he do now, Clive wondered. Will was not someone to double cross. He thought he'd call Winston. He thought Winston was the only friend he had he could talk to about all this. He glanced at his watch calculating what time it was in London. He gave up and decided to ring anyway. This was so very important. He heard the phone pick up.

'Hi Winston, how you doing?' said Clive trying to be upbeat.

'Good, thanks. Sun shining on you too I guess. Sure is quieter with you and Kaylah out of London. And how's that

271

baby nephew of yours doing? You two start taking him on international holidays young, he'll be wanting them the rest of his life, you wait,' he chuckled.

'Winston, I ain't called for no reason,' said Clive impatiently.

'Alright, alright. What's up then, bro?' asked Winston.

'That fella Will has just called me up. Wants me to be his drugs fixer over here now. I just want out, you know I do, but you know how persuasive he can be. He's one scary dude,' said Clive.

'Hey! Don't get so worried. Will's deluding himself to think he can rule the world. Now what does he want you to do?' asked Winston.

'Fix up a drugs delivery for him, here in Istanbul, would you believe. Receive a parcel, then send it on by parcel post. He made it sound so easy. He's got the parcel coming here to my hotel, tomorrow. What do I do?' asked Clive as Winston went quiet, clearly thinking what to say.

'No way can he know what you do or don't do about his stuff from where he's sitting in his flat in Tottenham. One more drug delivery that don't make it to his London empire ain't going to ruin Will's world. He's got so much going on he hardly knows what day of the week it is. The guy's losing it Clive. You listen to me. If you don't want to do it, you don't do it. But are you sure, Will pays well?' said Winston.

'I'm sure, Winston, I want out,' he said.

'Well, just think of a good reason why it all went wrong and send Will a text. No way can he check it out. Why not be out of your hotel when the stuff's delivered and say the police got it. Don't get involved man,' said Winston. None of the suggestions rang as plausible in Clive's ear.

'He'll suss that one out and then I'll be in for it when I get back. He knows how to find me,' said Clive.

'OK, use that guy you said might help you get free of all this. What's his name? The spook you told me about. Can you reach him?' suggested Winston.

'Him, I don't like the man,' said Clive.

'Yeah, well, you've got nothing to lose by testing him out. You'll earn his duty to protect you by putting this on to him,' said Winston, this time sounding much more convincing.

'Yes, I'll do that. I've no other option open to me. I'd be covering my back too. Then all I have to say to Will is that the border people were waiting and took it. Nothing I could do about it,' said Clive, warming to the idea.

'See, you got yourself an answer. Enjoy your holiday! Any idea when you're back?' asked a now cheerful Winston.

'No, not just yet, a week or so I guess. I'll call you when I'm back in town,' he said, the thought of when they might return not actually having crossed his mind until Winston mentioned it.

After his helpful call to Winston was over, he looked for Dave Stephen's number in his phone contacts and gave him a call. He filled him in on exactly what Will had told him. This time, Dave was civil and sounded warmer, listening intently. Maybe, he just thought me another loser before, a drug dealer he despised.

Dave told Clive to leave the matter with him. The parcel would be intercepted as it arrived at the hotel. Clive's job was to lie low, to keep out of it and just to forward on any messages from Will directly to Dave who said he'd know what to do with them. Dave went so far as to venture that he thought Will's days as a drug baron were numbered, but added cynically, there would no doubt be someone else in the wings just itching to take over.

It was already early afternoon when Will's text with all the details came through. Clive acknowledged its safe receipt and then, not allowing himself the chance to change his mind, immediately forwarded it on to Dave Stephens. Dave responded with a brief thank you message coupled with an assurance that the matter would be fully taken care of and a reminder that his promise to Clive made in London still stood good so long as he delivered on his side of the deal.

Now all Clive had to do was to see out the consequences of having betrayed Wicked Will. One tactic he

273

was certain of – moving quickly back upstairs, he decided whatever happened downstairs, he was going to stay well away from the hotel foyer for the rest of the day.

36

Big Harry had been a loyal England Football supporter since as young as he could remember. His dad was into scrap metal, and with the modern obsession of recycling and the insatiable appetite of a world that would buy any old metal going, his father was doing very nicely.

Harry had just celebrated his twenty-fifth birthday before leaving Plymouth, his dad buying him a red Audi with wide wheels. It wasn't new and Harry wasn't worried where it had come from. All said and done, he was well pleased with it. Family loyalty was a big thing with the McNamaras. After that came loyalty to one's mates, one's local football team, – Plymouth Argyle – and one's country – England – in that order.

Harry hated the way England was in decline. There was no political leadership worthy of the name in his view. All had sold out to liberal thinking and had forgotten the people they were supposed to represent. In recent years he'd found a movement with a voice he could agree with. Soon after the English Defence League came to birth early in 2009 Harry had, as a young teenager duly signed up.

He thought it was cool to be part of a modern media-savvy outfit. They said it how it was and were prepared to take to the streets. He had no problem persuading his like-minded Plymouth friends to travel with him at weekends to rallies and demonstrations up and down the land. He liked the honesty of the anti-jihadist ideology and the anti-immigration stand they took. When the EDL all too soon fell apart, he'd looked round for something to replace it and in the newly formed Britain First Democratic Party, he believed he had found a worthy successor to call his own.

Racism and Islamophobia were second nature, a basic instinct, but to get political change he was coming to understand the need for it to be covert and unexpressed if it were to be effected. The EDL, he thought, hadn't held back, and in so doing lost their way and ultimately collapsed. Now, the BFDP leadership understood these things. They stood for the silent majority, the ordinary English people, and knew how to speak to them and for them without alienating wider future support from signing up. Things were definitely on the up as far as Harry was concerned.

Being well-built, having a naturally strong physique, further strengthened by working with weights in the gym and taking anabolic steroids (though he kept quiet about that), he soon came to the attention of the political leadership. His powerful presence was quickly seen to come combined with an aggressive personality; he was seized on and invited to head up the BFDP South West England Division.

It was his piercing dark-blue eyes that settled it for the local political party scout. He had that ability to look at someone until they were paralysed, like a rabbit in the headlights. He was a natural, a born leader. However, all this more serious political interest was never allowed to interfere with his sacred mission, being a loyal England supporter.

The trip to Istanbul was important to Harry. The match itself against Turkey didn't rate highly in his opinion. It was just a pre-season friendly and he thought it had been arranged out of political correctness, by people who hadn't got the heart of football properly in focus. He couldn't put his finger on it exactly, Turkey mattered to someone, maybe the pro-European lot, maybe the pro-immigrant crowd or even those who thought Muslims were a good thing. But, to his mind a match against France, Germany or even Spain would have been many times better. The long and expensive trip out had to be offset against the positives, after all he had his closest mates with him and where they went together there was always excitement and fun to be had.

He'd nearly come to blows with the plane stewards when some smart arse little 'Paki' guy in a window seat ended up sitting near them. Harry thought parts of the country had been taken over by such people and he loathed them. If he had anything to do with it, he would keep the

South West of England pure. It would be for the English, allowing only for the local identities of Cornish, Devonian, and that of the other old counties of the West Country to remain to bring local colour. The Padstow Mummers or the Ottery St Mary annual running of flaming tar barrels weren't to his liking or taste, but he could live with such traditions in the future vision of the England he saw lying ahead and almost in reach.

The hotel where they were staying was conveniently located near the Galatasaray Stadium in Beyoglu, Istanbul. Harry looked forward to the match that coming Friday. He always enjoyed a game, even when he and the lads had a kick around in a local park. Matches gave him the adrenaline rush he needed and he knew this ground and occasion would not disappoint.

The Galatasaray Stadium was the home to a Turkish team that had won over fifty domestic trophies and were the only Turkish team to have won the European UEFA cup. He knew that all 52,000 seats would be sold and the stadium would live up to its heady atmosphere. Local Turkish fans were known to be some of the most fanatic in the world, the noise they made the loudest anywhere. Harry would be sure to give someone at the match a good hiding they wouldn't forget.

The few days of waiting before the game were taken up with finding places to drink whilst escaping the attentions of the ever watchful eye of local police who seemed to have been assigned to them since they left the airport. Harry and his mates had come early because Stu Brown, the group's youngest member had announced his forthcoming wedding. Stu and Penny had known each other since school and were getting wed when they got back. Penny had especially asked Harry to keep a watch on him as she knew Stu liked to get totally hammered given any excuse. So far, thought Harry, no-one had got anywhere near being hammered, small portion beers were all they had managed to procure. The heat just made everyone lethargic and they had not managed to find any night life to brighten their stay either.

Harry was all for an outing to liven up the pre-match waiting time and decided on the Thursday afternoon it was time to look for some presents to take home. They usually left shopping for presents until back at the airport, but this time, he told the lads, they'd got plenty of time and they'd get the chance to explore the best market out.

Taking the tram, they headed for the Grand Bazaar. Every now and then someone would step out and try to persuade them to buy their wares. Harry was getting annoyed by their persistence and found himself getting into the habit of physically pushing them to one side if they got in his way.

In one of the ancient markets called Hans, whilst Stu was choosing some jewellery for his fiancee back home, a shoe polisher, with his eyes on the shoes rather than Harry, made the mistake of standing in front of Harry, and bent down before him. Harry roared with laughter.

'How I love it when they bow down before me,' he cried, his friends catching up and crowding round. The man had brought him temporarily to a halt. Then Harry felt his shiny black Doc Marten boots being touched and looked down.

'Bugger off now mate. You're in my way. Speak English?' he said.

The man was persistent and the brushing continued. Then he stood up in front of Harry with his outstretched hand.

'Twenty five Lira,' he said.

'Push off you beggar,' Harry repeated.

The man wasn't going to move, and waved his hand under Harry's nose. He moved in closer. That was a mistake. Harry looked round, smiled at Stu, then suddenly dropped his forehead on the bridge of the man's nose and watched as he fell to the ground.

'There's one idiot in every city I go to,' said Harry. 'Walked right into me he did.'

Harry stepped over the prone figure of the fallen man, clutching his bleeding nose and trying to get up. By then a couple of the other stallholders had begun jabbering and pointing at Harry.

'Time to move on, don't want to start a party until after the match,' Harry declared.

A couple of turns and they were hidden away, lost among handbags and leather goods. A short while later they emerged back into the open air and hot sunshine in Beyazit Square.

'There's a university here. Looks more like a fort,' one of the group observed. They walked through the crowds without further incident, passing the university and ending up facing another hugely impressive building.

'This sign says this mosque was built to remember Suleman the Magnificent. I remember being told about him at school. That guy gave Christians a real whopping. Any of you lot been inside a mosque?' asked Harry.

The stony silence told Harry none of them had and none of them were keen to do so. Here was a chance for him to show who was boss, he thought. They never like going outside their comfort zone. This will be an education.

'Come on. We're paying a visit,' Harry called out, leading the way, the others feeling unsure.

They found the whole complex intimidating. The mosque itself was surrounded by a wall, outside which were many ancillary buildings, evidently used for all manner of peripheral religious activities. The entrance was located by following the crowds. It was, rather surprisingly, tucked away to the side, some distance from the central dome of the main building. Harry looked up at the soaring minarets, having to admit to himself they looked rather impressive. Once inside, the air was cooler. They were expected to remove their shoes, and seeing that everyone else did so, his entourage followed Harry's lead and followed suit. They moved into the mosque interior. It was a huge space beneath the central dome. It exuded a sense of powerful calm and symmetry.

'Like being in church,' said Stu, sensing the religious atmosphere.

'Better get used to it then, with your wedding coming up,' laughed Harry. People started to turn round and stare at them. Harry stared back, choosing to ignore their tut-tutting.

'OK lads. When in church we show a little respect. Remember you're from a Christian country. Let's show them what we're made of. They shuffled slowly forward across the central space. Then they were standing before the amazingly decorated coffins of Suleyman, his daughter and two of his successors.

'Once went to Westminster Abbey,' said Harry. 'We know how to remember important people too,' said Harry.

They re-wound their path and returned to their shoes, relieved to see they were still where they had left them. As they strolled back outside into the sun, Harry began to share his reflections, something a leader needed to do with his men, he told himself.

'That, my friends, is as good a mosque as you get. Don't be deceived, they are not usually fine buildings like this. Usually, when they're built in England, they are annoying. They start off in people's houses and cause noise and traffic problems. Before long, they look to build somewhere else and end up taking prime sites away from city centres. They become the focus for ghettoes, hotbeds of anti-British sentiment.' He paused, making sure they were listening.

'All the Muslims want to live by their mosques and they push up house prices near them and drive away the local people who have lived there for centuries. They start by coming to take our jobs, then with their religion they try to take away our souls as well. While you're here, just you remember where you come from and the pride you have in being English. These are things we have to fight against. Someone has to take a stand. Let's go and find some beer.'

37

Kaylah knocked on Clive's door only to be told he had a headache and would spend the rest of the afternoon sleeping it off. She left him to it and took Jacob downstairs with her, this time carrying him, leaving the buggy in her room. There were still a couple of hours before supper and she decided to pass the time in the lounge and people watch, observing the new arrivals and departing guests.

It was interesting to Kaylah what kind of people came to stay in a hotel like this. Were they here for holiday or business? It was fun to try and guess. She was also quite good at striking up conversations with people she didn't know and Jacob was proving to be a real icebreaker. Being black was sometimes the one thing that made her feel an outsider, marginal, in the borderlands, but having a baby let many more people than she might have imagined share a conversation. It might be superficial, but that didn't matter. It was a positive social exchange and that was what she needed.

No sooner had she sat down in the comfortable hotel lounge, than the waiter appeared and asked her what she would like. She settled for a fruit cocktail. Whilst he was away preparing it, her eye caught a tourist magazine and a page advertising Turkish and Middle Eastern rugs and carpets. She remembered Ali's telephone offer of help to sell such rugs through a contact he had in Berlin. She'd dismissed the idea out of hand when he'd mentioned it, but looking at these rugs now, colourful and desirable, she thought again. At the right price and marketed in the right way, they could really sell. She used her phone to photograph the page to explore later. Her orange cocktail, complete with paper umbrella on a stick, arrived with a smile. She gave her room number and signed a chit.

She looked at the receptionist and wondered what it was like to work with all these very different people coming to the hotel. An elderly couple, possibly German, were asking a lot of questions, but the receptionist remained endlessly courteous. Kaylah wasn't sure she would have sufficient patience for work like that. She considered once again her own increasingly urgent need to get a job when she got back. Surely her mum could help with Jacob whilst she was at work, she thought. The need to generate some income by the autumn was pressing, the reality of returning to London could not be so very far away.

She was distracted from her reverie by a man in uniform who was trying unsuccessfully to leave a large parcel with the receptionist. He was in a hurry and wanting a signature, but the receptionist continued to give her attention to her German couple, waving him away with her hand. He was getting more impatient and looking outside where his delivery van was now holding up traffic. An incident was building as Kaylah watched and she wondered how it would be resolved. This was definitely more interesting than staying up in her room.

Just then a man in a concierge uniform marched in through the front doors. She hadn't seen this particularly well-built man before. Surprisingly, he took the delivery man by the sleeve, still desperately clutching his large parcel, and frog-marched him back outside the front door. Kaylah continued to watch as a spectacle began to unfold.

The delivery man looked most unhappy that the concierge was dealing with the receipt of his parcel when, from his wildly gesticulating arms, he clearly wanted to take it inside and get a different signature. From the glances the man kept giving to the traffic still building behind his van, he knew he was onto a loser and in the end gave up, handing the man his parcel and accepting the concierge's signature, before mouthing something Kaylah couldn't of course hear as he leapt back into his van.

At this point, Jacob was beginning to make a noise, so Kaylah stood up to walk round with him to try and quieten him. She moved towards the front door to see better what might happen next. The van driver now in his van was shouting at the impatient waiting drivers, before finally pulling smartly away.

Kaylah was then puzzled by what she saw happen next. The concierge, rather than walking back into the hotel, was walking away from the hotel carrying the large awkward parcel to a waiting Land Rover; he placed the parcel on the back seat and climbed into the front passenger seat, taking his uniform cap off as he did so. How very odd, Kaylah mused.

Turning away, she spotted that the receptionist was now free and looking around for the delivery man. Kaylah walked over and told her what she had seen. A puzzled look spread across her face; she asked to be excused, picked up her desk phone and asked for the manager.

Listening in on the ending conversation, it sounded to Kaylah like a theft had taken place. The usual concierge was called over. He explained that he had been urgently called to collect some suitcases which in the end had been delivered to the wrong hotel. He hadn't seen anything of another concierge. Kaylah noticed he was so very different in build, it very definitely wasn't him who had taken the parcel, and she told the receptionist so. The receptionist vaguely remembered the interruption, but nothing more. She explained to her manager that a German couple had arrived who were wanting to make a complicated booking arrangement over several weeks, but in the end the couple had decided to go elsewhere.

Jacob was beginning to make more noise and other people were starting to look disapprovingly in their direction. She felt like staying put to make the point that Jacob had as much right to be there as they did, but it was a battle not worth fighting and Kaylah decided to go back upstairs and see how Clive was. She took the lift and as she strolled along the marble floored corridor she thought what she had just seen had been so very entertaining, maybe it had even been a sophisticated theft. It would be the first thing she would tell Clive about. It would no doubt amuse him.

Clive invited her into his room. He fetched her a glass of water and sat on the bed, leaving Kaylah and Jacob the easy chair. He was more than interested in her story and declared that he was only sorry to have missed out on all the excitement. Inside, he knew exactly what had really gone on and felt guilty he couldn't say more to his sister. From what she had said, he deduced that the German couple were there to distract the receptionist and prevent the delivery man making his delivery and the usual concierge had been called away on a diversionary errand.

Clive knew the big guy in a concierge uniform had been briefed to intercept the parcel. Wicked Will's drug consignment had been intercepted and Clive had turned away. At one and the same time, Clive knew he'd done the right thing, but inside he feared that in spite of all the assurances Dave Stephens might give, a real threat to him for what he'd done remained. He knew Will never forgot those who double-crossed him. He began to worry, but was determined not to show his feelings to Kaylah.

By the time they'd finished chatting, there was a knock on the bedroom door. Clive jumped up in alarm and then tried to calm himself.

'Yes, who is it?' he called out.

'Lena, just back from work,' she replied.

'Come in,' said Clive, opening the door to her, 'finished earlier today then?'

'Yes, are you two alright? Been out?' asked Lena.

'Fine, except Clive was feeling a bit under the weather and has had an afternoon in his room,' said Kaylah.

'But I'm feeling OK now. Just a headache, migraine. Probably the heat,' Clive explained.

Lena sat next to Clive on the bed. She looked like she had something she wanted to talk about.

'We need to talk about Ali,' Lena said. 'We haven't had much joy so far, now have we? We need to try again. Thinking about what he told you when you two spoke last, he's clearly on a mission and with a group of his men. He's definitely not on his own this time. He found it difficult to find the opportunity to take and make his calls with you, which suggests he had people round him and had to await an opportunity to call you.'

'That makes sense,' said Kaylah.

'We don't think we've got much time. All I can say is that Ali's mission involves a large amount of explosives and that we in the security services are very concerned that a lot of innocent people might get hurt. We had a lucky break when a van load was intercepted on the main road near Ankara, but they'll be sure to try and replace their loss. We're all on the highest alert level. So we need to ask you to try again. OK?' she said, not so much an enquiry but an expectation. Kaylah knew she had no choice and nodded her agreement.

'We ought to do this now while I'm with you. Might make it easier if I just put this up in front of you.' She pulled a Tablet out of her bag and flipped it open, entered a password and a work page headed up, 'Ali Conversation Check List' instantly appeared. So this is what she has been working on today, thought Clive.

'Basically, it is all very straightforward. No different to last time. But this time, mention Jacob more and that you'd love him to be able to see his dad just once. We know that he mentioned that as a special request when he sent the parcel of gifts to you in London. Tell him you want to make it easy and that the Grand Bazaar might be the best place, plenty of people around, a labyrinth of ways for him to approach and escape. It's somewhere you know and it's nearby. It'll tempt him. From what we know of his personality profile, we think that will be enough to entice him. If he doesn't like that idea, mention the open square behind, the Beyazit Square. That will, for different reasons, also appeal. He'll be able to see around him and spot you some way off. So that is what you do first,' Lena said, her finger pointing down her typed list of bullet points.

'Then what?' asked Kaylah who had spotted the first bullet point 'Jacob' with subheadings, 'i Grand Bazaar' and 'ii Beyazit Square'.

'You're overlooking one thing. Ali doesn't know we know he's here in Istanbul,' interrupted Clive.

'I've thought about that. There's no easy answer, but you'll have to tell him you had an anonymous call from

London warning you that Ali might be in Turkey and to be careful,' Lena suggested. 'I can't think of anything else.'

'It won't work,' said Clive. 'Kaylah would do better to blag it. Say you saw it on the local news. He won't know any different, now will he?' suggested Clive.

'You know what, I think you're right. Why didn't I think of that?' said Lena. 'Let's go with Clive's suggestion, Kaylah.'

'What's this about timing?' asked Kaylah pointing to the next bullet point.

'Yes, timing is going to be vital. We need to control the time Ali comes to meet you as tightly as we can. You can argue for the time windows we will give, on the basis of Jacob's feed times, whether it's true or not, he won't know any different. He'll accept that coming from you. What we want you to tell him is that Jacob will be having his morning feed and sleep first thing. A meeting around 10am would be best as you will need to get him back to the hotel by around 12 otherwise, you will say, he starts crying nonstop for his next feed. If he doesn't bite at the time, suggest the afternoon. We think he'll want a quick meeting as soon as he can and then get back to what he's planning to do,' concluded Lena.

'What will happen then, when we meet?' asked Kaylah anxiously.

'And how will you keep these two safe?' interjected Clive.

'That's vitally important, but I don't want us to run too far ahead of ourselves. Believe me, we've got that well taken care of. Let's just focus on the task in hand, getting Ali to come out of hiding. Are you ready to make that call again, Kaylah? We'll look at these matters after the call. I don't want to fill your mind with too much detail all at once. We must make the call. Many innocent women and children's lives hang on what we are about to do. If you can help save all these people's lives, well, that's the most important thing, isn't it?' she said.

Kaylah couldn't find a reason to say no and thought that the sooner she got the next call over with, the better. She passed Jacob to Clive and positioned herself to see Lena's list. She dialled up Ali. This time he picked up.

'Hi Kaylah. I've been thinking about you,' he said. 'I'm just taking a break, a quick walk round the block. It's not so hot at this time.'

'I was thinking Ali. I saw your name on the TV news. Is it true you're in Turkey? If so, is there any chance you could see Jacob, even briefly before we leave? It's just that one day I'd like to tell him his father saw him and I helped it to happen for him. Jacob's an absolutely gorgeous baby. He's beautiful, has your eyes, has curly brown not black hair. He's doing really well. I've told him about you, though I know he doesn't understand. Everyone says he's cute. I'd really like him to meet his dad, just once. That's why I called you,' Kaylah said making her case as instructed, holding Lena's Tablet open in front of her.

Lena leant forward and gave Kaylah a thumbs up. There was a pause whilst Kaylah waited. She knew Ali was thinking hard. She could almost hear his brain turning things over.

'Big risk for me Kaylah. I have to be sure it's safe,' said Ali.

'Well, why don't you choose somewhere you feel happy with? How about the Grand Bazaar? I've been there already, lots of people around,' she suggested. '

'Not so sure about that. Bit enclosed. No, I don't think so,' he replied.

'Well, if you don't like that, how about the Beyazit Square, near the University. That's not so far for me either. It's a big open space if you feel more comfortable with that. It has to be somewhere I know and feel safe with you too you know,' she said in a matter of fact tone. There was a pause.

'Yeah! That'll do. I know it. There's a tall flagpole by the fort-like entrance to the university at the northern side of the park. Whenever I've seen it, they have a giant red Turkish flag flying from it. Take Jacob there,' Ali told her, 'that's where we'll meet.'

'When?' asked Kaylah, 'When can you make it?'

Lena looked across at Kaylah anxiously, jabbing her finger at the times on her tablet. But, Kaylah knew Ali better than Lena and she knew he would come back and negotiate with her. Besides, she also knew he would feel more in control if she asked him when, handed him control in the conversation.

'It has to be tomorrow morning,' Ali said, 'I can't say why. Early is best.'

'Jacob has a sleep first thing, but if he sticks to plan, and he's a very easy baby, I should be able to wheel him over in the buggy for about 10am. Is that OK with you? I'll need to get him back to the hotel soon after 12, he'll be due his next change and feed by then. Clive's here helping me. I might bring him along too,' said Kaylah.

'No Clive,' he said.

'Oh,' said Kaylah, momentarily thrown.

'No Clive if you want Jacob to see his dad,' Ali insisted.

'OK. Don't worry. You know me. He can find something else to do tomorrow morning,' Kaylah said reluctantly.

'And I'd rather you didn't tell him you're seeing me tomorrow,' Ali added.

'OK. I'll just tell him I've got to do some personal shopping. That will set his mind at rest, he'll be fine with that,' she said.

Ali said he had to go and Lena gave a thumbs up again, and the call ended, with Kaylah saying, 'Until tomorrow at 10am then. I'll call if there's a problem with Jacob, but I'm sure there won't be. Thanks. Bye.'

Lena asked to be excused a moment. Clive heard her on her mobile as soon as she was in the corridor outside the bedroom door. The first few words were clear, then she moved out of earshot.

'It's Lena. Did you copy that? Meeting fixed 10am Beyazit Square by the flagpole outside the University entrance, old fort building.' There was a pause as she listened to whoever was speaking at the other end.

'First part of Operation Turkish Delight is go. Also, Ali let slip he was busy tomorrow afternoon. Think we might know what that means – there's no time to lose. This'll be our one and only chance to draw him out into the open.'

38

It was just before supper, Thursday evening and the four were to eat together at their student Apartments. The café-restaurant on site meant they didn't need to venture out again, which everyone agreed suited them just fine. Adam knew he had to call Krish and as the four finished the last of their drinks, Adam looked across at Raqiyah and excused himself saying he had to phone someone.

'I'll come with you,' Raqiyah offered, and rose from the white-top square table to follow him. They made their way up to Adam's room. Adam didn't want to make the call where there was any likelihood it might be overheard.

'I'd better do it,' he said, as he dialled Krish.

'Hi Adam, everything OK? How are you feeling today?' Krish said cheerily.

'Much better. The medication, much as I don't like taking it, has really made a difference. I called because I want to talk to you about Ali Muhammed.' Adam detected a pause at the other end.

'OK, are you sure about this?' asked Krish, pleased by the call, but genuinely concerned at the stress it might place on Adam.

'Yes. I'd rather tell you what I think and get some straight answers back from you than continue to live with the stress of all the uncertainty. I don't think you've been entirely frank with me, Krish. The time has come for some honesty, some straight talking,' Adam said, surprised at how assertive his voice was.

'Look, I'd rather chat with you face-to-face about this. Is it OK if I come over now? I know it's evening, but I don't work regular hours and this sounds important,' Krish suggested.

'That's fine by me. We can meet in the café here, the one on the top floor. It's open and it'll be quiet. Oh, I want Raqiyah with me when we meet,' Adam insisted.

'That's good. I'll see you in about half an hour. I'll come straight up and find you both.' Krish ended the call.

Adam summarised the conversation for Raqiyah, though he hardly needed to, she'd overheard everything. They took the stairs up to the top floor rather than wait for a lift and found a quiet table near the window which offered a fine view north over the roof tops of Beyoglu.

'Just think, somewhere amongst all those buildings is Ali Muhammed,' Adam said calmly, pleased his medication seemed to be working a treat.

Krish arrived sooner than they thought, looking less formal than Adam had seen him before, dressed in a light, crisply-ironed, colourful shirt and dark-blue trousers. Perhaps he had been relaxing when he took his call. He saw them and smiled, joining them. Drinks were ordered from the tired waitress. The café area was quiet and she left them to it. Small talk followed – talk about the city and its sights, how the visit was going, and so on. Only when the drinks arrived did they begin to address what was really on their agenda.

'Krish, to cut to the chase, what I really want to ask is whether you know Ali Muhammed is here in the city or not?' asked Adam, leaning forward in his chair. Krish eyed Adam questioningly, as if unsure what to say.

'Right, look, what I say next, I want the two of you to keep entirely to yourselves. I'm taking a big risk here and need to know I can rely on you both. Otherwise that's it, end of conversation,' replied Krish.

Adam and Raqiyah looked at each other and both nodded to Krish.

'Yes, we know Ali is here in Istanbul. Don't ask how we know. We have ways of knowing and even I don't get told everything. I apologise Adam, for not telling you, I kept this from you. It was necessary, and I was told not to. I was only to keep an eye on your well-being, to be in contact with you whilst you were over here, just in case you might be useful to us in the event we needed someone to reach Ali. To be frank, there were some in my office who thought because you had been held so long by IS yourself, perhaps you were in league with Ali, and it was too big a coincidence to think both Ali and yourself had turned up in Istanbul at the same time without there being some ongoing connection between the two of you. Personally, I have to add that was never my opinion, but it strengthened the overall case that we should, that is UK security services, keep an eye on you and your well-being whilst you are here,' said Krish.

'Thought so, worked it out I did. When we bumped into Kaylah Kone in the Grand Bazaar, it just hit me. No way could it be a coincidence. But, Kaylah being here. She can't be here because she has a student placement on Islam. Her being here must be because someone has deliberately brought her over. Who? Ali? You?' asked Adam.

'What I have to say now really must be kept under wraps. We know the Israeli Secret Service have got a hold on her and have brought her here to try and lure Ali into the open,' Krish said, with a look of concern on his face.

'She's here with her little baby. You must be joking! She didn't look like she was on a serious mission. What kind of risk are they being exposed to? Does she know it, or like me is she also being kept in the dark?' said Adam.

'She knows it. She knows exactly why she's here. We are working with her brother Clive to keep as close an eye on her as we can. It's the Israelis who have created a situation here, not us. They used some leverage to get her and her baby to come to Istanbul and at some point, if they haven't done so already, they will have asked her to call Ali, to get him to contact her. They have the lead on chasing Ali down. Their strategy has some merit in that we know Ali wants to see his child. You have to remember we are seeking to avoid a major terrorist incident here which threatens not only significant loss of life, but might even lead to wider international ramifications. This could play out badly for the UK if it goes wrong,' said Krish, realising he had stepped well over a line in the sand somewhere in sharing this.

'But, to put a baby at risk like this,' interjected Raqiyah.

'Welcome to the real world of murky espionage and state security,' said Krish uneasily. The reply did little to satisfy either Adam or Raqiyah.

'That's not to say I like what they are doing. Kaylah is in the hands of her Israeli minder. It is their job to look out for her. So far as you, Adam, are concerned, we think, given the return of your post-traumatic-stress this week, it is only fair you are not made more anxious by all this and there is absolutely nothing we expect of you,' added Krish trying to play things down. '

'That's fine, except I am feeling more my well self, with the help of the medication, and if I had half the chance I'd like to get at Ali and see that Kaylah and her baby are not exposed to any harm,' he added.

'I'll take that to be an offer of help from you, which is appreciated, and if need be, we'll come back to you on that. So far as Kaylah is concerned, I share your expression of concern for her and Jacob. Look, the demarcation lines are quite clear. We have to leave Kaylah to the Israelis. If you try and do anything, you might simply make things more dangerous, both for her and yourselves. Understood?' he said addressing them both.

'But we are already involved with her. We met her by accident and we'll meet up with her again, probably tomorrow,' said Adam.

'I suggest not,' said Krish, knowing instinctively this was one argument he wasn't going to win and, to be honest, if he were in their shoes, he'd probably do the same. Nonetheless he was seriously worried what Adam might end up doing. He also began to think that his own plans hadn't seriously considered the well-being of the Kone entourage who were, after all, also British citizens. He'd need to pick that question up again back at the Consulate.

The conversation went back and forth for a further ten minutes, before Krish looked at his watch and said he needed to get back to the event at the Consulate he'd left earlier. It would be poor form if he didn't show for the final speeches and farewells at the evening dinner being hosted for business leaders. Then he was gone. It was getting late.

Adam looked across at Raqiyah. She instinctively knew what he was about to do next. He picked up his mobile and gave Kaylah a call.

'Hi Kaylah, Adam.'

'Hi, Adam. So nice a surprise seeing you this morning. I wondered who would ring the other first,' she offered.

'Well, I did! How has the rest of your day been?' he asked, 'Enjoying the sights of Istanbul?'

'Came back to our hotel actually. Clive had a headache. He's OK now, but to be honest it's nice to mix sightseeing and resting up,' said Kaylah.

'I wanted to chat because I've been thinking. Neither of us are here by some weird coincidence. I'm here because that's just the way my uni placement planned out, but you are here because someone manipulated you to be here. I'm not supposed to, but I'm ringing because I don't want you or your baby to end up in danger,' he said, more bluntly than he intended.

'What do you mean by "not supposed to", sounds like someone's pulling your strings too,' retorted Kaylah on the defensive.

'Sorry, I didn't mean to say it quite like that. What I meant is, I know what it's like to have the security services steering what you do. I had my fill of it last autumn. They have their own agendas and at the end of the day they don't particularly care about people like me and you so long as they achieve their own goals. They don't care, Kaylah, the bottom line is they don't fucking care,' said Adam, making his point.

'Adam, I'm feeling quite safe actually. I'm being well looked after and Clive's here with me too. Thank you for your concern, but I have to look after myself,' she countered.

Jacob was crying in the background and both knew the conversation would need to end.

'Call me if you need to,' said Adam, 'and take good care. Watch your back Kaylah. Bye.'

Kaylah was unsettled by the conversation. She suddenly felt isolated and exposed in a foreign land. She'd not only put herself in the firing line, but Jacob was being brought into things that really he oughtn't to be. What kind of mother was she? She began feeling guilty and worrying that she had committed herself to the wrong thing tomorrow.

Later as she lay on her bed, sleep just wouldn't come. She had nagging doubts about whether she was doing the right thing. Ironically, as she herself tossed and turned, it was one night when Jacob didn't even stir once, he was totally at peace.

39

There was a hurried urgency as people gathered for the 6am meeting at the security HQ, Tel Aviv. No-one minded getting up early for this kind of meeting. Everyone arriving was carefully screened before admission. Official passes were only part of the entry-check process. All had to stand still and submit to iris recognition scans before security would finally let them in. Some then grabbed coffees and a notebook as they made their way inside. None of the more important visitors carried anything. Few words were exchanged, the air electric with anticipated risk, as visitors made their way upstairs.

Since yesterday afternoon it had become clear that Ali Muhammed's terrorist operation in Istanbul would be allied with wider Kurdish attacks, probably in Ankara and these were considered to be imminent.

Anna Simonsson knew that things had moved up and way beyond her level, and those currently assembling in the operations room on the top floor of the building were senior strategists together with political as well as military leaders. These were people who had the authority and power to take decisions and make things happen. The government trusted their discretion and ability to fix things, to deal outside the world of polite diplomacy and handle the mess of the 'realpolitik' to ensure everyone else slept soundly in their beds at night.

At first light people had begun to arrive. It was almost time. Anna glanced at her monitor screen. At 06.25 precisely, she switched it off and set off to join the meeting. People who made the mistake of leaving on an unattended computer faced serious disciplinary proceedings. She'd seen it happen. Anna glanced around the room. This morning she thought it unlikely she would be asked anything in the meeting, even though it was her own technical and eavesdropping skills that had provided much of the information everyone would be relying on. Even so she had to be ready for any questions, as one of the gathered experts on hand. There were six of them like herself, officially present as 'Advisers'.

A quick count and she made it fifteen people around the conference table, nine men and six women. Within a minute she had identified a number of mathematical symmetries in the male to female seating arrangements and in the ratios of grey, green and blue uniforms. It was something she had to do to keep her anxiety levels manageable. Her mind always found it easy to be playful with numbers and forms, it was never the same with words or human relationships. Some people called her autistic, she just saw herself as different and found inner satisfaction, if not pride in her unique assortment of personal traits and skills.

She switched from her playful mathematical exercises to focus on the unfolding business, the real purpose in being there. All were ready. The Chair, Rebecca Levi, the Administrative Head of Security, was calling everyone to order. She was sharp, precise, slim built if not thin, wearing a white blouse and dark trousers, her matching jacket hanging over the back of her chair. Black and silver gunmetal-rimmed oval-lensed glasses sat in front of a head framed in short white curly hair. No-one could miss her.

There was but one agenda, she told them. After the situation had been precisely delineated by her in a crisp, punchy manner, she signalled for the lights to be dimmed. The wall behind her that served as a screen flashed a series of photos in quick succession – vehicles, faces, an apartment block in Istanbul and a map of Istanbul with possible targets identified by red flash shaped symbols.

To interpret these, she called upon Moshe David, Head of Security and Intervention Services, to speak. He explained with characteristic clarity in a detectable American Bostonian accent what everyone was seeing in the images before them. In a matter of a few minutes all present had no doubt that a major IS terrorist attack would be made on Istanbul, in all probability that very Friday afternoon.

'We have so little time,' Moshe David said, drawing his presentation to an end with a sigh and a tilt of the head, 'but I have anticipated our meeting by alerting certain diplomats and special forces personnel that their services may be urgently required. I have also taken the liberty to talk with my opposite number in Turkey, but I have to say, our conversation was not very encouraging. We cannot count on our Turkish friends being ready for what needs to be done today. Their Security Group Delta overseeing this have done no more than simply raise the state of alert and put more police and soldiers on the streets. It's pathetic, really – it's as if they are waiting for catastrophe to befall them. My conclusion is, that if anything is to be done to prevent Ali's terrorists, we are the only ones capable of acting with the necessary speed and precision. I rather see it like this: someone needs to lance the boil and then apply the antiseptic, before it infects the whole body. Please let me tell you in outline what I propose and then I'll take questions.'

He picked a glass of water as he stood there, taking a couple of sips, before replacing it carefully and deliberately back on the circular absorbent place mat with a star of David motif on it. Anna noticed how he had placed it exactly on the centre. She liked that. Her eye was caught by what she saw and she found herself assessing the regular distortions to the six pointed star caused by the passage of light through the water. Her attention returned to Moshe as he began speaking again. She looked up into his serious face.

'Outside the political sphere, there are two direct actions we can take ourselves. The one may obviate the need for the other. First, we can lance the boil, we can liquidate Ali. Ali provides the leadership for this IS mission, though we believe there is a Turkish local leader who has joined forces with Ali, but we have no doubt Ali is still very much the one in command. If we hit him and take him out, we may well neutralise the IS attack. So the first option we have is to authorise an attack to take out Ali.' He let this sink in.

'Let us consider next how realistic this option is. Unfortunately our earlier attempts to get Ali all missed him, albeit by a narrow margin. Drone attacks on locations in Mosul were unsuccessful. Some say he was lucky. I say, he's used up his luck and a much more precise and certain opportunity now presents itself to us.' There was a quiet shuffle here and there in the room. He pressed on.

'The information to mount an attack on him in his four vehicle convoy as he headed north into Turkey a week ago, came through just that bit too late for us to be able to do anything. Now, he is based in an apartment block in the Beyoglu district in Istanbul. We've identified the block. We still have two opportunities to get Ali, thanks in part to the excellent work of one of our operatives from London who has successfully arranged for Ali to be drawn out of hiding at 10.00 Turkish time.' He stopped and pressed the remote in front of him. An image of a fortress-looking building across what looked like a large green square appeared on the screen.

'This is our first chance. This is where we anticipate he will be this morning. Ali is desperate to see his baby son who was born to British citizen, Kaylah Kone. Our agent has persuaded Kaylah to take her son here to Beyazit Square and show him to Ali, here, by this flagpole. The phone calls to make this arrangement took a while to take place, but the final message we have is that Ali has agreed to meet up, to see his baby son here at 10am Turkish time.' He used a red laser beam to point to the exact spot.

'It just so happens we are able to have a driver take and place a special forces sniper in position right here. We can use one of our tinted window vehicles to keep things absolutely discreet. Our man is 100% confident that a fatal shot is possible. It is within a range and distance allowing for almost 100% predictability and offering the necessary good exit route for our people. At this point in time they are about to move their vehicle to where they need to be to take Ali down. You need to know we have decided not to notify the Turkish authorities and no-one must know about our unilateral action. It is the kind of thing we have done successfully before in different parts of the world and I'm confident we can do what is necessary here. What is needed is for this committee to give its authority to proceed.' He folded his arms and looked around the room.

The Chair, Rebecca, intervened. She said she would not let it go to an immediate vote on a show of hands, without first calling for some more background information she felt those present needed to have before proceeding to the step of authorisation. She nodded to a man, probably still in his thirties, sitting opposite her.

As a political analyst, Isaac Jacobson stood up to address those gathered. He hoped people wouldn't mind but he found it easier to express himself standing. He was a little man with twinkling eyes and known to have the sharpest political mind of anyone in Israel. His particular field of expertise was the politics of those countries to the north of Israel, stretching across from Iraq to the Balkans.

'Thank you Chair. I think all of you present will have worked out that if a major attack by IS and the Kurds takes place the potential fallout could be very significant. Potentially, we might see the instability currently present in so many neighbouring nearby countries spread further into the borderlands of Europe itself. The stability of Turkey, a member of NATO, ally of the USA, is often taken for granted. Let me tell you, we can no longer make that assumption. The millions of refugees entering that country, the recent polarisation of political parties, the hardline secularism of the ruling party, and the increasing frequency of internal acts of terrorism have tilted the balance. If Ali and his IS team achieve what they have in mind, Turkey, the stable bastion and bridgehead with Europe, could be lost. Turkey today is a straw man waiting to burn.' He paused before continuing.

'Think about what this means. If Turkey falls apart, it will become harder for our American friends to find somewhere to base their planes, friends of Israel will be pushed further away, and we should no longer think that in the future they will still be ready to help us when we need them. In sum, the political dynamic is at tipping point. A successful attack by Ali Muhammed could do far more harm than we might think at first glance – but the reality is a few

300

explosions and casualties from another IS attack might tip things right over the edge. We need to view stopping these imminent attacks as critical.'

With that he sat down and there was a silence around the table. The Chair, Rebecca Levi, asked Moshe to spell out the full package of preventative measures he had in mind. It would be better to hear them all before coming to any decision.

'Whether we are successful or not in taking Ali down this morning – after all he may simply not show – there are further measures that can be taken. We do have a second option which is daring, but possible, using our new extended reach drone capability. This would involve a precise targeting of the first floor of the apartment block where we believe Ali and his terrorists have a base in Istanbul. Our Turkish opposite numbers in the Security Group Delta are talking about making a raid there tomorrow, Saturday. They think they have both the time to delay and see Saturday as advantageous in avoiding disturbance to Friday's Muslim holy day activities,' Moshe said dismissively.

'They were candid about this and said they are preparing their special forces troops to do this in the early hours of Saturday morning. They think it is soon enough to send in military personnel in an early morning raid. In their experience pre-dawn raids work best. We have a difference of opinion. Our intelligence suggests we need to act now. To conclude, I think we have two actions to authorise. The first, to kill Ali by sniper at Beyazit Square at 10.00 hours. Failing this, the second, to launch a drone attack to burn them in their nest. If Ali survives the morning, we get a second chance to finish him and his team by taking out that part of the apartment block at midday. That's it chair,' and with that he sat down.

Questions were taken. Logistics were checked. Likely collateral scenarios anticipated and political responses gauged. By 07.00 Israel time, Rebecca was checking her watch and said it was time to vote.

Both proposals were passed by a unanimous show of hands. No minutes were kept of the meeting. As everyone began to move, Moshe David was already on his way out of the door, his mobile pressed to his ear, a sniper at the other end getting ready to move into place.

40

'How about hiring bikes today?' said Adam. 'It's forecast to be sunny and dry; no surprise there then. It's a great way to see the city. We could do with some physical exercise. I can recommend it!'

All agreed it was an excellent idea. After talking to the reception desk downstairs, Bilal made the necessary phone call to book the bikes from a local bike rental shop they pointed him to which was only two blocks away. Adam suggested he might ring Clive to see if he would like to join them. No-one objected. When he called, Clive immediately jumped at the idea, so Bilal had to call the bike shop again to book five rather than four bikes. It was no problem, the man said. Clive said he was keen to see where they were staying in Beyoglu and asked for their address, saying he would come straight over by taxi and should be there to meet them by 9am.

As Clive climbed into the yellow taxi taking him across to Ataturk Academic Apartments he thought how fortuitous Adam's call had been. The idea of letting Kaylah go off to meet Ali struck him as highly risky, but Kaylah and Lena had it all sewn up between them. Kaylah had told him that Ali didn't want him there, and he'd gone to bed the previous evening wondering what on earth he could do to see the two of them stayed safe. He could see in Kaylah's face she was apprehensive, but her mind was made up.

Clive told himself he had no intention of staying right out of it, but didn't feel he could say anything or do anything to help. So, when he told Kaylah he was going cycling round the city with Adam and his friends, Kaylah was pleased for him and he had the perfect excuse, so long as he could persuade the others to go in a particular direction, to use the ride to keep half an eye on his vulnerable sister and baby nephew without her knowing it.

All Kaylah had said as he left was that he was to enjoy himself, not worry about them, and she'd see him when he got back. She made light of seeing Ali, saying the visit would all be over in a couple of hours, done and dusted. Clive wasn't convinced by her show of bravado, but she was unshakeable in her resolve to go through with it. He began to feel angry with Lena for her influence over his sister. Did Kaylah always have to fall prey to people so easily? She'd finally said that when she got back to the hotel after seeing Ali, she might use their baby-minding service so that she could make use of their spa facility.

Clive arrived to find the four students waiting by the front door. The thought crossed his mind that with a fair wind his own plans to start student life in the autumn might mean he'd be enjoying life like they were. After politely exchanged greetings all of them set off to walk to collect their bikes. As they moved away, Adam got chatting to Clive. Clive very quickly told him what was happening that morning and how concerned he felt about his sister going to show Jacob to Ali.

'Anything might happen. I don't trust Ali and I'm amazed she does. As a father he's lost all his rights to access so far as I'm concerned,' said Clive expressing his feeling rather more strongly than he intended.

'Let's hope it all goes off OK,' ventured Adam.

'The Israeli woman, Lena Bloom who is with us on this trip and who fixed this up for us, she said they'd make sure they were safe. But how's she going to do that? I haven't even seen her this morning. I feel really bad because I feel complicit in this whole thing and so fucking helpless. I was asked to support this use of Jacob as bait idea. I've gone along with it so far, but I feel so guilty. I couldn't live with myself if anything were to happen to them this morning,' said Clive.

'Is there anything we can do?' asked Adam. 'How about I ring my contact at the Consulate?'

'No. No. We could make things worse. Last thing I want now is to make Ali do something drastic. What I'd really like to do would be for us to cycle at a distance near the park where they'll be well out of range, not so they'd be aware of us, just so as to keep half an eye,' suggested Clive.

'I'd go along with that. Where is this all happening?' asked Adam.

'You may know the place. Beyazit Square,' said Clive.

'We were shown it earlier in the week. It's where the University of Istanbul has its prestigious entrance,' said Adam.

'That's exactly where the meeting is to happen, right there,' said Clive.

'That's quite a big square and there's lots to see. It's not so far for us from here, so why not? The others will just follow where I lead when it comes to bikes, just wait and see! They've got no fixed plans, no destinations in mind,' said Adam.

It took a full half hour for them to get their bikes, what with finding helmets to fit, paying the right deposit and understanding what time they had to return the bikes to the shop. They settled on a three hour hire, promising to be back by twelve-thirty. Adam led the single line of five bikes, enjoying as he always did the feeling of freedom that being on a bike provided. The air was hotter than he'd expected, but it wasn't uncomfortable and it wasn't long before they were heading across the Ataturk Bridge and then turning left following the line of the Golden Horn before swinging south into the city.

It was nearly 10am and when a café offered itself, the girls and Bilal were already keen to pull up and buy some cold drinks. Adam and Clive looked at each other and said they'd go round the square and rejoin them in a few minutes. The group split up and Adam led Clive in a circular anti-clockwise route around Beyazit Square. Clive called out and Adam pulled up. They were on the southern edge.

'I think I see them,' said Clive.

In the distance Kaylah's buggy was immediately visible. There was no doubt it was her. She was walking slowly away from them towards the University's entrance and fort-like structure, a view Abdul had been so proud to point out to

Adam and his group when they had first arrived. That now seemed so long ago.

'Do you see Ali?' asked Adam, lifting his sun glasses to see if he could better make things out.

'That could be him, what do you think?' said Clive, nodding slightly right.

'Reckon so,' said Adam. 'Everything presently looks straightforward from here. I thought you said, by the flag pole, but he's walking towards them.'

'Must be keen to meet up,' said Clive.

'Let's carry on cycling around the perimeter of the square. They shouldn't notice us. If everything looks OK we'll go and rejoin the others at the café,' suggested Adam.

They set off, again Adam leading the way, both with helmets and dark glasses back in place. Whether it was Clive or Adam who spotted it first would be argued over later, but the metallic blue BMW with tinted windows up ahead caught their attention.

'My mate Winston once had one of those cars, just like that one,' Clive said as they approached.

The car was facing away from them, parked against the kerb, the engine idling. It all happened so quickly. The rear window wound down just a few centimetres and the unmistakeable business end of a gun poked out. Not far, not more than eight inches, but far enough for Adam to know exactly what it was. Clive saw it simultaneously and understood immediately the direction it was pointed.

'No,' he yelled, accelerating his bike and overtaking Adam.

Adam watched as Clive's bike got ever closer to the car, edging to within inches of the curb, before hitting the projecting gun with his front handlebars. There was a crack as the jolted gun went off on impact. The collision had clearly damaged the end of the weapon and a clumsy attempt was made to try and withdraw it back behind the car's tinted window. By now the driver was bringing the engine into life and pulling rapidly away into the traffic, the gun finally having disappeared from sight. Then it was over and the car and its gun had gone.

In the collision Clive had fallen to the ground. He complained about his arm hurting and when Adam looked down at his bike, the front handlebar had been pushed out of alignment. There would be no more riding today.

'You OK?' he asked.

'You see that. The guy had a gun pointed towards Kaylah and Ali. What else could I do?' Clive said.

'Think you'll need to get that arm seen to. Haven't broken it have you?' asked Adam, feeling shaken himself.

'No, I don't think so. Just grazed and cut up a bit. I'll clean it up when I get back,' said Clive, rubbing himself down.

Clive then looked across the Square to check on Kaylah only to see her standing alone by the buggy. She looked distressed. There was no sign of Ali.

'No harm in making our way over to her now, I suppose,' said Adam.

They wheeled their bikes across to a distraught Kaylah. When she saw them she ran across to them in evident fright.

'He's taken Jacob! He's taken him,' was all she could say before collapsing on to the ground.

41

Ali had got to hold his baby son Jacob. When he'd asked Kaylah if he might, she was unsure what to say, but she didn't try to stop him when he reached in and picked him up. As Ali gazed upon his son in evident delight and pride, she saw glimpses of the same Ali she'd fallen under the spell of. Perhaps Ali looked a little more worn than before, but he seemed very much the same guy she had spent so much time with in London the previous autumn and, without realising it, she once again felt lulled into a feeling of safety by his presence.

To any observer there was a strange normality in these two parents enjoying their new baby in the park. At the same time Kaylah felt a huge sense of unreality. The whole situation was bizarre. She was at an assignation with a terrorist on a mission in a foreign land and in a park surrounded by strangers. In the moment she began to think like this, she began feeling terrifyingly isolated and entirely vulnerable on her own with Ali. How she wished Clive had been able to come, and where was Lena who had promised to watch over her? She could find no more words to say to Ali other than the briefest acknowledgement as to why she was there.

'You asked to see him and I agreed to do it,' she said.

'I know. A child should see his father,' he replied.

Ali marvelled at his new son, unable to quite believe the baby he was looking at was actually his. Jacob's eyes and the shape of his head echoed his own. He held him closer and told Kaylah how beautiful he thought their son was. He rocked Jacob back and forth and began to speak words in Arabic to him Kaylah couldn't follow. He began to think how he could take his son away from Kaylah, something he hadn't planned through and began to realise he just couldn't do it.

Kaylah felt increasingly uneasy. She looked around. There was no sign of help nearby if she needed any.

'I think I need to go now,' she said to Ali, and made to reach for Jacob.

Ali was poised as if a statue, held spellbound by indecision. It was then there was a noise which made Ali start and look round. Instantly he knew what it was. He didn't say anything, but turned and began running quickly away towards the corner of the park. He was still holding Jacob, Kaylah left with her arms outstretched towards him as if pleading with her hands for him to stop and come back. But he didn't. He didn't even look round and in seconds he had made his exit, turned the corner, gone from sight, taking Jacob with him.

Kaylah's body wouldn't move. She was frozen under the hot sun. Not knowing what to do, she grabbed the empty buggy and looked again. Perhaps he would be coming back. Yes, he just wanted to show Jacob something, that was it. He would be back in a minute. The seconds passed and the fear returned. Then the wailing started, the wail that said her baby had been torn from her and she could do nothing. It came from deep inside wrenching at her stomach as it came up and through her throat. Tears filled her eyes. In the misty haze, she saw two cyclists approaching, then Clive and Adam were with her.

'He's taken Jacob. He's taken him,' she cried as she collapsed to the white burning pathway. 'What do I do? Help me, help me, please, please,' she begged.

It was pitiful and desperate. Words meant nothing. Clive and Adam looked at each other, hoping the other could offer a solution, both realising that they had stepped into hell.

Adam reached into his pocket. He desperately needed some more medication. His anxiety levels were building and he felt frozen to the spot. He could not bear the thought he might be an added burden and quickly found and swallowed two Lorazapan tablets as the doctor had suggested he do if he felt himself heading into a crisis.

Clive meanwhile had, despite his grazed and bleeding arm, cradled his arms round his sister and was guiding her to a nearby seat. Adam, trying to be helpful, picked up Clive's bike and wheeled it along with his own over to where the two were.

'We need to get help, Sis,' Clive said. 'Suggest you ring Lena, now,' he said.

'You do it Clive,' she said, putting her head in her hands, after she'd passed him her mobile. Clive looked at Adam.

'Lena's the Israeli woman who's been looking after, sorry, fixing things, up to now. Think she'd better find a way of sorting this one out as she promised,' explained desperate sounding Clive.

He called up the number and had almost given up when she picked up.

'Hi, Kaylah,' she said.

'It's Clive here. Big problem. She met Ali and he's run off with Jacob. Hope you meant what you said when you promised nothing would go wrong, that you would look after us. We need your help and we need it now,' he said, bluntly.

'Clive, tell me what's happened,' she said, her concern evident, disrupting her usually smooth conversational manner.

'What, you don't know already?' Clive asked, his rising anger getting hold of him.

'Kaylah was meeting Ali to show him Jacob in Beyazit Square by the flagpole on the north side. That I know. A security car with one of our guys inside left here earlier. The two said they would be there to keep an eye on them,' said Lena, Clive immediately putting two and two together.

'Well, no sign of any security guys or help in sight. Please, please help us. Kaylah's distraught,' he said, desperately wanting her to help.

'What are you doing there Clive? I thought Ali said you were to keep away,' she asked.

'I was out for a cycle ride, nowhere near them,' he lied, not wanting to take any blame, 'but then I saw her in the Square all alone, just her and the buggy.'

'Look I'll send a car, straight there. I'll come myself, pick her up. Take her back, and have a word here as to what we should do. I'll meet you back at the hotel as soon as you can get there. OK?' she asked.

'Shall I call the police?' asked Clive.

'No, no, just get back. We'll talk about it back at the hotel,' Lena insisted, 'And on the way I'll contact our guys to find out what they say happened.' Clive, never one to be in a hurry to call the police, didn't argue.

'OK. How long will you be?' he said.

'Around twenty minutes or less. I'm on my way,' she replied before ending the call.

Adam was feeling the drugs taking a positive steadying effect.

'Sorry,' Adam said to Kaylah and tried to put a comforting hand on her quivering shoulder.

'Clive, now help's coming, I think I need to get back to the others. I've an idea. Why don't I take and return your bike. You can then stay with Kaylah and go back with her in the car to the hotel,' he offered.

'Good idea. You might have to sort out the handlebars being out of alignment. I'll square up any costs later,' said Clive.

'Nothing a few turns of an Allen key and a spanner to the headset won't fix. Shouldn't cost anything. No worries,' he said. Clive wasn't listening. His mind was focussed on his sister, now crying inconsolably.

'You go, we'll be fine now,' Clive responded quietly, taking charge, 'Catch up with you later, and thanks.'

Adam picked up Clive's bike and began walking awkwardly, a bike in each hand, heading back to find his friends.

Lena, meanwhile, was upset. Her unruffled professional demeanour had been shaken and undone. She felt responsible for and even tainted by the catastrophe and, though she hadn't said so to Clive, betrayed by her colleagues, her trust in her security colleagues too for that matter. As soon as she stopped speaking to Clive, she booked a car from the Consulate car pool and headed out, but not before calling her boss on the handsfree. When he picked up, she didn't hold back.

'Have just had a call. Moments ago Kaylah's baby son was kidnapped by Ali Muhammed. You promised me the two guys you sent out would get Ali and take care of the two Brits. Where the hell were they?' she shouted.

'There's been a hiccup, our guys have just called in. They got unlucky. We're not sure how it happened, but they got hit and had to get out. We get another chance at Ali. He can't be that lucky!'

'A hiccup! Look, you told me when I got Kaylah to cooperate, they would be safe. It's a bloody nightmare! A mum has had her baby kidnapped! How does that play out in your book? What are the Brits going to say about that when they find out about your bloody hiccup?' she said, not letting up.

'Calm it Lena, you're not normally like this. Steps are being taken to remedy the mistake. Our guys know where Ali and the baby are headed. They've got an hour to get the baby back. So just cool it, look after the Brits. Reassure them and I'll call you about delivering the kid back to its mum. No more to be said for now,' he said plaintively.

Lena had to end the call; she was already approaching the Kone's hotel and was wondering where to park up. In the end she didn't care and threw the car onto the pavement out of the traffic right outside the hotel door. She fully expecting there'd be a traffic penalty and she smiled at the pleasure she would feel imagining it landing on her boss's desk. Striding into the foyer she couldn't see Kaylah or Clive, but the helpful receptionist looked up from her queue of waiting guests to signpost her upstairs.

Lena slowed her stride, deciding to take the stairs. She realised that this was going to be difficult. No amount of training prepared you for telling a mother that your people

312

were responsible for the loss of her baby. Kaylah will be in shock, angry or hysterical, she thought; whichever, and she dreaded the pending encounter.

She decided that her boss had given her a line to use, the hope that there would be good news within the hour. That would be what she would emphasise. They needed not to lose hope. But what about Clive's wish to alert the Turkish authorities. She couldn't allow that. It could lead to unpredictable responses in the next hour when she believed the attempt to rescue Jacob would take place. She decided she would play for time, sitting with them the full length of the hour, sharing the time as if it were a hospital waiting room and the subject was having critical surgery.

She arrived at Kaylah's door and could hear the wailing inside and she couldn't shut it out, it touched her very soul. Hesitating, she plucked up her courage, told herself to do her duty, and knocked twice. The door was immediately opened by Clive. Kaylah's face, being dabbed by wet tissues, was a picture combining loss and pain. It was going to be a most difficult hour and Clive looked at her with the burning hate of a man deeply wounded and looking straight at someone he believed to be personally responsible. She felt his gaze was a justified rebuke, knowing inside that never before had she ever done anything quite so reprehensible.

Lena began by asking Clive if she could sit with Kaylah for a few minutes. Taking the initiative, she asked if he could see if he could get them all something to drink. Glad to be doing something useful, he asked what everyone wanted and disappeared through the door heading downstairs to the bar. Lena sat on the bed and put her arm over Kaylah's shoulder.

'I'm so sorry, if I'd had any idea this would happen, believe me I would never have suggested you meet. But please, try and be patient, I don't know what went wrong in the Square, but I've been told that our guys think they know where Ali has gone and are going now to get Jacob back. That's all I've been told. We have to be patient. Try really hard to wait out the coming hour. I'll stay here with you until the call comes,' Lena said quietly trying her best to inspire some hope into the situation.

Kaylah couldn't speak, her head bowed low and deep sobs shaking her body. Lena thought she had registered what she said but couldn't be sure, and so when Clive returned she went over what she'd said a second time.

None of them knew how to make the time pass in a bearable way, the tension waiting for news was so great. The drinks of mint tea and orange juice lay untouched on the tray brought to their room by a puzzled but discreet waiter, who quietly disappeared as quickly as he'd arrived.

At midday Lena's phone rang. She picked it up and decided to take it outside in the corridor. It was her boss. 'I don't know how to tell you this, but there's been an almighty explosion to the north of you in Beyoglu. It's where an IS attack cell HQ is located. As I speak emergency services are going to the scene. I think you should prepare your friends for bad news.'

42

It took a bit of skill to wheel two bicycles in the same direction through busy pedestrian thoroughfares when one bike had an out-of-alignment handlebar. By the time Adam got back to the café he thought his friends would be angry at being kept waiting for so long. He needn't have worried, they looked up from their drinks, all smiles when they spotted him coming and as he approached made jokes about what he'd done to lose Clive.

'No wonder you cycled on your own last year,' said Bilal, 'you would lose anyone you'd take with you! Now what have you done with Clive?' He spotted the twisted handlebar, adding in a tone of concern, 'What, did he fall off?'

Adam ignored him. By now everyone was looking at him, seeing the need for some kind of explanation for the missing Clive. Adam quickly briefed them, telling them that there had been a problem in the Square. A meeting arranged between Kaylah and Jacob's father had gone wrong and the father had gone off with the child. Clive had stayed back to look after Kaylah and get some help to sort it out.

Adam reasoned it would get all too complicated if he started to explain about Ali and the reason for the meeting and he certainly didn't want to start talking about gunmen in cars lining them up in their sights. He told his friends that it was time to start thinking about returning the hired bikes and that he might need their help to back him up if they were to avoid losing the deposit on Clive's bike. They settled up the drinks bill and headed off, knowing it would take all of the next hour to push the bikes back to their start point.

Adam asked Bilal to take a turn pushing two bikes as he needed to make a call. Bilal was happy enough to help. Adam was desperate to get a call in to Krish to tell him what had been happening and see if Krish could do anything further to help. The more he thought about it, the more urgent Kaylah and Jacob's situation seemed. As he re-lived the distress he saw in Kaylah, he was now feeling every second wasted was a moment too long. He called Krish. It was 11.30am.

Krish listened to Adam over the noise of the busy traffic. This time Adam did not give a sanitised version. He told Krish every last detail, especially about the gunman in the back of the car. Adam had a good memory for vehicle details and reeled off the colour, make and first part of the registration.

Krish interrupted. 'You sure about the plate? Only it's a diplomatic number, sounds like one of the cars from the Israeli Consulate to me.'

'Well that starts to make sense,' said Adam. 'That Lena woman has been trying from the first to use Kaylah and the baby as bait to trap Ali. I reckon they were out to shoot Ali down as he stood with Kaylah and the baby. How cynical is that?'

'Looks like your cycling companion Clive spared them that one. I have to admit he certainly showed some courage and quick thinking to get the result he did. Sounds like they had to do a quick abort mission. Someone's going to have a very red face. They sped off you say?'

'Yes, but while this was going on, Ali's taken off with the baby. Can you do anything? We're talking British citizens here, people you are supposed to look out for when abroad,' pushed Adam.

'It's complicated in that Ali is the child's father. Don't suppose you know which direction he headed off in?' enquired Krish.

'No. It all happened so fast. After Clive got ahead of me, hit the projecting gun barrel and then crashed to the floor, I caught up, helped pick him up off the floor. He wasn't hurt, a thumped arm and some cuts and bruises, nothing really. By the time we both looked up, there was only Kaylah there. Ali and Jacob had gone leaving her and an empty buggy. She was totally distraught, Krish. It was painful to see it.'

316

'The shortest route of exit from where they were was somewhere behind the flag pole near where they met up I guess. I'm going to see if we can get a couple of our people out looking for them now. No time to lose. I'm also going to get straight on to the Israelis. We need some answers as to what kind of game they are playing here. It looks like they had a very dirty assassination in mind. At some stage we will need to tell the Turkish police, but let's see if we can find out more first. Where are you now, Adam, and where are you headed?' asked Krish.

Adam explained that the four of them were heading back with the five bikes and it would take around an hour. Clive was returning to their hotel with Kaylah. Adam's own group were walking together heading north. Krish checked out how Adam was feeling, thinking that he was performing incredibly well, given the state he was in a day or two earlier. Adam explained he'd had to take a double shot of the tablets he'd been given and that had boosted him.

Adam rejoined the others after the call. He told them he'd called the British Consulate to ask for their help and that they were hopefully sending out a couple of guys. Raqiyah and the others thought Adam seemed in control and had taken a good decision. However, inside, he began to feel he might need to pop another tablet before long. At the same time he feared sliding into drug dependency. He slipped his hand into his pocket to make sure the reassuring packet of Lorazapan was still within easy reach.

They walked back over the Galata Bridge and into Beyoglu. They still had the length of a few streets to go, when there was the sound of a massive explosion somewhere ahead of them. Pigeons flew up above them in alarm, people began looking at each other and then pointing between the buildings where a dust cloud was beginning to rise. '

'An explosion, over there,' said Bilal in alarm, pointing where everyone was looking.

They looked at each other and then decided to just keep walking and deal with getting the bikes back. As they approached the hire shop, the sound of emergency vehicle sirens filled the air as vehicles rushed to the scene of the explosion.

The bike shop was quite near to where it had happened, and they could see the apartment block had been badly damaged. It looked, through the dust, as if the whole first floor had been ripped apart. Dazed people were standing in the street, policemen in uniform trying to use tape to create a cordon sanitaire. The good thing was that the bike shop assistant was so absorbed in what was happening on the street, he took the bikes without looking at them and handed them back their deposits, Adam taking Clive's in his absence.

'What do you think caused it?' asked Sophie. 'Do you think there'll be another one?'

'Don't know, it's hard to tell and we can't see the back of the building which may have been the centre of the blast. There's nothing we can do. We're just spectators,' said Raqiyah.

'There's grey dust blowing everywhere. It's messing my trainers,' said Sophie.

A fleet of ambulances were lined up, the first ones were filled with stretcher cases. The local police were now being supplemented by more serious-looking military figures in flack jackets, metal helmets and carrying machine guns.

'I think it's terrorist related,' said Adam, 'and I don't think we should hang around. We're either going to end up being picked up as suspects or we'll get told to move off for being in the way.'

'OK, I suggest we head back to our Apartments,' suggested Raqiyah, to which there were nods of assent all around.

Adam was looking at Twitter feeds on his phone, and then switching to Breaking News. Then he saw something Reuters had posted of news coming in of an explosion in an apartment block in a residential area of north Istanbul. The report suggested the explosion may have been the result of terrorists being the victims of an explosion of their own making as they prepared for some kind of attack elsewhere in the city. Adam shared the news with his friends.

318

The only terrorist I know of round here is Ali Muhammed, thought Adam, and if he came straight back here with baby Jacob I hate to think what has happened to that child. For now there was simply no way of knowing.

The four turned, moved away and were back at the Apartments by 1pm. After allowing time for each to return to their rooms, they agreed to meet up in the downstairs café at 1.30pm and catch up whilst having something to eat. As Adam's latest medication began to wear off, he no longer felt like having a meal.

43

Ali was holding Jacob. His mind was thinking impossible thoughts and dreams. How could he keep hold of him? When he heard the unmistakeable sound of a nearby passing bullet, followed almost instantaneously by the distant crack of a firing gun, his instinct was to protect the lives of himself and his young son.

Without thinking he just ran, ran fast, straight for the nearest exit-route, trying not to shake baby Jacob too much as he ran. No further shots came and he questioned whether he'd really heard it, but there could be no doubt. On further reflection it sounded like a marksman, a sniper, and he concluded someone was on to him and it was just too dangerous to look or go back.

Once in the busy streets, he was just another figure in the crowd and he slowed his pace, walking briskly, purposefully back towards Beyoglu. He didn't know what to do next. He needed help with Jacob. Very quickly he'd realised he was in no position to look after him and it wouldn't be long before Jacob would need milk and changes. His only thought was to call Zaid.

'Zaid, I need your help,' he said.

It was a difficult story to explain, but Zaid offered the help of his family and said he would come and meet Ali. He was concerned that time was getting tight. The teams would need to start gathering their equipment and setting out between 1pm and 2pm. He was particularly feeling hard-pressed because he and Ali would need to be ready to leave soon to get to the Galatasaray stadium. Zaid gave directions to his family's apartment and told Ali to make his way straight there. He'd call through to say they were coming.

Thirty minutes later Ali arrived and was let into Zaid's flat. Jacob was stirring. Ali explained that this was his son and that a shot had been taken at him whilst he had been with him and he'd run for cover carrying Jacob to safety.

The baby was a problem none of them wanted and Zaid was getting anxious. It was time for the first team, the Galatasaray group to get ready and leave, and Ali seemed hopelessly distracted.

'Ali, look here. I'll take the two lads to the Stadium. You see to your baby here. My wife will take care of him. She has three young children. It will be an honour. If need be, she will see your son gets back to your family in Mosul. Come on, we have to leave him here now. Are you with us or not?' he said, moving to leave the apartment.

'Zaid. I'll go to the Blue Mosque instead. You know what to do at the Stadium. You'll be fine. Go now and get in place. The Blue Mosque group could use another person who knows what to do, it's a more complicated mission,' said Ali.

The two embraced and then Zaid headed off to gather the lads, three explosive vests and automatic, rapid-fire, handguns. It would be 11.45 by the time the three of them had collected their equipment from the flat and set off to get themselves in place at the stadium in good time. Theirs was the first attack group to move out.

Ali meantime talked to Zaid's wife who did not seem at all fazed at taking on an extra little one. Whether her feelings were genuine or not, Ali had no way of telling.

'His name is Jacob, my son,' he told her.

'Jacob,' she repeated. 'I will look after him as my own and if it is the will of Allah, I will ensure he is safely delivered to your family in Mosul,' she reassured him. 'Go now.'

After a quick final glance at Jacob, Ali walked across the street and headed towards their apartment base to get ready. He glanced at his watch. The men should have sorted and prepared all the explosives and weapons to take with them by now. He started going through the programme in his mind – Zaid's group of three should be on their way, the other twelve waiting for him to arrive. He wondered how they would take his sudden change of plan, knowing no-one liked last minute changes when it came to the final stages of a mission. As he turned the final corner he spotted Omar's al Britani looking out for him from the first-floor window. Seeing him, Omar's face disappeared again back inside. Ali surmised he'd probably gone to tell the others that he was about to arrive.

Ali never made it across the road. The force of the blast caught him and threw him back. He lay on the street unable to get his breath, his ears ringing, only knowing he was still alive. He couldn't hear what was going on and the one side of his head had been hit, his one eye unfocussed. Dust was everywhere.

Instinctively he knew what had happened. In Mosul drone attacks felt just like this. His mind went back to earlier attempts to attack him and the drone attack on the hospital killing his brother Mo and little five year old Ahmed.

As he lay on the road his mind flashed further back to the time as a younger man when his father had been shot on a Mosul street. He thought his own time to die hadn't come yet. He forced himself up off the hot tarmac, and saw blood on the road where he had been lying. Blood was dripping from his head to the ground. He blinked to try and clear the sight in his right eye, the blood filling it as it ran down from his forehead.

Gently he touched his head, feeling over it, detecting wet gashes as he did so. He looked at his hand now covered with blood. He concluded he had either been hit on his head by some piece of flying debris or had been thrown hard to the street by the blast. He told himself the injury was not serious.

Instinct kicked in. He must get off the street quickly or he'd be picked up. He pulled his open jacket off and bound it round his head and with faltering steps retraced his way back to Zaid's flat he'd left just moments earlier. The windows were broken, but no-one inside hurt. Zaid's sister pulled him inside. She called for help and an older lady came and sat Ali down on a stool before removing his jacket from his head to look at his injuries.

'I'm a nurse. Sit still. Let me see here,' she said, taking control. She called for a First Aid box from the other room. With scissors she hacked at Ali's hair, and working from behind him, wiped his head, a bowl of water and bloody rags piling up on the floor beside her.

'I'm putting stitches in myself, unless you want to go to the hospital? I thought not. Just I've no pain relief for you.'

'Go on, do it,' Ali said, 'Tidy it up. I must get on.'

His ears were still buzzing from the blast, but his eye once washed from the blood that had clouded it was able to see clearly again. He'd been lucky, only scalp wounds. They bled a lot, but that was all. The stitches would soon stop that. He got up to go outside as soon as he was allowed, one of Zaid's jackets now replacing his own. He heard the sirens outside before he saw them and knew they were headed this way.

No weapon or explosives, no men left of his own, he was now a fugitive. He went over to the window where once glass had been and gazed across the street. First, he saw where he had fallen, the crimson blood marking the spot. Then he gazed up at the apartment which was no more. He knew at that moment, no-one inside would still be alive. It was over.

But Zaid's team had surely left well before the blast, he calculated. If they'd left on time, they'd be on their way to the stadium. There was no point trying to join them now. What could he do? Unlike them, he hadn't even a ticket to get into the ground, let alone the capability to achieve anything. They'd be alright, that was something, he thought.

His heart sank as the full scale of the failure of his mission began to dawn on him. One success at a football match would be just another footnote in a series of other recent attacks. Today would no longer be part of a campaign designed to tip the balance in IS's favour. He thought he needed to alert their Kurdish friends. They'd need to make their own decision whether to continue or abort. He picked up his mobile and called his CO.

'Ali Muhammed here,' he said.

323

'Salim Ismat,' he replied, before formal Islamic greetings were exchanged between them.

'We have suffered a setback. There has been a leak somewhere. A drone attack has destroyed us, killed all but four of us. You have a traitor somewhere,' said Ali thinking on his feet. 'I'm injured, and only one of the attacks is still going ahead. Do we tell our friends in the north to call off their mission?'

'If indeed this is a disaster, it is the will of Allah. I will talk to our Kurdish friends. Do not let yourself be taken alive,' he said, before the line went dead.

Ali had to think fast, but his head was hurting and thumping now. He asked for painkillers but was told there were none. He looked at Jacob but knew he could do nothing for him. Zaid's wife told him she would look after him as one of her own. She was anxious that he should leave now, the area would be crawling with police and army very soon. She was worried the police would soon be knocking door to door. She wanted Ali out.

'Zaid has a bicycle in there,' she said pointing to a room beside the front door, 'Take it, now go. Allah be with you, inshallah,' she said.

Pointing to his head, she pulled a cycle helmet from the cupboard. He grabbed it. It would hide his hacked hair and stitched head from casual inspection, even disguise his appearance. The bike would give him the chance to move away from the area and Ali was reminded of his earlier escape from London. His spirits lifted as he wheeled the bike outside, round the corner out of sight. He climbed on and headed east in the direction of the Caliphate. Once again Ali was a fugitive on the run, only this time it wasn't so far to go to be back amongst friends.

44

Big Harry was in his hotel room. He unpacked his shiny black Doc Martens with the steel toecaps. It was really important to turn up at a match looking smart, a credit to one's people. He double-tied the laces and rolled the bottom of his jeans down over them. They now looked like an ordinary pair of smart shoes. Match preparation followed a well-rehearsed ritual. It wasn't that he was superstitious or anything, it just felt right when everything was in order. The final piece was his dark-blue blazer. It had wide stripes, making him look distinguished and it went well with his white 'England's Glory' emblazoned T-shirt he'd got the proprietor's missus to iron for him overnight.

He stared in the full-length mirror. Fingering the lapel, he remembered he'd acquired the jacket from a charity shop whilst studying his engineering degree at Plymouth University. His dad had told him engineering was the thing to do if he was going to take over the family scrapyard business one day. His grandfather had started it off after the second world war, now his own father was looking to the future. Trouble is, thought Harry, as he continued to gaze at his reflection, too many people think people like me are just thick. One day they'll come to realise the truth, I'm going to inherit a business and I'm handsome and intelligent to boot. Maybe vain too!

Harry grinned as he turned away from the mirror and glanced at his heavy metal watch with its steel strapping. It was nearly time to head for the stadium. Years of experience had taught him to prepare well before a match. It was essential to set out and turn up early at a stadium. People who didn't and turned up late got hassled, kept out of the ground or didn't know the danger they were in until too late. Going to the ground followed a well-oiled routine – a time when all of them needed to stick together, walking in line, each in his place, Harry in the centre and all watching out for each other.

Places like Italy were the worst to visit, knives got used. The old Eastern-Block countries weren't so bad, they had respect for hard guys on the right. But Turkey, you could never tell, he mused. Who knows what this afternoon will turn out like? Friendly matches tended to be low-key, but you never knew. They needed to be one step ahead, they didn't want to get caught out in a fight not of their own making in a place where the odds were so numerically and culturally stacked against him and his mates.

He was the first downstairs, leaning on the bar, waiting for the others. They'd found a family-run restaurant with rooms upstairs. It suited them fine. Nothing was too much trouble for the owner and his staff once Harry had made a few things clear about their stay. Tell people how it is, Harry reckoned, and there never was any trouble. Five minutes later, the others, all wearing matching white T-shirts had joined him. The seven of them were heading out for the Galatasaray Stadium, or Turk Telekom Arena, as people seemed to call it locally.

The group took control of the pavement as they headed out into the afternoon sun making for the nearest yellow 'Taksi' rank just a block down the street. Between them, they took two taxis and headed north in convoy arriving at the ground by 1pm giving them a planned window of two hours before kick off. Harry asked his driver how they got back to their hotel after the match, but the driver only vaguely waved towards the main road opposite the stadium. Harry wasn't going to get more from this guy. He paid up and the two yellow cars sped off.

Looking around them, this was some busy place. High-rise apartment blocks were on every side; a huge multi-lane dual carriageway arterial road flyover carried streams of incessantly noisy traffic nearby. They moved in closer to the football ground and found a bar that suited them. They had some time to kill before they could get inside. Harry suggested they take the table out on the street where they

326

could see what was going on. Lagers were soon bought and all began to enjoy the combination of lager and sunshine. Soon their conversation began to get noisier as they considered the merits and defects of their favourite players. The young waiter who spoke reasonable English came out to try and ask them to quieten down, his anxious manager looking on from inside.

'Just go and tell your boss that we're from England and it was the English who first brought football to this godforsaken land. Ask him if he knew that. Ask him if he knows that Istanbul's Fenerbahce Stadium is built on the site where the English first taught you Turks how to play football. Ask him that.' Harry knew the very mention of Galatasaray's rival's ground would be enough to wind-up most people, but the lad, from the look on his face, knew when he was already beaten.

'OK, but can you be more quiet please,' he repeated.

Big Harry pushed back his chair, stood up and towered over the lad, his eyes staring hard at him. It was enough to send the lad back inside. The matter of noise levels in the area sorted, it was time to move anyway. They had a whip-round to raise the money for the drinks, Stu told to go and pay at the bar. They waited whilst he disappeared to settle up and then they all began moving towards what was, they agreed, a spectacular modern venue. The stadium looked like a flying saucer which had somehow found a place to land in the crowded cityscape. For a national stadium they thought it looked small. This was no Wembley stadium. Even so, as they walked towards it, its huge dimensions began to tower over them.

They moved inside. Here their tickets were closely scrutinised before they were eventually directed towards where the small area of England supporters had been corralled. Harry thought they must be expecting trouble, he'd never seen so many soldiers and policemen supporting the local stewards and more looked like they were arriving by the minute.

As he watched, every now and then a policeman would pull a supporter away from his friends and with his accompanying armed soldier carefully looking on a few paces off, thoroughly search him. They're worried about something, Harry's instinct told him, and he cast a gaze round him to check out he wasn't missing anything. It paid to be watchful at all times. He sensed there was something else in the atmosphere not normally present for a friendly match.

Time soon passed on these occasions and it had gone 2.30pm when Harry next glanced at his watch. The fast food kebabs they'd bought on their way in, dry to their taste, had long been finished as their group hung around in the interior precincts avoiding the programme sellers and other hawkers. Looking to the stadium's interior, the steep banks of bright-red seats promised an intense atmosphere.

Harry had carefully organised his group's seats so that they could be near one of the entrance/exit tunnels. He always did the ticket buying. In recent years grounds had been designed and managed to ensure supporters were kept stationery during a match, with particular attention given to keeping rival fans apart from each other, but Harry had learned that a bit of careful internet research before booking tickets ensured he could be sure of his group having some control of their own movement in spite of the built-in constraints. He was good at exploiting opportunities to create an impression, to let the locals know who was boss.

As they found their way to their seats he felt pleased with his choice. The view of the grass below was excellent and they were but a low jump from getting into the tunnel beside them. It annoyed him there were so many CCTV cameras everywhere he looked, even in the tunnel. If they were working as they should, these could limit options open to them if they needed to let people know they were here. Maybe today, all the physical stuff would be on the pitch, he thought. He was cautious and only took carefully calculated risks, the more so when abroad, on someone else's turf.

The stadium often hosted national team matches and had much loyal local support. Harry had to admit that the

Turkish turnout, with most of their ranks of supporters wearing red, was impressive. Those clad in white made up only a small, much quieter gathering.

The few remaining empty seats in the stadium were filling fast in the final minutes before the teams appeared on the pitch. Only a relatively small area of the stadium around them was occupied by England supporters and he eye-balled a number of faithful regulars he recognised, having spotted them nearby. Maybe they would all meet up in town later. They usually did.

Harry was making one of his periodic sweeps of the stadium crowd, just as the two lines of players were coming on to the pitch to make their formal presentations and hear the anthems, when long experience told him something he was looking at was not quite right.

Most people at this point made their way quickly to their seats. Time was of the essence in the final moments before kick-off, but there were three local guys still hanging around in the entrance way to his right, messing around with their bags.

They were ridiculously overdressed for such a hot day. The two younger guys were being told something by a slightly older one. Perhaps they had stuff to sell, he wondered. Then he realised that couldn't be so. People who press against a sidewall like that are trying to be invisible. Could be drugs, was his next thought. Time for a second opinion. Harry nudged Stu.

'See those three in the tunnel. Odd don't you think?' said Harry quietly. Harry always thought Stu had a special gift for reading situations and getting it right, and valued his second sight, as he called it. Stu fixed his eyes on them, immobile.

'They're not security are they?' he asked, not lifting his gaze, 'because they're armed, weapons under their jackets. They keep looking to the pitch, as if waiting for the formal parties to line up in front of them.'

'Don't like it. Could be a bunch of bloody extremists for all we know,' said Harry.

'They are, Harry. I'm certain. Brace yourself for trouble. The young lad at the back. He's scared witless, he just dropped that black rolled up cloth. Only one team I know goes for black banners and they don't play football,' commented Stu.

Harry watched some more, precious seconds ticking by. His pulse now racing, he was convinced they had weapons and maybe suicide vests too. He rapidly considered their options. They were too near them, there was no bloody cover to be had. The three were so busy eye-balling the approaching football teams marching on to the pitch that Harry and Stu's observations passed unnoticed.

The players would soon be lining up just in front of them. Harry reckoned himself to be as hard as the next man, but he felt a fear he'd never experienced before. He thought of himself being maimed or killed by flying shrapnel, blinded even and he felt something he could only call raw-edged fear eating at his insides.

He looked at Stu, Stu who was totally dependent on him, Stu who had come here in part to celebrate his stag weekend and Harry remembered it was his promise to Penny, his missus-to-be to watch over him. Harry's mind had never thought so hard so quickly. He looked at the low wall in front of them. If he called them all to lie down behind it, what would that look like. In any case, what protection it afforded wasn't enough. Harry looked around to see what obstacles might undo his idea of a quick dash to get them before they got him and his mates.

In the end he knew he had only really got one option and not for the first time he would have to trust his mates to unquestioningly leap into attacking these three. All depended on them simply doing it when he gave the word. He got the immediate attention of all his group, using the well-tried and tested touch shoulder method he always employed. They looked his way, and he nodded down the tunnel, ensuring they too had read his thoughts and homed in on their target.

'Let's get them,' he ordered firmly but quietly. The familiar words usually triggered the launch of a fist fight with rival supporters. His friends would know exactly what such a command meant. They'd get in there fast before the opposition knew what hit them. It was all about getting the other person before they had the chance to strike one back at you. These three looked easy and they wouldn't expect to be jumped on from the side.

They were still not looking in his direction, observed Harry, as he led the way and dropped over the low barrier and into the tunnel not three paces from them. His eyes scanned for police or security to be doing their job, but none were anywhere nearby. Most were staring at the gathering players on the pitch, approaching them for the National Anthems. Harry's heart rate accelerated, adrenaline was released in great bursts of uncontrollable energy, his senses heightened in a state of ecstatic awareness. He needed release.

'Our boys in white are in danger of their lives from those three in the tunnel. We jump them now or it'll be too late. Just follow me. Now! Now! Now!' cried Harry to those nearest him.

Harry led the way over the sidewall into the adjoining tunnel with a side jump that all his training in the gym made look smooth and practised. The three guys heard the sound and the two younger ones turned, desperately clutching under their oversize coats to pull out their guns, but it was too late.

One yelled 'Zaid!' to alert the older guy still looking in the direction of the pitch. Harry crashed into him and bundled him to the floor, Harry's knee riding up under his ribs. He knew his lads would be very close and they'd have taken down the other two. Then he yelled out, realising that a deadly peril could at any moment destroy them all.

'Pin their arms, pin their arms, suicide vests, they've got suicide vests. Pin them down and hold them, as if your fucking lives depend on it,' he commanded.

The three were duly flattened, spread-eagled and Harry gave Zaid an introduction to his right boot, the steel kissing the side of his head with a noticeable clunk. He glanced at the other two lads, his mates holding and hitting them. Terrified, all three had let go of their guns, dropping them to the floor and were jabbering away, probably pleading for the onslaught to end. They were wasting their breath, any movement and they got another fist to the face. There were shouts from behind them in the tunnel as a soldier and a policeman ran up, their weapons pointing at them.

Harry gesticulated to explain what they were doing. He had a moment of panic, wondering if the guy would comprehend the situation or trigger an explosion. To his surprise and utter relief the soldier understood, nodded to Harry and then explained to the policeman what was happening. The soldier moved in, pointing his machine gun at the three on the ground, kicking away their discarded hand guns, whilst waving the policeman to stay back, as he moved in close to take a look at what they were wearing.

'Hold them, hold them. Not let move,' he said in broken English.

Harry told his guys, repeating the soldier's words, 'Hold them still as if your very lives depend on it.' The three on the ground were not offering any resistance, any fight had long gone out of them.

By now other soldiers were running towards them. Two at a time were sent forward to replace Harry's men. Then Harry's guys were waved urgently back down the tunnel, first three, then two and finally Harry and Stu who left Zaid groaning beneath them on the ground. The last to walk back down the tunnel was Harry himself, to find he was now Harry, the hero of the hour, soldiers and policemen lining up to shake his hand.

It was strange, Harry thought, this must be how the winning team felt as they left the pitch at a match end, the applause and cheers resounding around them. It was a good feeling, and he slowed his pace, time to re-collect his poise, adjust his jacket and show some British pride. Then Harry was worried, he could see that all this fuss might mean they'd miss the match.

He was right to worry. The seven of them were escorted in line to a waiting police minibus, then driven fast to a nearby police HQ. As they were such unlikely heroes, the police stared at them, time and again. To their eyes these English supporters didn't add up.

The following hours were spent in the taking and signing of statements with the aid of an interpreter, until finally they were told they would shortly be leaving. Mint tea, Turkish coffee and sweet Turkish cakes were brought in, though Harry could have murdered a beer.

They were told that a press conference was being convened for 6pm and the world's waiting media wanted to photograph them and ask some questions. They were warned the reporters were wanting to meet the 'have-a-go-heroes,' as they were already being called.

Harry had a word with his lads and they decided to give it a go. The senior Turkish army officer interrupted him.

'A message of appreciation for what you have done has already come in from 10 Downing Street and our own Prime Minister who was here watching the match wants to come and thank you personally. Oh, yes, and in case you were wondering, the friendly match ended in a 2-1 win.'

'Who for?' asked Harry.

'The only downside I have to report this afternoon – your team won, and you lucky guys have lived to celebrate it!' A well-practised roar went up from Harry and his mates.

45

The drone missiles were precise, surgically accurate, a new model built with US help and recently introduced, its design addressing the voiced political requirement to try and overcome the embarrassment of excessive collateral damage. Politicians didn't like having big civilian losses to explain away. Nonetheless all trace of make and any clues as to the missile's source had been carefully erased in its production. The three low-flyers despatched were a quarter of only a dozen such drones kept aside for secret use in sensitive locations. No-one except their controller knew where each one released was targeted and where they were at any one time.

At 12 noon on Friday 20 August, the first drone proved its accuracy as it went in through the first-floor kitchen window of the Beyoglu apartment block, detonating milliseconds later as it touched the far-wall of the kitchen.

Instantaneously, all the interior dividing walls were taken out, pulverising the room, dividing plasterboard into a million deadly shards, in an explosion so strong no-one inside would have known what killed them. The force lifted the ceiling sending everything flying upstairs including the occupants on the floor above. The floor below bowed down perilously. Water started spurting and hissing from shattered pipes, spitting into the grey dust, which made seeing or breathing impossible, before beginning its search downward for somewhere to escape.

There was no-one left alive to try and force an exit through the apartment front door. Had they wanted to, they'd have had to look for it first. Amazingly, the still-intact white door was now lying in the rubble and glass on the car park below.

The second drone hit a storeroom in the car park area as simultaneously the third hit the container on the articulated truck still parked down below.

All people claimed to have heard later was one big explosion, but in reality the second and third drones simultaneously detonated the IS stores of ammunition and explosives, and these together destroyed the whole of the back of the building where the visual impact of the damage was far worse. Some claimed to have heard some kind of hum or whoosh in the air beforehand, but no-one knew what to make of it.

The drone controller tapped away on his keypad to send a text to Tel Aviv. 'Packages successfully delivered. Ground observations are required to verify desired outcome.'

An encrypted message was immediately sent to the Israeli Consulate in Istanbul asking for on the ground local intelligence as a matter of urgency. Meanwhile, back in Tel Aviv, members of Israeli Security gathered round their monitors waiting for the first news and intelligence reports to come in. They didn't have to wait long.

The Turkish authorities were sending messages back to their own HQ on easily tapped frequencies. Unknown to them, the constant chatter from the first on-scene emergency services was being picked up word for word back in Israel. When they reported they had not yet been able to find any survivors on the first floor and the first bodies were now being recovered, there was a cheer in the Tel Aviv office and high fives between anyone with a colleague nearby with whom to share the mission's apparent success.

Further news came in only slowly. Local Israeli observers verified the total destruction of the first floor in the Beyoglu apartment block and the destruction of the IS explosive storeroom which had caused the most extensive damage. Media officers in Tel Aviv were already creating their own stories of an IS terror campaign having gone wrong with an, as yet unexplained, explosion destroying their capability in Istanbul. With luck no-one would know there had been any foreign involvement and in any case it would be forever denied.

The Israelis knew that waiting for verification of the IS body count and identification of remains would take weeks, but to try and speed the process along, they sent an urgent message through to ask the Turks if they could offer any assistance. Their provision of expertise was welcomed and an Israeli forensic pathologist, together with an explosives scientist were allowed to join the embryonic Turkish team facing the grim task of collecting and working on the body parts.

Now positioned in the intelligence front-line, they were the ones best placed to answer what everyone wanted to know, 'Did we get Ali Muhammed?'

All knew however, that any conclusive answer to a question like that would have to wait. Only a lucky break, a quick visual of what was left of the dead man would verify what everyone hoped was true. In the meantime, with all the waiting, well-satisfied staff in Tel Aviv began to drink more coffee.

Meanwhile, back in the police HQ in Istanbul, there was a sudden outbreak of panic and subsequently pandemonium. It was one thing for everyone to be on a heightened state of alert in case of terrorism, but this attack when it came had been a surprise to everyone.

People were asking each other why a block of flats had been the target. Could someone somewhere have had a lucky escape from an IS attack, with the terrorists suffering a catastrophic explosion of their own making?

On hearing the news, the Istanbul Police Chief, Adem Rahman, remembered all too well Israeli Intelligence had suggested the Turks take on attacking that very block today, believing tomorrow to be too late. It was Chief Inspector Kizilay's Security Group Delta who had told him he could delay until Saturday. Personally, he had been the one who refused to believe the Israelis.

The first thing he did was to call his deputy to order the preparations they had in hand for tomorrow's pre-dawn raid to be immediately stood down. So far as he was concerned, the coincidence of Israeli insistence and explosion were too close to one another to be simply called an IS accident, but so far as public discussion went, the IS accident account was definitely going to be the only storyline going out. He had no wish to see himself hauled before yet another interminable internal disciplinary enquiry. The very thought depressed him.

Now was a time for action and he knew he had to call Police HQ in Ankara. They would have already had some preliminary reports sent across, but he needed to speak directly to his opposite number in Ankara, Chief Inspector Kizilay, and then to the National Internal Security Chief, Hakan Turan. He shut his office door and went to sit behind his desk to make the necessary calls.

'Kizilay,' came the reply.

'Adem Rahman, Istanbul, speaking.'

'Glad you called. I hear there's a situation at your end today,' said Kizilay who had already had a call from a contact.

'Yes, but it's been dealt with. Early thinking is that the IS cell we were monitoring and going in to neutralise at first light tomorrow have saved us the trouble by having a problem handling their own explosives. Emergency Services at the scene report total devastation of the IS hideout with, as yet, no known survivors,' said Rahman hoping that his interpretation of events would be accepted.

'It's always helpful to have the terrorists dead. How many do you think have been taken down?' asked Kizilay.

'Too early to say for sure. The apartment's interior must have contained explosives too in addition to those stored outside. Everything inside is a mess, debris mixed with body parts and a small fire hasn't helped. As yet the structure's too dangerous to move around in, and we'll need to talk to the local authority about demolition in due course. We've evacuated the whole block and got all the neighbours either to hospital or safely escorted offsite,' Rahman explained.

'I think you've been very lucky, IS had something major lined up and it's gone down,' said a seemingly satisfied Kizilay.

'But we heard it was all lined up with Kurd attacks to take place in Ankara,' said Rahman. 'Anything happening at your end?'

'We're on highest state of readiness here, and what has happened at your end will facilitate getting the necessary permissions to set up extra road blocks and street searches here. The Police and Defence Ministries have just agreed to my request for extra overtime for the next week,' said Kizilay.

'I hope you have the same luck we've had here. In all probability a major attack has been thwarted and all the terrorists have been killed,' said Rahman now feeling more upbeat.

'You wait, you'll get a medal for this, Adem!' he chuckled. 'Keep me posted on what you find. I'd better go, we've got a large number of Kurdish sympathiser addresses to visit here today,' concluded Kizilay. 'After what's happened at your end, we can go in heavy here.'

When Adem Rahman put the receiver down he felt happier. Ankara were happy. The crisis was passing. He decided to make his second call to the National Internal Security Chief, Hakan Turan.

'Adem Rahman, Istanbul. Just wanted to brief you on later events here, Hakan,' he said.

'Yes, good, I was expecting you to call,' said Hakan.

Adem gave Hakan the same report he had just given his police opposite number Kizilay, but Hakan was more searching in his reply.

'I think we need to know a lot more here. First, early examination and analysis of the photos of the scene your guys have sent over suggest that there were three explosions, and I'm asking myself how come? One IS act of carelessness is possible, but I don't see it. I can't see how the container on that lorry blew up either as a consequence of an explosion in the flat, or the storeroom simultaneously went up as a result of the explosion in the flat. It's improbable, even impossible to believe. It can't be all as it first appears, Adem. You need to be looking at other explanations here. I'm sending my best

338

field officer over to join your team for a detailed examination of the site.'

'We've already had an offer of help from the Israelis. They've got two experts on their way,' Adem Rahman added, feeling vulnerable.

'Hmm. Now that's quick off the mark. They know more than they're letting on. I recall it was the Israelis who were pushing us to go in earlier on that apartment block. I think they've been having a little party of their own making. Oh, I dare say, if they nipped an attack in the bud, our leaders won't want to say anything about it. If they didn't, then you and I won't want to say anything about our timeline cock-up. But, you listen here carefully. Personally, I want that investigative team to check out for third party explosives. I'm pretty certain they'll find them. You'll need to ensure there are no press leaks on this one and all the investigative people you set to work have to be trusted to obey your orders. Understand me?' ordered Hakan.

'OK, I hear what's required. I'm on to it, Sir,' said Rahman.

'And, if things aren't tidied up properly, be sure the mud will come back to stick to your boots. Just remember it was you who delayed the search on that block, it was you who messed up, so make certain you tidy up properly and keep me fully in the picture,' Hakan added with all seriousness.

It was almost 3pm and Adem Rahman thought he'd have a break and order coffee. He never had the chance. A call came in from the Galatasaray stadium where Turkey were about to play England.

'They didn't all die at the apartment explosion,' said the local police inspector at the stadium. 'With the help of some English fans, we've picked up three IS fighters with guns and suicide vests here, inside the stadium. A major disaster has been averted. It's all safe here, no casualties. The match is going ahead, it's what the Prime Minister here wants.'

'Any idea of ID on the three?' asked Rahman.

'Sorry to have to report they are radicalised Turkish nationals. We've had our eye on Zaid Abbas for some time, the other two are youngsters. Zaid's address is the block opposite where the Beyoglu explosion took place. Suggest you get a team over to thoroughly search it,' he suggested.

'Thanks. We've had another lucky escape. Congratulate your men,' said Rahman.

'Will do. We're keeping the English fans with us for the time being. The Prime Minister wants them with him for the post-match press conference. Suggest you watch it, you'll find it fascinating,' the inspector said.

Adem Rahman ended the call. He was worried by this latest news. He then called his man on the ground at Beyoglu to make the necessary search of Zaid's home, ordering him to report back once he'd gone inside to brief him step by step on progress.

'Take great care on entry, we don't know what you will find and I don't want any casualties. Scene of Crime Officers will need to go in before everything's contaminated. This is an opportunity to find out more of what's going on in this city. Don't screw it up,' Rahman barked.

The brief call was then followed by return calls to update Ankara and then finally, Adem Rahman was able to order his coffee. As he sat down again at his desk, he clutched his hot sweet-smelling drink in both hands thinking hard. If three had escaped the explosion, how many more were there? And where was Ali Muhammed? He was no longer sure Ali was amongst the dead or that all the day's dramatic news had yet come to an end. The coffee was good, but not so good it made him any less anxious.

46

As soon as Adam was in his room he put on the TV and watched as the serious face of the Turkish television news reporter spoke from outside the block they had just left. The fire brigade were clearly hosing down a fire. It looked small and under control. Adam could make out from the accompanying revolving text news banner at the bottom of the screen that so far eight bodies had been recovered, some believed to be foreigners.

Omar al Britani's name appeared on the screen. Was he one of them? Adam couldn't be certain. There were many injured, mainly walking wounded, people in neighbouring flats hit by flying glass. The rolling subtitles showed the letters IS repeatedly and Adam suspected this was indeed where Ali had been staying. In the dirty world of liquidating terrorists, he wondered whether this could have been a deliberately targeted allied attack, rather than someone in IS simply being careless as they prepared explosives. He'd never know. He'd seen enough, switched off the TV and went to re-join the others downstairs.

Raqiyah looked up as she saw him approach. She was on her phone and put her hand over the mouthpiece to speak to him.

'It's uncle Abdul. Checking to see we are all OK. He's heard of the explosion on the news,' she whispered. The other two were talking quietly together and waved Adam over to them. Adam sat down. He'd taken another tablet before leaving his room and he was already registering its calming effect. He picked up a Diet Coke they'd bought for him. Bilal spoke first.

'Why is it, Adam, trouble seems to follow you around?' he said only half-jokingly. 'You were so right to be apprehensive about coming. We've ended up having more excitement than any of us bargained for. I think we ought to let folks at home know we're all alright, just in case they are picking things up on the news and we start getting a flood of concerned parent calls.'

'I already have,' said Sophie, looking up from her mobile, 'they liked my earrings.'

'I'll put something mundane on Facebook later. That way it'll be less likely to worry my parents, it's normal-like,' said Adam.

Raqiyah came off the phone and joined them, sitting next to Adam.

'Uncle Abdul's so sweet. He was all apologetic for his city letting us down, frightening us with extremists. He wants to make it up for us this evening and is sending Mustafa over to pick us up later. It's over to his home for supper tonight. I told him that would be nice. It's not like we've anything else planned or anything, is it?'

'I don't like to say such things, but there's one question on my mind that just won't go away. Do you think Kaylah's baby was in that blast if Ali had taken him?' asked Adam.

'Why don't you phone Kaylah. See if there is any news, ask if we can help in any way, or at least send her our love, poor thing,' said Sophie.

'Yeah, think I will. Won't do any harm. No, I'll speak to Clive, I can tell him I've got his bike deposit back,' said Adam.

'Don't think he'll be thinking of his bike deposit just now. Ask after Kaylah, whether there is any news,' suggested Raqiyah. Adam knew she was right.

He picked up his phone and walked away from the others and over by the main door to make the call where it was quieter. Clive picked up immediately.

'It's Adam. Any news on Jacob, Clive? We were all wondering,' he asked.

'No, not yet. You get the bikes back OK, no hassles?' Clive enquired.

'No problems there. I've got your deposit to return to you. But what did Lena say she'd do?' asked Adam.

'Have you heard? There was an explosion,' Clive told him.

'Yes, we were near. Heard it first, then saw it, right by the bike hire shop,' said Adam.

'Lena told us to expect bad news. She asked for an hour to try and get her people to track Ali and Jacob down. It's now mid-afternoon and we've heard nothing. Kaylah's in pieces, beside herself with worry. I don't know what to say or what to do. This is the worst day of my life, Adam,' he said sounding miserable.

'I'll call my friend at the British Consulate, then call you back. They may have news,' said Adam.

'But Lena didn't want us to ...,' but Clive's words were lost. Adam had gone.

Returning to the others, Adam told them there was still no news and he was going to call Krish again. Personally, he thought the Consulate should be giving Kaylah and Clive advice and support in a situation like this. Krish will know what they should do, he said. He began walking back towards the door as he dialled the number.

'Hi Krish, any news on Jacob, or Ali for that matter?' asked Adam.

'No, afraid not. It doesn't look good. We sent a couple of guys out, but nothing so far. At the site of the explosion in the apartment it looks like there were no survivors. We keep getting reports of bodies being removed, but as yet, no identities. The one good thing is no baby has been found. No mention of Ali either, but don't rely on anything you hear in the media at this stage. There's a lot of speculation going on. The Turks have now sealed off the area around the Beyoglu apartment and are not letting anyone near.' He paused to check Adam was hearing him.

'What I've done is send one of the best female support workers we have here over to see Kaylah. She'll give good advice, support and practical help from here on in. It's the very least we can do. I've also booked a conversation with the local chief of police at 5.30pm. It was the only way I could get to reach him, by adding my name to his list of people booking calls with him. I'll keep you posted as to any news I get. What are your own plans?' Krish asked.

'Looks like Raqiyah's uncle Abdul is looking after us with dinner at his home tonight. Krish, if we can help in any way, you will tell us, won't you?' Adam said.

'I'll call you. News has come in that three IS terrorists were caught at the Galatasaray Stadium this afternoon, apparently by some English football supporters. The Consular Commissioner has gone over to join them for a news conference to happen around 5pm. They're being given a heroes' reception for what they've done. The three terrorists are all confirmed to be Turkish, so no help to us at this stage finding Ali, but I've asked the Commissioner to find out what he can. Even though we've not found any trace of Ali yet, there's almost certainly some link between them and Ali. Maybe they'll know something. Speak to you later. Bye,' and Krish had gone.

Adam couldn't think there was much else he could do. He felt for Kaylah in her pain and the continuing uncertainty as to what had actually happened. The probability that Ali, Jacob and all the terrorists had died in the apartment weighed heavily on them all. The four friends talked amongst themselves as to the likely course of events.

Perhaps Ali had had second thoughts about any terrorist attack once he'd seen his handsome baby son and simply decided to lie low. But how would he do that? He'd need help, at the very least somewhere to stay and hide. He wouldn't have any experience of looking after a tiny baby just six weeks old. Jacob would be crying for feeds and changes. A new born baby needed bathing and fresh sets of clothes. The more they thought about it, they couldn't see how Ali and Jacob could make it. Where else would he have gone except back to his hideout. In the end all they could do was wait for news as to the discovery of more bodies, a baby's body amongst them.

They put on the café TV at 5pm, clicking on to the local Turkish news channel. A press conference on the edge of the

344

Galatasaray pitch was about to start. Seven English football supporters wearing white England T-shirts were lined up standing behind the key speakers sitting in front of them on the row of chairs. In the middle of the seated group sat a bald-headed, large man beaming from ear to ear, a distinctive striped jacket over his white shirt and the name 'Harry McNamara' on a printed card before him. A senior Turkish Police spokesperson, with the name badge 'Adem Rahman' and the Turkish Sports Minister completed the set. Before them was a table bristling with microphones. The assembled press were ready. The Police spokesman, Adem Rahman began to speak. He began in Turkish, a man with a clear look of relief on his face. Then, turning to Harry, he spoke in English.

'Mr McNamara, would you mind telling those watching what you saw and then what you and your friends did.'

Harry was clearly up for this, seizing the moment giving him the kind of attention he inwardly craved. He had hardly stopped beaming since the police had taken the pressure off him and his mates.

'Certainly. Can I begin by congratulating the England players on their win this afternoon. Well done lads,' Harry said.

'What did you notice before the match, Harry?' asked the police spokesman.

'There were these three geezers. It was obvious they weren't there for the football. They were hanging around in the entrance tunnel, messing about. I guess it was because they were so over-dressed and in the wrong clothes I noticed them,' said Harry.

'What do you mean, "in the wrong clothes", Harry?' the police chief prompted.

'None of them were wearing red and on a hot day they had these bulky jackets on. It was Stu here who thought they had guns under their jackets. Well, it was all wrong. They were all wrong,' said Harry.

'So tell us what you did,' encouraged Adem Rahman.

'Well we weren't going to wait for them to get us. We jumped the wall and got them to the floor and gave them a good hiding,' said Harry.

'"A good hiding",' repeated Adem Rahman with a puzzled look.

'Yeah. I mean. We held them down, all seven of us, taking an arm each, until your boys in blue came to take over.' Harry leaned back, satisfied he'd told them how it was.

The Minister for Sport then spoke up.

'People sometimes judge people by their appearance. Let today be a lesson to us all. Behind every football supporter there lies a hero. Today, we have discovered seven heroes who have shown extraordinary courage and saved countless lives. We don't know whether these terrorists would have been successful in killing our footballing stars, in killing scores of innocent supporters or indeed attacking our Prime Minister and his distinguished guests. But what we do know is that this afternoon's pre-season friendly match has revealed a new and deep level of friendship which we shall always honour. Thank you my English friends. On behalf of the Turkish Government and people, thank you.'

The press conference concluded with questions, but nothing further was learned through them, other than a question asking the Minister if they might expect further similar attacks. The minister simply reminded everyone to remain vigilant. The city was still on the highest state of alert and the forensic work at the site of the apartment where IS had been hiding up had yet to reveal all its secrets. It could well be there are still extremists in our midst and everyone must be on their guard, he told them.

The TV news programme then switched to the site of the apartment in Beyoglu where both the fire and police on-site investigation leads were standing together side-by-side ready to give their interpretation of events.

In the meantime, Mustafa had arrived to collect the four students in the university minibus. He'd joined them, without them even noticing him, so intensely were they watching the screen. Adam turned to Mustafa and after greeting him, asked if he would translate what was being said on the TV for them.

Apparently investigators had only been able to begin a proper search when the small fire from a fractured gas pipe had been fully extinguished. Even so, the site remained very hazardous and progress had to be made carefully for fear of collapsing floors from above or below. The fire officer praised the bravery of his force. He then said that they had now been able to go through and search the entire area of the first floor flat that had been destroyed. In the fire spokesman's opinion, they had found all the bodies and a total of twelve individuals had been removed from the apartment. Some were very badly mutilated by the explosion and forensic help would be needed to assist with identification. A number of walking wounded, from neighbouring flats, mainly people hit by flying glass and falling masonry, had been taken to hospital. Reports suggested none were in a life-threatening condition. The police officer then took over.

The police officer reported that a specialist scene of crime team had just been given permission by the fire service to begin their work onsite. Already they knew that one of the bodies was suspected to be that of IS terrorist Omar al Britani. If so, this was excellent news. A major threat to national security had been destroyed. There was no reason to believe, after enquiries with neighbours, that the other eleven bodies were those of anyone other than terrorists, but formal identification would take time.

He then turned to the flat itself. Some kind of explosion had occurred within the flat. What had caused it had yet to be ascertained. Several weapons had been found in the flat which confirmed it was indeed a terrorist base. He had directed the forensic team to look at what was left of an articulated lorry outside. A camera shot showed the container on the back now looked like the carcass of an expensive firework. It was all metal shards facing outwards, like a giant metal flower, the top of the container entirely gone. A lot of the blast had gone upwards, the officer said.

He pointed to a third explosion that had taken place in an outside store. Again, little was left of the store except a few scattered bricks at ground level surrounding a large crater. Mustafa said the police officer had a theory. He might be proved wrong, but he thought the terrorists had set their timing devices incorrectly or they had been faulty, and for that reason there had been a simultaneous explosion at the three points, sounding like, to all who heard it, one big explosion.

Mustafa was thanked for his translation. One more thing, he added, was that expected attacks in the capital Ankara had not happened, something the police spokesman personally attributed to public vigilance and police pressure. A huge police and army operation was now in place to ensure there were no further threats to internal security.

Their attention moved from the TV to the waiting minibus outside. It was time to go to Abdul's house and supper. Adam was troubled. If Jacob had not been found, maybe he was still alive, and Ali himself might also still be in the land of the living. What, he wondered, was being done to locate them? No-one had said anything about him. Was Ali still out there somewhere and what was he doing?

47

Ali only cycled as far as the nearest pharmacy where he bought the strongest, over-the-counter, painkillers he could buy. On his bike once again, he soon stopped, deciding he needed to get himself a hoodie of some kind. He couldn't wear his cycle helmet all the time and he needed something to hide the throbbing hairless bloodied mess the one side of his head had become.

There was a clothing store with jeans and T-shirts displayed and he decided to go inside. He rested his bike against the glass-fronted shop. The assistant inside had had a long hot day and was yawning. He didn't take too much notice of Ali which suited him just fine. In a few minutes he'd found what he was looking for and handed over his payment. The red top with Turkey written across the front was handed him in a plastic bag.

Once outside, he hung it from his handle bars to wear later before moving off again along the coast road, the busy Besiktas Cad. He could only manage to go slowly. He was feeling shaky and in pain and only gingerly entered the fast moving line of traffic. He'd only been pedalling a few minutes when he saw to his right the Imperial Gate to the Dolmabahce Palace, a grand building, constructed at the time of the Ottoman Empire's decline. He saw it as a last architectural goodbye to the old Caliphate as it was on its way out, another footnote in history.

Passing the perimeter of the grand palace he came to a halt and knew that before pedalling further he needed time to collect his thoughts and come up with a plan. It was as if all his energy had been drained from him. A feeling of light-headed listlessness was overwhelming him. The one side of his head and face were causing him a lot of pain and the end-of-afternoon sun was still hot, dry and sapping. It was not the time for a long cycle ride. He pulled over into the shade of a tree near the palace and sat down facing the road, resting his back against the solid tree trunk.

After a while he plucked up his courage and took hold of his cycle helmet and tried to ease it off his head, but the congealed and drying blood, together with the swelling made it agonising. More pain killers were taken. He waited for them to take effect.

Making a second attempt at removing his helmet, he prised his index fingers under the headband, working them round the contour of his head. It was not coming free. In the end he just grabbed the black helmet in both hands and wrenched it free, seeing as he did so hair and blood clinging to its interior, the pain causing him to cry out. Immediately fresh red blood started dripping again. He had nothing with which to stem its flow and watched it pitter-patter on to the dust beside him as he bowed his head.

He hadn't noticed, but an elderly lady had cautiously and quietly approached him. She asked if he was alright. He nodded. Maybe she thought he'd had an accident. She passed him her half consumed bottle of water which he eagerly drank from. Then, reaching in her large bag, she eventually found what she was looking for and passed him a packet of paper tissues. Before he could lift his head to say thank you, she had gone. He couldn't see her. Clutching the tissues in his hand, he noticed she'd left what remained in the water-bottle standing in the dust beside him.

Ali sat against the tree no longer wanting to move, his weight supported by the solid grey trunk. He needed that support. It was not just his head, but his whole body was filled with a great weariness. What had become of him, he thought, to bring him to this? He thought of his father, seeing him again shot in the hot dust of a Mosul Street, an image so vivid, that even though several years had passed, it was as sharp as ever in his mind. His father had been a strict man, though not perhaps by the commonly applied strictures of Muslim family discipline, nor by the standards of IS. He'd frequently beaten Ali as a boy and a young man, trying to urge him to make something of his life, never getting the result he'd wanted to beat into him.

What indeed had he made of his life? An unfinished engineering degree at Mosul University? A failed attempt to destabilise the United Kingdom by a half-hearted attack on Armistice Day? A family depleted by the killings that came because of his military service in IS? His father would not be proud of him.

He'd been glad when he saw him shot. It had given him his freedom, so he thought. But his freedom had soon turned to dust. His CO, Salim Ismat, had become his guardian in his father's place. Ismat never laid a finger on him, was always there to guide him. But, he thought in a moment of revelation, Ismat was cruel in other ways. His words were so sharp they could cut through anything anyone ever said. The control he exercised over himself and the others was subtle, yet absolute. He made me do everything I've ever done and I failed to ever question him and what he stood for. I liked his praise for being obedient and loyal, but where does blind obedience get anyone?

Ali looked up the road ahead, heading east, deciding there was no future for him in that direction. Certain arrest and what followed in the other direction. As he sat there, he realised he could never go back to the Caliphate. He was already dead in their eyes. He had failed catastrophically. Only a sentence of death awaited him back in Mosul.

A nearby mosque loudspeaker was calling the faithful to evening prayers. He was surprised it was that time already. A line of military vehicles passed him, loaded with soldiers who were headed into the heart of the city, no doubt to reassure the inhabitants that everything was still under control. Back in Mosul there would be no hero's welcome home this time.

Reflecting on his life, he thought what a poor Muslim he'd been. He hadn't prayed regularly, he had missed so many prayer times. What had he done to Kaylah Kone? He'd used her, groomed her to suit his purposes, enjoyed a

351

relationship with her, then left her with his child whom he could not support.

What of Jacob? He suddenly realised that Kaylah had given Jacob a name that was Muslim as well as Christian. In Islam, Jacob he recalled was a prophet, but Christians remembered him as the one who stole his brother's birthright. How ironic, he'd stolen Jacob from his own mother. What had he done?

He felt remorse, sorrow welling up deep inside. He had left Jacob with a family he never properly knew, abandoned him to an uncertain future and deprived Kaylah of the son he knew she loved. She'd trusted him by bringing Jacob to see him in Beyazit Square. His own father was harsh, but now he knew he too had been harsh and hated himself for it.

This war, he thought, this Jihad, was wrong. He no longer believed in it. It had made him into an abomination. Power and cruelty had supplanted love and mercy. He was a wretched, hideous, lowlife creature, a failure and the worst of men.

The mosque loudhailer suddenly stopped. A silence marked the end of the adhan, the call of the faithful to prayer. Ali threw his hoodie on. He'd made a decision. Slowly, he got to his feet and went over to the mosque, leaving his bike against the wall outside, the bloodied black helmet hanging on the handlebars.

First, he went inside to wash, the ablutions taking red water away from his face and hands and he watched it run over the white tiles until it disappeared down the drain. It took a while before he felt ready to enter the worship hall, his new red hoodie hiding him. The imam had already completed five of the cycles of prayer. He was late and thinking back over his failures, he realised there was no way he could make up for what he owed God.

By the time he had joined the line of brothers standing shoulder to shoulder facing Mecca for the few remaining prayers, he knew he was the last to arrive. He carefully moved his hands over his head, ears and face and began reciting the shahada, looking for comfort in submission to the oneness of Allah. He tried, he tried so hard, but found no peace and no God. When he wanted God to be his friend, when he most needed him, he didn't find him to be there.

Outside again, having no way back, he thought for a moment of turning traitor. It didn't take long for him to realise there was no future for him in that either. Going east or west, he was a dead man walking.

Pulling his bike from the wall, lost in his own despair, he mounted the saddle, headed back down to the main road, Besiktas Cad. Arriving at the T-junction, he was paralysed by indecision, whether to continue left towards Mosul or to turn right and hand himself over to the mercy of the authorities. Without realising it, he ended up going straight on and, with his hood pulled well over his head, didn't hear or see a coach fast approaching. He was hit without knowing it and went down, the bike pulled from his grasp, its frame dragged down, crunching under the coach's front wheels.

His arms were stretched out, broken, yet held by the coach's giant front. His still bleeding head, now knocked flat on one side, had new streams of red and white bodily fluid pouring from fresh wounds and out of his ears, nose and mouth. The coach instantly crushed and took him, carrying his disfigured form along in the air, dragging him a full half a block before coming to rest, leaving Ali's body lying in the dusty road.

When the driver realised what had happened, he quickly brought his vehicle with its alarmed passengers to a juddering halt. As the coach had slowed, Ali's body had slid slowly down from the white vehicle's bloodied front, falling on to the hot road below. He was dead before he touched the ground. Like his father before him, he too had met an untimely death in an ordinary street.

The local police arrived and took the driver's details. The Turkish coach driver was already in a state of shock, his hands shaking, but he insisted he was able to drive on. He'd already found a plastic bottle somewhere inside and with an oily rag had tried washing the bloodied coach down, ineffectually smearing Ali's blood over a still wider area of the dented front. Delayed traffic was building up behind and he resolved to make a better job of the cleaning once he'd dropped his passengers off at their destination.

Climbing back into his driver's seat, he moved off carefully to the side to allow traffic to pass, before giving a witness statement to the police. Their blue-clad uniformed colleagues gathered data, marked and photographed the road at the scene of death. This, another fatal road traffic accident, life's biggest killer of ordinary people going about their everyday business.

Minutes later, the ambulance crew placed Ali onto a metal stretcher, pronouncing him dead at scene, the attendant decided not to try and pull the hood back from the head for fear of detaching more of the face and jaw which were barely held together by the remaining flaps of skin and tissue. In any case the hood was full of blood and brain. Best leave the tidying up to the mortuary, he thought. After looking around to see they had not missed anything, they loaded the body on the stretcher into the back of the ambulance, leaving his mangled bike at the roadside and set off, no sirens this time, to take the corpse straight to the hospital morgue.

A fire crew had arrived and were already hosing away the last of the blood from the road surface. The street would shortly be allowing traffic to pass unhindered and the emergency crew would be free to move on to their next call.

Only when the road traffic victim's pockets were searched the alert ambulance driver found a driver's licence and asked his colleague whether this Ali Muhammed might be the one everyone was looking for. A call was made to the police and by the time they arrived at the mortuary, there was a police reception committee waiting for them to check out just who they had picked up from the roadside. The body, still on the stretcher, was taken inside for further examination in a more private area.

The police officer held a picture of Ali in his hand and looked down at the body, but such was the damage to Ali's head, he wasn't sure. He asked the ambulance man if it were possible to pull back the hood from the head in order to take

354

a better look. An attempt was made, but didn't help, only serving to make the officer feel sick.

Another search was made of Ali's pockets. This time a wallet, a smart phone, and a picture of a baby were found. Flicking through the wallet and flipping open the phone to make a quick search of contacts he discovered all he needed to know.

He turned away to compose himself and, after using the antiseptic cleanser by the door, took out his own phone from his pocket to telephone police HQ. It was just 9.30pm on Friday evening 20 August.

'We have him; Ali Muhammed is dead,' he said.

48

As the long hot afternoon in Tel Aviv moved into evening, the Operation Turkish Delight team's mood began to improve. Much to everyone's relief there was no news of any further terrorist activity in either Istanbul or Ankara. There were still many unknowns, but it was time to begin the first post-mortem review, time to go over the whole intervention to see what had been achieved, what might have been missed and what might have been done better.

As the high resolution pictures came in from the Istanbul Israeli Consulate over the past hours and were projected, they could see exactly the pinpoint devastating capability of the new drones. There was much excitement in the hushed conversation at the potential the improved weapons offered for countering extremist cells in urban environments. So often IS and their spawning terrorist spin-off organisations had tried to hide themselves away amongst hospitals, schools and in residential areas; now they could be reached. They had nowhere left to hide. The new technology promised a future of reduced collateral damage and just as importantly, much improved arms sales to carefully chosen allies.

Anna Simonsson made her way into the conference room for the final briefing of the day. It had been a long week and she was exhausted and eager to head home for what little remained of the weekend. The long hours of unbroken concentration had left her wrung out and she was utterly spent, only just hanging on. It was a one hour commuter trip to Jerusalem before she could unwind, refresh and prepare herself for another week, the beauty she found in looking at numbers.

She discovered there were just eight people still on duty at the Tel Aviv office. Since the immediate crisis had passed, all the senior military and political staff had excused themselves. Her new boss, Elias, was growing in confidence and a successful mission had clearly lifted him. With a smile of satisfaction on his face, in spite of the tiredness he felt, he called everyone to order. He had another strong coffee beside him as he began to address the gathered team.

'It is difficult to imagine it was only a short time, less than a week ago, that Anna brought me the news that Ali Muhammed was on the move again. She discovered he was in one of three vehicles of combatants heading for Istanbul. It was a carefully orchestrated mission of such audacity it could have destabilised Turkey, a threat to us all. In this venture, the Kurds had set aside their enmity, and had partnered IS for the first time. This small team of eleven IS men who left Mosul was reduced to nine by a lucky break when the Turkish police picked up two men in their van of explosives near Ankara. On arrival in Istanbul the remaining nine IS terrorists were joined at the beginning of this week by another seven Turkish terrorists, bringing the Istanbul force up to sixteen. We know a major assault on key targets was planned. The logistical support lost in the van near Ankara was replaced by a delivery in a container on the back of an articulated lorry. In sum: a unit of sixteen men amply resourced with weapons and explosives and backed by a Kurdish mission of indeterminate size. This was potentially the biggest and most dangerous threat to stability in the region we have yet faced.' He paused to take a drink from his coffee mug.

'Our initial response was to try and take down Ali Muhammed, the group's leader. One of our London operatives did a superb job in delivering him to a rendezvous in Beyazit Square where our special forces operative was provided with an ideal opportunity to liquidate him. Unfortunately, for reasons that are not yet entirely clear, some cyclists intervened and a rapid exit strategy had to be deployed. Putting it bluntly, the first part of our strategic intervention failed and we will need to hear from our colleagues in Istanbul to fully understand why.' Elias' face was a picture of dissatisfaction.

'Our second intervention, however, the use of three drones prior to the terrorists' departure from their hideout that afternoon was a significant, though not, I repeat not, a one hundred percent success.' There was an audible gasp from some of those present.

'The forensic team now at the site of explosions has two of our people helping the Turkish authorities. They have now made their first inspection of what is left of the interior of the hideout base in Beyoglu. Initial feedback tells us this: the targeting was 100% accurate, the destruction 100% what we had hoped for. But three terrorists had already left for the Galatasaray Stadium. A few minutes earlier and the drones would have got them too. Fortunately, the three were spotted by some English football supporters who acted the part of brave heroes, disabling them until Turkish security forces took over. Ali Muhammed was meant to be with them as the fourth member of that group, but apparently, owing to a last minute change in plan, he let them go ahead without him whilst he set off back to the hideout.'

'Do we know why he changed his plan?' asked one of the political advisors.

'We have a good idea what happened. As I have already indicated, and for reasons not entirely clear, the meeting we set up for Ali Muhammed to see his baby son went wrong. He made it to see his baby, but Ali may have heard a shot, he may have panicked. Whatever the reason, we know he ran off with his son, immediately leaving the Square and subsequently disappearing taking the baby with him,' Elias told them.

'You mean he kidnapped the baby from his mother?' asked Anna.

'Exactly. If we imagine what may then have occurred, it might have gone something like this, and I have to stress this is pure conjecture on my part. Ali knew time was tight and he had to get rid of the baby – find someone to look after it. He may have simply dropped the child off somewhere with one of his local contacts, as yet we don't know. What we do know is that he was delayed on leaving the Square and didn't get back to the hideout for noon when the drones went in.'

'He had a lucky escape then, making a total of four who escaped the drones, 25% of the attack force,' summarised Anna.

'Yes, he has a habit of making lucky escapes. We know he intended to be part of the attack at the Galatasaray Stadium, but none of the CCTV we've scrutinised so far shows he actually went there with the other three. Possibly, he had decided to attach himself to one of the other attack groups. Before we go any further, I want you to see this,' said Elias, reaching down to press the remote in front of him. A grainy, pock-marked, grey-white picture filled the screen. A wall could be made out with red smears and barely traceable writing upon it.

'This is a photo of the interior wall in the main room of the destroyed apartment. I've had Anna enhance it so we can see what the writing tells us. It really is impressive what she can do.' Anna smiled with satisfaction as Elias pressed the remote again. In the new image the writing immediately became legible with just a couple of areas left blank.

'This is Ali Muhammed's attack plan for Friday afternoon. He was highly organised, confident or foolhardy enough, depending on how you look at it, to write all his plans up and leave them there. We can see he had four targets lined up for Istanbul, simultaneous attacks to take place at 3pm this afternoon. So we were exactly right to intervene when we did, any later they'd all have gone and boom...' Elias let the drama of what might have been sink in.

'It was what Ali carelessly let slip to Kaylah Kone about the meeting arrangements that alerted us to the fact we had no time to lose. Indeed, to have waited until the Turks were ready to raid the flat at first light on Saturday morning as they wanted to do, would have been far too late. In the light of what we know of IS plans and the embarrassment we have saved them I don't think the Turkish authorities will be kicking up much fuss. It would be just too politically embarrassing for them.' The political advisor nodded to Elias in total agreement.

'The plans tell us where the four strategic targets were to be. First, target A, the University of Istanbul. Second, the Blue Mosque. Third, the USA Consulate and fourth, the International Football match at the Galatasaray stadium. If you look here,' he said, pointing to the image, 'Ali has allocated four terrorists to each target and, from their names, it looks like he's mixed his own IS regulars with local Turkish sympathisers. The attackers had automatic weapons and high explosives, together with suicide vests. Had they succeeded, we'd be looking at many hundreds of deaths at least.'

'Do we know if the names on the wall tie up with bodies and prisoners?' asked Anna.

'Good question Anna. The veracity of the wall plan is verified by the fact that the three terrorists detained at the stadium are the three listed, minus of course Ali Muhammed himself. Those apprehended have already begun to talk and we have more names, but these will need to be checked and verified and DNA matched. The bodies found in the apartment will take a little time to identify, given the explosive force of our attack, but the forensics team are saying they think they have now recovered the clear remains of eight bodies, all young males. Identification on one of those less damaged indicates he was Omar al Britani, someone who joined IS from the UK and a person we're absolutely delighted to have taken out.'

'I'm sure the British Government will be just as pleased,' added the political advisor, 'as well as somewhat embarrassed at yet another home-grown terrorist hitting the limelight.'

'It is extremely likely the remains recovered will be forensically verified as those of Omar and the other seven listed fighters. The big question is, what happened to Ali?' said Elias.

'And the baby,' added Anna.

'Yes, the baby too. As I said, this is speculation, but I'm confident Ali would have tried to offload the baby. Bearing in

360

mind it is his son, he would have wanted, if at all possible, to place him somewhere he would be safe, with a sympathiser, probably with someone who'd be good looking after a small baby. However, he had very little time to do this, so the baby's fate remains a mystery,' said Elias.

'One of the local men could have signposted him to somewhere. Perhaps to one of their own families,' suggested Anna.

'Yes. Zaid was the local lead and we need to alert the Turks to follow that line of enquiry. My guess is they won't have made any connection between Ali and his son yet. Zaid would know. He would know why Ali didn't join him at the stadium. He would know what he was up to. He would have also known who might look after Ali's son,' said Elias thinking on his feet.

'So he could have dropped off his son and then made his way back to join the others at the flat, and knowing he was now too late to go to the Galatasaray stadium, decided on going to another target and he left Zaid to lead the Galatasaray attack,' said Anna.

'But he probably didn't get back to the flat before the drones went in,' said Elias, following her train of thought.

'Yeah, but he might have been nearby. He might even have been one of those hit by flying debris and glass,' added Anna.

'We don't know. Imagine the scene. Ali has sent off three to the Stadium. He's on his way, going to join his remaining force of eleven poised to head out, but he can't. They're taken out. What does he do next? Does he go back to his son? Does he try to escape? Does he have a second safe house to go to? Perhaps Zaid's? He needs an IS sympathising family to hide him. Or maybe he has a vehicle and heads off east?' said Elias, scratching his head.

'No, he hasn't got a route back. What I mean is, he'd be going back to disgrace and execution if he went back to the Caliphate after what he'd done. He has no way back. He'd have no planned exit, it never works that way,' broke in the political advisor.

Elias' phone went. He glanced at it and asked to be excused, walking outside the conference room and into the corridor outside. Anna watched as he talked animatedly before closing the conversation and striding back to rejoin the waiting group.

'Sorry about that, but it's the news we've all been waiting for. Ali Muhammed was killed in a road traffic accident and pronounced dead at 9.30pm this evening. We could not have wanted a more satisfactory outcome,' said Elias with a smile.

The meeting quickly broke up, everyone eager to escape for the weekend. Anna was troubled, but by now she had no-one to share her thoughts with. What had happened to the baby Jacob? Did anyone care? Somehow this little baby had slipped from everyone's mind. It was as if he didn't matter in the grand scheme of things. It didn't count on any level to those who had just left. But to Anna's mind, the lost baby was the one last piece of the puzzle to be resolved. When everyone had gone, tired as she was, just as desperate to get home as the others were, she nonetheless dragged herself back to her work station and began to think inside as well as outside the box to search for an unaccounted for, missing baby.

49

Uncle Abdul was waiting outside his fashionable Fatih apartment as Mustafa's white minibus pulled up. The journey from the Ataturk Academic Apartments hadn't taken long. Upon arrival, Mustafa leapt out and ran round to open the van's side door for the four students to be let out. They looked around them at their new surroundings. Every time they went somewhere different in this city their eyes feasted on yet more, hitherto undiscovered, cultural treasures. Near Abdul's home, in the Fatih district, Mustafa had just pointed out the magnificent Fatih Mosque and round the corner from it, the twelfth century Church of Christ Almighty, the Pantocrator.

'Please, to follow me,' invited Uncle Abdul as he led them quickly inside. As they turned, Mustafa called out to say he'd be back around eleven and disappeared off in the minibus.

The interior of Abdul's home was cool and modest, the home of a successful and urbane university professor. Adam noticed it was clean and ordered, with tasteful decorations. Then there was a surprise as Abdul introduced them to his wife and two teenage children, a boy and a girl. In the middle of the room, a marble-top table was set beneath a sparkling chandelier. They all took their places, guided by Abdul, an ever-attentive host. He sat the girls down first, then pointed to where Bilal and Adam were to sit. He explained that his wife and children had eaten earlier and would be looking after the meal for his guests.

'Now you are here, let me welcome you to our home. You have been here not yet a week, but what a week and what a day! I am so sorry you arrived at a bad time for us. The TV has been full of the lucky escape the city has had today, events I know have not passed you by unnoticed. But look, we have some local dishes for you to enjoy this evening. I hope you like them.' Abdul looked over to the kitchen, indicating they were ready for the food. His two teenage children were waiting by the kitchen door to be summoned to bring in the first course. There was a little wave of the hand and two steaming serving plates of stuffed mussels were placed on mats before them. Abdul's wife brought in some bread.

'Midye dolmasi, a local delicacy, but with my wife's own stuffing mix with rice, lemon and spices,' Abdul announced.

Adam thought it smelled delicious and he realised how hungry he was. As they began eating, he recalled dinners his parents organised for visitors at home in Muswell Hill, except here he detected there was an added touch of formality, rather like formal dinners at the university. He felt he was expected to be on his best behaviour, a feeling that was to stay with him throughout the evening.

Here was a professor with his students, unable to totally step out of role. Accompanying the fine food was polite, fine conversation, covering predictable subjects – the status of university education in England, the political uncertainty in the Middle East, the outlook for the Indian and Chinese economies and the place of Turkey in Europe and the world. Abdul had much to say about everything and was quite capable of speaking for everyone.

The second course was introduced as 'Imam bayildi', a mix of tomato, aubergine, garlic and onion, baked with spices in the oven, all served with red wine, Abdul explained. This was followed by a fish course, a stew of sea bass and vegetables, whose name Adam forgot as soon as he was told.

It was at this point Adam began to find his attention wandering. This meal was all very well-intentioned but he couldn't forget Kaylah and Clive. He pictured them waiting anxiously and felt for them and wanted to know if there had been any news. Before the desert course was brought to the table, he excused himself from the table to make a call and asked for the toilet.

He called Clive as soon as he had closed the door.

'Clive, it's Adam. Any news yet?'

'No, nothin'. Lena told us when it happened we should have news within an hour, but it's now nine hours, innit! Kaylah's still out of her mind with worry. Don't know what to think. One moment we thought Ali had taken Jacob with him back to their hideout, the apartment that exploded and we were just about giving up hope. Then Lena calls to say that early indications were, but they couldn't yet be certain, only the bodies of terrorists had been found, neither Ali nor Jacob among them. She told us to remain hopeful. Since then we have heard nothing,' said Clive despairingly.

'I suppose that is better news, though not good news,' said Adam trying to find a bright side.

'Lena says we have to be patient and hopeful. That's not easily done, Adam,' said Clive.

'Did you hear from the British Consulate? I did call them,' asked Adam.

'Yeah! Thanks. A nice lady called. Very helpful. Coming again first thing tomorrow. Sounds like people are trying to do things behind the scenes, to find Jacob, though she couldn't tell us what they might be. I think they're sending a doctor over to see Kaylah later. She hasn't eaten or drunk anything since this morning. I'm worried sick,' said Clive.

'Let me know if you hear anything. Thinking of you both,' said Adam plaintively before ending the call.

Adam felt guilty going back to enjoy fine food and wine, but resigned himself to living with the contradictory feelings he so often felt he had to carry around with him. Raqiyah gave him a warm smile of acknowledgement when he returned to take his place at the table. The others were looking at the two plates of sweet Turkish pastries, dripping with orange honey, that had appeared for dessert. Orders for mint tea or strong Turkish coffee were being taken.

When the drinks arrived, they took their teas and coffees through to the subtly lit lounge with its rich, soft furnishings, resting on a magnificently large red Turkish rug, with little brass coffee tables for their cups. Abdul chose this point in the evening to offer them a programme for their remaining week in the city, saying they had as yet hardly begun to see all Istanbul's cultural treasures.

Soon he was waxing lyrical about the rich history of the many peoples, past and present, living in Istanbul and their different legacies. He spoke of yet more mosques, churches, museums and markets they simply must go and see. Maybe, he might arrange for them a boat trip up the Bosphorus and another down the Dardanelles. He asked if they would like him to arrange a timetable for their remaining time, starting Monday morning, so they had the weekend free and then finishing Friday lunchtime so they could have a final night together in the city before their flight home to London next Saturday.

How could they refuse? It would be churlish indeed to turn down such a generous well-intentioned offer and it was quickly agreed. The ever-willing Mustafa would be sent to pick them up at 9am on Monday morning. Everyone seemed delighted and Abdul was thanked once again, the man thorough;y enjoying his role of host.

Adam discreetly took another Lorazapan. He couldn't put aside the unsettling conversation he'd just had with Clive. He pictured Kaylah in her distress and the impotence he felt at not being able to do anything to alleviate her pain. Then he had a thought: it was about time he called Krish again. For a second time, he excused himself, this time saying he just wanted to make a call. He wandered out of earshot into the vestibule, pulling the lounge door closed behind him.

'Adam here,' he said.

'Hi Adam, how are you?' said Krish.

'We're being well looked after at Raqiyah's uncle Abdul's home in the Fatih district of town. He and his family have given us a fabulous meal served with lashings of generous hospitality and reassurance. But to tell you the truth my heart's not in it. I'm really concerned, Krish, to know what happened to Ali and Jacob? Have you any news?'

'We sent a couple of guys out looking for them but nothing has come to light. There's no news yet I'm afraid. In this game I've learned no news should be seen as good news,' Krish voiced, trying to instil confidence as he said it.

'Can't say I feel that way. But is anyone else doing anything? What about the Turkish police? Surely they will be on to this now? What are they saying?' Adam asked.

'Have you been following the news bulletins this evening?' asked Krish; Adam immediately wondered what he'd missed.

'No, not had a chance. Is there any news then?' enquired Adam.

'What's left of their apartment hideout has begun to give up its first secrets. We know that there were sixteen terrorists in all, that's including the three apprehended at the football stadium, but neither the bodies of Ali nor a baby have been found,' said Krish.

'That sounds more hopeful then. But are you talking to the local police? I mean if I was Ali, running an attack, first thing I'd be thinking would be, who could look after my baby whilst I'm busy. Has anyone asked who his group knew? Who was Ali's local contact? Someone needs to be conducting a house to house search. Surely one of those guys picked up would know what happened, where he is? What are they saying?' asked Adam.

'Adam, you're right. I'll get straight on to it and get an update from the Turkish police. I need to go. Will get back to you. Thanks for the thought. Enjoy the evening best you can,' said Krish as he ended the call.

As Adam rejoined his group, Krish was still thinking about what Adam had said. Adam surely understood Ali's mind better than many. The line of inquiry Adam suggested, to find out who the local contact was, someone minding the baby, made sense. In their total focus on the terrorists, he wondered whether some people had rather lost sight of the need to find a missing baby. He picked up his phone urgently and began making calls.

50

Krish Patel could be very persistent. He used the influence of the British Consulate to discover who the police officer handling the interviews of the three local suspects was and just before midnight he was put through to speak to him.

'Krish Patel, British Consulate here. Thank you for making time to speak with me. I won't keep you more than a minute, but we are very concerned here as to the whereabouts of a young British Citizen, Jacob Kone, a baby who may have been taken by Ali Muhammed, the lead IS terrorist. It is likely he was kidnapped and then passed to the home of a local IS sympathiser, immediately prior to the events of this afternoon. The baby hasn't been seen since midday and naturally fears for his well-being after such a time are being expressed. I really would be most grateful for your assistance in locating this child. I'm dealing with a very distressed family waiting for news.'

'Not sure I can help with that one, Sir. We've been very busy today as no doubt you've noticed. A baby, taken to the home of a local terrorist, you say,' the man replied, his heart not really into this late-night call.

'Please, can you tell me about the three men our English football supporters apprehended at the Galatasaray stadium. It may be they know where the baby is,' asked Krish, thinking on his feet and hoping a little gratitude would be shown for the part played by the English 'heroes' of the day. His comment touched home and elicited a more forthcoming response.

'Oh yes, your guys did well. The three terrorists, the leader, a man called Zaid Khan, had two lads with him, no more than college students really. Zaid lives directly opposite the apartment destroyed, a family man, has a wife and four children. His wife is an IS sympathiser too, poor kids. I ask you, what chance have they got? We've a team searching his flat now. The wife's asked permission to move out with the children to relatives for now. She doesn't like all the attention. What does she expect? We've known them and have been keeping an eye on them for some time. Zaid's been to Pakistan on training camps. You can never trust them after that, can you? Suspected extremists, now no longer just suspected, his wife won't be seeing him for a long time, you can be sure of that,' he laughed before continuing.

'The two lads with him, just lads led astray by the older man Zaid. Classic bit of grooming if you ask me. Both the boys come from middle-class professional families who hadn't suspected a thing. In shock now they are. Look, I have to go. I'm afraid there's nothing more to tell at this stage. No news on any baby that I've heard. And yes, everyone's really grateful to your football 'have-a-go-heroes', the policeman said.

'One final thing. Do you know the address of the relatives that Zaid's wife and children are moving to? There's just a chance she might know where the baby is,' asked Krish hastily, realising his chances of getting anywhere were diminishing by the second.

'OK, got it somewhere here. Hold on. The things I have to do for international cooperation,' he laughed, then the line went quiet.

'Yeah, here it is. 320 Kutulus Cad, she's given us. Expect someone from here will have already checked it out. She'll be moving there later this evening apparently. My colleagues say she's not a problem, not like her husband. She's got her hands full with her children and says there are more people to help with the children where she's moving to. They'll be watched for the rest of their lives, that lot. We can all have a relaxed weekend now this is behind us. Might even get to watch the football friendly on play-back TV. I missed it live,' he added, before this time finally ending the call.

Krish then thought he'd give Lena Bloom at the Israeli Consulate a ring. He needed to be up to speed before doing anything further. If anyone knew about Jacob Kone, she should, he reasoned. He glanced at his phone, the time now showing 10pm. He decided to call her before it got any later.

'Hi Lena, Krish Patel here. Any news yet on our young missing British citizen, Jacob Kone?' he enquired. He knew it was Lena's arrangement that had put Jacob at risk in the first place. Taking a formal approach helped him suppress the anger inside. He had to get along with her if he was going to get any help. 'We ourselves sent a couple of men from our Consulate out on the street to have a look round, but Ali and Jacob had long gone from Beyazit Square by then. Have you had any better luck?' he asked.

'No, but I've just heard Ali Muhammed is dead,' she countered.

'How? What happened? Are you certain?' he asked, not liking to be second in the know. It always felt like being put down a notch when it happened.

'An RTA, a straightforward road traffic accident, on the main road leading north and east from the city. He was on a bicycle apparently, got hit by a tourist coach, died instantly,' she said.

'Are you certain it was him?' asked Krish.

'His body was taken to the central hospital mortuary, initial identity checks confirm it was him – wallet, phone, etc. Looks like he'd just come out of the nearby mosque where he'd been at evening prayers. People in there think he was injured already, lots of blood from his head. You know what, no-one spoke to him and no-one even thought that he was Ali, in spite of all the news on TV. It makes you wonder doesn't it, what we're up against? Our latest guess is he was caught in the apartment explosion, but wasn't hurt so badly he couldn't try and make an escape. He didn't get far before his luck finally deserted him. Anyway, the detail can wait, main thing is he's dead. Excellent result all round, don't you think?' she said.

'But Kaylah and the baby,' said Krish, not believing he'd actually heard what Lena had just said.

'Look, you and I know that in the real world damage happens. Call it collateral, whatever. I'm sorry for Kaylah.

She's a nice kid. She'll get over it in time. It wasn't as if it was ideal, having a baby by a now dead terrorist. With Ali dead things have been tidied up, for her too I guess.'

'But Jacob? Any news?'

'To be honest, I don't think there's any real possibility of finding out what happened to the baby. There's every chance the baby's body is yet to be found. Ali was caught in a blast and we know he no longer had the baby later where he died. Kaylah, she'll just have to get on with her life, pick up where she left off. I'll see she gets back to the UK. We're grateful, we really are. She helped us big time. Without her, we wouldn't have taken them down. I'm sure we can let her keep the flat in London for as long as she feels she needs it, certainly until she gets back on her feet. I'll start sorting out return flights to London tomorrow when I call and see her. Have to admit, I'm not exactly looking forward to seeing her, she's so very distressed. I'm expected to be back at my London desk by Monday morning. How about you? What will you do now it's all over?' she asked.

Krish had long decided he did not particularly like the utilitarian thinking, career-minded, Lena Bloom. How could she think in terms of 'now it's all over' when baby Jacob was missing and Kaylah distraught. He knew she had no real interest in a difficult search for a missing non-national baby, dead or alive, hidden somewhere in Istanbul. She could leave that to Krish and his consular colleagues, and if not them, with the Turkish Police. That was where she would say responsibility now properly lay. Formally, a missing baby was not her problem, it was someone else's jurisdiction.

Krish was ready to end the call. Gritting his teeth he politely thanked her and made a point of the need to stay in touch regarding Kaylah and Clive's departure arrangements as well as being sure to let him know if she did by chance hear anything further about Jacob. Knowing Lena would no longer be any help, he realised it was time for him to make some further enquiries of his own.

In the Consulate he tracked down the security advisor, James, and asked him to come to his office bringing any local information he could gather on Zaid Khan's history in particular, but any other local IS sympathiser intelligence he could lay his hands on. Krish knew he would need to start by going over everything again, all the events of today, making sure he'd not missed some vital evidence. It could be a long night, but the fate of Jacob Kone deeply mattered to him and not just because he held a British passport.

At about the same time, lights were still on in the Israeli Consulate as Lena Bloom worked late. Krish's call had been an unwelcome reminder to her she had no news to take Kaylah tomorrow and, come to think about it, she didn't know how she was going to 'tidy up' on this one. Still holding the phone in her hand she began to have second thoughts about what she had actually just said to Krish Patel.

She heard her own words and began to hate herself. The work was taking its toll on her in ways she'd never foreseen when she took the post as a cultural attaché. Momentarily, she saw herself as abominable, uncaring, unquestioningly doing everything asked of her; she realised she'd fatally lost sight of important goal-posts. For too long she'd been told on the one hand how very able she was and how highly regarded; on the other hand she'd been performing all the tasks she was told to without a second thought.

At that moment and with the benefit of hindsight she realised she had committed the most terrible error in persuading Kaylah to take Jacob to Istanbul. It had had consequences she should have anticipated and now the damage was done. She resolved to return to the safe world of cultural promotion, no more cloak and dagger subterfuge for her; the significance of her own immorality in what she had done pained her.

The thought of seeing Kaylah and Clive in the morning without something positive to say filled her with growing apprehension, but she knew it went with her role to now help them 'move on'. She couldn't see her way through. Perhaps the baby's body would be found and handed in, who knows, but he certainly wasn't going to be found by her or her colleagues. Things didn't work that way, all Israelis in Istanbul had to be very circumspect and leave anything outstanding to the locals for now. She reasoned if Jacob was dead the uncertainty would disappear, and they wouldn't feel the need to hang around.

By midnight she'd had enough, so she collected her things, threw her phone in her bag and headed back to a room in the Israeli Consulate. The last thing she wanted to do was to go back to the All Seasons Luxury Hotel to a distraught Kaylah in the room next to hers. To go there wouldn't help her sleep at all, though she was beginning to wonder whether she would sleep again wherever she went.

Once back at the Consulate, she took herself off to a guest room where she could be alone. No sooner had she shut her door behind her when the phone in the room rang.

'Anna Simonsson here, Tel Aviv, HQ. We've never met or spoken before, but suffice it to say we both work for the same people. About Ali Muhammed's son, Jacob. Professionally, I've been told the file is closed, but personally I'm wide awake here wondering where that baby is, whether it's dead or alive. I need to know what you can tell me as I'm getting nowhere fast. As I read it, we've set up a situation in getting Ali Muhammed where there has been total disregard for this baby's life. Copy me?'

'I don't know what to say. I've followed orders and I've done my duty. Together we stopped a major terrorist incident or worse. What more can I say?' Lena replied, knowing as she spoke her words sounded hollow and devoid of human warmth. What, she wondered, was her work doing to her? There was a pause at the other end of the line.

'Anna, I can't give you anything useful. Local forces are in control. There's nothing more I can do. I honestly believe the baby to have died.' With that she heard a click as Anna ended the call.

Quite unexpectedly, Lena found tears beginning to well up inside and, so as not to let anyone hear, she thrust her face in the pillow on her bed as the distress and guilt at what she'd done took hold of her.

51

Krish was like a dog with a bone. As he was working away, he recalled his own family. How they had always been such a supportive unit and right behind him in good times and bad; not just his mum and dad, but also grandparents and numerous aunts and uncles too. Maybe the need to stick together came from having to try and survive as migrants in a new land. Family, he suddenly thought, is important and I don't think I could hold my head high again unless I do what I can to find Jacob for Kaylah.

When Krish had explained his feelings to James McGuigan, head of security, James had proved himself surprisingly helpful, providing him with access to all the data files he thought might possibly be relevant. James proved to be a warm, friendly and affable man. After a lifetime as a policeman in Newcastle, he'd not wanted to stop working and had found himself with, what he thought, was the ideal appointment for him at the Consulate. He knew a dedicated person when he saw one and was only too willing to help Krish all he could. Even so, by midnight James had long since gone off home, leaving Krish alone with his office light burning into the night.

Most of what Krish read was irrelevant, not likely to be connected to anyone knowing anything about Jacob, or if it was connected, he himself wasn't going to be the one able to make the connection. It was like looking into a fog, trying to spot the slightest chink of light. When he opened the file on Zaid Khan on his screen, he went through it with particular care. First he speed read it, his eyes quickly skimming the words, then he read it again line by line, slowly, letting every detail sink in.

This was Ali's Istanbul IS contact man, the man leading the local IS sympathisers, grooming them, and training them. Zaid was key, instinctively Krish knew it. Then he re-read carefully. Zaid first came to the attention of the Turkish authorities for minor thefts and drug deals as a young person and then everything on the file went quiet for four years.

The notes next had a record of him when he was seen at the front of a demonstration in Istanbul outside the USA Consulate protesting at the American use of Turkish airspace to mount attacks in 'Muslim' lands. For that he was picked up and questioned for forty-eight hours, before being released unbowed by the experience.

After beginning a degree course in pharmacy at the University of Istanbul, Zaid had failed to complete his studies because of a disciplinary misdemeanour. The note was vague as to what this was, but Krish noted a reference made to him being the ringleader, inviting radical speakers to speak to students on campus.

He'd left the university six years ago, had since married Maryam and they had had three children. They'd settled in the Beyoglu flat four years ago and Zaid was currently working on and off for a local food wholesaler, an importer of speciality foods from Pakistan. Occasionally he would be asked by his employer to travel to Pakistan and the file contained a note regarding possible radical links he might have in Pakistan and which needed following up.

Pushing the file to one side, Krish leaned back in his chair and decided to try and once again picture what Ali might have done with Jacob as he left Beyazit Square. Krish concluded, as he had before, that Ali's options were limited. Surely Ali had relied entirely on Zaid for his local contacts. In Krish's mind, the lads Zaid was with when he was apprehended didn't count for much.

It was Zaid himself, thought Krish, who was key, the one who had to know something useful. Someone ought to be asking him some serious questions about Jacob if they hadn't already. Maybe, in all the concern about terrorist attacks everywhere, no-one had asked, no-one had yet made any enquiries about what had happened to Jacob. It was time to phone his contact in the Turkish Police again, time of night didn't matter, he told himself.

A very sleepy voice picked up the call. Krish thought he had woken him. His contact said he was actually on duty at police HQ. Krish reacquainted him with the conversation they had had when he had called earlier and began to tell the guy that Zaid had important information as to the whereabouts of a missing British citizen. The longer the baby was missing, the greater the risk and time was of the essence in cases such as this.

Krish went so far as to ask the officer if he himself were a family man, and on hearing he was, began to play him a line. In the end the man reluctantly agreed he would go down to the cells himself and see that Zaid was asked some direct questions about the baby. He knew how to get answers from the man. He said he would call Krish straight back.

There was then nothing to do but wait. Krish decided to take a walk around the quiet British Consulate garden whilst he awaited a return call. Outside, it was still warm, the buildings radiating back the fierce heat of the day. Stars lit up the night sky in spite of the city's light pollution.

He sat himself down where Adam had not so long ago also sat whilst he waited to see Dr Arnold. As Krish waited for a call that never seemed to come, something nagged at his mind. He waited for the idea to form. Then he stood up, he knew what it was. Hadn't he just read that Zaid had three children, yet when he'd spoken to the policeman earlier he'd mentioned four? He ran back to his office and double-checked. He was right! Heartbeat racing, he grabbed his mobile, dialling through as fast as he could. He couldn't reach the policeman. Why didn't he pick up? Several times he called but there was no reply. In total frustration he eventually gave up.

He dashed back to his desk where he'd written down the address he'd been given, where Zaid's wife Maryam had said she was going later this evening, to stay with relatives. There it was, 320 Kutulus Cad. He tried the policeman again, but still no luck, and he began to think the man had either gone back to sleep or was deliberately putting off the matter and avoiding him.

377

In desperation he called James, head of security. Eventually, James picked up, a very sleepy voice asking what he wanted, reminding Krish it was 2am.

'I need you here now,' Krish said, 'I know where that baby is and we need to pick him up. Can you bring a car to the front gate asap?'

Fifteen minutes later, the car was outside and he went out to join it. Krish could see the end of James' pyjamas protruding below his trouser bottoms but didn't comment. He was just happy to see him there. Looking at his watch again, then his phone, Krish saw he had still had no reply from the local policeman and decided to give up on him. After explaining the situation, James McGuigan asked Krish what he proposed doing.

'There are two choices as I see it. We could do things properly through the Turkish police in the morning which may be too late, or we could take control and go straight there and try and take the baby back. Both are risky. Do you have any Turkish?' Krish asked, half expecting James to throw up his hands in horror at such a bold approach.

'Enough to get by,' he replied.

'If you're up for it, we'll go there now,' said Krish.

'Then I'll need to do a few things before we go. I'll get bulletproof Kevlar vests for us both, I'll pick up my gun, and these days we'll need to take a recording camera and leave a video-stream message feed so the Consulate know what's going on, just in case everything goes belly up. I've spent so long doing desk work recently, this evening makes a pleasant change. They can only send us for re-training if we get stopped. I've brought the car with the diplomatic plates, so we can be as bold as we dare. Give me five minutes to get what we need, then let's go. Can you put in the address for the satnav while I'm gone please,' said James, before dashing into the Consulate stores area.

Within ten minutes they were cruising slowly looking for the number of the apartment. The heightened silence between them was fuelled by the adrenaline pumping in both their bodies. Krish's searching eyes found the flat first, his

378

colleague braking, then driving past slowly to take a good look. He then went round the block and came past a second time. The third time he pulled up in a side street. James told Krish he was taking charge on this one. A time-check showed it was 2.30am and a quick glance round indicated that there were very few passing cars and no pedestrians about. The coast was clear.

'I always find the direct approach is best. Do it fast. Be clear. Go straight to the point. In and out quick. Krish, I want you to walk three paces behind me, and if anything happens to me just run. Here, have the car keys on you just in case,' ordered James, taking a strong lead.

Krish's pulse was racing. This was a huge, but calculated risk. He tried to find some calm, inner peace. It helped that James seemed so sure of himself. He waited whilst his colleague confidently rapped the front door and called out.

'Eminiyet Polisi, Security Police. Open up. Open now or we break down the door,' commanded James in a clear steady voice.

Krish wondered how he could do that for the door looked so solid to him. He looked up and down the street to see if James' shout and knock had woken any neighbours. All was quiet, even inside the flat. Krish wondered if, for the second time that evening, he would not get a reply. After what seemed like an interminable age the door slowly opened. A bewildered looking and clearly frightened young man peered at them from behind the barely open door.

'You have a baby here? Where is it? Bring it here now,' ordered James.

With one foot in the doorjamb preventing the door being closed, James, now off the street, chose this moment to produce his handgun. Only when he pointed it towards the youth were they let further inside. James was getting the desired effect and so far total cooperation was forthcoming. All the time though, Krish knew precious seconds were ticking by.

'This way. This way. Please no shoot. Wait here. Wait please. Women only. Please,' the young man pleaded.

The guy was really frightened and Krish wondered whether he might do something foolish once he'd disappeared from sight. Then he heard female voices talking on the other side of the door.

'Give me the baby now, or I go in,' demanded his colleague.

The boy was heard whispering quietly in Turkish; his face reappeared against the barely open inner door. Then the door opened more, inches, then just a few inches more and first a baby's head, then a blanket-wrapped baby was held out to be received.

It was Jacob, and Krish nodded to indicate this to James. There was more noise the other side of the door. It sounded as though more people were stirring and it sounded like very soon mayhem could break loose.

'Take the child, Krish, now,' ordered James, then more quietly, 'move quickly back to the car. Get in the back and wait for me.' Krish did exactly as he was told. No-one followed him, no-one as far as he could tell had seen him go round the corner and he got in the car as he had been told to, with a soundly sleeping Jacob cradled in his arms.

Then, rather taken by surprise, Krish looked up to see his companion had quickly joined him and was stepping calmly into the driver's seat. His hand was out to receive back his car keys and he had a smile on his face.

'I explained to them that they had done the right thing, that if they didn't say anything, then nothing further would come of this. They said they hadn't wanted to look after Jacob, it was one problem too many. Zaid had told them they had to. They were relieved I think that we took him, an additional burden they could well do without at this time. Let's go. Time to get away from here,' said James, starting up the engine.

'Not to the Consulate this time. We go straight to the All Seasons Luxury Hotel,' said Krish.

'You'll need to direct me,' he said as he swung the car round in a U-turn.

When they arrived, Krish asked his companion to wait outside. This was something he wanted to do himself. Still holding a silent Jacob, he walked up to reception and asked the young woman receptionist to call Kaylah's room to tell her she had a very special visitor coming to see her.

Krish left her making the call and took the lift straight to the first floor. Kaylah and Clive, still dressed from the day before, were standing in the doorway to Kaylah's room, looking towards the lift doors as they opened. He had a full view of their faces as he went out to meet them. In Krish's eyes, Kaylah's face suddenly radiated like a thousand suns, her tears sparkling as they fell, her smile broad and overwhelming. The kisses were showering down on her baby, instantly taken from him in her outstretched welcoming arms.

There was much waiting to be said, but the telling could wait a little longer and take many hours. Krish turned without leaving the lift. He called out as the doors were closing to say he'd see them tomorrow, later, in a few hours' time.

As he went to rejoin James, waiting outside, he felt a crushing tiredness begin to overwhelm him. Job done, he knew he just had to hang on until he was dropped back at the Consulate where he could now sleep to his heart's content.

52

Lena breakfasted slowly before leaving to see Kaylah and Clive. It was 9am and she knew she needed to get going. So, unable to put off the moment any longer, she took a waiting yellow taxi over to the All Seasons Luxury Hotel. Lena waved airily at the busy receptionist who was cheerfully greeting the latest arrival of visitors, then took the lift up to the first floor, strode out and tapped on Kaylah's door, taking a deep breath as she did so.

It was as well she did. Kaylah opened the door with a huge smile, her Jacob taking a bottle-feed in her arms. Lena had to look twice, then look again. She was speechless, overwhelmed.

'Krish brought him back. He just appeared with him in the middle of the night. Then like an angel, he vanished. Never explained a thing. Expect he's sleeping it off. He'll be round later. Said he would. Come in. We haven't had breakfast yet. Want to join us? Clive slept in the chair in here after Jacob came back. He just wanted to be sure, to be sure we were all safe,' said a very excited, ecstatically happy Kaylah.

Lena felt waves of relief wash over her. A grim encounter had been unexpectedly transformed. She could feel the tears of last night beginning to well up again and fought unsuccessfully not to let them show. She reached forward and put her arms round Kaylah and Jacob, both couldn't hold back their tears. The day was going to be better than Lena could have ever imagined. She'd need to talk to Krish at some point to know more. This was so surreal, so wonderfully unexpected. She looked at Jacob.

'How is he? Everything fine?' she inquired.

'Seems to be. Someone had changed him, must have fed him too. He's fine,' Kaylah said.

'We could get him checked over if you like,' offered Lena, realising as soon as she had said so, she'd need to find out from colleagues how to make such arrangements.

'We'll wait until we get home. When do you think we can go back, Lena? I mean we don't need to stay any longer, do we?' asked Kaylah.

'I'll get on to that. I'm travelling back tomorrow, Sunday. They want me back at work Monday morning in London. That's the way it is. I'll see if I can get you on the same flight, the three of you! Look, I had breakfast before coming over. I think I'll leave you to it and go back to the Consulate. I can get the air flight arrangements fixed up from there more easily. I don't think there will be any problem getting you on the same flight, I really don't. If there is, I'll call you straight away,' she said, and with that Lena was gone, pulling the room door firmly shut behind her, getting outside before more tears flowed in a flood of relief and guilt. Never again, she resolved, would she allow herself to be groomed into such dark and dirty territory as she had these past days. However, she quickly had to pull herself together as an incoming call flashed up on her mobile. It was from Anna Simonsson in Tel Aviv.

'I've just heard, Jacob's alive and all's well. Is it true? It was the saddest thing here how everyone just walked out of the meeting as if he didn't matter,' said Anna.

'It's true, wonderfully true, I've just been with them. I'm glad to tell you how happy and relieved that makes me feel,' and she sobbed uncontrollably into the phone.

'Me too,' said Anna. 'This has been easily the hardest job I've done. I didn't think I could carry on until I knew he was OK,' said Anna, holding back her own tears.

Back in the room, Kaylah finished feeding Jacob and passed him over to the seated Clive to hold.

'She didn't know we'd got Jacob back, did she? You should have seen the look of shock, then relief on her face. She couldn't hide it. I can guess how she must feel, poor thing. I sense she'd been under pressure without realising it, I ought to know! Let's go down to breakfast before we miss it. What a difference a day makes,' said Kaylah.

While they were down at breakfast, Clive looked at the front page of a local newspaper held by the man sitting opposite at a nearby table. The whole front page was devoted to yesterday's averted terrorist attack.

Clive got up, walked over to reception and picked up one of the freely available papers for himself. What he suspected, he now knew was true. The body photographed in the Central Hospital Mortuary was that of Ali Muhammed. He felt inexplicably sad and wondered how Kaylah would feel when he would tell her presently. Rejoining her at the table, he took her hand in his.

'Sis, I've got something to tell you. I think it's true, because I have just seen it on the front page of the newspaper. They say Ali is dead. The photo, look, it's of him at the hospital. From what I can make out, it says he died in an accident with a coach. Look there's another picture inside. I'll ask someone in a minute if I'm reading it right.' Clive looked at Kaylah. She seemed lost in her thoughts. After a few moments saying nothing, it was she who broke the silence between them.

'I half expected this would happen sooner or later. I never thought Ali would have a long life. How he lived, he could have died any time, and I had half prepared myself for such news. It's still a shock. I need time to think about it. I don't know what I feel, Clive, it's all mixed up. I'm fine, I really am. Just leave me to process this in my own time and in my own way, OK?' She let go of Clive's hand, and he knew it was alright.

Nothing further was said, but Clive noticed Kaylah's joy at having Jacob back had become somewhat tempered, the unbridled joyful edge she had earlier had been lost. He knew there was some loss and grief buried somewhere deep inside her. For his part, he felt able to step away from Ali. It wasn't like they'd been close and he carried a lot of anger towards Ali for taking advantage of Kaylah and leaving her the way he had.

Clive remembered he too had been used by Ali, taken advantage of back in London, but in spite of everything, there was still something there that made him warm to him. Ali was, he thought, rather like a child who had done a very naughty thing, but back in London, the twinkle in his eye and energy for life meant you still liked him.

Clive remembered lending him his own bike last autumn, the bike Ali had used to help him escape London, get back to Mosul. Before that Ali had taken Adam's bike. How strange, yet fitting, Ali had died on a bike. Clive felt he'd be glad to get back to London again. They'd spent long enough in Istanbul. They all needed to move on.

The rest of breakfast passed quietly. Neither Kaylah nor Clive had realised how hungry they were. As they were leaving the breakfast table around 10.30am, Krish walked in.

'I tried calling your rooms first, thought I might find you here. How is he?' he asked pointing to Jacob.

'Fine. Really fine. I don't know how to thank you, Krish. How did you do it?' said Kaylah.

'I had an idea where Ali might have dropped Jacob off. A friend took me round and I collected him and brought him to you. Simple as that,' he smiled.

'Do you know about Ali? I think the paper says he died in an accident. We wondered whether that's so?' asked Clive.

'Yes. I guess I should have told you last night. My apologies. It was very late. Ali died in a road accident. After everything had happened, he was heading away from the city last night. He'd been in a mosque for evening prayers, then cycled off, but was hit by a coach as he entered the busy main road and died instantly on the spot. The ambulance man thought it was Ali and called the police who later confirmed it was really him,' explained Krish.

'Thought so. Kaylah just needs a bit of time to think about that piece of news, but both of us want to go home now and, Lena, she popped in to see us earlier, she's arranging flights for tomorrow afternoon if she can,' said Clive.

'Oh, something else I forgot to do. I never called Lena to say I'd found Jacob,' said Krish.

'You should have seen her face. It was a picture,' said Kaylah smiling again, then mimicking Lena.

'I've got to head back to London tomorrow too, may even see you on the same flight,' Krish said.

'It'll be good to know you're watching over us,' said Kaylah, 'I don't know how to begin to say thank you for what you did. I'm forever in your debt. Thank you, Krish,' and she reached over and pulled the embarrassed Krish into a warm embrace.

It was time to leave and they said their goodbyes. Though he was invited, Krish explained why he couldn't stay with them.

'There is a reception party for the English football supporters at the Consulate at lunchtime. There's no doubt that, but for their quick thinking and courage, there would have been a major loss of life at the stadium. I've been called in to help serve drinks. It's a case of all hands on deck. I imagine the Consulate stock of beer will be considerably diminished by the time they leave!' Krish joked.

On his way back by taxi, Krish knew he had a couple of urgent phone calls to make. First, he got hold of Lena, who wanted a blow by blow account of how he'd done it. Her final tongue in cheek comment had been to invite him to join their own special forces in Istanbul, for he would have make a better job of things than they did. She didn't elaborate, and Krish realised she had said rather more than she had intended. He was glad to end on a better note with Lena. Her relief at the outcome was palpable, and Krish for one was pleased to see it.

Second, he phoned Adam, simply to tell him the good news of Jacob's reunion with Kaylah and to tell him about Ali. He didn't want Adam to see it in the media like Clive and Kaylah had. He thought he'd like to see Adam one last time in Istanbul, to chat things over before he headed back to London on the afternoon flight. When he suggested it, Adam jumped at the idea and they agreed to meet up 10am the following day, Sunday morning, over at the Ataturk Academic Apartments.

53

Kaylah, Jacob and Clive stayed at their hotel until the taxi arranged by Lena, arrived after breakfast, ready to take them back to the airport and the afternoon flight home. Lena was right, she was able to get them tickets for next day. Both felt a mighty sense of relief on heading for home.

Their time in Istanbul had been almost entirely overshadowed by the kidnapping of Jacob; the fourteen or so hours when he was missing had been a living nightmare that would never be forgotten, overshadowing a memory of the fantastic tourist sights the city had to offer as a visitor destination.

Jacob, for his part, never appeared to have noticed the adventures he had had. He was just the same, doing the things a young baby should do, his mother adoring him all the more, if not with a little more over-protection, keeping him close by at all times.

On arrival at the airport they had time for a lunch which Lena paid for, as indeed she had all the bills for their six-day-long trip. Throughout the taxi ride to the airport and during the flight itself, she never once ventured to mention what had gone so wrong with the missing protection at Beyazit Square after all the assurances she had given them beforehand. For her part, she was thankful that neither Kaylah nor Clive chose to mention it. Kaylah thought it, but kept it to herself, knowing her ability to trust another person would never be the same again.

Lena's Consulate bosses had never given her an adequate explanation for the failed attempt to take Ali out and with everyone's attention switched to the success of the three drones accurately finding their targets, the earlier failure was something she definitely couldn't begin to mention. A wall of silence greeted her every time. As she travelled she opened her Tablet and began composing a letter to her line manager in London. She wanted to be reassigned as soon as possible to straightforward cultural work, nothing more. Given the perceived success of her mission in Istanbul, there was every likelihood her request would be granted.

Lena made their airport exit run smoothly, using her diplomatic status and her air of confident authority to speed their passage through customs and on to the waiting British Airways plane. It was as if she couldn't do enough to help her charges – nothing was too much trouble. The 3pm flight took off precisely on time and the sense of shared relief once airborne was palpable.

The flight back enabled both Kaylah and Clive to take turns to catch up on some much needed sleep following yet another meal, this time served them by the ever-attentive air stewards. Although the flight took nearly five hours, they gained a couple of hours, putting their watches back.

It was a grey, cool, early evening as they stepped out of the plane onto the Heathrow tarmac. In the baggage reclaim area, as Clive retrieved their cases, Lena said she was leaving them to head to West London. She pointed out their waiting taxi driver holding up a 'Kone' sign, casting his glances left and right trying to spot his passengers to take back to North London. With a final wave of her arm Lena had gone. That would be the last time they saw her.

As their taxi driver headed into North London, Clive thought of his friend Winston. For a week they hadn't spoken, something unheard of. He was reminded of their last conversation, how Winston had encouraged him to phone his 'spook' as he put it, and he wondered whether Dave Stephens' promise to clear him of everything hanging over him would still be holding good, or whether the world of drugs and gangs would all too quickly bring his life crashing down around his head. It had been just six days away from North London, but it felt like it had been a lifetime. He felt a growing apprehension gnawing at his gut, the closer home territory approached. There was a newspaper left by an earlier fare on the back seat of the taxi and he picked it up to see if there was anything they'd missed.

Flicking through the pages, he saw there was a two-page spread coverage of the shooting of PC Bob Steer. A horse drawn bier carrying his coffin had processed the full length of the Hertford Road from Enfield to Edmonton and on to Tottenham High Road police station where he had begun his career. There had been a massive outpouring of sympathy and Clive felt sad, so very sad at what had happened. He dropped the paper, his mind still imagining the impact the drugs and gang world he knew all too well had had on a good man's life.

The taxi pulled up at Kaylah's flat first and dropping her and Jacob off. Lena had promised Kaylah that the flat was hers, rent free, for a full year, in fact until 31 August next year, all in gratitude for what she had done to help deal with a serious threat. Kaylah was glad for it and valued the independence, the new start, it gave her.

Kaylah assured Clive that she wanted to be on her own with Jacob in their own home that evening and that he needn't worry, they would be fine, he could go home. The taxi, now with just himself in the back, pulled away from the Crouch End flat and headed north for the last part of the journey to Edmonton.

A little more than ten minutes later Clive was dropped off in Cheddington Road. His mum and dad, hearing the taxi pull up outside, were there to welcome him. It was the warmest of homecomings. The experience, so unexpected, yet so welcome, felt like that of the prodigal son his father had so often spoken about in his sermons. He knew this was where he belonged and he knew he was loved by his family. In a few weeks, he told himself, he would go to college, a new life and a new world waiting to embrace him.

Upstairs in his room, his headphones lay on the bed, his familiar things all in their place. It felt so good to be back. He pulled out his phone to call Winston, then put it back in his pocket. The world can wait, he thought. He lay back on his bed, plugged in his earphones and lost himself in his favourite selected rap artists' music.

Later that evening, after his mum had served a delicious jerk chicken and rice and he'd told them all that needed to be told about Istanbul and the events they had heard about on TV, he excused himself saying he had some calls to make.

He rang Kaylah.

'You OK, Sis?' he asked.

'Sure. Just catching up on the soaps I missed. Got some ideas about a business venture I want to set up. Think I could trade some rugs and carpets online. Had an idea, but it can wait. I called mum and dad, said I'd come over tomorrow. Just needed space for Jacob and me tonight.'

'Until tomorrow then,' he said. It was the briefest of reassuring calls.

He didn't need to call Dave Stephens. Dave called him.

'Heard you were back safe and sound. Welcome back to old Blighty,' Dave said cheerfully.

'Thank you,' said Clive.

'Clive, I'm a man of my word, whatever you may think of me. When I offered you a fresh start I meant it. I have to admit I've had these thrown back in my face so often I thought you would be just the same, but your call from Istanbul last Thursday and the result, well that was just great. You did the right thing and it went down a treat back here. Just to put you in the picture, Wicked Will is old news. He was arrested on a range of drugs and violence related charges on Friday. There's also an investigation into an alleged murder of a local policeman he is thought to be responsible for. He's currently remanded in custody awaiting trial. Just wanted to say thank you for your help and take it from me, you will never be dragged into any of it. That's a cast-iron Dave Stephens' promise,' he said with sincerity in his voice.

'Thanks. I'm off to college in a couple of weeks, so life will take on a new start for me. Thanks again,' replied Clive and a second brief call was over.

Maybe he ought to call Winston, after all he's been a best mate. So the delayed call was finally made.

'Hi Bro! Just to say we're back,' he said.

'I know, had a call from Kaylah. Calling round to see her right now,' he said, much to Clive's surprise.

'Now look, she's had a hard time, you mind your step with her,' said Clive. He'd always figured Winston and Kaylah might get on.

'Picked up a new car while you were away, a mini. It's still a BMW, smaller than I've been used to, but nippy. Pick you up tomorrow, not too early. See what you think of it. Go down to Cliff's Cafe. Catch up on news. Things are just cool with me. I'm still one step ahead of the game every time! See you, good to know you're back.' Winston was his usual happy self cheered Clive.

'See you tomorrow Winston,' he replied and with that he'd gone.

Well, Kaylah had wanted to chat to Winston. Where will that lead, Clive thought. She could do worse. Then he had a strange thought. He remembered again that he'd once helped Ali, lent him his bed, this very bed, to sleep on last autumn. He'd lain right here where he was now. The ghosts of the past, they stay close to us, he thought, and with that he began to get ready for an early night.

54

Krish decided to take a taxi to Ataturk Academic Apartments. Those few minutes to himself gave him a chance to wind down, relax and think about what he would say to Adam. So much had happened in the past couple of days and in spite of having slept deeply in the short time he'd rested, he still felt a weariness and tiredness that he knew would take days to get over.

Before he'd left the Consulate he'd made a call to Lena and filled her in, in outline detail only, on how Jacob's rescue had been achieved. He was surprised to find that she wanted to talk at length and more personally than he'd anticipated – a warmer side to Lena showing itself. Probably, being a spook himself, he was someone she thought would understand, someone outside her own organisation she could offload to. Krish had mainly listened and that had seemed to be enough.

Lena described the pressure she had been under career-wise, describing what had been happening in the months earlier as a kind of grooming. Yes, she'd used that word. She now realised she'd acted against her better judgement in putting Kaylah and Jacob in harm's way. With hindsight she now wondered whether she could have lived with herself if anything had happened to them. Krish wondered whether, by the end of the conversation, she was really looking for a way out of the work she was in. And there it had ended, with polite thank you and goodbyes on both sides.

For the rescue of Jacob, he knew he owed Adam much. It was Adam who had spoken to him so persuasively the previous evening to suggest what Ali might have done with Jacob, and this in turn had prompted him to call in James and the two of them being able to successfully find, rescue and return the child safely to Kaylah.

He felt full of admiration for a guy who had been battling mental health issues, yet had managed to hold things together when it counted. There weren't many young people like Adam Taylor, he thought.

Maybe the press would start chasing Adam again as they had last winter after Ali's attack in London. They would want to know his story, why he was in Istanbul when Ali Muhammed was mounting another audacious act of terrorism. Krish could at least start to help Adam frame some answers for the questions that were bound to come, prepare him for the media-frenzy awaiting him back home. The yellow taxi slowed, he'd arrived, it was almost 10am, a Sunday morning, the heat and brightness of another summer day beginning to take hold.

Krish stepped out into the bright sunshine and walked through into the welcome area of the Ataturk Academic Apartments. There were a number of young people here and there, but a quick glance told him Adam was not among them. He pulled out his mobile and called Adam to announce his arrival and a couple of minutes later, Adam, accompanied by Raqiyah, were walking towards him.

'Have you had breakfast, Krish?' asked Adam.

'Well, no, come to think of it,' said Krish, feeling hungry at the thought.

'Come and join us then,' said Adam, leading the way into the café area. They all chose what to have and the three drew up their chairs round a table a little way off from the other customers using the café.

'You're not eating much,' remarked Krish, comparing his laden plate with their small fruit and yoghurt plates. '

'Suppose we had far more than we should have last night at Raqiyah's uncle's place. The food was really good and there was so much of it,' said Adam, 'but what we really want to hear from you is the latest news. It was such a brilliant thing, last night, that Jacob had been found. We managed to find some beers and toasted the news. Where was he found? Is he alright?'

'And how's Kaylah?' added Raqiyah.

'He was found in the care of a local mother who had three small children of her own to look after. She handed

Jacob over straight away once we'd found him and then Jacob was taken straight back to Kaylah, and as far as I can tell mother and baby are absolutely fine,' explained Krish.

'Perfect, just perfect,' said Adam.

'Adam, I don't think any of this would have happened the way it did without your call to me last night. It was only what you said you thought Ali would have done, that got us on the right trail. It was only that insight, in the end, that led us straight to him. So, I'm kind of here to pass on a huge thank you to you personally,' said Krish, taking Adam by the hand.

'And what about Ali? Where was he in all this? Was he with Jacob?' quizzed Adam.

'No, I guess you've not heard the news. Ali left the baby in safe hands and then made to escape out of the city by bike heading north and eventually east, but he didn't get very far. He died when a coach hit him on the road just a short distance north of here. He was pronounced dead at the scene by the ambulance crew. There's no doubt. Turkish police have confirmed it was him,' explained Krish.

'He'd run out of luck, I guess. He was nearly shot by a sniper in the park yesterday morning. I've thought about that lots of times since. Clive and I thought we were doing the right thing when we cycled down the man pointing his gun towards Kaylah, Jacob and Ali. Maybe we did the wrong thing? Maybe Ali might have been cleanly shot. Might that have been better? But he might have missed, he might have been happy to take out any one or all three for all we knew. And what about the impact on Kaylah if that had happened? Imagine seeing Ali shot right in front of you,' said Adam, lost for a moment in the reality of what might have been.

'Back in London last autumn, Ali led a charmed life, being able to escape back to Mosul like that. His time had come. He had nowhere left to run to did he? He couldn't stay. He couldn't change sides. He couldn't go back as a failure. I think he was in a way already a dead man,' said Adam.

'The coach driver who hit him says Ali came out of the side street straight in front of him. He didn't seem to know

394

which way he was intending to turn, left or right, away from the city or towards it and in the end went straight ahead right into the coach's path. There was nothing he could do, poor man,' explained Krish.

Krish noticed Raqiyah moving closer to Adam. Then she took his nearest hand in both her hands as if to comfort him. Adam did not move away and Krish wondered if he had started something in asking Raqiyah to keep an eye on Adam earlier in the week, when he'd brought him back from the Consulate and seeing the doctor.

'To be frank, Adam, I don't think we will ever truly know all the detail. You know from last autumn that enquiries into these things seem interminable and in the end don't answer all the questions we want to ask,' said Krish.

'How was the football supporters' reception?' Adam suddenly asked, changing the subject.

'Bigger than we'd expected. The visiting Minister from England at the match and the whole English team turned up, together with around twenty Turkish guests including some of their players. The Turkish Government PM, Sports Minister and all those present were immensely relieved at the outcome. Thankfully our guests at the Consulate last night didn't stay late. In fact they were all leaving around the time you and I had our conversation. Between ourselves, some of those English supporters who are currently being viewed as heroes are the least likely heroes I've ever come across. My view is there was a strong element of self-preservation combined with well-honed hooligan skills in what they did. But give them their due, it took some guts to have a go and take those three terrorists down. They'll get a hero's reception back in London too,' said Krish.

Raqiyah told Krish that they had another week left in Istanbul and that her uncle Abdul had put together a programme for them which they had all agreed to. Some cruising trips were included and it would be as much about relaxation as about learning, she added. Krish glanced at his watch and realised that if he were to get the 3pm flight to London, time was pressing. He made his excuses and once more thanked Adam, just as a taxi pulled up to whisk him away.

'I think I'm going to end up really enjoying this week,' said Adam, looking into Raqiyah's eyes. Though as soon as he said it, he felt insecure once again. He felt he was on some kind of crazy fairground rollercoaster, one minute up, the next plunging down. All he could do, he told himself, was hold on.

'That makes two of us then. Come on, let's find the others,' she countered. Then seeing the vulnerability in his eyes she grasped his hand with a big smile on her face and playfully pulled him up from his chair.

55

There was one thing that Kaylah wanted to do now she was back in London and she persuaded Winston to drive Jacob and herself over to Edmonton and drop her off in Windmill Road outside the Edwardian vicarage where Rev. Ruth Churchill lived. More than ever, more so than before she had left for Istanbul, she now realised she wanted to have a special service in the church for Jacob. She'd nearly lost him and thought she'd never see him again, and with his safe return she had deep within her the need to express some gratitude for the relief she felt. Never did she want to have to experience the pain of her child being taken from her again and in a world full of uncertainties she knew that her religious roots would provide her with some solace.

Wheeling Jacob's buggy up to the front door, she rang the bell. Moments later, the cheerful, comforting presence of Ruth Churchill filled the doorway. Ruth stepped forward and assisted her in getting the buggy up the steps and inside the vicarage.

'I hear you've been to Istanbul. That's quite an adventure for a mum with a new baby,' she said.

'I don't know where to begin really. It was more adventure than anyone would want. I ought to tell you why I went and what happened. Then you'll understand,' Kaylah said.

'But first, can I get you something to drink? What would you like? Let's go through to the kitchen. We can talk there,' said Ruth, leading the way.

'Last time I came I had some of your home-made lemonade,' remembered Kaylah.

'You're in luck. Phil made some more. Want some?' Ruth asked.

'That would be nice,' Kaylah replied, as she sat down at the kitchen table ready to tell her story.

'Such a lot has happened in the last ten days or so, I hardly know where to begin. We ended up in Istanbul supposedly on holiday, Clive coming too. But it wasn't like a holiday exactly. Lena Bloom at the Israeli Embassy had asked me to go because Ali Muhammed was going to be in Istanbul. Thinking back, I thought they wanted me as bait, to bring him out into the open, so they could kill him,' she stopped, shocked at what she had just said.

'When we left for Istanbul I never thought that would really happen. Don't you think that was naive of me? Also, they put me under pressure. They'd got me to look after a flat in Crouch End where I live. I didn't mind that. It's a nice flat, really nice, guess I didn't want to lose it. But then Lena made me feel obligated to help them. She made it all too easy, arranged the flights, booked the hotel, paid all the bills. If Clive hadn't come with me, I still don't think I'd have gone. But I know now, Clive was put under pressure to go as well. Anyway, the three of us, with Lena, ended up in Istanbul,' Kaylah said.

'So you didn't exactly go out of free choice?' asked Ruth.

'Can't say I can blame anyone else really. I could have said no and faced the loss of the flat, but then where would I go? Well, we went. It was a nice hotel. We started with some sightseeing. Then the strangest thing: in the Grand Bazaar, we bumped into Adam Taylor and three of his university friends, there on a placement,' said Kaylah.

'Adam comes back in a couple of days, at the weekend,' explained Ruth. 'You know he's my nephew, yes of course you do. His parents live in Muswell Hill, Jim and Sue. They were telling me about the Islamic Studies course Adam's doing at Exeter University and the summer placement he had to complete. Like any parent, they were worried about him being there. After what happened last summer, when he cycled through Istanbul and ended up a prisoner of IS, they thought going back there would just make him unwell. It hasn't been an easy year.'

'Adam seemed fine to me, and it was good to see him. I know he's on medication but he seemed to be managing OK. But it was all too much of a coincidence that Adam and me were together in Istanbul at the same time. Without realising it, I think we all got sucked into anti-terrorism initiatives to get Ali Muhammed killed. With hindsight I don't think I did the right thing when I agreed with Lena to take Jacob to meet Ali in a public park, but it was what she wanted. She was very persuasive,' said Kaylah, pausing briefly before continuing.

'Ali was pleased to see Jacob. He smiled. He was gentle with him, holding him with tenderness. Everything seemed to be OK, though I felt very vulnerable. I was beginning to feel I wanted Jacob back in my arms again. Meanwhile, unknown to me, Adam and my brother Clive were cycling around the perimeter of the park when they saw a sniper aiming at Ali. He was holding Jacob, a baby, and someone was still prepared to shoot. Then something distracted Ali. The sniper's gun went off I think. It was then it happened. On hearing the shot, Ali, rather than handing Jacob back to me, well, he took Jacob and ran off with him. I had no idea where he'd gone. They both simply vanished,' Kaylah paused in the painful telling of the moment.

'That's so terrible. You were left without Jacob. That's any mum's worst nightmare,' said Ruth.

'It was more than half a day later that Jacob was brought back. All that time I didn't know whether he was dead or alive. Later, I learned that Ali did in fact die, that same evening, in a road accident. You might have seen it in the papers?'

'I did. It got a lot of cover here,' said Ruth.

'After leaving Jacob in a safe place he was cycling away from the city when a tourist coach hit him. He died instantly, in the street. I still don't understand Ali. Part of him was warm and nice. He could be fun. I'm sure he tried to make certain Jacob was safe. Yet part of him was a secret, and he had a dark side. It was as if he were driven, even possessed by the ideas of others. He wasn't someone I'd call free, he was a dreamer tied to a strange set of Muslim ideas I will never understand. Where his ruthless side came from I'll never know. I used to hate him, I even wanted him dead, but now I don't know what I feel. Sorry for him I suppose. Ali was someone who'd lost his way leaving him open to others pulling his strings. That's how I see him now,' said Kaylah.

'Most people are full of contradictions,' said Ruth.

'That's a good way to describe him. Me too! But why I'm here is to pick up where we left off last time I came to see you. You said it would be possible to have a service of thanksgiving for Jacob and that's what I want. It's become really important for me. Do you understand? Can we do it Sunday week?' asked Kaylah.

And so it was agreed. Kaylah then went off to her parents' house pushing the still sleeping Jacob in front of her for the five minutes it took to get to Cheddington Road. She told them what she had in mind and wanted as many friends and family as she could invite to come along on the Sunday afternoon in ten days' time.

She thought her father Sam might object. There were lots of reasons why he should, and whether Shazee had softened him up already or not she didn't know, but he was all smiles. The family telephoned the church hall administrator next to the church and booked the space for a bit of a party afterwards.

It occurred to Kaylah that it was in that very place she had so many good, fun memories of her time with Ali when they'd worked last year at the asylum seeker Drop In. She decided that for her sake as well as Jacob's she would allow the good memories of Ali to remain in the ascendant, for one day she would need to talk to Jacob about his father.

Clive was out. After dropping Kaylah and Jacob off, Winston had collected Clive and the two had gone down to Cliff's café. Things were beginning to move on, thought Kaylah. Clive had more than once talked about going to college in a few weeks' time, his place lined-up. Winston had moved on too. When he came round to see her the night she had returned from Istanbul, he'd told her his life was different now.

A friend at a fast food outlet near where he lived had called him in from the beginning of September. He had his first job to go to. Kaylah too had ideas for developing a business in the coming months. The carpets and rugs she had seen in Istanbul would sell in North London, and if it could be done as an e-business there were profits to be made, of this she was quite convinced. She would get on to it this autumn. Something to look forward to.

Then the thought occurred to her that she would like to invite Adam, his friends from Istanbul and Krish Patel to the thanksgiving. She handed Jacob over into her mum's adoring arms, and excused herself to go upstairs to make the necessary calls to ensure everyone would be there.

At 3pm on Sunday 4th September, Holy Trinity Church was pretty well full. London's predictable ability to have warm sunny dry weather well into the autumn proved reassuringly reliable as everyone began milling into the church. Cars were parked all down the street holding up ambulances from the nearby ambulance station and annoying residents trying to get access to their homes. But everyone gathered inside the church was unaware of this in the excited happy chatter of the occasion.

Kaylah had asked Winston to sit beside her and he'd turned out in the smartest black and white tuxedo. Her parents and Clive had dressed up for the occasion and had brought with them many of their friends from Sam's Edmonton Green Tabernacle Church. Ruth scored a hit when she invited Sam to join her at the front and, setting theological niceties to one side concerning the role of women in church as he understood it, they stood side by side for the thanksgiving. Ruth stepped up to speak and the service began.

'We are here today to give thanks for the birth of this child, Jacob, with his family and friends, and to support his mother Kaylah in her responsibilities with love and prayer... It is God's purpose that children should know love within the stability of their home, grow in faith, and come at last to the eternal city where His love reigns supreme,' said Ruth.

Turning to everyone gathered, Ruth asked, 'Will you do all that you can to help and support Kaylah in the bringing up of Jacob?' In response everyone said, 'With the help of God, we will.' Ruth could see that Kaylah had tears of joy in her eyes.

Later, Kaylah's father, Sam, resplendent in a dark-navy suit and vermillion tie, led some extemporaneous prayers at the appropriate point, in response to which there were enthusiastic 'Amen' and 'Hallelujah' responses from the Afro-Caribbean members of the congregation present.

Adam, Raqiyah, Bilal and Sophie were sitting together three rows back. Kaylah waved to them. Then Kaylah spotted Krish Patel on the end having joined them at the last minute and she gained a cheerful wave back from him too. She was glad they were all there. They should all know what it meant to give thanks for Jacob today, she thought. Without them, and Clive of course, things might have turned out so very differently.

Behind them she could see some of her friends from Southgate Community College, one irreverently caressing a can of lager. With Winston on one side of her and her closest college friend Melissa on the other, as ever innocently playing with her mobile phone, she felt truly content.

Photos followed; Jacob dressed like a celebrity prince, bounced and paraded up at the front. No mention was made of Ali in the service, though in her mind's eye Kaylah saw him, or rather imagined him in the crowd smiling, looking on. That was how she wanted it to be.

Slowly people were leaving the church to walk to the hall next door, shaking Ruth and Sam's hands as they made their way outside. A van pulled up, a florist delivering the most enormous bouquet of autumn flowers into Kaylah's arms. There was a small card pinned on, with the message, 'I prayed for this child and the Lord granted what I asked, 1 Samuel 1.27 – With best wishes for the future and in need of your forgiveness – Lena'.

402

The short walk was slow and leisurely and the atmosphere happy and relaxed. Kaylah felt she had arranged something really positive for Jacob, a rite of passage she had been able to share with those who mattered most to her.

56

Exeter university was cranking up for the start of another academic year. The new students, the freshers, were being dropped off by anxious parents. The first of the returning students were also beginning to appear. Soon to join them were Adam and Raqiyah travelling down together from London on the Waterloo train. Since their return from Istanbul, Raqiyah had stayed on with him at Adam's home in Muswell Hill. He had taken her out to meet his friends in local pubs and taken her into London to see some of the sights. Suddenly, so far as everyone was concerned they were an item.

The month together had been broken only when she flew back to Oman for a week to visit her family, and it was then Adam had realised just how much he missed her. He was waiting, well ahead of time, at Heathrow Airport to meet her when she returned. Since then they'd been inseparable, and he'd known both a new contentment as well as a new companionship in his life.

This was something that had made the idea of returning to Exeter all the more appealing. She endlessly amused him: her laughter, her jokes, her teasing and her gentle touches. Since he'd had that episode in Istanbul, a kind of post-traumatic stress crisis, she'd been there at his side ever since. What a difference she'd made. He felt a renewed person and his attacks of anxiety were becoming less frequent. They were growing together.

Travelling down on the slow train, Adam's bike on board, panniers and bags on the luggage rack, they watched as the urban sprawl of London and its suburbs recomposed themselves into the green fields of Dorset and Devon, the single-line track offering a relaxed, charming and unhurried way to travel. She leaned against him and closed her eyes.

Adam looked up to his cycle pannier bag on the luggage rack above him, and reflected on the nearly complete placement assignment he'd managed to write about their time in Istanbul. What the university wanted to read, his objective observations about Muslim faith and life, was not what he'd really wanted to write about. In writing it, he realised he'd learned so much more than he'd anticipated.

Istanbul's kaleidoscope of different Islams, its secular state and accommodation of religions, its lively confrontation between east and west, the Sufis and the Sunnis, the Gulen movement and its opponents, the conflicts with Kurds and ISIS. His mind pictured the absorbing richness of sights and smells once again, the kebabs over wood charcoal, the calls to prayer, the cigarette smoke. Then he imagined the splendour of the Blue Mosque and the Hagia Sophia, the bustling Grand Bazaar with its teeming crowds pressing in on every side.

But did he understand better what drove Ali Muhammed to do the things he did? That was partly why, he told himself, why in part he had begun the course in Islamic Studies at Exeter. He'd kind of hoped he might, but wasn't sure. He recalled glimpsing Ali again in the Beyazit Square, the only time since events in London almost a year ago. Ali had taken the bait, come out of hiding to see his son Jacob. That was a big risk for him, thought Adam. He must have felt something for his son to do that, to take that bold step and Kaylah said he'd sent things to Jacob as well. That too would also have been hugely dangerous for him. Kaylah, she might have been easily manipulated by him, but she's not that naive. Ali could also be a very human guy as well as a very extreme Muslim guy. There was, he concluded, no one way to understand people like Ali.

He looked over his shoulder to check his bike was still OK and remembered how Ali and he had both cycled great distances on that very machine. Ali was, like himself, a cyclist. His mind then returned to when he'd been held prisoner in Mosul, in Ali's family compound and he felt he had an insight into someone who took his family responsibilities seriously. Ali wasn't all bad. So where had he gone so wrong? What drew him so into radical Islam? Perhaps it was the desperate power politics at work, utilising religion to its own poisonous ends. If so, then Ali might have been more a victim than a perpetrator. Who and what then was Ali Muhammed?

They passed through Salisbury Station, Raqiyah shuffling briefly, but continuing to sleep, nestling deeper into his shoulder. With the sound of a guard's shrill whistle they were on their way west once again, leaving part of the train behind in the station, only the few front cars continuing onward. He saw a church spire and wondered about religion. How it can be so positive, like when Kaylah got everyone together for Jacob's thanksgiving; and, yet so negative – driving Ali to lead terror attacks on ordinary people. Why? Maybe religions are like people, full of contradictions, but we have to learn to live with both, with contradictory people and contradictory religion.

Extremism, though is fear and terror exercised by desperate people, people who can see no other way. Maybe, even, extremism is where religion has failed to make an accommodation to a changing world, a last ditch stand in a default position it uses to defend a distorted image of its true self. Extremism feels like people losing sight of what a good faith is and choosing to make rigid dogmas and pronouncements about people different to themselves. It is the vestigial home – the hiding place of the lost soul. Where's the love of neighbour in that? What kind of God do they believe in? Adam's thoughts wandered down long corridors in his mind, searching for understanding, but just as he thought he might have grasped a truth, another corridor opened before him and into it he would go.

Ali had simply lost his way, Adam concluded. Then he became trapped. He was trapped and trained by his IS commander, who in turn was trapped by a monstrous regime based on fear and cruelty. Religion's a fall guy in this, one of extremisms many casualties, he surmised.

Now Ali Muhammed was dead, he had to admit he personally felt a sense of relief. Ali no longer haunted or threatened him. He could no longer unexpectedly reappear and threaten him. It had been a while since his image had appeared in doorways or in reflections to frighten him. The trauma of last year, when he'd been taken as an IS hostage, was hopefully drifting into the past and now he was free. Free at last, he said to himself, but even as he said it, he couldn't yet fully believe it.

He lifted his hand to Raqiyah's face and began ever so gently stroking her cheek. It made her smile. The new year could be nothing but good. Life was on the up. Soon they'd be back in Exeter, all set for a second year of student life. What could possibly go wrong?

57

Big Harry was in a state of confusion after the reception that had been provided for him and his mates at Istanbul's British Consulate. Never before had he been invited to give a speech in public as an honoured guest.

What he'd done was simply tell those gathered how it was and the simple direct approach had gone down well, better than he anticipated – he'd spotted the three guys acting suspiciously – he'd ask Stu for a second opinion and then they'd decided they had no option but to jump them before catastrophe followed. No, they hadn't really considered whether it would end in disaster for them. Thankfully no explosives had been detonated and the police had taken over minutes later. End of.

There were lots of kind words to listen to and many photos taken of them behind rows of bristling microphones. When, around 9pm that Saturday evening, everyone had started leaving he was quite relieved. They began another round of shaking hands as people said thank you again before moving towards the exit door and their waiting cars.

To be honest with himself, Harry didn't feel entirely comfortable being cast as a stereotypical hero and he was quite relieved when it was all over. His idea of a hero was something quite different. A hero was someone who was one hundred percent loyal to one of their own, stood by his mates and his people. These consular types were missing the point. Stu was standing next to him.

'Nice to be appreciated for once, eh?' said Stu.

'Suppose. But they don't know us. They're all knobs and tossers, glad to share in a free party where everyone pats each other on the back, saying, "haven't we done well lads",' said Harry.

'But we did do well, Harry, we did,' Stu added.

'Shit, we did. We only did what we had to, to save our skins. It was us or them. You know that. Those bloody Muslim fanatics hate us as much as they hate pork sausages. Probably more so. These people just don't get it. Right under their noses these guys watch a Muslim plot unfold before their very eyes, and all they think of doing is having a glass of beer and some nibbles. They just don't get it. Why the fuck don't they fight for the cause?' said Harry feeling himself getting worked up and hoping it didn't show too obviously. Someone at the Consulate had arranged some violin music to be played in the background, to help create the right atmosphere, and that too was beginning to make Harry irate.

'So what should be done, Harry? How are they to "get it"?' asked Stu standing in front of him.

'Just you wait. When we get back to England we'll need to organise to defend ourselves. If we don't, we'll lose even what's left to these bloody fanatics. England for the English, and all Muslims to be sent back home. That's how it will have to be. You've seen what it's like here. These political people need someone to make them stop and listen. You lot are not bloody listening,' said Harry looking around at his hosts. The last comment, said more loudly than even he'd intended, caused a few heads to turn in Harry's direction. The same faces quickly turned to understanding, if not patronising smiles, as soon as they saw who was speaking.

'Come on Harry, we've got a minibus laid on to take us back to our hotel. Let's have a few more beers there before our flight back in the morning. You haven't forgotten it's also my stag weekend,' Stu said.

'Yeah, and it's your last night of freedom before I hand you safely over to your missus, when we get back. Make sure you tell her I took good care of you. So definitely a few more beers, but not here. But you know what, Stu, I came here thinking the EDL, the English Defence League, in being so outspoken made a catastrophic mistake, which was why I liked the more subtle approach of the new Britain First Democracy Party, but now I'm not so sure. How the hell do you get anyone to take any notice of what's important unless you clearly and loudly "say it how it is" and take some direct action?' said Harry, Stu nodding as ever in total agreement.

'When I get back, things will be very different. Just you wait and see. All this publicity from what we've done today will have done us a favour. Then these ignorant bastards will have to sit up and listen for once,' said Harry.

A few minutes later the minibus took the heroic group back to their hotel near the Galatasaray stadium. Their hotel bar had received instructions from somewhere to provide as many free beers as were required, so rather more than just a few more beers were drunk. Finally, in the early hours and to the barman's evident relief, they noisily made their way upstairs to their rooms to sleep it off in the few hours remaining before breakfast.

Once back in England, they had another press reception waiting for them in London's Queen Elizabeth Hall before taking a routine coach from Victoria Coach Station back to the South West. It was a long day of travel. Harry said most of his goodbyes in Exeter, and found himself almost alone for the first time in a week for the last leg to Plymouth. Only Stu sat beside him, sleeping off the remaining effect of the previous night. Harry reckoned he could mark this trip down as one of the better, more interesting ones. They'd gone into the lion's den and come out smelling of roses. He'd come back feeling good, focussed, knowing what he had to do next.

As he glanced round at the faces in the Exeter coach station, he wondered how many of these white English really knew what a threat they faced. In Istanbul they'd met Islam and he knew now that it was them or us.

Thinking ahead, he could count on his family. He knew his grandfather and father would allow him time and space to develop his fired-up political interests. They shared similar views. They'd understand and be happy enough to focus on the family scrapyard business leaving Harry to do what was needed. But where to start? A leader had to be practical as well as idealistic, he reminded himself.

As the coach moved away he spotted a group of young people, students, he thought, and still on holiday. And then he had an idea. In a matter of a few weeks Exeter University's students would all be returning. They'd have a Freshers' Week. Now that could be a good opportunity. Where better to get some of the most able young people to start thinking radically? No-one will say no to a Britain First Democracy Party stand amongst all the other stands in Freshers' Week. He was certain there would be an Islamic Society table to turn over.

The South-West could see the awakening of an effective extreme right-wing party. Why not make a start here? A successful event could even catapult him into the national right wing leadership in the forthcoming autumn elections. He closed his eyes, not to sleep, just so that he could concentrate and formulate his ideas.

The coach was passing Ivybridge and nearing its final destination of Plymouth when his eyes opened and he knew what he would do. In his head he had planned it all out already, who would be there, the material they would take, the shake up and call to arms that would follow, and a broad smile settled across his face that stayed with him all the way to Plymouth and home. He was certain now the world would hear again from Harry McNamara.

Suggested
Book Group Questions

1. The life of Ali Muhammed, central in Flashbacks, features in IStanbul. How would you sum up Ali?

2. The key characters of Kaylah Kone and Adam Taylor are further developed here. What are the strengths and weaknesses of these two?

3. Turkey lies in the borderland of east and west, Europe and Asia. How important is the author's choice of setting? Do the novel's themes cross national boundaries?

4. Clive Kone is given a chance. What do you think of his story and that of his associates?

5. The institutions of the state, namely the police and security services, are given prominence in the story. What is your assessment of their role?

6. Harry McNamara appears on the scene. What do you make of his part in events and his character?

7. One of the themes is that of 'grooming.' Was Ali groomed by Salim? Was Lena groomed? Others? What makes someone either susceptible or resilient to grooming?

8. Do cultures, faiths and beliefs have positive and / or negative effects on people?

9. What does the reader take away with them?

Harry's England

J E Hall

The final novel in the trilogy moves the action
to the South-West of England where a right wing
extremist decides to stand
in a Plymouth parliamentary by-election.

Harry McNamara's experience in Istanbul has fired his
desire to change his country.

Harry's England is scheduled for publication late 2017

See website
http://jehallauthor.com
for
suggested book group questions
reviews
and further information